Books by Joy Nash

The Nephilim Series
Demons and Angels (2017)
The Night Everything Fell Apart

The Druids of Avalon series
Celtic Fire
The Grail King
Deep Magic
Silver Silence

Immortals series
The Awakening
The Crossing
Blood Debt

also by Joy Nash
A Little Light Magic
Christmas Unplugged
Looking for a Hero

www.joynash.com

Praise for Joy Nash

Silver Silence

"Spellbinding! Joy Nash combines her knowledge of Celtic lore with timeless legends and writes breathtaking romance of unconditional love amid a backdrop of lush descriptions and powerful magic." ~*Paranormal Romance Reviews* on *Silver Silence*

The Grail King

A Romantic Times TOP PICK! "Not since Mary Stewart's *Merlin Trilogy* has the magic of Avalon flowed as lyrically off the pages." ~*RT BOOKreviews Magazine* on *The Grail King*

A Little Light Magic

"One of those books that when you finish reading it, you have to turn around and start it all over again." ~*Bitten by Books* on *A Little Light Magic*

The Crossing

"Splendidly entertaining." ~*Booklist* on *The Crossing*

"Mac's personality is in full blaze. It is impossible not to fall in love with this man!" ~*Romance Junkies* on *The Crossing*

Looking For a Hero

"Oh man! A hilarious ride that had me falling out of my seat with laughter... Don't miss this story." ~*Romance Reviews Today* on *Looking For a Hero*

THE NIGHT
EVERYTHING
FELL APART

THE NEPHILIM: BOOK ONE
DEMONS AMONG US

Joy Nash

JOYNASH BOOKS LLC
Doylestown PA

The Night Everything Fell Apart
The Nephilim: Book One

Copyright © 2016 by Joy Nash
ISBN-13: 978-1-941017-01-2
Published by: joynash books, llc
              Doylestown PA, USA
Cover design by The Killion Group
Interior design by Joy Nash

First Edition: October 2016

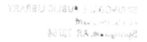

To my daughter:
first reader, social media wizard,
and advisor on everything magical

The Sons of God saw that the Daughters of Men were beautiful, and they married any of them they chose...

The Nephilim were on the earth in those days, and afterward, when the Sons of God came unto the Daughters of Men, who bore children to them.

Genesis 6:2,4

ONE

Arthur Camulus couldn't say it felt good to be back in England. To be honest, it felt like crap. And wasn't that bloody ironic? He'd spent years plotting his return.

At least, he thought he had.

Why was he here? He couldn't remember. His brain was that fucked up. It'd been hours, or days, or maybe even weeks, since he'd emerged from his Ordeal. Heat consumed his body; every nerve ending was ablaze. Opal lights moved under his skin. Stray sparks shot from his fingertips. He swiped his tongue across the roof of his mouth. His spit tasted of metal. He stunk of sweat and worse. If he looked down at his bare chest, he'd see blood.

Not his own blood. That much, he was certain of.

The first time his body had changed, the pain had been nearly unendurable. The second shift had been easier. His flesh was adjusting to its new condition. His mind? Fried. Horrors flashed behind his eyes. Shouts rang in his ears. The magic was his and yet it wasn't. He couldn't call it with any consistency or direct it once it responded.

He needed help.

The night was heavy with fog. How long until dawn? Hard to tell. Clouds obscured moon and stars. Night mist soaked his skin as he flew. Moorland, mottled with shadows, peeked through the haze below. To his newly-gained night vision, everything appeared strangely rendered in shades of gray and green.

It was difficult to keep steady long enough to orient himself. His wings were more awkward than he'd anticipated. Right and left refused to cooperate. Flight was dodgy.

The site was the highest point for miles around. Even so, he only just managed to see past its protective wardings. He landed inelegantly, in a neglected garden. Here, the fog was thinner, sound muted. The old manor rose like a ghost, its windows like so many vacant eyes. He tilted his head and knew a rush of relief. There might be gaps—vast gaps—in the quagmire of his memory, but this place, at least, occupied solid ground.

Tŷ'r Cythraul. House of the Demon.

He willed his wings to melt into his back. Surprisingly, they obeyed. The lights under his skin faded. Breath hissed between his teeth as his body relaxed into human form.

His childhood home was an unassuming structure. Square and stolid, with a gray stone face. Four rooms below, five above. The attic, one large space under a steeply sloping roof, had once been Arthur's domain. His life here had been happy until that last, horrific night.

The front door—solid oak, polished to a high sheen— simultaneously beckoned and repulsed. Reluctant to face it, he pivoted, taking in the garden and its encircling stone wall, where his mother, in all her varied moods, had spent hours tending her plants. Now weeds overran the paths, feral herbs wrestled with gangly shrubs, and saplings choked the well pump.

Only the oak was unchanged. Its trunk, so massive that three men with outstretched arms could not have encircled it, stood near one corner of the house. Moss-covered roots spread out around the base like a treacherous welcome mat. Branches stretched over the roof, the tips scratching the slates.

I've come for the oak. With sudden clarity, the memory of it burst upon him.

Funny thing about memories. When they weren't your own, they had no context. Bits and pieces of his ancestors' lives churned about in Arthur's skull, like so much tornado-tossed debris. So many events, so many images. So many lost emotions. A thousand films playing at once, reeling past too quickly to absorb.

A dull ache pounded his forehead. He bowed his head and pressed his fingertips against it. *The oak,* he reminded himself. *The oak. What the bloody hell was he supposed to remember about the oak?*

Violent as lightning, one memory, one single lucid thought, flashed through his brain. He sucked in air. His eyes flew open. A morass of emotions—clawing, sucking, sickening—swamped him. He stumbled toward the oak and laid his left hand on its trunk.

Power leapt like a rabid dog. Too much, too strong: he couldn't control it. The magic savaged his brain, mauled his skull. Lifted his mind from his body. Desperately, he focused on the wood under his palm. He couldn't fail in this. He *would* not.

He swept his hand downward. The bark warmed. The ancient wood went soft. His fingers sank into it. Something slipped into his hand. He pulled the object out of the wood. Several seconds passed as he gathered the courage to look at it.

When at last he did, he knew. Who he was. What he was. Arthur Camulus. Human. Demon.

Nephil.

And he knew one more thing: he was in deep, deep shit.

TWO

Michael turned his phone sideways. The video enlarged to fill the screen, but it was barely an improvement. He couldn't quite make out exactly how the three human males were connected to the two human females. Frustrated, he backtracked and started another video. This one showed only two males, not a female in sight.

Interesting. How many different ways could there possibly be for humans to copulate?

"Abomination!"

The phone slipped from his grip and went flying into blue sky. It exploded overhead. A shower of sparks rained down. Each tiny light disappeared into the cloud under his feet.

Michael regarded his brother sourly. "F-f-f...*fuck* it."

It was difficult, almost painful, to form human profanity on his tongue. He wasn't even sure he'd be able to get it out until he heard the syllable explode from his lips. It gave him an odd feeling—energized and strangely satisfied. He sat up and grinned.

Raphael regarded him with undisguised horror. "*What* did you say?"

"Want me to say it again?"

"In the name of all that's holy, no!"

Gabriel, who was inspecting his fingernails while

seated atop a nearby puff of mist, fluttered his silver wings and snorted.

Raphael cast a baleful eye upon him. "Don't you start, too."

"Who, *moi?*" Gabe looked up, all wide-eyed and innocent. "Why, I wouldn't dream of it. There's certainly no reason for me to get involved just because you can't control Michael."

"It's got nothing to do with control," Raphael said.

Gabriel stood. "Come now, brother." Grasping his walking stick in his left hand, he smoothed the lapel of his linen suit with his right. "Angels aren't supposed to lie. Archangels, least of all."

The darkest thundercloud could not have rivaled Raphael's expression for pure fury. His robes whipped around his legs as if buffeted by gale-force winds. His hand landed on the hilt of his sword. "Are you accusing me of falsehood?"

"If the sandal fits," Gabe said, cheekily ignoring the oncoming storm. Fingers spread, he frowned down at his left hand. Sighing, he propped his walking stick up against a tuft of cloud and snapped his fingers. An emery board appeared. With the virtuosity of an artist, he applied it to the offending fingernail.

Raphael glowered. "Insolent brat."

"Insufferable bore," Gabe replied.

Michael sat back on his cloud, content to watch his siblings quarrel. Raphael would win, of course. Eventually. Until then, Gabriel could drag out a squabble from here to eternity.

His brothers could not be more different. Raphael, eldest, was the golden boy, with shoulder-length blond hair and a blindingly handsome face. He was, in Michael's private opinion, the pompous back end of a donkey. If he'd ever seen Raphael wearing anything but sun-bright robes, gold-wrought sandals, and a gilded, belted scabbard—Sword of Righteous Vengeance sheathed threateningly inside—Michael could not remember it.

Gabriel, the middle brother, was pale. Skin white as parchment, eyes silver-grey. He invariably dressed in a white linen suit, white-on-white striped shirt, skinny silver tie, and white shoes and socks. His hair was clipped short and was—surprise!—pure as driven snow. He carried a white, silver-handled walking stick. A pair of diamond stud earrings, set in platinum, gleamed in his lobes.

The argument went on. And on. And *on.* Bored, Michael snapped his fingers. A new smart phone appeared in his hand. He bent his head over the screen and occupied himself scrolling through website after website. He just couldn't get enough of this human porn thing. The Earth's Internet was full of it. And cats. For some reason, always cats.

He was so absorbed in his...erm...research of the human realm that he didn't notice the altercation had ended until a shadow fell over him. He looked up to find Raphael staring him down.

"May I help you?" Michael inquired.

"What," his brother intoned, "is that infernal human device?"

Michael quickly shoved the phone into the back pocket of his jeans. "It's called a smart phone. Almost all humans have one. They carry them everywhere."

"Whatever for?"

"To connect with each other. Send messages and trade pictures and videos and...shit."

Raphael did his baleful eye thing again.

Michael shrugged.

"Hmph." Raphael waved a hand. "Humans would be

far better served by casting off their...what did you call them?"

"Smart phones."

"Humans would be far better served casting off their smart phones and speaking directly to Heaven."

"I'm sure that would be ideal," Michael hedged, "but I can tell you it's not likely to happen this millennium. The next millennium looks doubtful, too. From what I've seen, humans aren't all that interested in celestial matters. Sin consumes them. It's really very interesting—"

"I sent you to Earth to fight sin," Raphael said tightly. "Not to wallow in it."

"I have to know my audience," Michael protested. "Humans are very emotional. They'll fight about anything. Power, money, parking spaces—you name it. And if they're not fighting, they're fu—"

"Cease! I'm thinking you've come to know your audience far too well." Raphael looked Michael up and down. "And what in Heaven's name are you wearing? Where are your celestial robes?"

Gone. Michael found denim pants to be surprisingly comfortable. He'd shrunk his righteous sword down to a deadly six-inch switchblade, now hidden in his sleeve. He was equally pleased with his Doc Martens and the frogged military jacket he'd picked up in a vintage shop in SoHo.

"You don't have a problem with Gabe's Earth garb," he said. "What's wrong with mine?"

"You're wearing black, for Heaven's sake. What kind of self-respecting angel wears black? And hides his wings?"

"One that's undercover," Michael said testily.

Gabriel tittered behind his hand. Raphael shot him a glare. Gabe sniffed and turned his head.

"Undercover is one thing," Raphael said, "but dignity must be preserved."

"I don't see why."

Raphael gave a flap of his golden wings. Robes fluttering behind him, he glided a circle around his brother. Touching down once more, he crossed his arms. "Disgusting garments. Get rid of them."

Like hell I will, Michael thought, and then flushed. Human obscenity concerning copulation and defecation were one thing. Invoking the underworld was perhaps going a bit too far.

"Forget my clothes," he said. "Don't you want to hear my field report?"

Raphael heaved a sigh. "Of course." He waved a hand, swirling cloud mist into the form of a throne. His celestial buttocks settled upon it. "Proceed."

Michael rose and bowed.

Raphael inclined his head in reply. "Have you located Cherub Fortunato?"

"Regrettably, no. And believe me, I've looked all over."

"Odd." Raphael's shining brow creased. "I wonder where he might have gone. He's definitely not up here."

"He's probably just floating around Earth, oblivious. You have to admit, the little guy isn't exactly the most intelligent of angels."

"Heaven knows that's true. When the Almighty was giving out brains, Fortunato thought He said 'pains,' and made himself scarce."

Michael chuckled. "He's as lucky as his name, though. And very soft-hearted. He'll be fine."

Raphael contemplated a moment longer, then shook his head. "I suppose you're right. Fortunato has always been a curious sort. He probably just got distracted. I expect he'll turn up eventually." He leaned back and steepled his fingers. "Very well. Continue. What sin did you find rampant in the human realm?"

"The usual trouble in the Middle East—that's a given. In other areas...let's see. Your typical wars here and there, along with the expected number of refugees fleeing each conflict zone. Species extinction continues unabated. Greed and gluttony is on an upswing. Racism, sexism, and xenophobia holding steady. Murders and thefts are, surprisingly, slightly down. As for illicit sexual congress—"

Raphael held up a hand. "Please. No details."

Michael shrugged. "In that case, I guess that's about—oh wait. There was one other thing."

"Yes?"

"It's not really about sin, per se. It concerns the Nephilim."

Raphael snorted. "If those abominable left-handed demons are involved, you can be sure it's a sin. What evil are they up to now?"

"The Druid clan, descendants of the Watcher Samyaza, has a new adept. A male. He emerged from his Ordeal two days ago."

"What do I care about that? Nephil dormants become adept with regrettable regularity."

"Not like this, they don't."

"What do you mean?"

"This particular Nephil went rogue," Michael said. "Defied his alpha, abandoned his clan, and entered his Ordeal alone. No guide, no mentor, not one scrap of assistance. And yet he survived."

Raphael waved a dismissive hand. "So he's insane now. Nothing need be done about it. He won't last long enough to become a problem."

"Well, that's just it. He's not insane. At least, not fully. He emerged from his Ordeal with his mind mostly intact. His demon powers are rapidly escalating. He can't quite control them yet, but—" Michael shook his head. "It's amazing, really. Arthur Camulus is—"

Raphael's chin jerked up. "What did you say?"

"I said, the new adept is sane. Mostly."

"No, not that part. The other. His name. What is his name?"

Michael regarded his brother quizzically. "I told you. It's Arthur Camulus, Nephil of the Druid clan. Descendant of Samyaza, leader of the fallen Watcher angels."

Raphael jumped to his feet and paced, golden robes swirling about his ankles like a small tornado. *What the—?* Michael had never seen his brother so agitated. He shot a questioning look at Gabriel. Gabe raised a hand, palm up, and made a face.

"It cannot be," Raphael muttered. "Cannot be, I tell you. Arthur Camulus is dead. He died as a boy of twelve. Seven years ago."

"You are...misinformed," Michael said carefully. "I assure you, Arthur is very much alive."

Raphael whipped around to face him. "Even if he were alive, he's not yet of age. He'd be only nineteen. A full year short of attempting his Ordeal with any hope of survival."

"I'm not sure of Arthur's age." Michael's eyes tracked his brother's progress to the edge of the cloud and back again. "I only know he was living with the American branch of the Druid clan. In Texas, of all places. I gather he took exception to his clan's alpha." He gave a grunt of distaste. "Mab. A nasty piece of work. I can see why he rejected her as his guide—she enslaves every dormant she brings out of the Ordeal. Anyway, some two weeks ago Arthur snuck out of the Texas homestead and ingested a dose of cocaine that should've killed him. He got as close to death as possible without actually crossing over."

Raphael resumed his chase to the end of the cloud. "Arthur survived his near-death-seeking only two weeks ago? It should have been months before his Ordeal came upon him."

Michael was getting dizzy, watching his brother's frantic pacing. "In the traditional scheme of things, yes, a Nephil Ordeal usually comes two to three months after the subject's near-death. But I gather cocaine speeds up the process. If the dormant survives, the crisis arrives almost immediately. Some idiosyncrasy of Nephil physiology, apparently."

"Disturbing. Very disturbing. When did Arthur emerge?"

"Thirty-two hours ago."

Raphael passed a hand over his eyes. "Go back to Earth. Immediately. Keep an eye on him. Arthur Camulus, a Nephil adept." He shook his head. "Blessed God in Heaven."

"I don't understand." Michael looked from Raphael to Gabriel. "Who is Arthur Camulus?"

Gabriel slid off his patch of mist and onto his feet. "Yes. Who is he?"

A pained expression crossed Raphael's countenance. "It's not who Arthur is, precisely. It's who his ancestor was."

"All right," Michael said slowly. "I'll bite. Who was Arthur's ancestor?"

"Merlin."

"Merlin the Sorcerer?" Gabriel said with some surprise. "Camelot and all that?"

"Yes."

"So?" asked Michael.

"So," Raphael replied tightly, "Merlin the Sorcerer was the most powerful Nephil ever to walk the Earth. If Arthur Camulus is alive, he's Merlin's only living direct descendant. He's heir to Merlin's memories and magic.

Magic, I might add, that Merlin gained by surviving his own Ordeal unguided." Raphael pinched the bridge of his nose. "And now, if Arthur has done the same..."

"So what if he has?" Michael asked. "It's not the end of the world or anything. Nephilim have no souls. Their existence is finite. Wait a century or so, and Arthur will be in Oblivion."

"It's the damage he could do before he dies that I'm worried about," Raphael said. "You want to talk about the end of the world? Back when Merlin was alive, he managed to push humanity this close—" He pinched a bare inch of air between his thumb and forefinger. "—to destruction. Utter and complete destruction."

What? If the world had once been in danger of ending, this was the first Michael was hearing about it. "When was this, exactly?"

"Thirteen hundred years ago."

"I don't remember a crisis of that proportion during that time period."

Gabriel approached, eyeing his eldest brother curiously. "Neither do I."

Raphael's gaze slid away. "Yes, well. You two didn't know about it. I didn't choose to inform you. I handled it alone." He cleared his throat. "As thoroughly as I could, anyway."

"What's that supposed to mean?" Michael asked.

"It means I acted to ensure the world's continued survival, all right?" Raphael dragged a hand through his golden curls. "I thought the issue was over and done with."

Gabriel's brows rose. "Hardly. We all know how the Almighty has set up the universe. No solution is unassailable."

"The Loophole Edict," Michael said.

"Yes. Exactly. The Loophole Edict." Gabriel's

expression turned uncharacteristically serious. "Nothing is certain. Possibilities always exist. No matter how sure a thing seems, or how impossible, there's always a way to do it. Or undo it, as the case may be."

"Exactly." Raphael sank down on his throne. "This young heir of Merlin could easily overreach himself, just as his ancestor did, and undo all my hard work. In fact, given the magnitude of the power Arthur now has within reach, it's more than likely he'll misuse his magic. Or worse, lose control of it completely."

"And if he does—" Gabriel tucked his walking stick under one arm and flicked all ten fingers outward, like a bursting star. "Kablooie."

Michael regarded Raphael uneasily. He'd never seen his overconfident elder brother so troubled. "If you're that worried, maybe we should wake the Almighty and seek His guidance."

"No." Raphael's head jerked up. "No, no, and no. I forbid it. Two thousand years ago, before the Almighty went down for a well-deserved nap, He gave me two simple commandments." He counted them off on his fingers. "One—don't disturb him. Two—the Apocalypse is not, under any circumstances, supposed to happen until He wakes up." He shuddered. "If I have to wake Him early, Heaven help me."

There was a brief moment of silence while Michael and Gabriel absorbed this information.

"Then...what are we going to do?" Gabriel ventured.

"I don't know yet," Raphael said. "But I swear to you both, by Heaven's holy gate, I will come up with a plan."

Somehow, Michael wasn't reassured.

***

Arthur had found his mother's touchstone.

He took a quick step backward, as if needing to distance himself from the immensity of his achievement. His foot slipped on the moss; he only just managed not to fall. He staggered to the center of the garden and dropped heavily onto a stone bench. Long moments passed before his breathing slowed and his stomach settled.

He examined the stone with shaking hands. A three-rayed star shone within a translucent blue moonstone. The carved apple wood setting resembled an intricate tangle of vines. An unbroken silver chain passed through the carving. A distant memory called—Arthur's own this time. He was in his mum's arms, swatting at the stone. He'd wanted it for himself. His mum had laughed and said it was not yet time.

Well, it was past time now. He dropped the chain over his head. He might have searched for a new touchstone for his magic, but this one, passed down through generations of his line, was the best tool to focus his magic. Now that he'd found it, he would...

He frowned. His goal was...what, precisely? The image of a woman—blond, tall, eyes like jade—appeared in his head. She was waiting for him.

But who was she? *Where* was she? Why did it matter so damn much? Sod it all, he couldn't remember. His ancestors' memories were murky rubbish. Memories of his childhood, however, were unfortunately clear. His gaze darted to the house. *Leave,* screamed the voice of his terrified younger self. *Leave.*

He was halfway to the door before he even realized he was in motion. He was on the front step before his brain registered a protest. He flung open the door and stepped into a narrow hall. Parlor and dining room to the right, library to the left. He strode straight ahead into the kitchen.

The shock of it hit him like a slap across the face. The room was in shambles—furniture overturned, floor strewn with shattered glass. Cabinets hung open. The calendar above the icebox, stuck to the wall with a tack, hung askew. His mother's valise, the one with the embroidered roses, stood upright by the door.

Dark splatters covered it all. Floor, walls, furniture, even the ceiling.

Blood.

He didn't know what he'd expected, but it wasn't this. Nothing had changed, except that his parents' corpses no longer lay in a heap on the floor. Mab must have disposed of the bodies. Maybe she'd returned to search for his mother's moonstone. Luckily, she hadn't found it.

Mab hadn't killed his parents, but she'd shown up soon afterward. She'd claimed Tristan's diamond touchstone right off his dead body. It had become a decoration on her whip handle. For seven years, each time Arthur had seen his father's gem, each time he'd felt the lash of the whip's hellfire, his hatred of his clan's new alpha had burned hotter. Maybe that was why, while the rest of his brain seemed to have turned to muck, his memory of Mab remained clear.

The farmhouse table lay on its side, a rusty smear slashing across the spot where Arthur had eaten his daily porridge. On the floor nearby, a larger stain marked the place where his parents' bodies had fallen. Their blood, dead and dry, was all that was left of them.

Anger and grief, helplessness and hopelessness, rushed in on him. A high-pitched tone rang in his ears. The shriek escalated with each labored breath. It twisted inside his skull, scraped through his brain. He pressed shaking hands to his ears. No good. The noise was inside his head.

His stomach turned. Wave after wave of unreality assaulted him. Everything around him turned...strange. Unreal. *Where was he?* He looked wildly about the room. Enamel sink, copper counter, oak table. Stained floor. Suddenly, none of it looked familiar.

Sweat broke out on his forehead. Where was he? How had he gotten here? Why had he come? Acid panic burned in his veins.

Get out. Get out now.

And go where? He couldn't think of a place. He didn't, he realized with lurching dread, even know his own name.

Who the hell was he? What was he?

Air. He needed air.

He crossed to a window. The glass was muddy. He grasped the sash and shoved. It didn't budge. He looked closer. What he'd thought was mud was blood. A thousand droplets of dried blood.

He balled his fist and smashed the glass. A jagged edge sliced his thumb. He staggered back, staring at the crimson trail running down his forearm. His heart banged. His lungs worked like a bellows. The blood ran to his elbow. Dripped to the floor.

Crouching in the garden, peering in the window. A tall man, a Nephil. Pale and gaunt. The hem of his black cape brushed his knees, the edges of its crimson lining like streaks of blood. A ring on his left middle finger bore a golden face as its signet. It looked like its wearer... Lips pursing, eyes blinking...

Dark gold hellfire, whipping from the Nephil's hands, sharp as a blade. Slicing through Father's neck. Blood spurting. Spattering the window. Father's body, crumpling. Falling, falling...

The murderer and his ring, both smiling...

The scream began in Arthur's gut. It pummeled a path

from his diaphragm, to his ribs, to his throat. His lungs sucked air. His mouth opened, but his cry emerged in silence. Living, shaking silence, vibrating so fiercely his tendons threatened to separate from his bones. Power streamed through his body. It blasted from his hands. Pure white light, consuming everything in its path. The kitchen, its contents, its memories. For an eternity, or perhaps only for an instant, there was nothing but brilliance.

And then there was only nothing.

He fell as if dropped by an unseen hand from a great height. His hip struck something solid and pain shot down his leg. He lurched to his feet. His knees buckled. He grabbed the edge of the sink.

Long moments later, he righted a fallen chair and lowered himself into it, rubbing the lingering pain in this thigh. When his breathing had slowed and his heart was no longer pounding like a drum, he stood. He looked— really looked—at the room around him. And froze.

His brain struggled to make sense of what his eyes saw—or, more accurately, what they didn't see. His parents' blood—on the floor, on the table, on the window—had vanished. The squealing echo in his skull was gone, too. Silence—pure and ominous—remained.

He passed his hand down his face. *What the fuck was going on?* He'd done magic again, without planning, without knowing, without even being aware of it until it was over. Once again, his memory had failed, reducing his life to dark and ragged fragments.

It wasn't the first time he'd blacked out since his Ordeal. Far from it. His time as a Nephil adept could be described as a few islands of lucidity engulfed by a sea of darkness. Simple exhaustion? A natural learning curve? Insanity? With no guide to teach him, he couldn't know.

His fingers closed on the moonstone. He'd pinned all his hopes on it. He could use any stone as a focus to his magic, but a gem handed down through his ancestral line offered the greatest advantage. He'd hoped his mother's stone would end his blackouts. But here it was, in his possession, and he was no better off than before.

Coming so abruptly back to himself, to the aftermath of magic he couldn't remember calling, left him on the edge of panic. And there was something else...or, rather, *someone* else, wavering indistinctly in the back his mind. His own memory? A fragment of a long-dead ancestor's past? Whichever it was, the jade-eyed woman never wandered far from his awareness.

He heaved the table upright. It teetered, then thudded into place. Roaming the kitchen, he set chairs on their legs and retrieved fallen cookware. He swept up shattered crockery and emptied it into the rubbish bin. He *would* remember, he told himself. He had to.

He stacked two chairs, broken beyond repair, in a corner of the room. He placed his mother's valise, unopened, beside them.

His head jerked up. Fine hairs lifted on the back of his neck. The noise was slight. Nothing more than a faint creak on the back stair. Every muscle tensed. His palms tingled. He shifted onto the balls of his feet, listening.

Footsteps, descending. Pausing. Someone—or something—was in the house. A cold drip of sweat trickled down the side of his face. Mab? No. The Druid alpha would never sneak. But who else could have gotten through her wardings?

The back stair gave out in a corner of the kitchen. Arthur moved toward it on silent feet, mentally tracing the intruder's path. Nine steps down from the upper hall to the landing. A tight turn then another ten steps down to the kitchen. Once on that lower stretch, his descending quarry would be effectively trapped.

He inhaled. Druid magic, cast with any measure of control, felt impossible. Magic common to all Nephil clans, however, seemed much more doable. Shifting into demon form, even that first, harrowing time, had been instinctive. Casting hellfire also came fairly easily. He only had to think of it to have it spring, burning, to his fingertips. Actually aiming it at a target was more of a challenge.

A creak sounded in the stairwell. The intruder had resumed his descent, with a cautious footstep on the landing. Another pause. Another squeaking tread. A figure appeared...

Arthur surged up the steps. With a snap of his wrists, hissing fire streaked into the narrow passage. His aim was pitiful. One white streak hit the ceiling. The other struck the wall. The recoils bounced, whip-like, to wind about his adversary's neck. Arthur leaped back, stumbling down the stair, pulling the firelashes with him.

His captive bounced down the last three steps and landed hard at his feet.

It was a woman. A blond woman, dressed in blue jeans and a flowery, flowing blouse. She gagged, clawing at the hellfire wrapped around her throat. Her eyes—wide and jade green—met his. Her lips parted.

"Arthuuuuuuuur—"

Recognition slammed into his brain. Followed by pure, primal terror.

"*Fuck!*"

He dropped to his knees. He hauled Cybele into his arms even before he'd managed to banish the last sputter of his hellfire. Her body sagged across his thighs. Her eyes rolled up, and her head lolled to one side. She went limp.

"No," he rasped. "*No.*"

He ran a shaking hand over her head, her shoulder. He flattened his palm against her chest. Her heart was beating. He clung to the sensation. The rhythm was rapid and none too steady. His own heart stuttered.

Was she breathing? His firelash had left an angry red welt across her throat. It didn't look like he'd crushed her windpipe. But her chest...it wasn't moving.

"Damn it. *Damn* it. *Fucking* damn it." He grasped her shoulder and shook. Nothing.

He tried again, harder. Her head snapped forward. A rasping sound—her lungs abruptly sucked air. Her spine arched with the force of it.

Arthur's rush of relief was so intense, it caused black spots to dance before his eyes. Cybele's exhale shuddered out of her lungs. He froze, waiting. An eternity passed before the next breath came.

"That's it." He held her tightly and rocked her back and forth on his lap. If he'd had a soul, he might've even uttered a prayer.

"Breathe, damn it. *Breathe.*"

Perhaps Heaven was watching. If so, he was sure it was laughing. Cybele's third breath was a choking gasp. Fear closed Arthur's throat. His arms were banded around her ribs. Too tightly? He forced himself to loosen his hold.

He lowered her onto the floor. Her lips parted. With trembling hands, he cupped her face.

"Come on," he muttered. "Come on..."

She sucked in a breath, and then expelled it in a bout of fierce coughing. He rolled her onto her side and pounded between her shoulder blades. When at last the hacking subsided, he eased her onto her back. She was definitely breathing. But her chest rose and fell in an erratic rhythm.

"Cybele." She gave no indication she'd heard. "God

damn it, Cybele. Wake up."

This time, her eyelids fluttered. He tensed, willing them to open. They didn't. Her complexion was deathly pale, her lips a faint shade of blue. *Fuck.* Her hands were like ice. The red stripe across her neck might as well have been a lash against his own back.

He couldn't bear to look at what he'd done to her. He gathered her into his lap and cradled her head against his chest. She shivered. His ran his hands up and down her arms, generating friction. If he could have brought her right inside him and given her all his heat, he would have done it.

A sick feeling settled in his chest. He'd remembered Mab, that bloody bitch, but somehow, he'd forgotten Cybele. How the *hell* could she have left his mind, even for an instant? She meant everything to him.

"Don't you dare die," he muttered. "Don't you *dare.*"

He didn't know how to heal with his magic. He tried anyway, pouring all the life energy he could muster into her body. His effort seemed to help. Her shuddering abated. The blue tinge of her lips yielded to a pale pink.

Her next inhale was less of a gasp and more of a wheeze. Her lips parted.

"Not...dying." Her eyelids fluttered open. Their gazes locked. "Not even...close."

He swallowed. "Are you sure?"

"Harder...to kill...than tha—" Another coughing fit took her.

"Bollocks," he muttered. "Not again." He urged her to sit up and lean forward, his hand on her nape.

She held up one finger. "Just...give me...a sec."

The coughing abated. Her hand fluttered downward, as if it weighed too much for her arm to support.

"Take your time," he said. "Take all the time you need."

She nodded. Several long moments passed. Finally, she raised her head. "Better," she said. "I think."

He examined her more closely. When his gaze fell on her neck, he tasted bile. He might have killed her with his blind strike. If he had proper control of his magic, she wouldn't have stood a chance. His mind started to run with the scenario. Ruthlessly, he choked it off.

She's not dead, he told himself. *Not. Dead. Not dead, not dead, not dead.* Color had flooded her cheeks. Her breathing was still uneven, though. He grabbed her wrist and pressed the pulse point. Weak. He frowned at her eyes. The pupils were dilated.

She blinked up at him. "Dang it, Arthur. Quit looking at me like that."

His chest eased a fraction. If she had enough energy to tell him off, she wasn't dying quite yet.

"Don't look at you like what? Like you're bloody lucky to be alive? Sweet Lucifer, Cybele, what were you doing, sneaking down those steps? You scared the piss out of me."

"*I* scared *you*? What about me? Next time try looking before you attack."

"Rubbish. You should've let me know it was you."

Her green eyes flashed. "Give me some credit. I'd have to be dumber'n a bag of rocks to call out before I knew…" She sucked in a breath. "…before I knew—it was y—" She dissolved into another round of coughing.

"Fuck. I'm sorry. You're right. It's my fault." When she started to reply, he shook his head. "Quiet. Don't talk. Just breathe."

She pressed a fist to her chest and nodded. When the coughing finally stopped, she looked up and offered a wry smile. "I think that's the first time you ever apologized to me."

He snorted. "Don't accustom yourself."

"No chance of that."

Her complexion appeared almost normal now. He searched for something mundane to say. He settled on, "I've never seen your hair like that."

Her long blond hair was ruthlessly braided and wrapped tightly around her head. She usually wore it loose, the curls hopelessly tangled.

"I didn't want it getting in the way." When his gaze dropped again to her neck, she grabbed his face and guided it to her mouth for a quick kiss. "Don't look. It's nothing."

He tore his lips from hers and set her back at arm's length. "It's not nothing."

"The sting's already going."

She probably wasn't lying. The welts had faded somewhat. Still. "I could've killed you."

"You didn't. I'll be fine." She pressed her forehead against his chest and inhaled. "You smell nice, Arthur."

Her accent, a low-pitched Texas twang, soothed him. "I couldn't possibly," he said. "I'm filthy."

"I don't care. It's you." Her arms tightened and he felt dampness on his chest. His heart lurched. Cybele, crying? That was a sight he'd never seen, not once in the seven years he'd known her.

"I was so scared, Arthur. I thought...I thought you might not have survived it."

He smoothed a hand down her back. "You won't get rid of me that easily."

He felt her smile. "Thank the ancestors."

"But—" His mind, having pulled back from the edge of panic, was beginning to work again. "How did you follow me here?"

"I didn't." She slid out of his lap, gently disentangling herself from his grasp as she rose. She swayed a bit on her feet. He jumped up and reached for her, but she waved him off and sank into a chair. She rested one forearm on the table. He rose and claimed the chair beside her.

"I got here before you did," she said. "But I was exhausted. I fell asleep upstairs. I didn't hear you until—" She looked around the room. "Until you started cleaning up, I guess." He saw the moment when she realized what else had changed. Her eyes widened and snapped to his. "What happened to all the blood?"

"Gone."

"Gone how?"

"I'm not exactly sure," he admitted. "I just know I did it." He didn't give her time to protest his pitiful non-explanation. "How did you know I would be here? I didn't know myself, not until a couple hours ago."

"Oh, please. There was no way you weren't going to come here."

He supposed he shouldn't be surprised she'd anticipated his movements. Cybele possessed keen intuition. Female Nephil dormants, unlike males, acquired some of their magical powers before entering the Ordeal. Cybele's talent was stronger than most and she'd worked hard to develop it. But even aside from intuition and magic, it wasn't surprising Cybele had guessed he'd be here. She knew him better than anyone.

"I came here because I remembered this." He touched his mother's moonstone.

She focused on the gem. "It's beautiful. Whose is it?"

"My mum's."

"It's been here all this time? Mab never found it?"

"My father hid it. He'd stolen it from my mother when he found out she'd been having sex with—" He swallowed. "Well. My parents weren't lifebonded. They both had other lovers. But then my mum took up with a Nephil from another clan."

"She slept with a rival?" Cybele tilted her head and searched his gaze. "You never told me that."

"I know." He looked away. "I couldn't bear to think about it, let alone talk of it. If she hadn't done it, they'd both be alive today. My mother's lover was the Nephil I saw that night. The one who killed her and my father."

"Oh, Arthur. Why didn't you ever tell me?"

He shrugged and avoided her gaze. "Too ashamed, I guess. And angry."

"You shouldn't have had to deal with that alone."

"There's nothing you could've done." It killed him, even now, to admit out loud what his mother had done.

"I could've listened."

"I know," he said quietly. "Before that last night, I hadn't realized what had been going on. A few days earlier, I'd noticed my mum's touchstone was missing. When I asked her where it was, she just shook her head. Yesterday I saw my father's hand sliding it into the trunk of the old oak in the garden."

"You *saw* it? Yesterday?" She leaned toward him. "You mean in an ancestral memory? Your father's?"

"Yes. It was as if I was behind his eyes, looking out."

"Arthur, that's fantastic! Have you seen memories from other ancestors? What about Merlin's?"

"No. Not his. I've tried, but..." Merlin's were the memories Arthur most wanted to recover. But was it even possible? Not one of Merlin's descendants, in all the hundreds of years since the great sorcerer's death, had received his memories.

"It'll come." Cybele's voice rang with a confidence Arthur didn't feel.

"They never came to my mother. Or any of my other ancestors." He paused, hesitant to voice a fear he couldn't seem to put to rest. "Maybe Merlin's memories are gone."

"What? That's not even possible."

"It could be."

"You can't know that."

"No," Arthur said. "I suppose I can't." It was only a feeling he had. A cold, tight knot in his chest.

They both fell silent. The wind gusted, sending a chill into the room. Cybele frowned at the broken window. "That wasn't like that before."

"It broke when I tried to open it."

"Looks more like you put your fist through it."

"I might have." He looked down at his hand. The cut he'd gotten when the glass shattered was already closed, the scar rapidly fading. A Nephil adept didn't suffer much with non-magical wounds.

"So you don't remember anything at all from your ancestors' lives? Besides the memory from your father?"

"The memories are in my head. But they're all jumbled up. I see bits and pieces, but nothing distinct enough to sort out."

"They'll clear," Cybele said. "They have to."

"I hope so. But even if they do, my magic—" He exhaled. "Let's just say it's giving me a spot of trouble."

"No surprise there. You passed through your Ordeal without a guide. Of course it's going to take longer than usual to figure things out."

The last thing Arthur wanted to discuss was his Ordeal. Abruptly, he changed the subject. "Why did you leave Demon's Hollow? We agreed you'd stay in Texas until I came back for you."

"Yes, well, that was the plan, wasn't it?" Cybele said. "But with two weeks gone, I didn't dare—"

"Two weeks?" Arthur stared. "Two bloody weeks? What the fuck day is it?"

"You don't know?"

He shook his head.

"March thirtieth."

He swore. "I had no idea. I...time doesn't exist within the Ordeal. And since I emerged..." He hesitated, not wanting to admit the larger part of his recent memory was a black abyss. He glanced out the window. "It's been too cloudy to see the moon." He leaned in. "What happened after I left?"

"The first day, nothing," Cybele replied. "I'm not sure Evander even knew you were gone—he was too busy in bed with Raven and Tempest."

Evander was Cybele's father. Arthur had never heard her refer to him by anything other than his given name. She hated him, with good cause. He wasn't Mab's thrall— he'd been adept before she rose to power and he had never challenged her authority. But he might as well have been enthralled for all the arse-kissing he did. He was as cringing and cowardly as his daughter was passionate and brave. Arthur had to assume Cybele took after her mother, a witch who'd died before Cybele was old enough to remember her.

Evander's job was to look after Demon's Hollow's witches and dormant offspring. In actuality, he spent most of his time drinking or loitering in bed with one or more of the witches.

"What about Draven?" Arthur asked.

"He had that big shipment coming in," Cybele said. "And clients waiting for him to package it up and send it out. He wasn't paying much attention to anything else. It wasn't until a couple days later, when Evander finally got out of bed, that he realized you'd skipped out. The shit hit the fan then."

"He called Mab back from Houston?"

She snorted. "Not at first. He was too afraid. He and Draven spent a day searching the swamps. When they didn't find a trace of you, Evander finally broke down and sent a message to Club Tartarus." She studied the scarred table top. "Mab flew in that night. With Rand and Hunter, of course." She bit her lip. "And...and Luc."

Luc was Cybele's twin. Arthur had tried to talk him into running and facing his Ordeal alone, as Arthur intended to do. Luc had rejected the idea, opting to stay with the clan and accept Mab as his guide.

And who knew? Perhaps Luc had made the wiser choice. Death or brain damage were the expected outcomes of an unguided Ordeal, and avoiding the Ordeal entirely was an even worse option. If a Nephil dormant reached the age of twenty-five without experiencing a near-death experience and subsequent Ordeal, the cells in his or her body mutated. A deadly cancer was the inevitable result. Without the Ordeal, a Nephil couldn't expect to survive past thirty.

"How did he look?" Arthur asked.

Cybele shuddered. "Horrible. Pale. Grim. He's lost weight. I can't stand to look at that damn collar around his neck. Or the thrallstone embedded in it." She gave her head a swift shake. "Let's not talk about it. I was telling you about Mab. She threw a hissy fit when she found out you'd gone rogue and taken a couple eightballs with you besides."

Arthur had stolen the cocaine from the clan's stash. A dormant needed to trigger the Ordeal with a near-death experience. A drug overdose worked just fine. Normally two or three months passed between recovery from an NDE and the start of the Ordeal. Mab, in the course of her illegal drug trade, had discovered that cocaine decreased the transition interval to just a few days. It was a dangerous proposition, more likely than the natural process to kill the dormant who tried it, but she preferred the control it gave her. As for Arthur, the quick route had been his only chance at escape.

"Did she question you about me?" he asked.

"Of course," Cybele said tightly. "After she got done screaming at Evander and Draven, she started in on everyone else. Me, Zephyr, Auster—even the witches and the younger dormants."

"What did you tell her?"

"I played dumb. She didn't blink. We've been careful, Arthur. She's got no idea how close we are."

"Or how powerful you've become." At Arthur's urging, Cybele had practiced her magic in secret.

"All the adepts searched for you," she continued. "Even the ones from the club. After three days, Mab finally admitted you'd gotten away. She said you were either in the middle of your Ordeal or dead. She said she'd find you—or your body—eventually."

She fell silent, picking at a cuticle with her thumbnail.

He covered her hand with his. "And then what?"

She shrugged. "Then nothing. Mab went back to Houston with Rand and Hunter. Before she left, she told me to be ready for my NDE when she came back in a couple weeks. I waited five days for you. When you didn't come, I ran."

Of course she had. Cybele would never sit tight and wait for the axe to fall. "Could Evander have followed you?"

"Not a chance." She looked down. "But Luc..."

A chill ran through him. Nephil twins were linked in ways Arthur didn't completely understand. With Luc enthralled to Mab, his connection to Cybele was dangerous. "Luc would have known the exact instant you left Demon's Hollow."

Cybele chewed the inside of her cheek. "I'm sure he did. But he didn't try to stop me. And he didn't follow. Do you think...do you think maybe he's not completely under Mab's thumb?"

"It's possible," Arthur allowed, though he didn't believe it. Mab embedded a thrallstone, a sliver of her own ruby touchstone, into every thrall's collar. The collar couldn't be removed until either master or slave was dead. Every time one of her thralls used magic, Mab knew what he was doing. When a thrall was in extreme distress, she could sense his thoughts as well.

Thinking of Luc as an enemy felt like shit, but Arthur couldn't ignore the facts. "If she questions Luc about you, he won't be able to lie. Not while he's wearing her collar."

A flash of profound pain, quickly masked, passed through Cybele's eyes. "Even if Luc does tell her when I left, that's all he knows. He doesn't know where I am now."

"I hope you're right."

Cybele sighed and pushed to her feet. "Are you hungry? I have food. And I brought extra clothes for you. Clean jeans, boxers, and as many shirts as I could stuff into my backpack. I figured you'd probably need those the most."

That was certainly true. When he didn't have the presence of mind to pull off his shirt before he shifted, his wings ripped it to shreds. And presence of mind had been in short supply lately. "Thanks," he said.

"I'll fix us something to eat."

"I need to get cleaned up. Is there water in the house?"

"No."

"I'll try the garden well."

Arthur left the house and all but attacked the rusted pump. He doubted Cybele was hungry. What she wanted was space. What he wanted was to feel human again.

THREE

Maweth bounced and bounced, careening off the shining curves of his prison. He tried angling his batwings for a somersault, just to spice thing up. Honestly. He was bored out of his skull.

Not quite bored enough to wish for a visit from his master, though. *Bastard.*

For the millionth time, he lectured himself on how stupid he'd been. After thousands of years of demonic existence, you'd think he'd be too wily to stumble into a trap. But who could blame him for being distracted? He'd been massively stressed out for the past couple centuries. Earth's population was exploding. So many people, coming to so many ends.

He blamed his captivity on the lights. They'd been all rainbows and sunshine. So pretty. So sparkling. So unlike death. They'd caught his fancy. He'd reached out to touch them and...bam!

Damn alchemy anyway. It was very deceitful magic, constructed with the elements of metal, fire, and blood. What Maweth had thought was light was really a mirror, a dazzling quicksilver mirror, fused alchemically with salt, flame, and a drop of blood. Though the mirror was solid, the quicksilver it was made of moved like a liquid, swirling and reflecting all the colors of the rainbow. Very pretty. The dazzle had lured him. He'd approached and poked at the mirror with a finger. Before he knew what was happening, he'd been inside the blasted thing. Where there were no rainbows, just dull gray walls. And no getting out, except when his new master called.

To make matters worse, his master was a Nephil. Nasty creatures, Nephilim were, at the best of times. The occasion of Maweth's capture was not the best of times. The Nephil who'd caught him had been steamed when he realized Maweth couldn't do what he wanted him to do.

Maweth thought then that he'd be set free. No such luck. His master was very adept at changing his plans to suit unexpected circumstances. He'd quickly found an alternate use for his captive's talents.

All that had taken place, Maweth estimated, four months ago. Ninety-nine percent of that time had been spent in utter boredom. The rest had been spent doing things he'd rather not dwell on. Right now, his master was occupied with the fruits of one of Maweth's labors. Which was another thing he'd rather not think about.

He started to hum, adding a grunt every time he struck the concave surface that defined his world. He tried a double backflip. The inside of the mirror was a little tight for the maneuver. His body splatted flat, arms and legs spread, his nose pressed to the mirror's surface. His master's office, its lines curved in fish-eyed distortion, loomed above him. As he pushed himself off the wall, the office door swung open. A familiar, black-garbed figure stepped into view.

His master. Vaclav Dusek, Nephil adept and alpha of the Alchemist clan.

Ah, shit.

Maybe, Maweth thought hopefully, just maybe, Dusek had other things on his mind. Paperwork or something.

Nope. The Nephil stopped at his desk. Maweth's

stomach lurched as the mirror lifted, dangling on its chain. His world spun wildly. He braced himself for the inevitable command.

"Maweth. Come."

With a sigh, he somersaulted out of the mirror. He landed on the desk with a flourish he was sure would've earned a perfect ten in the human Olympic Games.

"You called, oh Master my Master?"

Usually Dusek chided him for his petty sarcasm. This time he didn't. He smiled instead. At least, Maweth assumed the smug curve to his master's thin lips was a smile. Dusek was pleased about something. His latest thrall, no doubt.

Maweth was right.

"Success, Maweth," the Nephil said with an expansive air and a generous wave of his left hand. The gold ring on his middle finger caught the light.

Maweth repressed a shudder. Dusek's ring, fashioned from alchemical gold augmented by a drop of his own blood, was creepy as all get out. In the place where a normal signet ring would've had an initial or a stone, there was a face instead—a perfect reproduction of Dusek's countenance. The golden face could change expressions, blink its eyes, and even, on rare occasions, open its mouth and speak. The thing gave Maweth the willies.

"Stunning success. It took longer than I had anticipated, but the result was well worth it. Your latest dormant recruit not only survived her Ordeal, but revealed herself to be a member of a clan I hadn't previously mastered. Vodou magic. The elements of flesh, blood, and breath. Quite a prize."

"Bully for you," Maweth muttered.

"I now possess the magic of three clans. Five elements of magic respond to my call. The next recruit awaits his

Ordeal." He rubbed his hands. "Soon all nine elements of Nephil magic will be mine to command."

He replaced the mirror on the desk. "When they are, I will unite the magic fractured by Raphael so long ago. Have you located my next candidate yet?"

Next victim, more like. Maweth had actually been looking forward to that question. "As to that," he said, "I regret to inform you that while you were gone, you missed not one, but two prospects."

Dusek frowned. "How can that be? I've not been gone long enough for anyone to complete a transition."

"Yes, well, it seems one clan has figured out how to shorten the transition. Instead of taking months, the Ordeal arrives just a few days after the NDE."

Dusek muttered a curse. "Which clan is that?"

For most of his existence, Maweth had paid scant attention to the Nephilim. He'd always known when a Nephil died, of course, since the creatures were half-human. He also knew when one almost died. Which was why he was in his current predicament.

Young, dormant Nephilim were indistinguishable from their human counterparts, until they passed puberty and survived a near-death experience, or NDE. After those milestones, they entered a period of transition leading to their Ordeal. It was Maweth's job to help Dusek locate these vulnerable, transitioning dormants.

"The new adepts belong to the Druid clan," he said. "American branch, currently residing in Texas. Involved in illegal sex and drug trades."

"I am aware of Mab's operations. Proceed to the point."

"I'm getting to it. The point is that while you were occupied with your new thrall, two Druid dormants ingested a crapload of cocaine. When they didn't die, their Ordeals came on within days. They're both adepts now."

"And enthralled to their alpha," Dusek muttered. "Making the bitch that much more powerful."

"Well," Maweth said. "As to that. Not exactly."

"What do you mean?"

"Mab's enthralled one of the new adepts, true enough. But the other went rogue. He faced his Ordeal alone."

"And survived?" Dusek said. "He must be mad now."

"No. He's not. At least, not any more insane than his ancestor was." Maweth paused for dramatic effect. "The new adept, you see, is a direct descendent of Merlin the Sorcerer."

"*What!?*"

Ah, but it was sweet, witnessing Dusek's shock. Maweth grinned.

"Not possible," Dusek said. "Merlin has no living heirs. The last of his direct line died seven years ago. I should know. I was there."

"Mab was there, too," Maweth said smugly. "Looks like she came away with the prize, in the form of one twelve-year-old dormant."

"Arthur Camulus was dead. Utterly and completely dead. I saw his body."

"Did you?" Maweth grinned. Oh, but he was enjoying this. "Think again, because the boy's a man now and he certainly looks alive to me. He's fairly glowing with power." He paused. "Druid Nephilim are masters—and mistresses—of illusion, are they not? Mab, especially?"

Maweth watched understanding dawn in Dusek's eyes. Enraged, the Nephil slammed his fist on his desk. Maweth hopped nimbly to one side.

"That damned cunt tricked me," he spat.

Maweth nearly clapped his hands. His master was so incensed by his rival's seven-year-old deception Maweth half-expected to see steam hissing out his ears.

He hadn't had this much fun in months.

"Where is he?" Dusek's tone was as quiet as it was dangerous. "Where is Arthur?"

"Not sure," Maweth hedged. "He met his Ordeal in the States, but soon after emerging he took off over the Atlantic. Toward Great Britain, I think."

Dusek snapped his fingers. "Tŷ'r Cythraul."

"House of the Demon? Where's that?"

"It's where I sent Arthur's parents to Oblivion." Dusek made a sound of disgust. "Tristan Camulus was a pitiful alpha. Couldn't control his lover, much less his clan. He entertained odd notions of democracy. Made him weak. He was almost too easy to destroy." His expression darkened. "I'd cultivated Arthur's bitch of a mother for months. She'd agreed to run away with me and bring her son. Arthur was to be mine when he came of age. My thrall, my bridge to Druid magic."

"Sympathies," Maweth said, rather insincerely. Really, this Arthur kid had had a lucky break. Maweth wouldn't wish Dusek on his worst enemy.

Dusek jerked his thumb. "You. Back in the mirror."

"So soon? But—"

"In," he ordered. "Now."

A vortex caught Maweth's body, tossed it aloft, and turned it into something akin to an oily black liquid. The inky tornado whirled across the desk to the mirror, which quickly sucked it inside.

Maweth's body exploded from the whirlwind, smashed into a wall, and then bounced onto the floor. He lay on his back for a moment, trying to catch his breath.

Outside the mirror, Dusek's distorted form turned and stalked out of the room. The Nephil must be very unsettled—he'd left his office door open. That almost never happened.

With a sigh, Maweth clambered to his feet. Frowning, he brushed at the oily residue the vortex had left on his robe. There was a particularly stubborn spot...

A sparkling flash broke over him in joyful, iridescent splendor. Maweth's head jerked up. What the—?

Forgetting the stain on his robe, he flew to the edge of the mirror. He couldn't believe what he saw through the swirling quicksilver. A flying creature had entered Dusek's office, via the open door. It zipped around the room—to the bookcase, to the chandelier, to the desk—propelled by gossamer wings.

The newcomer was blond and rosy, his pudgy body draped in unraveling swaddling clothes. He might've been a human baby—he was about the right size—except for the wings. And the shiny gold ring floating just above his head.

Maweth's jaw dropped so abruptly and so widely that he was obliged to put one hand under his chin and push upward to close his mouth. A cherub? A freaking cherub? One lacking a brain, apparently. No self-respecting angel— not even the most dimwitted cherub, he'd heretofore thought—would venture into Vaclav Dusek's lair.

Amazed, he watched the celestial creature zig-zag across the room. The angel flew close to a window, catching a ray of light with its buzzing wings. The effect was dazzling.

"Pretty," Maweth murmured.

"Ooh!" the angel exclaimed. "Shiny!"

The cherub dove toward the desk, directly toward Maweth. His prison jumped as the little guy landed. A moment later, a chubby palm slapped the face of the mirror, momentarily turning everything dark. Then the palm lifted and a sweet, round-cheeked face, weirdly distorted by the shifting surfaces of the quicksilver, took its place.

Baby blue eyes peered intently into the mirror's depths. "Is somebody in there?"

Maweth grinned and waved up at him. "Yes," he called out. "Somebody is."

"Ooh. Who are you?"

"Why don't you come in here and find out?"

***

Cybele Herne had bought thick slices of beef at a shop in the village. She'd told the butcher she wanted it so rare that it dripped. It did. She ate her share in a sandwich. Arthur devoured his plain. He'd put on the clean jeans she'd brought him, paired with a blue t-shirt she'd always liked. His dark hair, wet and in need of a cut, was slicked back from his face.

He looked, in short, normal. Like her friend, her lover. Not at all like the wild-eyed stranger who'd attacked her.

"Does it help?" she asked.

He slanted her a glance, his gray eyes troubled. "The meat, you mean?"

She nodded.

"Some."

Better than not at all, she supposed. Adepts newly emerged from the Ordeal experienced an overwhelming urge to spill the blood of weaker creatures and eat their raw flesh. In Demon's Hollow, Mab encouraged deathlust and feeding. After every Ordeal, a few local humans, and a good deal of cattle, were found with their heads ripped off and their bodies mauled.

One of the Texas dormants, Clayton, had transitioned about six months after Arthur's arrival in Demon's Hollow. Arthur had been appalled at the slaughter Clay had strewn across the countryside. In Britain, Arthur had told Cybele with a shaking voice, a new adept ate raw beef until the deathlust faded.

When Cybele had witnessed Arthur's disgust, she'd been filled with shame. Though why that should be, she didn't know. She'd been taught that humans were little more than resources to be used and consumed by Nephilim. The only humans given any bit of respect were human witches, whose distant echo of Nephil blood allowed them to bear full Nephil young. But this odd British boy, a year younger and almost a foot shorter than Cybele, had caused her to question everything she thought she knew.

His opinion of the human race could not have been more different from Mab's. Voice vibrating with conviction, Arthur declared that humans weren't to be used by Nephilim. They were to be protected. This ideal, handed down through Arthur's line for generations, had originated with his most famous ancestor, the sorcerer Merlin Ambrosius.

Cybele had been skeptical at first. But slowly, Arthur had persuaded her to his point of view. Luc came to believe as well. At least he had until Mab crooked her little finger at him.

And look where that had led him. *Oh, Luc.*

She shoved the thought away as she rose and collected the dirty plates. They rattled in her hands as she walked them to the sink. It was hardly worth the bother. She couldn't wash them. The tap was dry. She stood for a moment, staring down at the bloody remnants of the meal. An old linen tea towel hung over the front edge of the sink. Had it been draped there for the past seven years? The thing was insanely normal—a souvenir from Stonehenge, printed with an image of the famous stones.

"Is the plan still the same, then?" she asked.

Arthur's voice was tight. "I don't see how it can be

anything else. If I don't defeat Mab, she'll give you to Rand."

The thought of Rand guiding her through the Ordeal, taking control of her body and mind, was nauseating. Not quite as bad, though, as imagining Arthur dead. Mab had tolerated Arthur for seven years, biding her time until she could force him into the Ordeal under her control. She'd wanted him as her thrall, wanted control of his magic. Now that Arthur was a free adept, with the promise of Merlin's magic within reach, Mab would work to enslave or eliminate him as quickly as she could.

"I could attempt the Ordeal on my own," she said. "Like you did."

"No," Arthur snapped. "You will not."

Cybele flinched. She turned and leaned against the sink. To her surprise, Arthur had left the table. He stood on the other side of the room, palms braced on the wall, head bowed.

"Are you okay?"

"I'm fine." He turned and pressed his spine to the wall. She wanted to go to him, put her arms around his neck and press her cheek to his chest. She wanted to feel like she was free to do that at any time, and he would welcome her.

She stayed where she was. "The Ordeal was awful, wasn't it?"

His expression hardened. "Leave it, Cybele."

She bit her lip. "Leaving it" wasn't much in her nature. "Forcing it" was more her style. But in this instance, she found herself backing down.

"So," she said. "It's to be a challenge." She eyed his rigid shoulders. "Can you win a duel?"

He made a harsh sound. "I don't know. Maybe."

His uncertainty left her cold. If he couldn't defeat Mab,

there were only two other ways things could end up. Arthur would be dead, or he'd be wearing Mab's thrall collar. She wasn't sure which outcome would be worse.

But how could he possibly win, if he didn't believe he could? She approached him slowly, hating herself for her caution. She'd never felt cautious around him before. But then, she didn't know this new Arthur. Oh, she'd known the Ordeal would change him. She wasn't an idiot. But somehow she hadn't expected him to be so...harsh.

She stopped, close enough to feel his body heat. He watched her with wary eyes, unmoving. She didn't like that reaction at all. She resisted the urge to brush a wisp of hair out of his eyes. She gave him a small smile instead. He didn't return it.

The pad of her finger brushed his mother's touchstone. A spark of magic leapt. The star inside the gem glowed brighter.

Arthur covered her hand with his, pressing it against his chest, the pendent under her palm. His eyes met hers. His gray irises, light in the middle, with a darker ring around the edge, looked like ice.

"I promise you," he said urgently. "I will give the last drop of my power, and my body's last breath, to see you safe." His fingers tightened, squeezing almost painfully. "But I have to warn you. You need to be prepared. I might not be able to defeat her. I might end up dead. Or wearing a collar."

She forced her voice to remain even. "You don't think your power is strong enough?"

He released her and paced to the other side of the room. "Oh, it's strong enough. The trouble is, I can't control it."

"You'll learn."

"Maybe. Given enough time. Time and... Hell. I have

no idea what it'll take. I can throw hellfire, obviously, but constructing a glamour?" He spread his hands. "I can't create even the simplest illusion."

"I can teach you."

He shot her a look. "I'm not sure that's the best idea."

"Why not?"

"I won't have you within striking range. Not until I'm sure I won't hurt you. Right now, calling magic is like trying to shoot a single leaf off a tree with a hand grenade."

She turned and leaned against the wall, in the spot he'd occupied just moments ago. The plaster was still warm from his body heat.

"A grenade might do the trick in a duel," she said. "It might even be better than a direct hit."

"No." He opened a cupboard, frowned at the boxes and cans inside, and then closed it again. "The advantage would be Mab's. She'll slice me in half before I can even summon so much as a spark of hellfire."

"What kind of sad-ass talk is that?" Honestly, Cybele felt like strangling him. "How the hell are you going to win if all you think about is losing?"

"We need to think about it." He swung around to face her. "We need to plan what you'll do if it happens."

She crossed her arms. "No. I won't discuss it. Because it's not going to happen." Someone had to believe that, since he clearly didn't.

And she *did* believe it. She'd always believed in Arthur, from the first moment she'd laid eyes on him. No matter that he'd been twelve years old and shivering, eyes blank with shock and grief. When she'd looked at the British boy Mab had brought to Texas, she'd felt her magic stir for the very first time. Tingling in her palms, spinning in her brain. A hum in her ears and a strange vibration in her chest. Yes, she'd known. Even though he was a dormant, and only a male, she'd sensed a rare and powerful magic. It hadn't surprised her at all when she'd learned Arthur was Merlin's heir.

And that was before he'd filled her mind with his strange notions about the human race and his duty toward it. Before he'd helped her step away from Mab and discover her own strength.

"The ancestral memories will help," she said now. "Once you can see them clearly."

He laughed, an ugly sound. "If I ever see them clearly."

"You saw one strong memory. It led you to the moonstone. More memories are bound to follow." She paused. "Can't you make out anything else at all?"

"Snatches. Bits and pieces. Nothing makes sense."

"Anything about Merlin? About his staff?"

"Not as far as I can tell."

Merlin's staff was legendary. It was said the sorcerer had fashioned it from several different types of wood, all twisted together. He'd placed his touchstone, a crystal orb, at the staff's apex. It was possible the staff was nothing but a myth, or, if it had existed, that it had been destroyed. But Arthur's father, Tristan, had believed the staff was real and still whole, lying beside Merlin's bones in the cave where he met his end.

The trouble was, Nephil and human legends put the sorcerer in many different locations at the end of his life. Half a dozen Merlin "gravesites" were scattered across France and Britain. Tristan had visited them all during his lifetime, often with his young son at his side. He'd discovered nothing.

Arthur dragged his palm down his face, then didn't seem to know what to do with his hand. He clenched his fingers into a fist. "If only I could remember Merlin's final days, I'd know where to go next. I can't go running around half-assed, without any direction at all."

"It'll come," she said again. "You just need time."

"Time we don't have. Damn it. Mab has every advantage. I've got nothing."

"That's not true. Mab didn't survive her Ordeal alone. Only you and Merlin have done that."

"I'm hardly Merlin."

"No. But once you remember—"

"Damn it, Cybele, don't you think I've been trying?" He spun about and slammed his fist into the counter. "Will you please get off my fucking back?"

She sucked in a breath. She and Arthur were no strangers to bickering, it was true. Sometimes she thought they fought more than they got along. But the Arthur she knew didn't snap and curse. Didn't look at her as if she were poison.

He dropped into a chair. Leaning his elbows on the table, he pressed his clasped hands to his forehead. "Shit. I'm sorry. I didn't mean that."

"Two apologies in one day." Cybele tried to keep her voice light, but it just came out shaky. "What's next? The end of the world?"

He glanced at her. "I'm a mess."

She sat down beside him. "You'll pull out of it."

He lowered his hands to the table. "I sure as hell hope so. How much more of this can I take? My brain is chaos. There's nothing in there to hold on to."

She covered his hands with her own. "Hold onto me, then."

With a sudden movement, he turned and drew her into an awkward hug. She went down on her knees before him. He buried his face in her neck.

"I held onto you during my Ordeal," he said. She felt his tears, hot on her skin. "You were my anchor, my guide.

You kept me sane."

"Oh, Arthur." She threaded her fingers though his hair, her thumb stroking his cheek. He looked up and their eyes met.

She felt a tugging sensation in the vicinity of her heart, drawing her to him. To safety and, at the same time, to turmoil and danger. It had always been this way. Arthur was a magnet to her iron. She'd long since stopped wondering why.

She kissed him. Their lips brushed and clung. But only for a moment. His hands came to rest on her shoulders, easing her back. When she made a sound of protest, he pressed his forehead to hers and sighed.

"Thank you for finding me," he said. "Thank you for knowing where to look."

"I always will," she murmured.

He kissed her again, open-mouthed and hard this time. She melted into his arms. His palms slid down to her buttocks, urging her up off her knees. She straddled him awkwardly. He scraped the chair away from the table to accommodate her. She pressed her lips to his neck and licked the sweat from his skin. He cupped her breasts, teasing her nipples with his thumbs. His cock, straining against his jeans, prodded the inside of her thigh. She caught her breath on a hot roll of desire and opened her legs wider.

His hips came up off the chair. They both groaned. Cybele grabbed the hem of his shirt and yanked. He nipped the side of her neck. She spread her palm on his stomach. His muscles contracted under her hand. Her fingers dipped lower, past the waistband of his jeans, her nails barely scraping the tip of his engorged penis.

His entire body jerked. Breath hissed through his teeth. She smiled and concentrated on slipping the button.

He caught her hands. "Not here. Bedroom."

"Yes."

She swung her leg over his lap. He surged to his feet. Their limbs tangled. Arthur went down hard on one knee, while Cybele pitched forward, landing with her stomach across his thigh. She flung a hand out to stop her fall. Her palm slapped the ground.

"Ow!" She scrambled to her feet. "Dang it, that hurts."

Arthur stood and reached out to her. "What's wrong?"

She blew out a breath and showed him her hand. "Looks like you missed some of the window glass."

A jagged shard protruded from the fleshy mound at the base of her thumb. She grasped it with her opposite thumb and forefinger and yanked it out. Blood oozed rapidly from the cut, trickling in a narrow stream across her palm. "Damn. Its deeper than I thought. Get me a rag or something, will you?"

Arthur didn't move. She looked up at him. He'd gone motionless, his gaze fixed on her hand. His breathing was harsh.

"Arthur? Are you all right?"

"No. I...your blood." He shuddered. "It's so...beautiful. I want...to see more of it. All of it. Spilling into the ground—" His skin darkened, lights pulsing just under the surface in opalescent shades of blue, gray, and green, lit by a touch of crimson.

Was he shifting? Her head jerked up. Their gazes clashed. His eyes had turned red. They seemed lit by a light burning in his skull.

He looked at her with an odd expression, as if he didn't recognize her, as if he'd never seen her before. Fear squeezed her chest. How could she have forgotten? Fresh blood could trigger deathlust in a new adept. Arthur had warned her he was out of control. She hadn't really believed him. Yes, he'd attacked her on the stair, but he hadn't known who was there. She couldn't believe he'd ever actually want to kill her.

She was an idiot. Because she'd bet money that right now, right here, he wanted to kill her. Deathlust, hard, cold, merciless, shone in his eyes. A low growl vibrated in his throat. The fine hairs on the back of her neck lifted. His scent, raw and elemental, terrified her.

Every muscle in his body spoke of his tenuous hold on his lust to kill. Cybele fisted her bloody hand and whipped it behind her back. Her heart pounded against her ribs. Her legs felt like so much jelly, but she knew better than to cower, or turn and run. Instead, she stiffened her spine and met his gaze squarely. Slowly, slowly, his eyes tracking her every movement, she backed away.

His body went even more rigid, if that were possible. A sheen of sweat broke out on his brow.

Their gazes locked. "You're shifting," she whispered.

A flicker of the Arthur she knew showed in his eyes. The tip of his tongue darted out from between his lips. His jaw clenched. "I...can't...control it."

He closed his eyes. Cybele moved back another step. Her butt hit the sink. Without looking, she felt along the edge. Her fingers closed on the old tea towel. She fumbled with it behind her back, winding it around her injured hand, pulling the ends into an awkward knot. Half-turning, she pulled it tight with her teeth.

"I've covered it," she said.

His eyes slit open. His body jerked, but his feet stayed where they were. His chest expanded in a slow breath. He exhaled even more slowly.

"Any better?"

"The cloth helps. But not with the scent. Or the sound."

"Blood has a sound?"

"I hear it. Rushing. Calling. Mocking. But maybe..." He swallowed thickly. "Maybe the noise is in my head. Maybe...my brain is damaged. Permanently."

"It's not," she said sharply.

"You don't know that." He arched his back, hissing through his teeth. "I've got to...to get away."

The opal lights under his skin were a wild, shifting swirl. A red glow consumed his irises and pupils. His body was changing, seeking its demon form. Cybele wasn't a stranger to the shifting. She'd seen the adepts of her clan change countless times, mostly from afar. This shift was different. For one thing, it was so close, barely an arm's length away. And it was Arthur.

He labored over each breath. Sweat drenched his shirt. He staggered toward the door, shucking the garment over his head as he went. He flung it behind him and wrenched open the door.

He threw himself headlong into the night. By the time Cybele followed him out the door, he was at the garden gate. He gripped the iron bars with both hands, flung back his head, and groaned.

It was a low, inhuman sound, infused with primitive pain. As the cry died away, he turned and dropped into a crouch, head bowed. Cybele stopped some ten or fifteen feet away, her hands coming up to cover her mouth. She wanted to look away. She couldn't. She could only stand, transfixed, while Arthur changed.

The skin over his shoulder blades melted. Wings emerged, slowly at first, then with a rush of power. The joints snapped open, charcoal feathers fanning wide. Under his skin, a dark rainbow of color ran wild.

He straightened. Drops of sweat poured down his torso, shimmering like jewels. He lifted his head and looked at her. She resisted the urge to shrink back. Arthur loved her. He would find control somewhere, somehow, rather than do her harm. She had to believe that.

He pinned her with his crimson gaze. He stood, still and silent, for what seemed like an eternity. He made no move toward her. His eyes didn't even flick toward her bandaged hand. Cybele took that for a good sign.

"That looked...painful," she said.

"Like being flayed alive." His voice was low and rough. "The first time...was much worse."

"This is the second time?"

"Yes." He grimaced. "Or maybe the third. I don't know. Cybele, I..." He dragged a hand down his face. "I have to go. I want...I need...to kill."

At least they were in the countryside, where livestock likely outnumbered humans. "Go," she said. "Do what you need to do."

"I don't like leaving you alone."

"I'll be fine."

"If Mab comes..."

"She won't. Not this quickly, anyway."

"But if she does—"

"I'll hide," she told him. "You know how good I am at that. I've fooled her for years. Now get out of here."

He searched her gaze and gave a tight nod. With a powerful stroke of his charcoal wings, he took to the sky.

Cybele's breath caught. Arthur—his body, his power, his unwavering loyalty—it was almost too beautiful to bear. The cloud cover had broken. She craned her neck, tracking his shadow against the stars. Her eyes lingered on the sky even after he disappeared.

Neck aching, she looked down at the ground. Alone again, she felt deflated. Enervated. Terrified. Hopeful. Exhausted. *Damn.* She was one hot mess.

She sank down on a bench, her emotions churning

emotions. She'd been so afraid that either the cocaine or the Ordeal would finish Arthur off. She'd been equally frightened that, without a guide, the magic would burn out his brain. Or turn him into someone she didn't recognize.

He's fine, she told herself. At least, as fine as he could be given all he'd been through. He was nothing like Luc.

She bit back a sudden rise of nausea. Oh, *Luc.*

The last few months had transformed her brother into a stranger. A hard, desperate stranger. Cybele couldn't shake the feeling that she was somehow responsible for it, at least in part. She and her twin had been close until last year, when Mab had started showing Luc special attention. He'd left Demon's Hollow to work at Club Tartarus in Houston. He'd assisted Draven when the Columbian runners came ashore. And he'd gone to Mab's bed. The thought of it, even now, made Cybele's stomach roll.

Around the same time, Cybele and Arthur had become lovers. In six years, Arthur had never once been permitted to leave Demon's Hollow. Now, taking advantage of Cybele's expanding skill with illusion and concealment, they snuck away from the compound at every opportunity. For the first time, Cybele had distanced herself from Luc. If she'd told him what she and Arthur were doing, and he'd told Mab, there would've been hell to pay.

She'd felt guilty keeping such a big secret from Luc. If he hadn't been away from Demon's Hollow so often, she might not have been able to do it. On the days when he was home, Cybele did everything she could to avoid him.

Maybe, if she hadn't been so wrapped up in Arthur and their burgeoning physical relationship, things might have gone differently for Luc. She might've put more effort into convincing Luc that Mab was only using him. Or Luc might've listened to Arthur. He might have gone rogue, rather than enter the Ordeal with Mab as his guide.

Of course, if Luc had gone rogue, he might be dead now. Was death preferable to a life as Mab's thrall? She didn't know. She could only hope that if—no, not if, *when*—Arthur killed Mab, Luc would be set free.

And Arthur *would* kill Mab. Even though she was only a dormant, Cybele could sense the depth and breadth of his magic. The sheer magnitude of it took her breath away. He was an adept, with no ties to any guide, with the magic of Merlin within reach. All he had to do was claim it.

She'd never seen anything so beautiful, or so frightening, as his shift from human to demon form. Her own magic—and her body—couldn't help but respond. Oh, how she wanted him. She wanted to open her palm on his chest and absorb the heat of those dark, shifting lights. To sink her fingers into the velvet luxury of his wings. She'd lick his skin, press her nose to his stomach and inhale his musk. His cock would harden against her breasts. She'd open her mouth on his stomach and taste the salt of his sweat. When her senses were filled with him, he'd place his hands on her head, his fingers curling into her hair. He'd urge her down to her knees. And she'd go, willingly.

Damn it all, just thinking about it made her horny as all get out. Abruptly, she stood and paced the garden path. Her entire body was ablaze. Oh, why couldn't she be in bed with Arthur right now, screwing his brains out?

Her head snapped up. Something was screaming. Cries of pure terror floated toward her on the breeze, from the direction toward which Arthur had flown.

A human cry? It sure sounded like it. But maybe she was wrong. She wrapped her arms around her waist, suddenly very aware of the dawn chill.

FOUR

Honestly. Some creatures were just too stupid to live.

Maweth studied the round-cheeked cherub as he flitted back and forth, exploring the confines of the mirror.

"Wow!" The angel bobbed before him, wings whirring. "It's so much bigger on the inside."

"Not really." Maweth lay on the floor, against the curved wall. "You shrunk when you dove in."

The cherub flew down and landed in front of him. "What kind of place is this, anyway?"

"A mirror," Maweth replied. After a brief pause, he added, "See this wall? It's liquid but—" He rapped on it. "It's solid, too. Quicksilver, mixed up with salt, flame, and blood. It's made with magic. Alchemy, to be specific."

"Oh." The cherub nodded soberly and blinked.

Maweth was momentarily taken aback by the stunning blue sparkle. The little angel had the most beautiful eyes he'd ever seen.

"I'm Fortunato," the cherub said after another few seconds. He plopped down on the floor.

"You're lucky?" Maweth snorted. "Probably not, if you're in here."

"No, I mean my *name* is Fortunato, silly."

Maweth had never in his long, long existence—never ever, not even once—been called "silly." It was a novel sensation. He sat up a bit straighter. "Well, then, Lucky—

you don't mind if I call you Lucky, do you? Fortunato is such a mouthful." At Lucky's nod, he continued. "Why in the world are you here?"

"I flew in." He laughed in delight, kicking his feet and unraveling his swaddling clothes. "You saw me."

Maweth laughed with him, until he realized the comment hadn't been a joke. Lucky really was a dim one.

The angel bounced up onto his dimpled feet. Gathering his wrappings, he tried to tie them more securely around his torso.

"I mean," Maweth enunciated slowly, "why are you here at the Institute?"

Lucky looked up. "The Institute? What Institute?"

Oh, brother. Conversing with this angel was like swimming upstream. Through rapids. With weights tied to both legs.

"The building we're in," he explained. "It belongs to the Prague Institute for the Study of Man. What are you doing here?"

"I'm in Prague? Is that very far from Paris?"

"It's not exactly in the neighborhood."

"I got lost," Lucky said. "Crashed into a goose or something and got all turned around." He swiveled his head, peering over one shoulder at his wings. "I think I've lost a few feathers."

And a few brain cells. "You shouldn't have come in here, you know. The Institute's no place for an angel."

"But the front gate was so pretty. And it was open. I just flew in."

"You just...flew...in," Maweth repeated, shaking his head. Into the lair of the nastiest, most powerful Nephil on the planet. "Hell on wheels. You need a keeper, you know that?"

"Why, that's just what Raphael always says. Do you

know Raphael?"

Maweth blinked. "You mean the archangel?"

"Yes. That's him."

Maweth knew *of* Raphael. Every metaphysical creature knew about the Steward of Heaven. But... "Know him? No." He hesitated. "I'm not exactly on speaking terms with angels."

"That can't be true." Lucky waved a pudgy hand in front of Maweth's face. "Yoo-hoo! I'm an angel, and you're talking to me."

"So you are." Maweth said, bemused. "And so I am."

Lucky looked around. "Are you alone in here?"

"Not any longer."

The angel fell flat on his back, laughing. "You're so funny," he said, popping back up again. "What's your name?"

"Maweth."

"Maweth? That's a funny name. Except..." Lucky's forehead wrinkled. "Wait a minute. Doesn't that mean d—"

"Death." It just figured the first spark of intelligence Lucky exhibited would go there. "Yes. Yes, it does. That's exactly what it means."

"But—you're not dead. You're alive."

"Not really," Maweth said. "I exist. That's not exactly the same thing as being alive. I'm a demon, you see."

The angel's eyes went round, like two shiny blue marbles. "A demon? I know about demons. They consort with evil people and get them to commit even worse sins. They're big, mean, and—" He brought his hands up to his forehead and wiggled his index fingers. "—they have horns. But—" The little angel lowered his hands and blinked. "*You* don't have horns."

"Yeah," Maweth said. "I guess I'm different that way."

"But—you just can't be a demon. You're nice!"

Maweth rolled his eyes. *That* old stereotype again. "What law says demons can't be nice?"

"Um...celestial law?"

"A bunch of xenophobic bullshit, celestial law is." Suddenly incensed, Maweth jumped to his feet. "I'm telling you, demons are as nice as the next guy. Or at least," he amended, "we can be, when we want to."

Lucky looked up at him a little uncertainly. "If you say so. But you do wear an awful lot of black."

"It's just a color."

"Not a very friendly color." His brow furrowed. "And your face looks kinda like a skull."

"Not my fault," Maweth said with a scowl. "I am what I am. Not everyone can be pretty like you."

Lucky's wings perked up. "You think I'm pretty?"

Give me strength. "Of course I think you're pretty. Because you *are* pretty. By any objective standard ever conceived."

"Oh. Thanks, I guess." His cheeks puffed out. "So, then. If you're Death, does that mean you kill people?"

Oh for the love of— Maweth threw up his hands. "Why," he complained loudly, "does everyone always assume that?"

"Um...because it's logical? By any objective standard ever conceived?"

Maweth doubted the dimwitted cherub would recognize a logical construct if it flew up to his face and punched him in the nose. Lucky did, however, have an impish sense of humor. Maweth liked him all the better for that.

"No," he said. "It's not logical, because it's not true. I don't go around killing people. That's a vicious human lie."

"Really?"

"Yes. Really. The truth is just the opposite. The human

race created me."

Lucky's eyes widened again. "They did? Why?"

"To cover their tracks. They ate some stupid apple and death was created. The next thing you know, they invented me, the personification of death, and blamed me for the whole sorry episode." Maweth made a sound of derision. "And you know what? They've treated me like bull crap ever since. They curse me, defy me, avoid me, run from me, and fight me. Oh, sure, some of them actually come looking for me, but only because they think I can solve all their problems. As if I could." He turned and slammed his fist against the wall.

"Ouch." He shook his hand. "It's so unfair. Humanity pulled the whole Grim Reaper mythos out of its collective behind. And now, because of them, I'm stuck here in this blasted mirror."

Lucky blinked three times, his long eyelashes fluttering. Otherwise, he seemed unfazed by Maweth's outburst. "Um...how?"

"How what?"

"How is it because of humans that you're stuck in a mirror?"

Maweth slumped against the wall. "Because of the rotten reputation they've pinned on me. That's why the Nephil wanted me."

"A Nephil?" Lucky blinked. "I know about Nephilim."

"Do you?" Maweth snorted. "Then you should know to stay away from them, for crying out loud. Soulless beings with no hope of an afterlife tend to get crazy ideas. The one who caught me—Dusek—wants to live forever. He thought imprisoning me would do the trick." Maweth snorted. "Idiot. Doesn't work that way."

"The Nephilim are bad people," Lucky said. "Very bad."

"Well, I don't know if all of them are bad." As a victim

of prejudice himself, Maweth always strove to give the other guy the benefit of the doubt. "I only know the one. And yes, he's a rotten bastard. Dusek is the Alchemist clan alpha. His ancestor is the Watcher Azazel."

Lucky nodded vigorously. "I know about Azazel, too. He's the fallen angel who invented war. Raphael banished him from Earth. Forever."

"Too bad he didn't banish all Azazel's descendants while he was at it. Dusek's a creep. And don't get me started on that ring he wears."

"What's wrong with his ring?"

"It's made of alchemic gold. It focuses his magic. It's got a face instead of a stone. A face that looks just like him."

"That sounds creepy."

"Creepy doesn't begin to describe it. The face moves. Blinks its eyes and opens its mouth. It's like the thing's alive." He shuddered. "Maybe it is."

Maweth pushed off the wall and onto his feet. "So. Delightful as it's been chatting with you, you probably should be going."

Blink. Blink. *Sparkle.* "Oh, really? Why?"

"Are you serious? Because of Dusek. He can't see into the mirror, but even so, you don't want to be here when he shows up."

"Oh." Lucky looked around doubtfully. "But...are you sure? I hate to leave you here all alone."

"I'll manage," Maweth told him. "Just go."

"Well...all right. If you really insist."

"I really do."

Lucky zipped into the air. For a moment, he hovered. Were those tears in his blue eyes? Ridiculous. "Good-bye."

Maweth's eyes felt funny, too. He made a shooing motion with his hands. "Go."

The cherub nodded. With a buzz of iridescent wings, he sped toward the surface of the mirror. The quicksilver bent like a trampoline, then, with a *pop!* Lucky went through.

Maweth sighed and flopped down on his back. Strangely, he was already missing the little—

The quicksilver bowed inward. *Pop!* The cherub reappeared. He swooped down to the bottom of the mirror and flopped down on his chubby butt.

"Hi again," he said.

Maweth couldn't believe it. "What are you doing?" he exclaimed. "Why are you back?"

"Well," Lucky said. "About that. I decided I don't want to go yet. You're too lonely."

"But...I'm used to being lonely," Maweth said, more than a little nonplussed. Lucky was worried about his feelings? How unspeakably sweet. A warm glow expanded in his chest.

He squelched the heat. "Look, you have to go."

Lucky crossed his arms. "No. I don't think I do."

"Of course you do!" Maweth exclaimed. "You can't possibly stay with me."

The angel blinked his innocent baby blues. "Oh, yes, I can."

***

It might've been a damn sight better, Lucas Herne thought, if he hadn't survived his Ordeal. And he'd tried to not survive it. He wasn't sure which was more humiliating—that he'd attempted to die, or that he'd failed.

Or that he wasn't—most days—sorry he'd taken the coward's way out.

Even after all he'd been through, during his Ordeal and after, Luc didn't quite want to be dead. It was, he supposed, only natural. A Nephil's survival instinct was incredibly strong. When no afterlife waited on the other side of death, a person tended to cling to the few years on Earth he'd been given. Much as Luc fantasized about Oblivion—its peace, its beauty, its goddamned nothingness—he couldn't honestly wish himself there.

He could, however, wish he'd never been born. He wished that with all his heart.

A door slammed. He turned toward the sound.

From the outside, Mab's warehouse looked like a tumbledown wreck. It could've been a barn thrown up some fifty years ago and since forgotten. The structure stood on a slight rise of land, surrounded by swamp.

It was easy to imagine a stiff wind knocking the place over flat. The illusion was that good. Rotting wood and peeling shingles were, in actuality, concrete and metal. The sagging doors were reinforced steel, guarded by both Druid wardings and an excellent human alarm system.

Two men emerged from the warehouse, carrying the last of the cargo. Dressed in camo gear with AK-47s slung across their backs, they looked like bad news on its way. Luc wasn't impressed. Arms crossed, he watched the pair stow the merchandise in the back of a dirty white van. Two dozen 19-kilo bags of turf fertilizer, the kind commonly sold at any home and garden chain retailer. At least that was what the printing on the bags said.

The payment, tight rolls of hundreds stashed in a black backpack, lay on the ground at Luc's feet. The boss of the two—Luc knew him only as Buzzard—was a ridiculously overstated character: massive biceps, shaved head, a jaw that could cut steel. He carried, Luc estimated, seven hidden weapons in addition to the semi-automatic in full sight.

Luc, by contrast, was unarmed. And alone. He felt not

the slightest trepidation. The van's tailgate slammed. Buzzard gave Luc a curt nod. The man was no idiot—he'd been buying from Mab for a couple years now. Luc didn't think Buzzard quite knew who—or what—he was dealing with, but he knew very well where a fight would get him. He climbed into the driver's seat without a word.

The other idiot—a strutting fool with more hat than cattle—didn't have the sense of a frog. Instead of heading straight to the passenger door, he stopped, turned, and pointed his weapon at Luc's head.

Luc raised his eyebrows.

"Throw the pack this way," he said. "Nice and easy."

Luc didn't move.

"Now, I said." The rifle's muzzle jumped. "Or I'll—"

"Hornet!" Buzzard leaned out the van door. "Get in the fucking van!"

"In a minute. After I get what I want."

"Fuck, no. We talked about this. Don't piss him—"

Buzzard's warning was lost in a barrage of rifle shot. Luc felt each bullet strike—most of them in his chest and stomach, one in his right shoulder, a couple in his limbs. One dead center in his forehead, which hurt like a motherfucker. The rest weren't much more bother than blackflies.

Magazine exhausted, Hornet stood, chest heaving, mouth agape. Far from falling down dead in a puddle of his own blood, Luc was still standing and hadn't moved so much as an inch.

"Wha—?"

Buzzard was out of the van, arm half-extended, eyes darting nervously between Hornet and Luc. His face flushed beet red. "Damn it, man, I'm sorry. Hornet shouldn't'a done that. But fuck it, he's new, he don't know—"

He cut off as Luc's eyes swung toward him. Swallowing hard, Buzzard inched backward, feeling behind him for the van door. Once he located it, he scrambled into the van, slammed the door, and cranked the engine.

Blood dripped from the holes in Luc's body. It trickled downward, staining his shirt and jeans. He looked up. Anger colored his vision. The bayou took on a red cast. His skin tingled, dark opal lights gliding just under the surface. His demon nature was rising.

He did nothing to stop it.

Buzzard's tail lights disappeared around a curve, the squeal of his spinning wheels swallowed up by cypress, moss, and mud. Hornet jerked his head back toward Luc. Luc's wings unfurled, ripping through the t-shirt he hadn't bothered to take off. The shredded cotton cloth fell away. Hornet's jaw went slack. A violent shudder passed through him.

"Holy fuck. What are you?"

His legs gave out. He fell on his knees in the dirt, trembling hands extended. A gagging sound emerged from his throat. The stupid slob was trying to beg. Or, maybe, pray. Hell of a lot of good either would do him.

If he'd had any balls at all, he would've taken off into the swamp. No one was stopping him. Not that he would've gotten far. In Mab's playbook, one strike and you were out. Permanently.

Luc probably should feel sorry for the poor bastard. He didn't. He hadn't felt much of anything—other than self-loathing—since his Ordeal. Nothing else was left. Nothing but the weight of wood and stone around his neck.

Arthur had warned him. Luc hadn't believed him. He'd believed Mab when she'd told him he'd stand as her equal.

He'd been a fucking fool.

He eyed Hornet. The man was curled up tight,

blubbering like a goddamned infant. He sobbed harder as Luc approached. Hardly worth the trouble of killing, but the trouble Luc would bring down on his own head if he let this pitiful excuse for a human escape wasn't something Luc wished to contemplate. He leaned down and grasped the dealer's ears with both hands. Lifting the asshole's head a couple feet off the ground, he gave his neck a tidy twist.

His legs kicked. Luc let go. For a moment the body teetered, as if wondering which way it should fall. It decided on face-forward in the mud.

Fool should've run. Or at least screamed. Should've fought like a madman for every damn second separating his miserable life from Hell. What was that poem Arthur was so goddamned fond of?

Rage, rage against the dying of the light...

Luc nudged the corpse with his boot, heaving it over onto its back. Hornet's mud-caked face bore an expression of imbecilic surprise. Had he really thought death so unlikely? He was a drug dealer, for fuck's sake. He should've been expecting it.

Luc flicked his wrists, calling his hellfire. Sparks of green gathered in his palms. One good blast combusted the corpse. Flesh and bone burned, until all that was left of Hornet's sorry-ass life was a heap of muddy ash.

Luc stared at the remains for a long moment. Eventually, he came back to his surroundings. Insects buzzed, frogs croaked. He looked down at his body. The bleeding had stopped. The wounds were already scabbing over. Pain—at least the physical variety—was gone.

How many humans had he killed in the past couple weeks? Ten? Fifty? How many of those had he mauled, before disgust had overwhelmed his bloodlust? It hardly mattered. He was Mab's weapon now, whether she stood beside him or on the other side of the Earth.

He stood beneath the branches of a water oak. A faint rustle sounded above him. *Fuck.* He closed his eyes and let his demon body fade.

When he was fully human again, he opened his eyes. Without looking up, he said, "Get down here, Zephyr."

A skinny teenaged girl, all long limbs and awkward grace, immediately dropped from above. She landed on her feet without so much as a stumble. Flipping a thick auburn braid over her shoulder, she peered up at him. "How'd you know it was me?"

He regarded his half-sister with exasperation. "What other dormant could spy without me noticing?"

"Cybele."

Luc flinched. Of course, Cybele. Cybele was the reason Zephyr was so stealthy—Luc's twin had been giving clandestine magic lessons to their half-sister for a year or more, since the first flashes of the girl's magic appeared. Now that Luc was Mab's thrall, this was dangerous knowledge for him to have. Mab had been furious when Cybele disappeared without a trace. If the alpha discovered Zephyr's magic promised to be almost as strong...

Luc scowled. "Damn it, girl, you shouldn't be following me. Not during a pickup. Those men would kill you soon as look at you." After they raped her, but he didn't add that.

"Those two? Come on. If you couldn't tell I was here, they sure couldn't. Besides," she added, "you wouldn't've let them hurt me."

Damn right. He'd've murdered both of them just for looking at her. "You shouldn't be out here. Where's Auster?" Auster was Zephyr's twin.

She made a sound of derision. "Playing video games.

It's all he ever does anymore." Her brows drew together. "I'm bored without Cybele here." She watched him closely. "Know where she is?"

"No. And I don't want to."

Her green eyes, so like Cybele's, betrayed her fear. "She went after Arthur, didn't she?"

Luc let out a long breath. "I reckon she did."

"Think she found him? You think he's even alive?"

"I have no idea. Come on. Let's get out of here. You shouldn't have seen me kill that human."

"Maybe not." Zephyr looked older suddenly, well beyond her thirteen years. "But...I'm glad you killed him. He was horrible. And I'm glad I finally got to talk to you. I've missed you. I was afraid when you came back, you wouldn't care anymore."

"Of course I still care," Luc said. "About you and about Cybele." And that was the truth, he realized with a start. Maybe his emotions weren't quite as dead and buried as he thought. He wasn't sure if that was a good thing.

A shadow passed overhead. He looked up sharply. Three dark shapes glided above the trees. His heart plummeted.

Zephyr's gaze followed his. Color drained from her face, rendering her freckles even more prominent against her pale skin. "Mab's back," she whispered. "With Rand and Hunter."

Luc jerked his head toward the house. "Go. Now."

He didn't have to tell her twice. With a frightened glance skyward, Zephyr ducked into the vegetation and scampered away, cloaking her path with illusion as she ran. He wished he could follow. But for Luc, escape was impossible.

He was Mab's thrall. There wasn't enough world in which to hide from her.

FIVE

A man lay in the grassy verge, his head a few feet from the rest of his body. He'd been a big bloke, middle aged and round-faced. A laborer with muscular chest and arms, and a stomach running to fat. Now the bloody mess of his muscles and sinew spilled across the road. One leg had been mauled quite thoroughly. The femur bone had been broken and its marrow sucked out.

The last of the poor sot's blood leaked hotly from his body. Wisps of steam rose, wraith-like, from the congealing liquid. Arthur turned away, doubled over, and vomited on the grass.

This time, he had no memory of the killing.

The last minutes floated in darkness. He tried to look past it, to the moments just before. He remembered leaving Cybele at Tŷ'r Cythraul. Her blood had triggered his deathlust, but the urge to rip the head off of something had diminished as he put distance between them. He'd hoped that this time, he'd remain in control of his magic.

As he'd flown, he'd sifted through the ancestral memories churning through in his brain. Try as he might, he could see nothing beyond the single vision of his father hiding his mother's touchstone. His frustration grew. The deathlust returned. He tried to resist. But in the end, the urge to kill overwhelmed his resolve. He'd turned his attention to the ground, searching for a victim.

Thankfully, he hadn't been near a town. Dawn had just been breaking. A wash of golden light bathed the countryside. As the sun peered over the horizon, Arthur had spotted a massive bull, grazing alone in a fenced pasture. He dove for the creature.

Halfway to the ground, he'd become aware of seething anger. Not his own anger. The emotion had been pouring off a man he'd not previously noticed. The bloke was engaged in repairing the stone fence that separated a pasture from the road. He spat curses as he worked, spewing an ugly mess of hatred and petty grievance. He hated his boss, his wife, his lover. His mates were goddamned motherfucking losers.

As Arthur hovered above him, the laborer hefted a large stone. His grip wasn't true. The stone slipped from his grasp and smashed into his leg. Bones split with a sickening crack. He collapsed, screaming. His agony washed over Arthur in a beautiful, brutal wave.

Even now, in memory, the dead man's pain called to Arthur's demon nature. Doubled over, with his back to the corpse, he fought it. Beads of sweat dripped down face. He swallowed thickly. Dark lights shifted under the thin skin on the back of his hands. His eyes burned. The black tips of his wings were just visible in the periphery of his vision. Any human unfortunate enough to catch a glimpse of him would likely need therapy for years.

With an effort, he pushed his body upright. He dreaded turning around and looking again at the corpse.

He did it anyway.

Blank eyes stared at him out of the disembodied head. Had he gone for the kill instantly? Or had he toyed with the injured man? The former, he thought. He remembered hovering on the cusp of a dive, his entire being focused on the man's ugly mood. Pain, fear, anger, hatred—such emotions were opiates to a Nephil. He remembered the deathlust burning in his heart. Itching on his palms.

And then...nothing.

Arthur felt heavy, as though he'd added the dead man's weight to his own. He turned away, to look past the stone wall, and farther, into the pasture. His nausea returned. He grabbed the top of the wall.

The bull lay no more than thirty feet away, as bloody and dead as the man. Its massive head, like the man's, had been ripped from its body. One shoulder had been chewed to the bone. So he'd killed both, Arthur thought dully, and remembered neither. Damn it all to fucking Oblivion. He'd survived his Ordeal, but what did it matter if he couldn't control—or even remember—the magic he'd won?

His shoulders slumped. His conscience burned. He'd betrayed every lesson his father had ever taught him. What would Tristan say, what utter disgust would he feel, if he could see what his son had become?

For the first time in seven years, Arthur was glad his father was dead.

***

Maweth and Lucky were seeing who could bounce the highest, without using wings, when the office door opened.

"Shhh!" Maweth slapped his palm over Lucky's mouth. "He's back."

Lucky's eyes widened. Tentatively, Maweth lifted his hand.

"But it's only been a couple of hours since we got back from—mmmph."

"Quiet." This time Maweth kept his palm in place until Lucky nodded. He hauled the cherub to the back wall of the mirror. "Don't talk. Don't move, either."

Lucky was right. For crap's sake. What was Dusek

doing up? The three of them—Dusek, Maweth, and Lucky—had been out all night. The misadventure had started just after sunset. The master had mounted the stairs to the roof, shifted to demon form, and taken off into the sky. He'd flown from Prague to England, the quicksilver mirror dangling from his neck the entire way.

Two miserable hours of swaying and bouncing. Lucky'd gotten so seasick, he'd heaved. Dusek had spent half the night searching for Arthur. Maweth had expected fireworks once he'd been found, but to his great surprise, the Alchemist hadn't confronted the rogue Nephil. He'd simply hidden in the shadows, watching him, until dawn.

At daybreak, Arthur killed a bull. While he was feeding, Dusek found his own breakfast. A human male. The poor slob hadn't had a chance. Dusek swooped in and ripped the man's head clean off his body. Blood and guts sprayed every which way. Then the master chewed a hunk of thigh, snapped the bone, and sucked out its marrow.

Lucky, who'd only just recovered enough to lift his head, had been sick all over again. Even Maweth had been shaken by the viciousness of the kill. And considering Maweth's vocation, that was saying something.

He sighed. You'd think he'd be used to death by now, for crying out loud. Currently, an average of nine human beings died every five seconds. Maweth was aware of the agonizing last seconds of each expiring life. Even so. He'd rather bear witness to a full year's worth of normal deaths, than experience just one of Dusek's unnatural kills.

The flight home had been just as nauseating. Maweth had hoped Dusek would spend a little time digesting his unholy meal, but no. Here he was, all bright-eyed and bushy-tailed, at barely— Maweth glanced at the ormolu clock on the sideboard. Barely noon.

The Alchemist wasn't alone. Dr. Shimon Ben-Meir,

archeologist and adjunct professor to the Institute, accompanied him. Maweth sat up. Interesting. For the past six months, Ben-Meir had been on an expedition in Ethiopia, on the site of the ancient city of Axum.

The Israeli scientist was as academically brilliant as he was handsome. His common sense was a bit deficient, though, in Maweth's humble opinion. A more astute man would have realized by now that his boss was a demon.

Shimon, dressed in khaki pants and jacket, carried a hard-sided suitcase. Dusty and disheveled, his body fairly vibrated with fatigue and excitement. Maweth edged a bit to one side, craning his neck for a better view.

Gently, as if handling a crate of eggs, the archeologist laid his suitcase on Dusek's desk. He withdrew a ring of keys from his breast pocket and proceeded to open what Maweth considered to be a ridiculous number of locks.

The top lifted to a nest of foam peanuts and crumpled newspapers. Moving those aside, Shimon extracted a colorful, cloth-bound bundle and set it on the desk. He banished the suitcase to the floor while Dusek cut the cords to reveal a crude wooden box.

"I excavated the relic three days ago," Ben-Meir said. "I made no mention of the discovery in the expedition log. There is no photographic record, either."

Dusek glanced up at him, before returning his attention to the box. "You had no trouble taking it out of the country?"

"Some small delay at customs. Nothing a handful of Euros could not remedy."

"Very good. Show me."

Shimon produced a pocket knife. He slid the blade under the lid of the box. Dusek, palms resting on the table, leaned close, blocking Maweth's view.

Frowning, Maweth rose off the floor, trying to see

around his master's bulk. Lucky followed him, wings abuzz. "What's he doing?" the cherub whispered loudly. "Shush."

The archeologist lifted a number of flat stone fragments from a cloud of lamb's wool. He set the pieces one by one on the desk, matching the edges like a puzzle. The fragments formed a rough rectangle, about twenty by thirty centimeters. Etchings covered its surface.

"A surprisingly complete specimen," Dusek said.

"Yes," Ben-Meir replied. "Intact but for a few perimeter fragments. It was excavated from a strata dated to the first century of the Common Era. The stele itself, however, is clearly much older. I believe its provenance is Egypt's Old Kingdom. Twenty-third century B.C.E."

"Excellent." Dusek retrieved a magnifying glass. He bent close, examining the tablet's markings.

"You'll recognize this symbol as the cartouche of the Pharaoh Teti," Ben-Meir said, pointing to a lower corner. "The piece, I believe, is contemporary to his reign."

"Some five thousand years ago," Dusek murmured. "The correct era."

"Translation will be my highest priority. My starting point—the reason I left Axum so precipitously—is here."

Maweth flew higher, angling for a better view. His head bumped on the mirror's ceiling. He barely noticed.

The archeologist's finger hovered over a pair of concentric circles. "Many of my colleagues would identify this glyph as an early notation denoting the sun god Ra."

Dusek's fingers, until now spread flat on the table, curled. "But you would not."

"No. I recognized the truth immediately. The glyph doesn't represent Ra or the sun. It is an eye." The archeologist straightened. "The eye of the Watchers."

SIX

It was full daylight by the time Arthur returned to Tŷ'r Cythraul. The clouds had moved off, revealing a sky of brilliant blue. He stumbled as he landed in the garden, going down hard on one knee. He remained in that position, head bowed, wings brushing the ground, fighting the horror of what he'd become. It was a long time before he felt calm enough to raise his head.

He caught a glimmer of light in the attic window. He rose and allowed the morning breeze to cool the heat of his demon nature. His wings melted into his back. The dark opal light under his skin faded. His humanity reasserted itself.

And he felt...incomplete.

The sensation took him by surprise. When he'd shifted for the first time, during his Ordeal, his demon form had been a nightmare. He'd reverted to his human body with mind-numbing relief. Since then, a subtle shift had taken place. Now his human form felt like a pair of favorite jeans, slightly shrunk in the wash. Vaguely uncomfortable, but not tight enough to get rid of. You wore them, hoping they'd stretch out, unwilling to admit they never would.

It seemed incredible that he'd been away from Cybele and Tŷ'r Cythraul for only a few hours. It felt as though an eternity had passed. Ironic, considering how little he remembered of his travels. He glanced again at the attic window. Was Cybele awake, waiting for him? Or asleep, her body soft and unaware?

Both scenarios made his cock jump. He was fiercely glad she was here. At the same time, he fervently wished she was somewhere else, somewhere safer. He mocked himself with a grim laugh. Consistency of emotion didn't have the upper hand just now.

He shied away from the thought of Cybele seeing him in his demon form. He wasn't sure why that embarrassed him. She knew what he was. Hell, she was the same—or would be, after she came through her own Ordeal. Neither of them could help what they'd been born to.

And yet a part of him wanted to run from her. Fly into the dawn and leave her behind without a word. He'd have done it, too, if he thought she'd be safer without him. Unfortunately, she'd be only more vulnerable alone. Mab would find Cybele, and force her into the Ordeal with Rand as her guide.

If Arthur didn't claim that role instead, there were only two ways Cybele could avoid becoming a thrall. The first was death. The second was an unguided Ordeal. Arthur would die before he allowed Cybele to face either of those horrors.

He was, once again, covered in blood. It streaked his chest and arms, spattered his jeans. The scent of it infused his brain with images of death. He wanted to kill again. Craved the visceral sensation of flesh and sinew ripping from bone.

He went to the well. The pump worked a bit more easily this time. Water spilled into the stone trough. He scrubbed his face and torso as best as he could, and then ducked his head beneath the stream. The shock cleared his mind. He began to feel, marginally, like himself. Whoever the hell that was.

He entered the front hall on silent feet. To his left and right lay the parlor and the library. After a brief hesitation, he entered the library. So many hours spent here. His father, alpha of the Druid clan, had been a Nephil of profound power, as well as a scholar and philosopher. He'd been a master of the three Druid elements: stone, wood, and water. Weather had obeyed his command, and his illusions had been beautiful and intricate. When he called his deepest magic, his illusions became reality.

Even Tristan's magic had its limits, though. Druidry could transform illusions into reality, but only on a small scale. It couldn't cause the moon to disappear or create a mountain where none had been before. In addition, Druid transformations were restricted to the physical realm. Druidry couldn't affect the stock markets or bring about world peace. It couldn't change a person's core beliefs or cause them to fall in or out of love. And the transformations lasted only a short time. After a time—a minute, an hour, a day—the new reality faded back into the old.

Arthur's father had stressed the history of their race and ancestral line. Samyaza, forefather of all Druids, had been the leader of the Watcher angels. His offspring, like all the Nephilim, bore the curse delivered by Raphael. Nephilim possessed no souls. Their lives were limited to one hundred twenty years, after which they passed into Oblivion.

Another facet of the curse encouraged instinctive hatred among Nephilim of rival tribes. Where Nephil clans intersected, violence and a struggle for domination was inevitable. Each clan wielded a unique fragment of Heavenly magic inherited from their Watcher ancestor. Raphael's curse was designed to insure those fragments of magic were never reunited.

The Nephilim who survived Raphael's vengeance spread out all over the Earth. Samyaza's descendants migrated to the European continent and became the Druid priests of the Celtic people. Other Nephil lines traveled east, west, and south, but no matter where they settled, their magical powers soon elevated them to positions of honor in the local human cultures.

Nephilim did not reproduce easily, and birthed few females, but through the millennia, the clans endured. Matings of a Nephil male and female produced Nephil offspring, and, because human witches were distant descendants of Nephilim, the offspring of a Nephil male and a human witch also perpetuated the line. Nephil dormants were indistinguishable from human children. Because of this, dormants who grew up apart from the clans often were unaware of their heritage.

Unawares lived short, precarious lives. If a chance near-death experience triggered their transformation from dormant to adept status, they were catapulted into the Ordeal without a guide.

Insanity and death soon followed. But unawares who never experienced an NDE fared no better. A dormant who reached the age twenty-five without transitioning experienced cellular mutations. The result was terminal cancer, with death before age thirty a certainty.

Most aware Nephilim, living among their own kind, viewed the human race as a commodity to be used and discarded at whim. Arthur's ancestor, Merlin, had challenged that notion. Merlin had viewed humans as his beloved brothers and sisters, worthy of love and protection. It was a radical, even heretical, notion.

Merlin's life remained shrouded in the past. For reasons unknown, none of his progeny had inherited his memories. Before Arthur's birth, his mother, Alwen, had been Merlin's last living direct descendant. This was why, Arthur knew, his father had mated with her. Tristan had hoped his own vast power, combined with Alwen's heritage, would produce a child strong enough to inherit Merlin's memories and magic.

Had his father's efforts been in vain? Time would tell, Arthur supposed. He left the library and wandered into the parlor. It was a large room, with twin fireplaces and comfortable seating. A round table and six chairs nestled in the curve of a bow window. The sideboard bore decanters of whiskey and port, still half full.

He remembered this room alive with the laughter and camaraderie of his father's relations. The London kin had visited often. He'd been in awe of Percival, his father's tall, austere uncle. Brax and Avalyn, his father's younger twin siblings, had treated Arthur like a little brother. Less frequent, but no less welcome, had been the visits of his Scots kin, Morgana and Magnus. The twin brother and sister had been much alike, with shocks of white running through their black hair, and accents almost too thick to decipher. Collum, another Scots cousin, had been a warm, jovial sort. There'd been other relations as well, and several human witch consorts. Their faces and names were all jumbled in Arthur's memory now.

Unlike Mab. Arthur remembered her from his early years most distinctly. She and Evander had come to Tŷ'r Cythraul rarely, and only when summoned by Tristan. The last visit had occurred a year before Arthur's parents' murder.

Arthur, on the cusp of adolescence, had been struck almost speechless by the American's harsh, voluptuous beauty and the huge, raw ruby nestled sensuously between her breasts. Her eyes were a vibrant shade of blue, her hair, pin-straight and pure black. Her American accent, a

Texas drawl, had sent shivers up his spine.

Despite Mab's blatant sexual appeal, or perhaps because of it, Arthur hadn't trusted her. She was like a poisonous spider or cobra: beautiful, but deadly.

His instincts had always been bloody excellent.

He returned to the kitchen. This room was the worst. It was where it had happened. Cybele had left an oil lamp burning near the stove. He wished she hadn't. The flame cast flickering shadows on the walls and ceiling. He could almost feel his parents' murderer creeping up on him.

He stared at the spot where the blood had been. His mother had been acting oddly for several weeks before that fateful night. She'd been away from the house more than usual. Even when she was home, she'd seemed withdrawn. Twice he'd seen her crying. When he'd asked her about her moonstone—or rather, its absence—she'd pressed her lips together and turned away.

On the morning of that last day, his parents had argued. His father had left the house angry. His mother, agitated, had shut herself in the parlor. She still hadn't emerged when night fell. His father remained absent as well. Arthur climbed the steps to the attic, where he lay awake in his bed and wondered what was going on. The window above the front door was open. The sound of the knocker startled him out of his brooding. His father would hardly request entry to his own house. Had another of Arthur's kin arrived, unannounced?

He sat up, listening to low voices drifting up the stairway. A man's voice, his accent placing his origin someplace in Eastern Europe, blended with Alwen's proper English inflections. He couldn't hear what they were saying, but a moment later his mother appeared on the stair. *"Pack a bag,"* she'd told him. *"Quickly."*

He'd ask where they were going, but she vanished

without answering. It was clear something wasn't right. Arthur went to the window and, after a moment's hesitation, opened the sash. It took only a few minutes to climb onto the roof and swing himself onto a sturdy oak branch.

As he jumped to the ground, a black shape, wings spread, descended from the sky. He let out a sigh of relief. Father. He had already started forward, ready to call out as Tristan landed in the garden. But when Arthur caught sight of his father's face, the greeting died in his throat. He'd never seen such rage.

Tristan disappeared into the house. Shouts erupted inside. Arthur could make out only a few words. "*Traitor,*" his father growled. "*Ingrate.*" That had been his mother's voice, high-pitched and barely recognizable. "*Fool.*" That pronouncement had been uttered in the mocking voice of the stranger.

Arthur crept to the kitchen window and peered in. His mother stood by the hallway door, her valise clutched in one hand. The stranger stood beside her. He was very tall, as all Nephilim were, but almost unnaturally slender. A black cape, the edge of its lining a slash of crimson, hung from his shoulders.

Tristan stood across the room, facing them. "Alwen." His voice was calm. "Step away from that bastard."

"No. I'm leaving with him."

"With a rival? Are you mad?"

She might be, Arthur realized suddenly. Her eyes certainly didn't appear quite sane.

"You are a Druid," his father continued. "You cannot take your magic away from your line, and use it for the benefit of a rival clan. The very thought is repugnant. I will not allow it."

"I am not your thrall," his mother spat. "We are not

bondmates. And yet you think you own me. Why, you've even stolen my ancestral stone. I'll never forgive you for that."

All this time, the stranger remained silent, a small, mocking smile playing on his lips. Arthur's eye was drawn to the ring he wore on the middle finger of his left hand—the dominant hand of all Nephilim. The ring was gold, lit from within by a glow of magic. Where a stone might have been, there was a face instead. It was, Arthur realized, the stranger's exact likeness. Even from across the room, there was no mistaking it.

"I took your touchstone for safekeeping." His father moved a step closer. "You know why I did it. Precisely because of this. Because of him." Tristan held out his hand to Alwen. "All you need do is send him on his way, and I will put it into your hand."

"You expect me to trust you? After what you've done? You're a bigger fool than I thought." She picked up her valise with one hand and grasped the stranger's arm with the other. "Let's go," she said to the man.

"Of course, my dear." The rival Nephil placed his hand on the small of her back.

His father's strike was so sudden, Arthur hadn't even known it was coming. Blue hellfire erupted. At the same moment, Alwen threw herself—or was she shoved?—between Tristan and the stranger. The blast hit her neck, right under her jaw. For one frozen moment, her body seemed to hang in mid-air, head tipped back, arms flung out. Then a fountain of blood spurted from her throat. Her body crumpled to the ground.

"No!" Tristan's hellfire vanished. He flung himself down beside Alwen. Blood pulsed in waves from the wound on her neck. He slapped both hands over it. Life seeped through his fingers, turning his hands crimson.

Arthur, frozen outside the window, clapped his own hands over his mouth, trying to contain the bile surging up his throat.

The stranger laughed. "Are you trying to get all that blood back into her body? You'll not do it. You've killed her, you fool."

Tristan's head jerked up. Slowly, his hands left Alwen's body. The pupils of his eyes glowed red. Opal lights skated under his skin. Hellfire spat from his fingers. "I'll kill you for this."

"I think not."

The stranger's hellfire erupted. It was dark gold, slender as a blade, and just as deadly. A thin red line appeared on Tristan's throat. His expression hardly had time to register its shock before his head tumbled from his shoulders. Blood sprayed from his neck, splattering walls, ceilings, furniture.

Arthur recoiled as his father's blood struck the glass of the window above the sink. He lost his balance; his tailbone smacked hard on the dirt. With a yelp of pain, he flung himself onto his hands and knees. His stomach heaved. He lost his dinner in the dirt.

He was on his feet almost immediately, dragging his sleeve across his mouth as he dashed across the garden, through the gate, and onto the moor. His only thought was to get away. Where he was going, he had no idea. About fifty yards out, a hand collared him from behind. He jerked to a halt. Twisting, he kicked out at a shadowy foe.

"Arthur." His opponent gave him a savage shake. "Get hold of yourself, boy."

He gulped air. It wasn't the rival Nephil. It was the American adept. Mab. Outspread black wings framed her beautiful, scowling face. He didn't trust her—was, in fact, afraid of her. But just then she looked like salvation.

"Wha—" He choked. "What are you doing here?"

"I sensed something wasn't right."

"It's—not." A sob forced its way up his throat. He swallowed it back. "Father—mother— Dead. A Nephil—a rival—killed them."

"Yes, I know. He's left the house now. He's searching for you."

"Who...is he?" He dragged in a breath. The air, though cool, burned his lungs. "Why—"

"Stay down," she said sharply, shoving him to the ground. "Don't move. Wait for me." With a pass of her spread fingers, an illusion of nothingness descended around his body. Anyone looking in his direction would see unbroken moorland.

He waited, trembling. After what seemed like an eternity, Mab returned. Without a word, she lifted him from the ground, spread her wings, and took off into the sky. He clung to her, dizzy and confused, all the way to Texas.

They arrived many interminable hours later. Dusk was falling as Mab landed. Arthur looked up at the rambling wooden house and the alien landscape of moss-draped trees surrounding it. He hardly had a chance to take it all in before Mab grabbed him by the upper arm and yanked him up onto a wide porch.

A glint on her finger caused Arthur to dig in his heels. "You're wearing Father's touchstone." He stared at the diamond, embedded in a ring carved of yew wood.

"Yes." She gave him a shove across the porch. "What of it?"

"It's mine."

She chuckled. "I think not, sugar. Tristan is dead. Soon I'll be alpha in his place. His touchstone belongs to me."

Your father is dead... Arthur had seen the murder with

his own eyes, yet it still felt unreal, as if the end of his father's existence was something that couldn't possibly have happened.

They stopped before the house's door, painted blood red. Arthur dug in his heels. "Who killed my father? Give me his name. His clan."

Mab's smile widened. "Come, sugar. Do you seriously imagine you can avenge Tristan? Against a rival Nephil adept?"

"Perhaps not now," Arthur replied seriously. "But someday I will. It is my duty."

Mab turned the knob and escorted him into a narrow entry hall. "Your duty is to wipe last night from your mind."

He heard voices. Mab steered him through the foyer, down a short hall, and into a kitchen. There, fifteen or more people surrounded a large table, sharing a noisy meal. As Mab swept through the doorway, pushing Arthur before her, an abrupt silence descended.

Arthur looked slowly about the room. Piles of dirty pots and dishes were stacked in the sink and on a long countertop. Crushed beer cans and empty bottles of whiskey littered the floor. A mirror, topped by a few lines of white dust and a razor blade, lay on a sideboard, amid a forest of liquor bottles.

The people sitting at the table were no less unsettling. A number of rough-looking males and scantily dressed females. There were children, too. The youngest was only a toddler, sitting in a high chair. The rest were a blur of curious faces. He saw only one of them clearly—a girl, perhaps a year or two older than Arthur. For some reason, in his mind's eye, she shone like a rare beacon.

Maybe it was her blond hair. Arthur had never seen anything quite like it. It was long and curly, a wild, unbound mane that was just one shade darker than white.

Her green eyes, wide and framed by nearly colorless lashes, reminded him of a jade stone his father had once shown him. Her expression was curious and thoughtful at the same time. Almost, Arthur thought in a daze, like she recognized him. But that couldn't be. If he'd ever seen her before, he was sure the memory of such a momentous occurrence would be seared in his brain.

Who is she? he thought.

Mab prodded him in the back. "Are you hungry, sugar?"

Arthur, startled, looked up into Mab's glittering blue eyes. His stomach turned. Hungry? Was she mad? Just the thought of food made him want to throw up.

"No," he said. "I'm not hungry."

"Good."

She gripped his arm firmly, just above the elbow, and propelled him across the kitchen. The audience at the table, still silent, tracked his progress. Before he quite knew what was happening, Mab had opened a door and shoved him down a flight of wooden stairs.

"Stay here," she said. "Until someone comes for you." The door shut. A key scraped in the lock.

The cellar was dark and, as far as he could tell, largely empty. The floor was concrete. Given the expanse of swamp Arthur had glimpsed as Mab landed, he could only assume some kind of magic kept the subterranean room dry. Or relatively dry, anyway. The air smelled strongly of mold.

When dawn broke, he found that one small window provided the only illumination in the space. He almost wished it dark again. Water pooled at the edges of the room, but in the center, the concrete bore rusty stains. Blood.

Three days passed, by Arthur's best estimation, before Mab reappeared. In the meantime, food and drink were delivered at regular intervals, set at the top of the stair by a woman with red hair. A witch, he thought, judging from her pentagram pendant and the spiraling tattoo on her left forearm. She also might have been deaf and dumb for all the attention she paid Arthur's questions. With nothing to occupy him, he paced the damp space, consumed by grief and fear, and wondering what was to become of him.

Eventually, the door opened, admitting an older Nephil male. He introduced himself as Evander, and took Arthur up the stairs. Mab was the new Druid clan alpha, Evander told him. When Arthur asked to speak with Mab, he was told she was tending her business concerns in Houston. Arthur was to live here, in Demon's Hollow, with his American kin. Perhaps the alpha would speak to him when she returned. Or perhaps not.

Arthur emerged from the cellar to find that the American Nephilim were as far outside his experience as it was possible to be. The adept males were a crude, rough set. Their witches were blatantly sensual creatures, who talked quite a lot, in an ear-piercing Southern accent Arthur could barely follow. There were several dormants as well, including two girls. One was only a small child. The other was the wild blond with the jade eyes.

Her name was Cybele. She was tall, taller than he was, and a year older. Her white-blond hair, most often seen flowing down her back in a riot of curls, mesmerized him. She usually went barefoot, haphazardly dressed in ripped jeans. She owned any number of delicate, flowery blouses.

She seemed not quite real, more like an elemental force than a person. An elemental force that was somehow already part of himself. Arthur didn't quite know what to make of his jumbled feelings toward her, so he did his best to hide them. He was wary around her. Initially, he discouraged her repeated attempts to make friends.

Even so, he thought she sensed the connection between them, too. It was there in the air between them, invisible, but as real as the electricity that heralded a lightning storm. Cybele, it turned out, wasn't easily dissuaded once she'd set her mind on something. She just wasn't willing to let Arthur go his own way. She insisted on being his friend, whether he wanted one or not. Truth to tell, he was grateful for her persistence. She was the one good thing in his bewilderingly strange new life at Demon's Hollow.

He had nightmares of that last night at Tŷ'r Cythraul. When he woke, Cybele was always beside him. Gradually, let her in. She listened gravely as he described, in halting tones, about the night his parents died.

She told him what had happened during the three days he'd been locked in the cellar.

He'd been stunned. Sick to the core. He hadn't wanted to believe it. Magnus, Arthur's Scots cousin, dead. The rest of his father's family had offered fealty and surrendered their touchstones to Mab. They'd accepted her rubies in return.

Mab had told Arthur's kin that he'd died with his parents, Cybele whispered. They'd believed her, because Mab had given them his body. Had they never considered the possibility the body wasn't his, that they'd been fooled by Mab's magic?

After learning the truth, he'd wanted to die rather than stay in Texas. If not for Cybele, he might have done himself harm. She was the one bright light in the darkness his life had become. She was his touchstone, his hope. And once again, she was here, with him, when he needed her most. Believing in him. Waiting for him.

He went to her.

***

"What's he doing?" Lucky asked in a stage whisper.

Holy shit on a biscuit! If Maweth weren't immortal, the cherub could've taken a decade off his life.

He darted a glance at Dusek. Shimon Ben-Meir had left the room at least an hour ago. Since that time, Maweth's master had remained standing motionless at his desk, gazing down at the fractured stone stele. Thankfully, he gave no sign of having heard Lucky's outburst.

Maweth breathed a sigh of relief. "I don't know what he's doing," he hissed. "And for the thousandth time, *keep your voice down.*"

"O-kaay." Deflated, the cherub fluttered to the floor.

A slight scratching sounded at the office door. Maweth came alert. Two visitors in one morning? Jeez-o-man, it was a regular circus in here today.

Dusek looked up, frowning. "Come."

A somber, skeletal youth stepped into the room. Maweth had seen him a few times before. Lazlo, a Nephil dormant, resembled Dusek to a disturbing degree. Not in the way of a son and his father, though. More in the way of identical twins. If the second of those twins had been born fifty years after the first.

Lazlo hadn't been born, however. At least, not in the usual sense. He'd sprung to life on one of the Institute's shadowy lower levels. It was there, in utter secrecy, that Dusek practiced his most powerful alchemy.

Maweth wondered if Lazlo—or any of his half-dozen "brothers" currently alive—realized the ultimate purpose of their existence. How could they not suspect the grisly truth each time one of them disappeared? And yet, as far as Maweth could tell by looking into their blank, golden eyes, they didn't suspect a thing.

Dusek regarded his visitor with an air of irritation.

"Lazlo. To what do I owe this unwelcome disturbance?"

The clone approached the desk, bowing low. "Beg pardon, Professor. I bring news of the new thrall. The Haitian."

Maweth let out a long, guilty breath. He'd helped Dusek locate the Haitian woman in her dormant state, shortly after she'd emerged from a near-death experience. Now she was an adept, enthralled to Dusek and imprisoned in the lower levels of the Institute. But what choice had Maweth had in the matter? None. He was as much a thrall as she was.

"What of her?" Dusek asked.

"She is...distraught."

Dusek waved a hand. "Only to be expected. Her rebellion will subside, eventually."

"With respect, sir, I fear she may do herself harm before she reaches that point."

Dusek's brows rose. "Impossible. She is restrained. Physically and magically."

"Yes, sir. But within the restraints, her Vodou magic runs amok. I believe she's trying to kill herself. Her magic blazes like a torch. Her head twists and jerks most violently."

"Indeed?"

"Yes, sir."

Dusek steepled his fingers, tapping them against his chin. The face on his golden ring opened its eyes. "Interesting," he said.

Several beats of silence ensued. Lazlo shifted on his feet and cleared his throat. "What do you wish me to do about her, sir?"

"What?" Dusek looked at him, as if he'd quite forgotten his presence.

"The thrall," Lazlo said. "The Haitian. What do you

wish me to do with her?"

"Do? Why, nothing."

"But sir—"

Dusek waved a hand. "Her little rebellion will run its course. Rest assured, she will not harm herself. At least, not permanently."

Lazlo accepted this pronouncement with a nod of his head. "Very good, sir."

Dusek nodded toward the door. "Back to your duties."

"Yes, sir." Lazlo backed respectfully out the door. He neglected, however, to close it completely. A slice of light shone between the heavy mahogany slab and its frame.

Dusek stood. As he did so, his gaze fell on the mirror. His eyes seemed to meet Maweth's. Though Maweth knew the Nephil couldn't precisely see him through the quicksilver, he couldn't stop himself from shrinking back.

"Maweth." Dusek snapped his fingers. "Come."

Holy crapoly. He directed a glare toward Lucky. "I've got to answer," he whispered. "Or he'll—" He paused. "Well, never mind that. Just stay here, and stay quiet. Quiet like the grave. Not a word," he added, in case the cherub had somehow misunderstood. "Not. A. Sound."

Lucky, his blue eyes enormous, nodded.

"Maweth! Now!"

"I'm here, I'm here." With a sigh and a popping sound, Maweth materialized atop his master's desk. He bowed, adding an ironic flourish. One took one's little pleasures where one could. "What is it this time?"

Dusek's gaze narrowed. "Insolent creature."

"Let me go," Maweth said. "And problem solved."

Dusek ignored the suggestion. "Arthur Camulus," he said, "isn't in his right mind."

Maweth blinked at the unexpected conversational gambit. "Um...and you're telling me this, why? If you recall, oh Master, I'm the one who informed you of Arthur's mental state. Not..." He checked an imaginary wrist watch. "...thirty hours ago, in fact."

"A mentally unstable Nephil is dangerous," Dusek said.

Maweth had to agree with him there. He had the living proof right in front of him.

"But one who's completely lost his mind?" Dusek mused. "Why, *that* Nephil might be easily enthralled. He could be a formidable tool."

Maweth eyed him uncertainly. "Well, then. I guess you'll have to wait and see if Arthur goes completely bonkers."

"No. I can't risk Arthur recovering his wits enough to control his magic. I need to drive him over the edge. Or rather, you do."

"Me?" Maweth couldn't hide his astonishment. "How could I possibly do that?"

"How indeed?" Dusek gave a thin smile. "You are Death itself. It could not have escaped your notice that when humans think about you too closely, they often lose their minds."

"Um, well maybe, but—"

"Arthur does not even have the possibility of an afterlife to console him. He knows his death will bring Oblivion."

"Well, sure. But even so, that doesn't mean I can—"

"You will go to him," Dusek said. "Cause him to stare you in the face."

"What good will that do? He's already seen me."

"His near-death experience came before his Ordeal, when he was brashly confident. Now, he's filled with doubt, torn by forces he doesn't understand, teetering on the brink of despair. You should have little trouble sending him over the edge into madness."

Maweth threw up his hands. "That's the craziest thing I've ever heard. It won't work, I tell you. Not with Arthur. That one's not afraid to die. Not before, and not now. Getting another look at me isn't gonna—"

"Silence!"

Dusek lifted his hand. The face on his ring snapped its eyes open. Twin golden beams shot out. They knocked Maweth on his butt even before he realized they'd hit him.

Fire ignited on Maweth's skin. The ring's unblinking eyes fed it. Golden flames leaped across Maweth's body, clinging and burning in patches of utter agony. He dropped to the desktop, writhing. Dusek leaned over him, an odd smile twitching his thin lips.

Maweth swatted at the flames. It only made them jump higher, burn hotter. "Ahhhhhhhhh! St-stooooop! Make it—stop—"

"Perhaps I will," Dusek said. "When you've learned proper subservience."

"Please." Maweth rolled and, even though he knew it was hopeless, swatted desperately at his robe, his skin, his wings. "I'll do it. I'll do anything." He hissed as the ring blinked and bits of golden fire combusted anew.

"Stop," he sobbed. "Just make it—"

"Stoooooooop!" The cry arrived with a popping sound. *"Stop it noooooow!"*

A sweet wave broke over Maweth's body. The fires sizzled and died, leaving nothing but cool bliss. *Heavenly* bliss.

Oh, crap.

He jumped to his feet and threw himself between Lucky and Dusek. For all the good that was gonna do. The cat was out of the bag now, and nothing was going to shove the spitting feline back in. Dusek stared at Lucky, his expression one of pure astonishment. It was rapidly replaced by a light of pure, evil calculation.

"You idiot." Maweth grabbed Lucky by the wings and shook. "I told you to lay low."

"I couldn't!" Lucky exclaimed. "He was hurting you."

"It was just pain. He can't hurt me permanently."

"Well, well, well." Dusek moved a step to the left, affording himself a better view of the cherub. "What have we here?"

"Oh, come on," Maweth muttered. Surely Dusek could manage something a little more creative than that.

"How long have you been hiding this creature?" his master demanded.

"Not long," Maweth said quickly. "Not long at all. And besides..." Surreptitiously, he extended one foot behind him. "He was just leaving." With a sudden jerk of his leg, he kicked Lucky off the desk.

"Oof." Lucky tumbled halo-over-heels then righted himself in mid-air, wings buzzing. "What the heck was that for?"

Maweth picked up a stapler and heaved it at him. "Holy crapshoot, Lucky. Fly! To the door. Get outta here!"

Lucky looked to the door, and back at him. "Leave you?"

"Yes. Go. Now!"

Thud.

Dusek was across the room, his hand on the door. The shut door.

Maweth's shoulders sagged. "Jumping Jehoshaphat, Lucky. You're an idiot. Do you know that? A dolt. A lunkhead. A moron, a clodpole—"

Lucky fluttered down beside him.

"—a numbskull," he continued furiously. "A bubblehead, a saphead, a nimrod—"

The angel sniffed. "For not abandoning you?"

"—a pinhead, a doofus, a lamebrain, an imbecile, a meathead, a—"

Dusek approached the desk. "Are you quite done?"

Maweth looked up and abruptly shut his mouth. His master smiled broadly. Showed his teeth, even. His eyes gleamed. It was an awful, awful sight. Maweth inched closer to Lucky. Snaking his left arm around the angel's shoulders, he pulled him tight to his side. Lucky clutched at his waist.

Several moments ticked silently by.

"An angel," Dusek said at last. "Well. One could hardly have predicted this turn of events."

No, Maweth thought sourly. One could not have, even if one had guessed at it for half of eternity.

The gleam in Dusek's eyes sharpened. He moved close. Too close, as far as Maweth was concerned. Lucky turned and buried his face in Maweth's robes.

"I see a new path," Dusek murmured. The face on his ring smiled.

That ring really, really creeped Maweth out. He averted his eyes from it. "Um...and what path would that be?"

With a smooth motion, Dusek reached out and plucked two feathers from Lucky's wings.

"Ouch!" Lucky cried, jerking around. "Hey! Give those back."

Dusek tucked the feathers in his breast pocket. His chin jerked toward the mirror. "Into the quicksilver. Both of you."

"But—" Lucky said.

"Now."

"But—"

"Forget it, Lucky. There's no arguing with him." With a swirl and a pop, Maweth dove into the quicksilver, pulling

Lucky after him.

Once inside, Lucky collapsed. "That was scary."

Maweth slumped on the floor beside him. "You're crazy, Lucky. You had a chance to get away. You shoulda bailed."

Lucky's blue eyes snapped with indignation. "Without you? I would never!"

Maweth didn't quite know how to reply to that. No one had ever really wanted to stay with him before. His boney chest ached strangely, and his vision went all blurry.

"Um...Maweth?" Lucky ventured.

"Huh?"

"What'd'ya think Dusek wanted my feathers for?"

"I have no idea," Maweth said wearily. "But I guarantee you, Lucky—whatever it is, we are not going to like it."

SEVEN

The stair creaked under Arthur's weight. When he gained the uppermost landing, he paused. The door was slightly ajar. The light he'd seen from the garden flickered behind it. The rhythm of deep, even breathing reached his ears.

Cybele was asleep in his childhood bed. The thought was unbearably arousing. And unsettling. This collision of his past and present lives threatened to knock him even farther off balance than he already was.

He pushed the door open. She lay curled on her side, in a tangle of white sheets, one hand tucked under her chin. Her braid, unwound from her head, lay across the mattress like a thick yellow rope. His old blanket lay in a dusty heap on the floor. No doubt she'd kicked it there. Cybele wasn't a restful sleeper. She wasn't particularly restful when awake, either.

The room, set under steeply sloping rafters, was very warm. Heat radiated from a small wood-burning stove in one corner. A battered copper stock pot sat atop it. Dormer windows, five on either side, threw daylight into the space. Other than the woman in his bed and an extra layer of dust, the attic looked much as it had the day he'd left it.

Low shelves lined the north wall. Arthur's father had built them to hold the books his son never seemed to be able to leave in the library. A desk and chair stood nearby, his old algebra textbook open atop it. A calculator, along with a lined sheet of paper bearing scribbled calculations, lay beside it. Arthur hadn't attended the village school; his father had been his tutor. While Arthur had loved history and poetry, and hadn't minded writing, he'd hated math. He could almost see his younger self seated at the desk, scowling at his miscalculations and wishing his father to Oblivion.

He winced at the memory. His boyhood innocence seemed criminal now. If only he'd known how idyllic his life was and how bitterly he'd mourn his father. A new wave of grief rose. He couldn't—wouldn't—allow it to break. The past, and all its associated grief, was as much a part of him as the blood in his veins. Like blood, spilling it would only make him weak.

He prowled to the edge of the bed, his eyes and his heart seeking Cybele. If not for her, his life in Demon's Hollow would've been unendurable. When he sank into black despair, she refused to allow it. She'd dragged him back into the sun.

He wondered what she'd thought when she explored the room, sifting through the detritus of his past. He had no doubt that she had. He smiled faintly, picturing her opening drawers and cupboards, and peering under the bed, before curling up atop it and falling asleep.

Dressed in her dark jeans and gauzy, flowery blouse, one cheek smeared with dirt, she looked the picture of innocence. She wasn't. No Nephil dormant, growing up in Mab's world, could possibly stay innocent. And Cybele was no child. She had, in fact, recently passed her twentieth birthday. She was a full adult by Nephil custom, ready to face her Ordeal. Arthur was younger. At nineteen, he wasn't even of age.

At this moment, though, the distance between them wasn't best measured in time.

She stirred. Inhaling deeply, she rolled over and sank more firmly into slumber. The loose neckline of her blouse slipped, revealing a pale shoulder. Arthur was no stranger to Cybele's body. Right now, though, it felt like a new wonder. Like something he was seeing for the very first time.

His gaze traveled over her body, taking in the swell of her generous breasts, the curve of her buttocks, the grace of her long legs. Whatever blood that was left in his brain drained south. It felt as though the top of his skull were floating several inches above the rest of his head.

He was hard, his erection straining against the zipper of his jeans. Flashes of what he wanted to do to Cybele careened through his brain. This was nothing new. Before they'd become lovers, Arthur had spent a full three years dreaming of Cybele. His nights had been plagued with images and sensations: silky hair brushing pink-tipped breasts, a smooth, rounded bottom in his hands, his fingers delving into the slick wetness between her thighs.

All his youthful turmoil, as fierce as it had seemed at the time, struck him as obscenely naïve. Dark lusts tore at him now—desires that in no way resembled the musings of his innocent youth. Demon urges, unholy yearnings sprung from his Nephil nature, infested his brain. Sweat and strength; ecstasy and violence. The things his demon mind envisioned for Cybele—and for himself—broke a cold sweat on his brow.

He gripped the bedpost, his fingernails pressing into the wood. He closed his eyes against a wave of raw lust. His body shook. He wanted to fall on her, claim her, use her.

It was a close thing, but in the end, his better nature—

his human nature—gained the upper hand. His fingers unclenched, and he drew a deep breath. The small victory over his baser self steadied him. He was a Nephil, there was no denying that. But perhaps he wasn't a monster. Or at least, not completely.

He sat on the edge of the bed, silent, not touching her. She sensed his presence, though, as she so often did when he was near. With a sleepy groan, she rolled onto her back.

Green eyes fluttered open. "You're back."

"Yes."

She came up slightly, supporting herself on her elbows. His eyes followed the sway of her breasts. When they returned to her face, he saw she was frowning.

"You're all wet. Is it raining?"

"No. I washed again. At the well." He hesitated, then added, "There was more blood."

"You...found something to kill, then?"

He tensed. "I...yes."

"That's good." She bit her lip. "What was it?"

"A bull." It was a cowardly partial truth, but he couldn't bring himself to say more.

Her eyes returned to his. He read relief there. "This was your second kill?"

He nodded.

"It should be easier to resist from now on."

Arthur wasn't so sure about that, but for her sake, he nodded again. Then compounded the lie by saying, "Yes. The deathlust is fading."

His gaze slid from her face, to stare at a gouge in the floor. His hunger for killing was far from fading. Despite the lives he'd so recently taken, he felt restless and empty, ready to kill again. Was this driving need for death normal? Or was it the product of his unguided Ordeal? He didn't know. There was no adept to ask, and his ancestors' memories, swirling chaotically in his skull, were no help at all.

"Hey."

His head swung back to her. She smiled, tentatively, and held out a hand. He studied it, but didn't take it.

Her smile faded. She let her hand drop to the mattress. "What's wrong?"

"How did you get here?"

"I told you, I knew you'd be coming here, and—"

"Not why did you come here," he said. "How? How did you get to from Texas to England? You don't have a passport."

"Oh, that." She made a dismissive gesture. "I didn't need one. I hitchhiked to Houston, slipped through airport security, and boarded the first plane to London."

His brows rose at this. "No one stopped you?"

"Of course not." She slipped her hand in her pocket and pulled out the tight bundle of alder shoots Arthur had helped her weave years ago. Nestled inside was Cybele's touchstone, a green peridot. "I had this, didn't I? And anyway, humans are amazingly unaware. Not one of them even blinked at my illusions, let alone saw past them. I landed at Heathrow, caught a train to Exeter, then a bus to that cute village on the edge of the moor. I walked the rest of the way."

He was impressed. Cybele's magic far surpassed that of any human witch. Arthur hadn't known many female Nephil dormants—the larger majority, more than eighty percent, of Nephil births were male. But he couldn't imagine that many female dormants held a candle to Cybele.

"You didn't have trouble seeing Tŷ'r Cythraul from the lane?" he asked. "Mab's wardings are strong."

She slipped her touchstone back into her pocket. "It

was a little tricky," she admitted. "But you described the house to me once—do you remember? That first night we snuck down to the beach?"

That had been two summers ago. The first time they'd been alone together away from Demon's Hollow. They'd sat on the sand and kissed for the first time. "I don't even know what we talked about that night," he admitted. "I mostly just remember kissing you. And how cheesed off Luc was the next morning when he found out we'd gone to the beach without him."

A shadow passed through Cybele's eyes. He saw her deliberately blink it away. Damn, but he was a sodding idiot. He never should've mentioned Luc.

She shook her head slightly. "I remember every minute of that night. Including what we talked about. But even though I knew what the house looked like, I almost missed seeing it. I walked up and down the road a half-dozen times, wondering if I was in the wrong place entirely. Then I noticed a clump of trees that didn't look quite right. You know? Like when you paste a picture onto another one and don't quite match up the edges. After that, the house practically jumped out at me."

"That's remarkable. I would've thought only an adept could see through Mab's illusions. And not easily, at that."

"I didn't have much choice, did I? I wasn't about to turn around and go home. I was so scared, worrying about you. Why didn't you come back to Demon's Hollow, like we planned?"

He ran his hand over his head. *Because I didn't remember Demon's Hollow. Or you, or Luc, or anyone else. Only Mab.*

"I don't know," he said. "When I came out of the Ordeal, my brain was rubbish." *Still is.*

"I was so afraid you were dead."

"I'm not. As you see."

"Yes." She reached out and touched him.

Just that tiny point of contact—the tip of her finger against his forearm—reignited his lust. His body tensed. His cock jumped. The attic walls seemed to spin. He closed his eyes, but the lack of sight only made things worse. The sound of her breath made him want to haul her into his arms. His lungs expanded with the scent of her. She smelled of the sky: vibrant and endless, with a hint of storm on the horizon.

He stood abruptly, turning his back. "Now that you know I'm alive, maybe you should leave."

"Leave?" Her tone conveyed utter disbelief. "Are you nuts? Where would I go?"

"Somewhere safe," he said.

"There is no such place. Arthur. Look at me."

He turned around. She regarded him seriously. "Even if there was a safe place, I wouldn't go. I'm staying with you."

"You don't know what I am now."

At that, her brows hiked up. "Of course I do. I've lived with adepts all my life, remember?"

"Not ones who aren't...who can't—" He blew out a breath. "Not ones like me."

"Aren't what? Can't what? What are you trying to say?"

He walked to the window and stared out over the moor. "My power...it's too much. It's tearing me apart. I'm afraid it'll rip you apart, too."

"You would never hurt me."

He pressed his forehead against the glass. "Not true," he said. "I already have."

He heard a sigh and a rustle of bedclothes. He imagined her untangling her long legs from the sheets and swinging them over the side of the mattress. Her footsteps approached. When she laid a soft hand on his shoulder, he flinched.

"This conversation is ridiculous," she said. "We both know I'm not going anywhere. Come on. Turn around."

He did as she asked. "Cybele—" Before his mind registered what was happening, she crossed her arms, grasped the hem of her blouse, and pulled it half-way over her head.

"No." He yanked her arm down. Her shirt fell back into place, but not before he'd caught a flash of creamy skin and a rose-brown nipple. *Dear ancestors. No bra.* He went still, his fingers tightening on her wrist, staring at the place where that damn sleeve had slipped off her shoulder. Again.

"Not a good idea." His voice was like rust.

She gave a huff of exasperation. "I think it's an excellent idea."

"It's not. When I'm not in my right mind...sexual lust...deathlust...it all feels the same."

Her eyes widened. "You can't possibly think you'll kill me.

He loosened his grip on her wrist and let her hand drop. "It could happen," he said.

Her brows came down. "Okay, yeah. That is kinda a mood killer." She studied him. "But maybe you'll calm down once you wash off all that blood."

"I washed at the well," he said.

"You did a half-assed job of it."

"All right." He headed for the door. "I'll take care of it."

She caught his arm from behind. "Let me do it."

He looked at her over his shoulder. "There's no water."

"Yes, there is. I brought it up earlier." She nodded toward the stockpot. "It should be hot by now. I've got clean towels, too." They were stacked on a chair nearby.

He hesitated.

"Arthur..."

Cybele had never been one for subtlety. The look on her face told him there was no chance of him slinking off into some corner to hide. If he went down to the library, or to the garden, she'd follow. Bugger it all, even if he fled to the other side of the globe, she'd be right behind him. To be brutally honest, he was—cowardly, selfishly—glad of it.

"All right," he said. "But make it quick."

He tracked her progress across the room. Why couldn't that damn neckline stay put? The slope of her shoulder showed through the tangled silk of her hair. He couldn't force himself to look away. Absently, she gathered all that hair into an elastic band she'd been wearing on her wrist, and then shrugged the drooping sleeve back into place. He felt the loss like a punch to the gut.

Lifting the pot's top, she picked up a cloth and dunked it in. Water splashed. "A little hot, but I figure that'll feel good." She glanced at him over her shoulder. "Well, step it up. Get over here."

His feet moved. Her scent reached out, gathered him in. A flash of dark excitement raced through him. The same sensation he'd experienced seconds before he dove to a kill.

Bloody hell.

She made a swirling motion with one finger. "Turn around."

He met her gaze briefly before obeying the order. He tensed as the wet cloth met his skin. She stroked his upper back. Hot water trickled down his spine. She was right. It did feel good. Way too good. He swallowed.

She swiped the towel across his lower back, just above the waistband of his jeans. He imagined her hands lower, cupping his arse. Her fingernails curling into his skin.

Another stroke, this time up his right flank and shoulder, and then down his arm. His breath grew ragged. When he closed his eyes, violent red light exploded behind his eyelids.

"You're so tense," she murmured. "Relax."

"I'm fine," he bit off. "Just get on with it."

He heard splashing as she dunked the cloth and wrung it out. Her hands trembled. He felt it when the cloth touched his back again. Even so, she washed a methodical path, back and forth, working her way from the top of his spine to his lower back.

This attempt at calm didn't fool him. Cybele wasn't fond of restraint. She was only careful when she was uncertain. Though he could tell she was trying to control her breathing, it wasn't quite steady. Neither was his.

She attempted conversation. "How much time do you think it'll take? To get ready for Mab, I mean."

This was not a subject Arthur wished to pursue. "Don't know."

The cloth paused. "We should talk about it."

"No," he said. "We shouldn't."

"Arthur—"

"Are you quite done?"

"Almost." She sounded as agitated as he felt. She dunked the cloth and wrung it out, and then came around his left side. When she stroked up over his shoulder and swiped the cloth down his chest, he snatched the rag from her hand.

"Enough."

"Not hardly."

He threw the wet rag onto the washstand. "It's early yet. Go back to sleep."

"With you?"

"I'm not tired."

"Well, neither am I." Her gaze traveled across his chest. He felt its touch more distinctly than he'd felt the cloth. "You're clean now. If we're not going to sleep, there are other things we can do."

He swallowed. "No."

She tilted her head and met his gaze. A smile tugged at her lips. "I say yes. You're in a crappy mood. You know what's good for crappy moods? Sex." Her lashes swept downward.

"Cybele, I—"

He cut off as her forefinger touched the center of his chest. Sucked in air as she dragged it slowly downward. She paused at his navel. His stomach muscles went rock-hard. He wanted that finger lower. In his mind, it was already there.

She withdrew her hand and smiled. "You don't want to talk, and you don't want to sleep. Not much else to do but make love."

Not true. There was plenty to do. He could explore the focusing power of his mother's touchstone. He could go out on the moor and attempt to throw hellfire without incinerating himself. He could fashion illusions that didn't fall apart with a sneeze. He could try to take those illusions one step further, into reality. He could reach into the morass inside his skull and pluck out an ancestral memory that would lead him to magic powerful enough to destroy Mab.

He should be doing any or all of those things. And he *would* be doing them, right this moment, if his magic didn't scare the piss out of him. It was just too strong. Or he was too weak. Either way, he wouldn't risk calling it in front of Cybele. What if his lusts caused another blackout? The thought of losing control of his mind and his power while she was nearby terrified him.

He had to get out—out of the room, at least. Arguing with Cybele, once she got an idea fixed in her head, was an exercise in futility. He'd seen that mischievous light in her eyes before. Often. It never failed to get him hard, and right now was no exception. Bugger it all, if he got any harder, his cock would snap off.

Leave. Turn around and walk down the stair.

He couldn't make his feet move the requisite number of steps toward the door. Cybele tugged her hair out of its elastic band and shook her head. He couldn't look away. She combed her fingers through the blond curls, separating the strands, and then let it drop into a wild riot about her head.

She bent forward from the waist, the heavy mass of her hair falling forward over one shoulder. Before his dazed mind registered her intent, she yanked her blouse over her head and dropped it on the floor.

She straightened. Once again, a sensation of newness washed over him. He felt as though he was seeing her bare breasts for the first time. High and proud, tipped with dusky nipples. Beautiful. Inviting. His nostrils flared; his palms itched. He wanted to stroke, to smell, to suck. Wanted to feel her life's blood coursing beneath her skin. Wanted to see it spill...

Fuck. "Cybele—" He gave his head a violent shake. "No."

"What's wrong?" The flash of hurt in her eyes was quickly masked. "Not interested in a dormant, now that you're an adept?"

He licked his dry lips. "That's ridiculous."

"Is it?" Her palms went to the small of her back.

He tried to ignore what the motion did to her breasts. "Yes. It is. If you only knew how much I want you right now—"

"Then what's the problem?"

"I don't want to hurt you."

"You won't."

She came a step closer. Like a fool, he couldn't back away. Of course, being Cybele, she didn't stop until the tips of her nipples brushed his chest. She tilted her head up—not far, since she was almost as tall as he. He searched her eyes, and felt himself tumble into a turbulent jade sea.

He gripped her shoulders. Did he have some half-baked notion that he was strong enough to push her away? Impossible. Her skin was smooth and warm, and slightly damp. Her scent enveloped him.

He was on fire with lust. His palms slid down her shoulders, stroked around to her upper back. He brought her flush against his body. She melted into him, fitting her body to his in that way she had that never failed to drive him wild. Her lips brushed his neck, kissing, then softly nipping.

He groaned. He felt her smile. Her arms encircled his torso, hugging him close. Her thighs cradled his rampant cock. She circled her hips and a shudder ran through him. Her strength, her scent, her need—it all wove in and out through his body. He couldn't—didn't want to—resist her.

"That's it," she murmured against the hollow of his throat. "Relax. Let me do everything."

"Cybele." He framed her face with his hands, urging her to look at him. "You don't know what you're asking."

"Yes, I do."

"You think so, but...you have no idea...what I'm like now. My magic...it's too strong for this."

"Why should it be? Adept males have sex with human witches all the time."

That was true enough. But most adepts didn't

experience blackouts. Gaps in their memories that involved blood and magic and death.

She mistook his silence for acceptance. "Don't worry so much." Her head slipped from his fingers, her hair slid over his chest. The tip of her tongue drew a line from his throat to his left nipple. She scraped the puckered point with her teeth. Sizzling lust shot straight to his groin.

She dropped to her knees. Her fingers worked his belt buckle. His zipper. He moaned as his erection sprang into her hand. When her cool fingers closed around him, his mind blanked.

He speared his fingers through her hair, gripping hard. She pressed a kiss to the underside of his penis and looked up at him through her lashes. Their eyes locked.

"Should I stop?" she asked.

"No," he rasped.

Holding his gaze, she licked. A slow, smooth sweep of her tongue, from the base of his cock to the head. All the while, her fingers teased his balls. He groaned. His knees threatened to buckle.

He was completely off balance, and yet, for the first time since exiting his Ordeal, he also felt centered. Grounded. With her. He needed this, he realized. Needed Cybele more than he needed breath or sanity. Maybe he could keep his magic under control long enough to make love to her.

No. He *would* keep it under control.

She parted her lips. His cock slid, wetly, into her mouth. Hot. So hot. His head fell back. A sound halfway between pain and bliss escaped from his throat.

She withdrew, but kept the tip of her tongue in contact. "Feels that good?"

"Fuck." Air hissed through his teeth. "There are...no words."

She gave a little hum of approval as she returned to her task. Bit by bit, the darkness inside him receded. Her tongue, her lips, the gentle scrape of her teeth—it felt like a benediction. He held on to the feeling as long as he could. Which was hardly any time at all.

Then he was hooking his hands under her armpits, dragging her up to her feet. He took her mouth in a deep, drugging kiss, tasting himself on her tongue. He filled his hands with her breasts, squeezing, pinching. She gasped. She slipped her hands into his jeans and grabbed his arse. He dipped his head, licking and sucking.

With shaking hands, he unfastened her jeans. He urged her across the room, backing her toward the bed. Sunlight streamed through the window. For one arrested second, he was mesmerized by the play of it on her hair. Until a slight movement at the corner of his eye snagged his attention. He turned his head sharply to peer through the glass.

"What?" Cybele leaned around him and looked out the window. "Is something out there?"

His eyes raked the branches of the oak. "Must've been a breeze," he said at last. "Moving the branches."

"Oh." She leaned against him, her back pressed to his chest, reaching behind to run her hands up his flanks.

He spun her around and tumbled her onto the bed. She laughed as they fell, grabbing his shoulders to pull him down on top of her. He all but tore off her jeans and underwear. She returned the favor. While he struggled out of his boots, she leaned over the side of the bed and fumbled in the front pocket of her backpack.

"Condom," she said, pressing the packet into his hand.

"Right." It was another testament to his fried brain that he hadn't thought of it himself. Nephil females didn't conceive easily, but there was always a chance it could happen. They'd taken precautions from the start. Mab would've gone ballistic if Cybele had fallen pregnant. And now, with everything so precarious? The last thing he wanted to worry about was fathering a child he wasn't in a position to protect.

He quickly rolled the condom on. Finally, they lay on the bed, naked and gasping, limbs entwined, his cock probing between her thighs. She was wet there, slick and welcoming.

"Can't wait," he gasped.

"Don't." Her fingernails dug into his buttocks.

He thrust inside her with a single deep plunge. Her inner muscles contracted like a fist. His breath deserted him. *By all the forsaken ancestors in Oblivion.* Her hips followed his as he withdrew. One of her knees hooked around his waist, opening her body even more. He slid back in.

She felt so damn good. She always had, from the very first time. And each time afterward. Every time he succeeded in making her gasp with pleasure, each time she whispered how she loved him, he lost another part of his heart to her.

She bucked beneath him, rolling her hips in sublime motion. He answered with deep thrusts, each one half-lifting her off the bed. She moaned her approval. He grew harder. She arched upward and opened her mouth on his chest, licking the sweat from his skin. He dragged in a breath. She smelled like musk and earth, fire and sky, rain and peace, all at once.

Their frenzy mounted. He bit her neck. Her fingernails scored his back. He hooked both arms under her knees. The new angle of penetration tore a cry from her throat.

"Fuck me, Arthur. Harder." She arched her back to give him even better access.

He took it. He'd never get enough of her. Never. She was his. Only his.

If you can keep her safe, a voice in his head taunted. *From Mab, from Rand, from her Ordeal. If you can't...*

No. He could. He would. He shoved fear of the future into the back of his mind and tried to anchor himself in the moment. He focused on Cybele—her heat, her touch, her face. Her eyes were shut. She was close to coming. He gripped her hips and moved faster. Plunged deeper. He'd defend her to the death, with everything he was, with every shred of magic he possessed.

And if it's not enough? If I'm not enough? If Mab wins... If Cybele becomes Rand's thrall... His ruminating thoughts hurtled him into a place of raw, burning anger. In the space of one breath to the next, his fury snapped into a towering blaze and hit flashpoint.

White light seared the inside of his eyelids. Cybele's inner muscles spasmed. Her body arched. She cried out. His cock was like granite. He grabbed the headboard with both hands, thrusting like a madman. She whimpered. He growled.

Another flash of light. His eyes opened to see the room dissolve in a shower of sparks. His body convulsed. Cybele called his name. He heard the sound of cracking wood.

His orgasm hit him like a small explosion. Pure sensation consumed him. His body convulsed. His ears rang.

The world went white.

***

This was not, Michael thought ruefully, his finest hour.

No self-respecting archangel found himself perched on a tree limb, eyes riveted on a bedroom window. Well, not on the window itself. On what was happening on the other side of the glass.

He should feel guilty. Curiously, he didn't. After all, Raphael had ordered him to keep an eye on Arthur Camulus. He was doing just that. Even so, it was rather disingenuous to claim his orders required him to watch a Nephil adept and his dormant female companion engaging in copulation.

Truly, his voyeurism wasn't appropriate. Not in this universe, nor in any other.

Michael didn't care. If he cared, he'd have to stop, and he wasn't remotely ready to do that. Inappropriate as his peeping might be, it was also interesting. Internet sex, he was discovering, didn't hold a candle to the real thing.

Besides. Raphael was probably overreacting about Arthur. His big brother did tend to create storm clouds out of the slightest wisps of fog. Michael had discussed the whole thing with Gabriel after Raphael had flown off.

It was true that Arthur's direct ancestor, the Nephil Merlin, had possessed far too much magic. The magnitude of Merlin's power had been a direct result of his unguided Ordeal. The situation had allowed the sorcerer to manipulate human events to a disturbing degree. For example, Merlin's powers of illusion had been so strong, he'd been able to substitute a fierce stranger into the bed of a loyal wife. The deceit had been so skillfully wrought that Lady Igraine hadn't so much as suspected she was fornicating with young, brash Uther Pendragon, rather than her own husband. At least, not until it was all over, and her lover's true face was revealed.

Merlin hadn't stopped with that little bit of mischief. He'd followed it up with stealing the offspring of Igraine and Uther's sinful union. He schooled the boy in all manner of war skills and forbidden magic. Eventually, via some improbable trickery regarding a sword and a stone,

Merlin had arranged for Arthur Pendragon to become King of the Britons.

True, King Arthur had been a fine warrior on his own merit. But no mere human, no matter how brilliant his warcraft, could've won battle after battle the way Arthur had. Not without the demonic assistance. This, Merlin had provided in spades. If King Arthur was a legend—and he was—he owed it all to Nephil magic.

Yes, Merlin had been very dangerous. In the end, though, he'd done himself in. Not much surprise there. Nephilim were, as a rule, their own worst enemies. Give them a little rope, and they'd hang themselves every time. Arthur, Michael suspected, would prove no different. In fact, he probably couldn't help it, even if he wanted to. As a Nephil, Arthur was, by definition, a cursed abomination. The soulless son of a fallen angel, to whom even Hell was denied. What could one expect of such a creature but sin? With no afterlife to look forward to, he was bound to create havoc on Earth.

Chilled by the thought of such mortal finality, Michael returned his attention to the window. Though every Nephil was bound for Oblivion, the two on the other side of the window didn't at present seem troubled by an existential crisis. On the contrary. To all appearances, they were having a very, very good time.

It only made sense, he supposed. If one was doomed to a fleeting, insignificant existence, one could be expected to seize life's every pleasure before the final curtain fell.

"Arthur! Oh, Arthur!"

His gaze narrowed. Nephil sex certainly appeared pleasurable. More so, even, than human copulation. No wonder. Nephil males were large, in all aspects of their anatomy. According to the Internet, size mattered.

Adjusting his grip, Michael eased farther along the tree

branch. His wings fluttered, assisting his balance. Arthur's sex partner was unlike any female—human, demon, angel, or Nephil—Michael had ever laid eyes on. She was tall and lushly formed, graceful and long-limbed. Her breasts were glorious when clothed. Nude, with rose-brown nipples on full display, they were mesmerizing. Her skin was like fresh cream. Her hair—long, blond, and curling—rivaled the sun.

Cybele. Arthur had called her Cybele.

He was rutting atop her, buttocks flexing with fierce purpose. Michael wasn't sure why Arthur had let things get this far—hadn't he stated, just moments ago, he was afraid of hurting her? Given the wild frenzy going on behind the window, that outcome seemed entirely possible. Arthur's control over his newly acquired adept power was sorely lacking.

Michael considered an intervention. He was certainly able to put a halt to the proceedings. He could even manage it in a way that wouldn't reveal his presence. He might have done it, too, if it seemed like Cybele was in distress.

She didn't appear to be. She looked, in fact, like she was enjoying herself immensely. Her hips met Arthur's thrust for thrust. She clawed at his back, leaving long red scratch marks on either side of his spine. Her head tossed back and forth on the pillow. Dear Heaven. The expression on her face was... *Dear Heaven.*

He moved another inch farther out onto the limb, angling for a more direct view. In that instant, her eyelids fluttered open. Their gazes locked. For one eternal moment, Michael lost himself in a moss-green sea. Then Arthur's head dipped. His mouth opened and sucked in one taut nipple. Cybele's body arched. Her lips parted. She turned her head away and let out a long, sweet moan.

Michael's breathing became decidedly unsteady.

"Fuck me, Arthur. Harder." Blessed be. Her voice. It was like amber honey.

Arthur obliged, driving deep into Cybele's body. Michael swallowed audibly.

His hand snaked downward. With trembling fingers, he unbuttoned and unzipped his pants. He eased his penis out of his briefs. Eyes riveted on the scene before him, he wrapped his hand around his shaft and pulled. Once. Twice. Again. And again.

Nothing happened.

Arthur's sex organ was a rigid log. Michael's was a limp noodle. Yet another grievance to lay at the feet of the Watchers. After the fallen angels had run amok on Earth, impregnating the daughters of men, the Almighty put down his holy foot. With all the righteousness of a farmer slamming the barn door after the cows had run off, He'd proceeded to remove certain functionalities from every un-fallen angel left in Heaven.

Michael could assume a fleshy body. No problem at all with that. It was just that an important bit of that flesh refused to work.

All he could do was watch. And yearn.

EIGHT

"Arthur?"

He half-grunted a reply.

"Arthur." Cybele poked her fingernail into his back. "Can't...breathe. Get...off me."

With a second grunt, he obligingly rolled to one side on the tilted mattress. The movement caused the bed's frame, which was already half-broken, to come apart completely. The headboard pitched backward, hitting the wall. The side rails and footboard, with no such support nearby, simply crashed to the floor. Cybele grabbed the edge of the mattress as it bounced. It settled with a thud.

Arthur slept through it all.

She drew a deep, much-needed breath. Oxygen rushed into her lungs. By all the stars in all the universe. By all the freaking ancestors in Oblivion. She'd wanted sex, and she'd damn well gotten it.

She'd just never known it could be like that.

Arthur's breathing slowed and deepened. He'd probably be out for a while still. She just hoped that by the time he woke up, she'd be able to wrap her head around what had happened between them. She pushed herself up on her elbows and winced. Dang it all, her shoulder hurt. It'd slammed into the headboard when Arthur had...

Her heartbeat accelerated, just thinking about all the things he'd done to her. And all the things she'd done back.

There were bite marks on her neck and breast. Bruises on her shoulder and hip. A deep, satisfying throb between her legs.

She tried to sit up. *Ouch.* She collapsed back onto the mattress. Her back ached, and the rest of her body felt like one big bruise. Getting to her feet was going to hurt. She'd made out better than the bed had, she thought with a spurt of amusement. At least she was in one piece.

They'd never actually done it in a bed before.

She laughed out loud. *That* caused a sharp, shooting pain through her ribs. She couldn't regret it, though. It'd been worth it.

She and Arthur had been lovers for almost a year. It would've happened a couple years sooner, if not for Mab. As a rule, the Druid alpha didn't much care what her dormants got up to, whether it was skipping school, smoking pot, setting fire to local homes, or screwing their brains out. Luc had certainly taken advantage of his freedom, pursuing witches and non-magical girls at every opportunity. There were never any consequences from local law enforcement or truancy officers. Mab's magic kept them away.

Mab had a separate set of rules for Arthur. He wasn't allowed to leave Demon's Hollow, not even to attend school. Evander and the other adepts left him alone, and the witches were told to steer clear of him. If he'd tried, Arthur might have made friends with the other male dormants. He ignored them instead, which only pissed them off. After a few fistfights—and worse—in which Arthur managed to give as well as he got, they grudgingly left him alone.

Through it all, the spark Cybele had felt when she first laid eyes on him never faded. Arthur was wholly outside her experience. He fascinated her. And he must be special, or else why would Mab treat him so differently than the other dormants? Why had she told his British kin that he was dead?

He was quiet and withdrawn, with a haunted look in his eyes that made her want to cry. He didn't eat much, but somehow still maintained a taut, wiry strength. She began following him everywhere, trying to talk to him. He ignored her at first. Then he'd told her to leave him alone. Of course she hadn't.

It'd taken real persistence to draw him out of his hard shell. When she finally broke through, finally got him talking about his life in England, she'd been stunned. He'd never been afraid of his parents, or any of his Nephil kin? He'd studied literature, philosophy, science, and math? He actually *liked* books, and wished there were more than paperback novels at Demon's Hollow? He wished he could go to school?

It was incredible. Cybele could read just fine when she needed to, and she knew how to add two plus two. She sometimes even showed up at school. Otherwise, her education came mainly from television and the Internet. She knew only the barest details of Nephil history. Arthur, it seemed, knew everything. And why shouldn't he? He was the direct descendant of Merlin, the most powerful Nephil of the Druid clan—perhaps the most powerful Nephil of any clan.

He hated Mab. He was certain his British kin would come to take him back to England. When Cybele told him they'd already come and had been told he was dead, the color drained from his face. When she'd told him one of them had challenged Mab and been sent to Oblivion, and that the rest had given up their touchstones and pledged fealty to their new alpha, his gray eyes had turned so cold she'd felt an icy shiver pass through her.

Arthur did everything he could to avoid Mab. Luckily for him, it wasn't hard. Mab spent most of her time at Club Tartarus, her exclusive and very expensive BDSM club in Houston. Demon's Hollow day-to-day drug smuggling operation was left to Draven. The oversight of the Druid dormants and the various witches who came and went at the compound was Evander's concern.

Mab was never absent, however, for a dormant's twentieth birthday. Soon after coming of age, a young Nephil was forced to ingest a near-fatal dose of cocaine. If the dormant lived, Mab guided the transitioning Nephil through the Ordeal. If the candidate lived, the new adept became Mab's newest thrall.

It was no secret Mab intended to guide Arthur's Ordeal. This was why, Arthur believed, she'd told his British relations he was dead. As Mab's thrall, Arthur's magic— the magic of the line of Merlin—would be in her control. Arthur believed that if his relatives knew he was alive, they'd fight to get him back.

Cybele wasn't so sure about that. She'd seen them, after all. After Magnus dueled and lost, none of the others had been willing to stand against Mab.

Through the months and years after Arthur came to Texas, Cybele's magic continued to grow. Whether Arthur himself had somehow triggered her awakening, she didn't know. She'd been the right age for it, but had felt nothing until she'd looked into Arthur's eyes. Luc, when he realized what was happening, had been jealous of her new power. Arthur, when she finally told him about it, had been thrilled.

At Arthur's urging, Cybele had kept the extent of her talent hidden. She'd shown Mab just enough minor magic to seem plausible, while practicing the more difficult tasks in secret. Magic wasn't easy. Self-taught progress was excruciatingly slow. Every time Cybele hit a snag, she wondered if she should go to one of the adepts for guidance. Every time, Arthur talked her out of it.

Arthur urged her to find a touchstone. She'd bought a pretty green peridot at a shop in town. He'd helped her gather alder shoots and braid them into a tight ball around the gem. When she'd started to experiment, using the touchstone to focus her magic, he helped her by telling her every last thing he could remember about his parents' practice of Druidry.

On her own, she probably would have given up. Because of Arthur, she'd persisted through every frustration. Bit by bit, her first, simple illusions became more complex. Her talent at deflecting attention grew. Arthur was beside her every step of the way, encouraging every risk, praising every success.

By the time she'd turned sixteen, and Arthur fifteen, she'd been irrevocably in love with him. It wasn't until three long years later, when they were absolutely sure Cybele could deflect the attention of every adept, dormant, and witch at Demon's Hollow, that they finally dared to make love.

It'd been the first time for both of them. They snuck out of the compound and ran down to the beach a mile away. The full moon, glittering on the still water, had been their backdrop. The sex had been memorable, even if it'd been cold, gritty, and over way too quick. But with practice—as often as they could manage it—things got better. A lot better.

Now, lying in Arthur's broken bed, Cybele took a deep breath and tried to relax. It was useless. The sheets smelled of sex, and the memory of what they'd done wouldn't let her go. Those memories were a jumble of excitement, fear, and blinding pleasure. Her back ached like crazy. Her skin was damp and sticky. She examined her arms and torso. More bruises were beginning to show. A day ago, she'd thought she knew what good sex was. She hadn't known a thing. But she did now. Dang it all, if sex got any better than last night, it would kill her. As it was, she felt like she'd been hit by a truck, after which she'd jumped up to run a marathon. She was especially sore between her legs. Not surprising. Arthur had pounded her practically to bits.

Her orgasm had probably wiped out half her brain cells. She'd blacked out—actually blacked out. Even now, several hours later, her body wasn't quite finished coming. Rhythmic aftershocks contracted her insides. Every nerve hummed.

Arthur stirred. She turned her head to look at him. The motion caused a twinge of pain in her neck. His eyes were closed, but darting back and forth under his eyelids, as if he were dreaming. His brow furrowed in a frown.

With a sudden motion, he rolled toward her. His chin, dusted with dark stubble, grazed her shoulder. His arm fell heavily across her torso. The contact stirred her senses into painful acuteness. Each square inch of her skin in contact with his sizzled. He was hot, as if a furnace burned inside him. His cock, still hard, prodded her hip. She inhaled, and the scent of him made her head spin. She wanted to do it again. She wanted more.

She gave a soft snort. *More?* The thought was ludicrous. Arthur had stretched her, shattered her, and flung the pieces to the seven stars. There couldn't possibly be *more.*

Except...Cybele was, after all, only a dormant. Her human body was too fragile to take everything Arthur's demon nature could dish out. Once she'd completed her own Ordeal—once she was an adept with a demon body of her own—then they would both find out exactly how much *more* there was.

The thought left her lightheaded.

Her gaze drifted to the window, where a brilliant blue sky shone through a lacy pattern of branches. The scene caused a snatch of memory to surface. She'd looked out the window earlier, during sex. The branches had been different. There'd been a shadow. She sat up, hugging her knees to her chest. No. Not a shadow. Just the opposite. There had been a soft glow. And a flutter of—she frowned—wings?

A sudden chill swept through her. Wings. Wings too big to belong to any bird. Nephil wings? Mab? No, it couldn't have been. Mab would never lurk outside a window. She'd stride through the front door, whip in hand.

And anyway, she realized now, the wings hadn't been black like Mab's. They'd been bronze. And Cybele had seen eyes—velvet brown, fathomless eyes. Mab's eyes were a piercing blue. It hadn't been Mab. She was pretty sure it hadn't been any of the other adepts from Demon's Hollow. Who, then? She was at a loss to explain.

Maybe a closer look would reveal a clue. Easing her body out from under Arthur's arm, she rolled off the mattress and came up in a crouch. When she tried to stand, pain stabbed her lower back.

"Aah!" She turned and dropped back onto the mattress.

Arthur's body jerked. He bolted upright, his head swinging toward Cybele. His eyes were open and dilated, irises nothing but narrow gray rings around the pupils. A sound came from deep in his throat: a terrifying half-snarl, half-hiss.

Cybele shrank back, her heart racing. Being frightened of Arthur was a new experience, one she didn't like at all. He was her best friend, her lover. She knew him. She trusted him. Or she had. Right now, naked and powerful, his body rigid and his eyes blank, she wasn't so sure.

His gaze passed over her. Did he see her? Probably not. Whatever he saw, she'd bet the farm it wasn't in this room. Something from his Ordeal? Some long-ago ancestral memory?

He looked right and left. His eyes glowed red, his skin darkened. He lifted his hands. Sparks of white hellfire zipped across his fingers. It gathered in his palms. Cybele ducked. The bolt sizzled past, just inches above her head.

"Arthur." She kept her head low, and her eyes fixed on his face. "Arthur. Can you hear me?"

If he did, he gave no indication of it. His glowing eyes darted about the room, looking for...what? Cybele faltered. What the hell should she do?

He's still Arthur, she told herself. And yet...he wasn't. Or, at least, he wasn't the Arthur she knew. His human body no longer encompassed everything he was. He was a demon now. A fearsome creature, filled with darkness and magic.

Careful not to draw his attention with any sudden motion, she eased herself upright. Gritting her teeth against the pain in her hip and ribs, she rolled into a crouch by the side of the bed. Arthur, peering intently at the window, didn't seem to notice.

He muttered a string of words, low and throaty, in a language she didn't recognize. He needed to wake up. Heart pounding, she rounded the bed to his side. Inching as close as she dared, she laid a soft hand on his shoulder.

"Arthur? Can you hear me?" She squeezed gently. "Whatever you're seeing, it's not real. You're asleep. Wake up."

He moved so quickly, she didn't even see him do it. She was on her back on the bed. His fist was in her hair, his arm across her throat, his lower body pinned her to the mattress. His cock was hard. He glared down at her, eyes aglow and teeth bared.

She lay utterly still, not even daring to blink. Her heart battered her ribs so loudly she was sure he could hear it. Their gazes locked. His eyes, burning red, regarded her with unnerving hatred. What—or who—did he think she was?

She licked her lips. His eyes followed the movement. His grip in her hair tightened.

"Arthur." She struggled to speak through the pressure on her windpipe. "Let me go."

When he didn't answer, she tried again. "Let. Me. Go." She swallowed. "Please."

His answer guttered low in his throat. "Break...your fucking...neck."

She forced all the authority she could muster into her voice. "Don't you dare."

Doubt crept into his eyes. "No?"

"No."

He frowned. "Why not?"

"Because...because I'm Cybele. You'd never—*never*—hurt me."

"I wouldn't?"

"No. You love me."

His brows shot up at that. "I do?"

"Yes."

He seemed to consider the information. "I...love...you?" He tested each word on his tongue.

The pressure of his arm eased fractionally. She drew in a breath. "Yes."

Something came into his eyes. A glimmer of awareness. Not full recognition, not yet. A willingness to believe, perhaps.

"Let me go, Arthur."

"Yes." His voice was oddly mechanical. "Let you go."

Cybele expelled stale air from her lungs as she watched Arthur come back to himself. It happened by slow degrees. First, he took his arm from her throat. Then his fingers loosened and slid out of her hair. His gaze ran over her face, her neck, her body. Not with any lascivious intent. It was more like he was taking inventory, checking her against some internal mental standard. Eventually, his attention returned to her face, and showed a glimmer of true recognition.

It was followed by an expression of pure, unadulterated horror.

"Fuck!"

He threw himself backward. He fell, sprawled on his ass on the floor. The next instant he was on his feet, stumbling toward the door.

Cybele jumped up. Her body protested. *Ouch.*

"Arthur, wait!"

He spun about. His eyes were wild, filled with self-loathing. His fists clenched and unclenched at his sides. "I've got...to get out."

"No." Pain shot through her hip. She stumbled, hissing through her teeth as she grabbed for the wall.

"What?" Arthur was by her side in an instant. He reached for her, but when she regained her balance on her own, he stopped short of touching her. "What is it?"

"Nothing." She clutched at his arm. "Just...my hip. I must've pulled a muscle or something. Help me sit down."

He lowered her to the mattress. His gaze swept over her naked body. Retrieving the blanket from the floor, he shook it out and draped it over her shoulders.

She looked up at him. "Thanks."

He scowled at the bed. "Did I do that?"

"We did it together," she said.

"Bullshit." He turned to face her. "There are—" He swallowed. "Bruises. Finger marks. On your arms and legs. And teeth marks..." He closed his eyes briefly. "Fuck." He moved away.

"Arthur—"

"I don't remember the bed breaking," he said. "I don't remember biting you. I don't remember...much of anything after I started to come."

"It doesn't matter."

He gave a short laugh. "Doesn't it?" He looked toward the door.

"Don't you dare leave."

"I can't stay." His voice was tight.

"Yes, you can. We need to talk about it."

He turned and leaned against the wall, regarding her with a dark expression. "That's a nasty bite I gave you. Right here." He circled his finger over his left breast.

She brought the edges of the blanket together. "Forget it."

"Forget that I hurt you? Not likely."

She made a face at him. "Don't be so dramatic. See those red lines on your shoulders? Claw marks. I did that. They were even bleeding earlier, before the Nephil healing kicked in."

"Your bruises aren't going to heal that quickly."

"They'll be gone soon enough."

"They shouldn't be there at all. We shouldn't have had sex. I told you—"

"I'm glad we had sex. Dang it all, Arthur, it was freaking glorious."

"Won't be glorious when it kills you," he muttered.

"Well, it didn't."

"It could have. I thought you were..." His gaze dropped.

"What? You thought I was what?"

"I don't know. I saw something...some memory, I think. Centuries old." He shook his head slightly. "Whatever it was, it's gone now."

"It'll come back."

"Maybe," he said. "And maybe if it does I'll just forget it again."

She blew out a breath. "You're being ridiculous."

"I'm not." He stalked across the room and bent to grab his jeans off the floor. "This magic...I might never be able to control it." He shoved one leg, then the other, into his pants. "I can handle it a little when I'm calm, but when I'm not—" He pulled up the zipper. "My brain—it goes blank. Everything goes wrong, and I can't remember how. Or why. Or even what I've done."

"You just need time to get used to it."

He found a shirt, one of the extras she'd brought from Texas. He crumpled it into a ball in his hands. "Maybe. In the meantime, you—"

"I'm not going anywhere," she said. "And you're not leaving me here alone."

He sighed. "No. Of course not. But we can't have sex again. It's too dangerous."

She hesitated. "We could be more careful."

"Cybele, I *was* being careful. My 'careful' nearly broke you in two."

She opened her mouth to argue, then, abruptly, shut it. "Okaaay," she said slowly. "Maybe you're right. Maybe we should chill on the sex. For now."

His brows shot up. "You're actually agreeing with me?"

She huffed. "You say that like I've never agreed with you before."

"You haven't. Or, at least, if you have, I can't remember when."

She injected a hint of humor into her voice. "Are you kidding me? I give in to you all the time." This was a bald-faced lie and a running joke between them.

He gave the answer he always did. "In what universe?"

She laughed, and he did, too. She was so relieved to see him smile, she nearly started crying. Which would've really alarmed him. She didn't cry.

She scooted to the edge of the mattress and fished her blouse off the floor. Abandoning the blanket, she shoved her arms through the sleeves, and kept her tone casual. "Just tell me one thing. Did you like it?"

"Arguing with you?" He shook out his crumpled tee.

"No, of course not. Did you like what we did? The sex? Um...what you remember of it?"

He paused in the motion of pulling on his shirt. "Now who's being ridiculous?"

"I'm not. You're an adept now, and I'm still just a dormant. I can't—"

"Cybele." He looked up, his eyes searching the ceiling as if reading something written up there. "You have to know by now that you're everything to me. Life and breath and heart and...well, if the Nephilim had souls, you'd be that, too."

She never cried. So why was her vision suddenly all blurry? "What did the Ordeal do to you? Scramble your brains?"

He pulled his shirt over his head. When he faced her again, a red flush burnished his cheeks. "Damn it, Cybele. Aren't you always telling me I should be more romantic?"

"Well, yes. But I didn't really think you had it in you."

"I've always felt this way. I've just never had the guts to tell you."

"You don't need to tell me. I know. Oh, Arthur, I was so afraid when you left. Afraid you wouldn't survive the overdose. Or if you did, you wouldn't survive the Ordeal. And if you did get through it, I was afraid it would change you."

"It did change me. But not in that way. Nothing in this life could change my feelings for you." His gaze slid away. "It's only—"

"Only what?"

"I don't know how long that life's going to be." He met her gaze squarely. "I don't know if I can defeat Mab."

***

Luc's thrallstone began to burn even before Zephyr disappeared into the brush.

The ruby lay, at all times, in unbroken contact with his skin. Mab had closed the twisted wood collar around Luc's neck before allowing him to exit his Ordeal. From that moment, his life had been hers to command. The stone, aided by the oak, made his magic her own.

Until it happened, Luc hadn't believed Mab would enthrall him. She'd promised not to. Despite Arthur's warnings, despite Cybele's pleas to listen, he'd stubbornly refused to consider the possibility she was lying. Why should he risk facing the Ordeal alone, as Arthur had urged? He'd already been in Mab's bed, where she'd let him do whatever he'd wanted to her. In his lustful stupidity, he'd believed he'd mastered her.

How could he have been so naïve? Mab's docility had been another one of her illusions, and Luc, like an idiot, had fallen for it. He was damn glad Arthur hadn't been in Demon's Hollow when Luc returned with Mab's thrall collar around his neck. Cybele's horror, and the pity in her eyes, had been almost too much to bear.

His shoulders tensed at the thought of his twin. Where was she? Didn't take half a brain to know that she'd run after Arthur, but did that mean Arthur had survived his Ordeal? Or had Cybele only hoped he had?

He couldn't blame her for leaving Demon's Hollow, Arthur or no Arthur. Cybele had always had more than her share of spunk. It was no secret that Mab had chosen her favorite thrall, Rand, to guide Cybele's Ordeal. Rand was a snakebit son of a bitch if Luc had ever known one. Of course she'd run.

What was amazing was that she'd gotten away with it.

The thrallstone burned hotter, sizzling like a branding iron. The pain was getting bad, real bad, but he fought it as long as he could. He wasn't sure why he still bothered. It was a pointless rebellion, one Mab could snap like kindling wood. And yet he kept at it.

Eventually, the compulsion to go to her overpowered his resistance. His feet moved him, against his will, to the north wing of the main house. Even though Mab spent little enough time in Demon's Hollow, no one dared enter her exclusive domain uninvited. Luc approached the shining black door, dread twisting his insides into knots. He hadn't been on the other side of that door since before his Ordeal.

His fear disgusted him. What could Mab possibly do to him that was worse than what he'd already endured? *Plenty*, a malicious voice in his brain whispered. *And you know it.* A cold sweat broke out on his brow.

He rapped on the cool steel. The door swung open into a room of red velvet, black leather, and shining chrome. Hunter, another of Mab's favorites, stood with his hand on the doorknob, smirking. When Luc stepped past him, he shut the door and turned the lock.

"'Bout time you got your ass here. Not smart, making her wait. She's madder than a rattler now, and I can't say as I blame her. Why in hell didya let Cybele get away?"

Luc gave no reply.

"Sure. Go ahead with the bullshit strong, silent act. Won't do you no good with her."

Luc's thrallstone flared so hotly, he couldn't suppress a gasp. Hunter laughed. "She's in the bedroom." Grabbing Luc's upper arm, he shoved him roughly toward a second black door. "I'm sure you remember the way."

Luc's hand shook as he turned the knob. He stepped into a larger room, one which could have easily held twenty people or more. Right now, it was empty. It was all the more threatening because of it.

A collage of oversized photos covered the walls from floor to ceiling. The subject was pornographic, with a general theme of bondage, punishment, and humiliation. Mab's personal toys hung on hooks or sat on shelves among the naked figures. Floggers, whips, rope, blindfolds, ball gags, anal plugs, collars, clamps. Leather cuffs, attached to gleaming chains, dangled from the ceiling and were attached to rings in the floor.

There was a room very much like this one in Club Tartarus. Luc had spent a good deal of the time since his Ordeal in that room, acting as Mab's submissive as well as taking a dominant role in the fantasies of some of the club's favored clients. The toys were only part of it. Illusion, terrifying illusion, was another part. And then there were the times Mab had turned her illusions into reality...

If not for his thrallstone, Luc would've turned tail and fled. Since that wasn't an option, he set his jaw and crossed the room. A second door was tucked in a corner. It led to a short hallway. Two more doors, to his right and left, were closed. The one at the end of the hall, facing him, was open.

He walked through it.

Mab sat cross-legged in the center of her massive bed, on top of a sable fur coverlet. A soft white spotlight shone down on her. Even knowing what she was, and what she was capable of, Luc couldn't help his body's reaction to his alpha's harsh, erotic beauty. There wasn't a straight man alive—except, maybe, Arthur—who wouldn't want to fuck her.

Her complexion was pale, her skin flawless. Brilliant blue eyes, framed by sooty lashes, gave her a sultry appearance, one accentuated by high cheekbones and full red lips. Black hair, pin straight and shining, fell to her waist.

She was very tall, of course, like all Nephilim. Her figure was proportioned to match, with generous breasts and hips. A black leather corset constricted her waist to almost waspish proportions, creating an illusion of delicacy.

Her massive ruby hung from its wooden chain. The stone nestled in her cleavage, pulsing like a heartbeat. Luc's thrallstone responded to its mother stone, matching its rhythm with its own burning throb.

Mab unfolded her legs. They were about a damn mile long, encased in black lace as far as her thighs. She rose to kneel on one knee, the opposite leg splayed wide, offering Luc a prime view. A blood red stiletto heel, propped on the bed, sank into black fur.

The room smelled like sex. Sweaty, explosive sex, recently completed. One whiff of the scent was a potent aphrodisiac. Instantly, Luc was hard and aching for it. Warmth crept into his face. He'd known both pleasure and humiliation at Mab's hands. Even though the bad had far outweighed the good, he was helpless to prevent his cock from near-combusting with lust for the sadistic bitch. It was the thrallstone, controlling his reaction. He knew that beyond a doubt. The knowledge didn't stop him from hating himself.

A figure separated itself from the shadows. Rand, a crystal tumbler in hand, strolled out of a dark corner of the room. He was naked, his penis half-erect. The ruby in his thrall collar was dark. That was a sign of his mistress's favor, but ultimately, Luc knew, it was but another illusion. Rand wasn't nearly as independent as he believed.

He saluted Luc with his whiskey. Ice clinked against the glass. "Howdy, cousin." He grinned as if he'd uttered a sly joke.

Mab waved a negligent hand. "Leave us, sugar."

Rand's smile turned to a scowl. No doubt he'd been looking forward to the party Mab had planned for Luc. He made no protest, however. With a respectful nod in his mistress's direction, he strode from the room.

Mab's eyes, in that unnerving shade of blue, raked over Luc. Responding to the slightest flick of her finger, Luc's thrallstone delivered an electric jolt to his throat. His muscles went rigid.

Her whisper vibrated both inside and outside his skull. "Where is Cybele?"

"I don't know, Mistress."

Her gaze narrowed. "Don't insult me."

Luc lowered his gaze to the floor. Black stone, polished to a dull shine. "I wouldn't dare, ma'am." That was true enough. What would be the point? Mab knew when he was lying.

"Sometimes I wonder." She swung her long legs over the side of the bed and rose. She smiled as she lifted an object from a low table.

It was a jeweled whip handle, carved from yew wood. The stones embedded in the shaft—gems of various colors and sizes—had once belonged to Arthur's kin, the British

Druids who had come to Texas in the wake of Tristan's death. After Magnus had lost the duel, the rest of the British line had been left no option but to accept Mab as their new alpha. Along with their pledges of fealty, Mab had demanded they give up their touchstones. In exchange, they had each been given a fragment of Mab's ruby, to be kept on their persons at all times.

The stolen jewels blazed to life. Mab twirled the handle once, like a baton. She smiled.

Luc knew that smile.

The bottom fell out of his stomach. The alpha tapped the butt end of her toy against one thigh. She moved closer, stiletto heels tapping on stone. When she passed to the left of him and circled behind, Luc kept his eyes trained forward.

"I don't know where Cybele went." He was ashamed of his trembling voice. He tried to force a semblance of confidence into his tone. "She'd hardly cozy up to me, now, would she? We've hardly even spoken in months."

"You don't need to talk to her, sugar, to know what she's up to."

The hairs on the back of Luc's neck rose. Mab stood directly behind him now. From the sound of her tapping whip, she wasn't more than a few steps away. A sound like whistling wind caused his entire body to tense. In his mind's eye, he saw a hellfire lash erupt from the jeweled whip handle. His body went even more rigid as he waited for the first blow to fall.

A flash of crimson hellfire whizzed past his right arm, raising hairs on his skin, missing his body by what felt like millimeters.

Her voice was deadly soft, inches from his left ear. He felt the heat of her all along his back. "When did Cybele sister leave? And, sugar? Don't tell me you don't know."

He swallowed thickly. "Wednesday. Just after sunset."

"That was three days ago."

"Yes, ma'am."

"And you said nothing to Evander. Or to Draven."

"No, ma'am. They...they noticed it themselves, the next day."

"And yet none of y'all saw fit to call me."

"No."

"How long?"

Luc licked dry lips. "I...I don't understand."

"How long have you known about Cybele's magic? How long have you known how strong she is?"

How long? He stuttered over the answer, dreading what she'd do when it emerged. "Five years. Or thereabouts."

"Five years." Her quiet rage made him flinch. "Five *fucking* years. And you didn't tell me."

It wasn't a question, so he gave no answer.

"Oh, sugar. You're gonna be so sorry. Take off your shirt."

He obeyed, shucking the garment over his head and dropping it to the floor. His back hunched. He knew damn well what was coming.

Even so, the first lash took him by surprise. It was a stripe of pure fire, laid across his upper back. Hellfire, formed by demon magic, enhanced by Mab's rage. A bullet or knife was like a whisper next to the pain of Mab's whip. Luc's body jerked with the shock of it. His spine arched. Air hissed through his teeth. His legs folded. He pitched forward, arms outstretched to break his fall. His palms slapped on the stone floor.

Laughter came from the doorway. Rand's malicious chuckle, Hunter's amused snort. "Pay attention, boys," Mab drawled. "Maybe y'all will learn something useful."

Luc tried to gather his wits and struggle to his feet. Before he could do either, Mab delivered a second blow at right angles to the first. The third strike scored his flesh from the top of his spine to his buttocks. On the fourth lash he collapsed completely, a strangled sob in his throat. The cold caress of her voice, licking his skull inside and out, was worse than any pain in his body. "Tell me, sugar. Tell me all about it."

"Cybele practiced," he gasped. "For years." He nearly gagged on the betrayal. "Arthur...Arthur encouraged it."

"And you didn't stop it."

"No, ma'am. I did not." It'd been foolish to keep their secret, he knew that. But whatever the distance between him and Cybele, she was still his sister. More than that, his twin. He didn't have it in him to betray her.

At least, he hoped he didn't.

"Roll over, Lucas. Look at me."

There was no question of defying his mistress's command. He rolled, hissing when the open wounds on his back struck the cold floor. He bit down on a moan, his teeth sinking into his tongue. He propped his upper body on his elbows, the taste of his own blood in his mouth.

Mab's eyes had gone red. They bored into his own eyes, looking past them into his mind. Her magic was like an icy finger stroking his brain. *She can't read my mind*, he reminded himself. But she could, as his mistress, read his emotions.

"You knew Arthur meant to go rogue." Her brows lifted slightly. "Did he try to talk you into doing the same?"

"Yes."

"But you didn't. Well. At least you have some sense."

Mab's shoulders went back. She widened her stance, long legs splayed like a threat. Dark opal lights flowed under her skin. Black wings, feathers sharp as blades,

emerged from her back. They snapped out to full length above her head.

Luc watched his mistress's transformation with increasing trepidation. The stolen gems embedded in the whip handle blazed with each tap against her palm. The single hellfire thong thickened and split in two. The process repeated itself twice more. Eight strands of fire danced before his eyes. The stone at his throat burned hotter with each pass. Luc's apprehension turned to panic.

"What have you to say for yourself, sugar? Do you beg for mercy?"

Luc opened his mouth and gave the reply he knew she expected. "No. No, ma'am."

Mab smiled. "Good answer."

The lashes whistled through the air. They fell on his stomach. Slashed across his chest. Gouged his thighs. Once, and again. And again.

He couldn't stay motionless through the torture. He twisted, he writhed, he screamed and begged. When the blows finally stopped, he knelt in a ball, his head bowed, gasping.

"Where is she?"

Luc raised his head. "I told you, I don't—"

"Enough." Mab lifted the whip. Its eight lashes thickened and split once more, forming sixteen twisted vines of fire. Then all sixteen lashes separated from the handle and dropped to the floor.

Luc watched in horror as the lashes hardened and thickened. They came together in a writhing tangle of scales and flesh and whipping tails. Brown and orange, alternating triangles, crackling red with hellfire. Curved fangs and forked tongues, spitting hisses.

Luc's mouth went dry. Copperheads. Illusion or reality? Impossible to tell. Mab's magic was that subtle.

"Where is Arthur?"

Luc truly didn't know. He could feel the pulse of his twin's life essence. He knew she wasn't close by, but more than that, he couldn't say. He was glad—fiercely glad—he couldn't tell Mab what she wanted so desperately to know. Vipers, no matter how venomous, couldn't kill a Nephil. But infused with magic, sparkling with hellfire, they could do a lot more damage than Mab's whip.

The serpents separated, surrounding him. "Ma'am. Mistress." Luc's voice was nothing but a croak. "I don't know nothing. Cybele is...lost to me."

"Dead?"

If he could've lied, he would have. He gulped a breath. "No. Not dead."

Several ominous beats of silence ensued.

"You know what, sugar?" Mab said at last. "That's a crying shame. A damn crying shame. For you."

Her arm sliced downward. Sixteen snakes, spitting hellfire, shot toward Luc. He tried to slap them away, tried to stop them from wrapping around his body, sinking their fangs into his flesh. It was no use. He was helpless against them.

Every slide of snakeskin on his skin left a trail of burning agony. Every bite sent the pain deep into his body. Venom dripped like acid through his veins. He screamed like a mindless thing, until one snake wrapped itself around his throat, cutting off his air. If Mab thought her snakes would force confessions from Luc's throat, she'd miscalculated. The pain was too much. It sucked every thought from his skull.

Darkness rushed in to take its place. Luc closed his eyes and welcomed it.

NINE

Arthur flew out over the sea.

He was out in the dead of night, far from human eyes. The last thing he needed was a video of strange phenomena in the skies over Devon, England going viral. Most humans would dismiss it as fake. But if Mab happened to see it, she'd know what it was.

His magic needed work. His mother's touchstone helped. He was getting better at manipulating hellfire—he could call it and send it where he wanted. Mostly. Fashioning it into more useful form, like a rope, whip, or net, was more difficult. But he was making progress.

He'd experimented with weather, a prime Druid skill. He was rubbish at it. Even given a heavy cloud cover, he couldn't manage a decent rain. He could maybe push some wisps of mist around high in the sky, but sending it down to Earth as fog? A bust. Hailstorms? Forget it.

Illusion was the most common form of Druid magic. Cybele was a deft hand at it. Casting glamour should've come easily to Arthur as a full adept. Somehow, despite years of watching Cybele manipulate illusions, the magic didn't feel natural. He had to hold an image in his mind while at the same time projecting it where he wanted it to appear. It was bloody tedious. Too little concentration, and the image didn't gel. Too much, and it became so sharply defined that it collapsed in on itself.

According to Cybele, projecting a static image was much easier than producing a moving one. Arthur worked on that for a time. He called up everything from trees, to ponds, to buildings and parked cars. The longest he managed to hold an illusion together was three minutes.

A corollary to casting illusion was the ability to deflect attention—becoming essentially invisible. This was Cybele's strongest skill. He flew into Dartmouth to practice this one, landing outside a pub. With Cybele's instructions ringing in his mind, he deliberately stood in the path of patrons entering and leaving the building. He could manage only a few seconds of obscurity before some bloke saw him and asked him to move.

Invisibility, he told himself, hardly mattered. When he finally faced Mab, there'd be nowhere to hide.

His first concern would be defense. Mab was decades older than he. She held tight control over powerful magic. He had to find a way to fight it. Yes, his touchstone helped focus his power outward, but he suspected he needed something more. He needed to look inward and try to make sense of the memories of his ancestors.

He tried. He nearly exploded his brain trying. Time and again he willed himself to *see*, to find the answer in the past. The memories, however, only grew murkier the more he searched through them. His frustration rose as his mind grew darker.

"Bollocks." He turned and slammed his fist into the pub wall. The brick cracked.

"Jesus Christ, mate. Are you okay?"

He turned to find a man, shirt half undone and none too steady on his feet, approaching from the direction of the pub door. The sot's path wavered, but he seemed determined to reach Arthur. Damn it all to Oblivion. How pathetic was he, that humans hurried to his aid?

"I'm fine," he said.

The bloke stumbled toward him, one hand outstretched. "Lemme see," he said. "I'm a paramedic."

"So? Fuck off."

He grinned. "Hurts that bad? Mush...mush...must be broken."

"I told you, fuck off."

"Just lemme see..." Moving more quickly than Arthur would've thought possible, the drunk lunged and grabbed for Arthur's wrist. Missing, he stumbled forward, practically into Arthur's arms. One arm went around Arthur's waist, the other clutched at his neck. He exhaled frying grease and ale into Arthur's face.

"Get. The fuck. Off me." Arthur tried to fling the human away. The bloke clung like a bloody limpet, grinning. His weight, his stink, his wide, smiling mouth...the drool slipping over his lips...

Suddenly it all was too much.

Arthur's anger and frustration hit boiling point. His hands went around the drunk's neck, thumbs pressing his windpipe. The bloke's mouth fell open. A gagging sound emerged. His lower body jerked like a marionette. The smell of urine permeated the air. Two bulging blue eyes, drenched with fear, stared up at Arthur.

And then everything went white.

The next thing Arthur knew, he was sprawled on his arse on the pavement. For a moment, he couldn't remember where he was, or why. Then memory rushed in. He lurched to his feet and looked wildly around.

The drunk lay face down, not twenty feet away. Arthur's stomach churned as he stumbled toward the man's motionless form. He heaved the bloke over onto his back. There were bruises on this throat, in the shape of Arthur's fingers. Fresh blood streamed from his swollen, broken nose.

Dead? No. The man's pulse was jumping. As Arthur straightened and backed away, his victim's eyes fluttered open. The drunk made a gagging sound, then rolled to one side and vomited a mixture of blood and beer onto the pavement.

A couple of humans, recently exited from the pub and very unsteady on their feet, stood gawking at him. The woman clutched her partner's arm and let out a strangled cry. The man fumbled in his pocket and pulled out a cell phone.

His wings were out, Arthur realized abruptly. When had he shifted? He couldn't remember doing it. He threw a narrow stream of hellfire at the phone, shattering it in the man's hand. Leaping into the sky, he shot out over the sea.

Damn it all to Oblivion. He didn't need this. He could only hope that, come morning, the three humans who had seen him in demon form would be too hungover to trust their drunken memories.

He circled endlessly above the choppy surf, too agitated to practice his magic, but reluctant to return to land. But even a Nephil's endurance had its limits. By the time a pale arc of light showed on the horizon, his wings ached with the effort of keeping his body aloft.

He set a course for Tŷr Cythraul. He landed in the garden, but couldn't quite bring himself to enter the house. Cybele would have a thousand questions. He didn't want to answer even one of them. The sight of the man, lying bloody on the ground, haunted him. How could he possibly defeat Mab? She was decades older than he, vastly more powerful. And she wasn't out of her fucking mind.

His wings melted back into his body. His skin became

human again. At least he was making progress with shifting. That was something, he supposed. The first few transformations in and out of his demon body had been excruciating. Now changing from human to demon and back again didn't hurt at all.

He sank down on the stone bench, leaning forward and bracing his forearms on his thighs. His mind was a dark blur of dread, and he was heartily sick of it. Sick of thinking, endlessly, and coming up with no useful solutions. Were Merlin's memories lost forever? And what of his other ancestors? They may not have been as powerful as Merlin, but their magic had been considerable. Why couldn't he remember anything?

He stared at the ground. The sun was above the horizon now, peering over the garden wall. One brilliant ray slanted into the clump of weeds a few feet in front of him. A sharp glint among the green leaves caught his eye. Frowning, he went to investigate.

It was nothing. Just a broken bit of mirror, the silvering on the back of the glass mottled with age. It'd probably been discarded years ago. Idly, he turned the piece over in his hands and peered into the glass.

He blinked and lifted his head. And was chilled to note that the sun was now almost as high as the roof. How bloody long had he been crouching in the garden, unaware of the passage of time? It had felt no longer than an instant.

Damnation. Not again. He looked around. To his relief, he saw nothing dead. But moving his head brought on nausea and fierce, spinning vertigo. He eased down to his knees and braced one hand on the ground.

The memory hit him like a gale force wind. His head came up. An instant later he was sprinting for the house. He pounded up the stair and burst into the attic. "Cybele!"

She bolted upright on the bed, her hair tumbling over her shoulders in wild disarray. "Arthur? Wha—?"

He stopped short, his heart pounding. "I remember something."

She sucked in a breath. "From your ancestors?"

"From Merlin. I think." His hands went to either side of his head, palms pressing as if to keep the memory from escaping his skull. "I mean, it has to be, right? It can hardly be anything else."

"Tell me."

She scrambled out of bed, grabbed his arm, and drew him down to sit beside her on the mattress. He hunched forward. His hands, dangling between his knees, shook. He laced his fingers tightly together.

"Are you okay?" Cybele's hand came to rest on his upper back.

"Yes. No." He expelled a breath. "Damn it, I don't know."

"Well. So long as we've got that straightened out." A bubble of laughter escaped her lips. The sound steadied him.

"Let's start from the beginning," she said. "What's the first thing you remember?"

"I was... I mean, Merlin was...walking. Carrying a pack and his staff. The shaft of the staff was oak, rowan, and yew, all twisted together. At the top, the branches separated to hold a stone. A sphere of colorless quartz, bigger than my fist."

"Go on."

"A woman was with me. She was...very beautiful."

"Of course she was," Cybele said dryly. "Was she a Nephil?"

"No. A witch. My student. More than that. I loved her."

"Merlin loved her, Arthur. Not you."

Her disgruntled tone made his lips twitch. "Right. Merlin had found Nimue in the forest, close to death. When she regained her strength, she told him that a year before, she'd been brutally raped. She'd given birth to an infant boy. She abandoned the baby at a monastery and went into the wilderness to take her own life. Nimue had considerable magical talent. Merlin decided to teach her to defend herself with it. In the course of awakening her power, he fell in love."

"Where did they go? In the memory, I mean."

"They circled a hill. There was boulder, split in two. They passed through the halves into an underground cavern. There was a wide pool in the cave, with an island in the center of the water. Merlin and Nimue made love on that island." His heart beat faster. "It was—"

Cybele cleared her throat. "Too much information, Arthur."

He flushed. "All right. Let's just say...it was good. Afterward, I—"

"*He*. Merlin."

"Yes. Afterward, Merlin fell asleep."

"What happened when he woke up?"

"That's where it gets fuzzy. The legends say Nimue trapped Merlin in that cave. I don't believe that—no human witch could contain a Nephil. But it's said Merlin died in the cave, alone. With his staff beside him."

He lifted his eyes to hers. "My father searched for Merlin's cave his entire life. He followed every story, every rumor, visited every place that claimed to be the final resting place of the great sorcerer. He wanted to be the one to find the lost staff. It wasn't to be. It's my duty to complete his quest."

Cybele's eyes flew to his. "Does that mean you know where it is?"

"Yes," Arthur said. "It does."

***

Maweth eased away from the attic window. His wings shook badly. He didn't quite trust them to carry him. *Crunchy poop on a cracker!* He was lucky Arthur had lingered in the garden long enough to find the spell. Double lucky the Nephil had been too distraught to see it for what it was.

He shivered. If Arthur had any sort of reasonable control over his magic, Maweth would be screaming in agony right now. He'd had a narrow escape. The thought sent a shiver down his spine. Scrambling up to the peak of the roof, he grabbed onto a chimney and waited for his limbs to stop twitching.

The twenty-four hours since Lucky's impetuous leap to Maweth's defense had been hell. Upon realizing he actually had an angel in his power, Dusek promptly took off for Wales, of all places. He'd visited a chilly cave—a place no Nephil, unescorted by celestial magic, could have entered. Fat lot of good it'd done him. He hadn't been able to get what he wanted from the place.

But Dusek wasn't one to let a little setback derail his cause. It was straight on to Plan B, a plan involving Arthur Camulus. Maweth thoroughly disapproved. The young Nephil was extremely unstable. Any scheme involving his magic was sure to backfire. He'd told Dusek as much. Had the stubborn Nephil listened? No, oh no. He had not.

Maweth gazed longingly to the south. He wanted to fly that way, rather than north to Dusek in Wales. An instant later, he was consumed with shame for even thinking such a thing. He couldn't, just couldn't, abandon Lucky.

Stupid angel.

TEN

"Tell me what your Ordeal was like," Cybele asked.

Arthur, startled, cut her a glance. Her green eyes gazed steadily back at him. Damn it, she was serious. "I hardly think a train station is the best place to discuss it," he said.

"I don't agree. We're stuck here in freaking Bristol for the next two hours. We have to talk about something. Or..." She gave him a pointed look. "We could just fly to Carmarthen."

She had a point, Arthur conceded. It was barmy to take public transport when they could fly. That, however, would require shifting to demon form and carrying her.

It was a risk he wouldn't take. Lust and unstable magic was a dangerous combination. Cybele already had the bruises to prove it. Even sitting on a hard plastic bench, shoulder to shoulder with her, was chancy. He was the driest of tinder, she the spark that could ignite him into a roaring inferno.

And now she wanted to talk about his Ordeal?

"You know why we can't fly," he said irritably. "Could you kindly quit nagging me about it?"

"Let's talk, then. What was it like, being that close to death? How long was it from when you took the overdose to when you entered the Ordeal?"

He kept his eyes trained on the travelers scurrying past the waiting area. "I don't wish to talk about it."

"Please. Can't we get past that?"

He shifted. Bloody uncomfortable chairs in this station. Knowing Cybele would needle and prod until she got at least some satisfaction, he conceded defeat. "All right. I'll tell you this much. The Ordeal defies description."

She rolled her eyes. "Not helpful, Arthur."

He shrugged. "It's all I've got."

She tipped her head back, as if patience lurked on the station ceiling. "Were you afraid?"

A sparrow flitted across the floor, pecking at crumbs. It must've flown in an open door. He hoped it managed to get out again. "I was scared shitless," he said. "A thousand times over. Only an idiot would be anything less."

"Oh." She looked at him, and then down into her lap.

He followed her gaze. She was twisting her fingers together so violently, he almost winced. He reached over and grabbed her hand. "Stop that."

Her next words came so softly, he had to duck his head to hear them. "I might not survive my Ordeal," she said. "Not all dormants do. Remember Colby?"

He remembered what the poor bastard's body had looked like when Mab had brought it out of the cellar and dumped it in the swamp. Arthur had been fifteen, Cybele sixteen. They'd both had nightmares for weeks.

His fingers tightened on hers. "You'll survive. I'll be there, guiding you. Every moment, until it's done."

"How did you endure it on your own?"

His mind shied away from the memory. "I'm not sure."

"Maybe..." She took a deep breath. "I've been thinking. Maybe I should just do it now. Before Mab catches up with us. Then we could fight her together."

He stared at her. "Please tell me you're kidding."

"I'm not. Even Mab can't stop an Ordeal. It would buy us time." She nudged her backpack with her toe. "I brought a couple eightballs with me."

"You have cocaine?" Her audacity astounded him. Though why it should, he didn't know. It was just the kind of thing she'd do.

"Yeah. I thought it would be good to have, just in case. What do you think?"

"Cybele." He struggled to find his patience. "Have you not been paying attention? My magic is so unpredictable, I can't even trust myself to pick you up and fly a hundred miles. I couldn't possibly guide you through your Ordeal. Not until I have more control."

She touched his arm. "Maybe guiding me would help. It might improve your focus."

"That," he said flatly, "is the single stupidest thing I have ever heard in my life."

"No, it's not. It's—"

He stood abruptly, throwing off her hand. "You have no idea what you're talking about. I won't discuss it. Not now, not later. Drop it."

"But—"

He spun on her. "The Ordeal doesn't improve focus. It destroys it. Obliterates it. It shreds every iota of control you ever had over your body and mind. It turns your brain inside out, stretches your bones until you think you'll snap apart. It's a howling maelstrom of violation, humiliation, and agony. You'll want to die. Every moment you continue living, you'll long for death that much more. You'll try to kill yourself. The Ordeal won't let you. And after you fail? That's when the torment gets worse."

He paused, chest heaving, sick dread spreading through him. "The way I am now, I couldn't guide you through a tenth of what you'd have to endure. And Cybele, if you died, if your brain fried, all because I'm a worthless shit who can't control the most basic magic..."

He was aware, through the haze of his agitation, of Cybele staring up at him, stricken. "I'm sorry," she whispered.

"Good. Now don't fucking ask me about it again."

She recoiled as if struck.

Shame flooded him. He was aware of several people nearby, watching their altercation with wary eyes. He dropped to his knees and buried his face in her lap. "Damn it, Cybele, I'm sorry. So sorry. Just—please. I can't...I can't talk about it. Please don't ask me to."

He felt her fingers comb through his hair. "Okay." The single word trembled.

He lifted his head. "No, it's not okay. I—"

A screech of pneumatic breaks sounded on the tracks. "Come on," she said. "Get up. Our train's finally here. And after all this drama—" She gave him a tremulous smile. "I refuse to miss it."

***

"For the love of Heaven, Raphael. Make up your blessed mind." Michael was none too pleased. The last place he wanted was to be called back to the clouds. Not when things were so much more interesting on Earth. "I thought you needed someone to watch Arthur."

Raphael waved a hand. "Gabriel will do it."

Gabriel? Michael clamped down on an unholy spurt of annoyance. "Why the sudden change in plans?"

"I need you elsewhere. There's a...situation."

"What is it?"

"Remember the missing cherub? Fortunato?"

"He hasn't turned up yet?"

"No. But I've received some further information. It seems Cherub Marius was the last celestial being to see Fortunato. They were playing a game on Earth and became separated. He's been searching for him ever since."

Michael frowned. "On his own? All this time?"

"I know. He should have informed me directly. But Fortunato's sense of direction is, shall we say, as deficient as his intelligence. Marius didn't want to get his friend in trouble. He thought he'd turn up."

"Where did he see him last?"

"In Paris. They were playing some human amusement called hide and seek. Fortunato hid, Marius sought. He looked all over the city and couldn't find him. He decided Fortunato must have wandered outside the boundary of the game, so he widened his search. A few kilometers outside the city, he found this."

From a fold in his robes, Raphael produced a feather.

Michael eyed the wispy bit of incandescence. "Fortunato's, I assume?" Among angels, the color and design of wings was as individual as a human fingerprint.

"Yes."

"Well. Good thing Marius found it, before it fell into the wrong hands." There was no telling what mischief that could cause. "Where was it, exactly?"

"Reims." Raphael slipped a hand into his robe. More feathers emerged, one by one. "Luxembourg. Frankfurt. At the German-Czech border."

Michael's brows rose. "Blessed be. How many feathers did Fortunato shed?"

"Five, that we've found. This last one was recovered in Prague."

Michael let out a low whistle. "From Paris to Prague? That's taking getting lost to a ridiculous extreme."

"Believe me," Raphael said sourly, "Fortunato is nothing if not ridiculous. He hasn't the sense God gave a flea. But that's not the worst of it."

"What is?"

"The last feather was found on the doorstep of the Prague Institute for the Study of Man."

Michael was sure that name sounded familiar, and not in a good way. "Isn't that place run by a Nephil?"

"Yes," Raphael said. "Professor Vaclav Dusek. Alpha of the Alchemist clan." He began pacing, golden robes swirling at his ankles.

Michael let out a low whistle. "Azazel's progeny." Azazel had been the most devious of the Watcher angels, the one who'd convinced his brother angels to rebel against Heaven.

"Yes. Azazel. The no-good troublemaker who taught mankind the art of war." A mottled red flush invaded Raphael's golden complexion. His voice rose. "The depraved scoundrel who taught womankind the art of harlotry." His fingers closed on the hilt of his Righteous Sword of Vengeance. "The disgusting degenerate whom I battled during the Flood."

Sklink! The blade scraped from its scabbard, and erupted in flames. "THE ACCURSED SINNER WHO—" Right arm outstretched, Raphael lunged.

"Whoawhoawhoa!" Michael jumped, barely escaping the righteous sweep of his brother's sword. "All right, all right, I get the picture. No need to start slicing up the clouds. Or me, for that matter."

Raphael froze, eyeing the sword in his hand as if wondering who'd put it there. With a sheepish expression, he straightened and sheathed his weapon. "Um...sorry."

"Don't worry about it. You're obviously carrying a bit of emotional baggage where Azazel is concerned."

"Yes, well, even Hell was too good for him. I sealed him into the foulest corner of Dudael instead. As for the Nephilim...the Flood was supposed to wipe out every last one of them. But somehow, it didn't."

"The Almighty's loopholes," Michael said. "Very frustrating they are at times. But that's neither here nor there at the moment. Tell me more about this Institute for the Study of Man. Is it simply a front for Nephil crimes?"

"No. Much as it pains me to admit, the Institute is a bona fide international center of learning and research. Ancient archeology, anthropology, that sort of thing. But I don't trust it. There's always been too much of an air of normalcy about the place."

"You do realize that makes no sense, right?"

"It makes perfect sense for a place founded and administered by a Nephil."

Michael supposed his brother had a point.

"And now this," Raphael continued. "An innocent cherub, vanishing into thin air, right on the Institute's doorstep. A Nephil getting his hands on an angel feather is bad enough. For him to kidnap the entire angel—"

"Aren't you jumping the gun a little? A single feather in the vicinity doesn't prove anything. Fortunato might've been merely passing overhead when he lost it. The whole thing could be a coincidence."

"Coincidence? There is no such thing," Raphael declared. "Marius searched high and low for more feathers. He found nothing. "I have a very bad feeling about this, Michael. I need you to investigate."

"You might've sent Gabriel and left me in Devon."

"I might have." Raphael's golden gaze narrowed. "If I didn't think you were enjoying your duties in England far too much. If you catch my meaning."

"Holy sh—" Heat flamed into Michael's face. "Are you saying you've been *watching* me?"

Raphael smiled thinly. "What I'm saying, little brother, is that you'd better watch yourself."

ELEVEN

They switched trains again in Cardiff. Two hours later, they arrived in Carmarthen. Or Caerfyrddin, as the Welsh called it. The small town was said to be the birthplace of Merlin. It was also one of the many places that claimed to be the location of his death. Arthur had told Cybele he'd been here as a boy, with his father, searching for his ancestor's grave. Had they been so close, after all?

The journey from Bristol had been awkward. After Arthur's outburst and subsequent apology at the Bristol station, Cybele had decided to give him some space. Unfortunately, space wasn't something she was exactly used to giving. She tried, though. She swore to herself that she'd let him be the first to start talking again. As a result, they hadn't spoken at all. Arthur sat by the window, jaw rigid, watching the landscape.

He wasn't angry with her, she knew. He was teetering on the edge of panic. She spent a good portion of the train ride berating herself. She shouldn't have brought up his Ordeal. He clearly hadn't wanted to talk about it. Would she never learn when to back off?

As they exited the train, Cybele drew a breath. Time to end this silent, moody bullshit. She eyed a sign bearing the town's Welsh name. Caerfyrddin.

"How do you pronounce it?" she asked.

Arthur glanced up at the sign. "Ki-air-*ver*-din," he said.

"It means 'Merlin's Fort.' It refers to a fort the Romans built on a rise of land outside the village. Merlin's cave is said to be under the hill. We might as well start looking there."

Well. He was a regular Chatty Cathy now. "How far out of town is it?"

"A couple miles, maybe. As far as I recall. Here," he said, reaching for her backpack. "Give me that."

She relinquished it and he hitched the strap over one shoulder. She fell into step beside him. He might be talking now, but he was still wound tight as a spring. They left the town center, passing by a cluster of newer buildings before reaching a country road. The fields on either side were dotted with sheep.

"There's a sign," Cybele said as they approached a crossroads. "Bryn Myrddin."

"Merlin's Hill."

The hill, surrounded by open fields and the occasional copse of trees, came into view soon after. A historical marker indicated a Roman fort had once occupied the site, its stones now completely gone. Though it was getting on to late afternoon, they hiked a wide arc around the base of the hill, looking for any depression or rock formation that might be the entrance Arthur had seen in Merlin's memory.

By the time they gave up the effort, it was dark. "It's been over a thousand years," Arthur said, surveying the landscape. "Probably a lot has changed."

"Damn, I'm a mess." Cybele shoved a limp strand of hair out of her eyes. Her jeans were muddy, her boots soaked from wading through a stream. "We must've turned over every rock, circled every tree, and peered into every fox den in a three-mile radius."

Arthur looked almost as bad as she did, but the dirt

and damp didn't seem to bother him at all. "There are a few places we haven't looked at yet."

"No way am I looking at them tonight," Cybele said. "I want a bath, a meal, and a bed. Immediately, and in that order." He shot her a look of annoyance, but she held firm. "Look at those clouds. It'll be pitch black out here soon. You might have adept night vision, but I don't."

He sighed. "All right. That farm we passed a while back had a bed and breakfast sign. We'll get a room."

At the B&B, their knock was followed by a protracted wait. Finally, a woman with wispy yellow-gray hair opened the door a scant three inches. She took in their grubbiness with a sour expression. "And what might you two vagrants be wanting?"

"A room," Cybele said. She caught a whiff of something meaty and savory. Her stomach rumbled. Arthur had her backpack slung over his shoulder. She pulled a handful of British pounds from the front pocket. "How much?"

"One room?"

"Yes."

"Fifty pounds," the woman sniffed. "Breakfast included."

"And dinner tonight?"

"Twenty more."

Highway robbery, but Cybele handed it over without comment. The woman shoved the notes deep in her apron pocket before pulling the door fully open. "I'm Mrs. Spencer."

"Lovely to meet you," Cybele said, with a hint of sarcasm.

Mrs. Spencer snorted. "American?"

Cybele nodded. "I am," she said. She nodded toward Arthur. "He's British, though."

Mrs. Spencer remained unimpressed. She eyed the

backpack. "And traveling light, I see. Well, come on with you then. This way."

She showed them up two flights of stairs into a short hall faced by three doors. The door on the right revealed a cramped bedroom under a steeply sloped ceiling. A double bed with a brass headboard and hand-knotted spread was pushed into one corner. A chest of drawers faced it. A framed photograph of a flock of sheep graced the wall above.

"Towels and such are in the dresser," Mrs. Spencer said briskly. "Bath's at the end of the hall. I run a proper house, I'll have you know. Quiet and tidy. I'll thank you both to keep it that way."

"Of course." Frowning, Arthur nodded toward the third hallway door. "Are there any other guests at present?"

She shrugged. "Had a foreign gent in there. He took himself off two days past. A historian." She frowned. "Odd ring he wore, too. He had a heavy accent—German, I think, or perhaps Russian. Not that I heard much of his voice. Wasn't much for tongue wagging, that one."

Mrs. Spencer's tongue, by contrast, seemed to be finally warming. "Just the family in tonight. Myself, the mister, and our grandson, Jack." She sighed. "Might as well tell you now, the lad's brain's not so quick. He's never said more'n a word or two here and there from the day he was born. But he's an angel otherwise," she added with a stiff glare, as if to head off any protest. "Good natured and a fine worker. A fine worker."

"I'm sure he is," Cybele murmured.

Mrs. Spencer gave a decisive nod. "That's that, then. I'll leave you to get settled. Supper's in an hour." She bustled off down the stair.

Cybele advanced a couple steps into the room. "Looks clean, at least."

"Cleaner than we are." Arthur dropped the backpack on the floor. "Just where did you get all that money, anyway?"

"Stole it from Evander, of course. Switched out dollars for pounds at Heathrow. I reckoned glamour and illusion wouldn't always be convenient."

He smiled slightly. "Always planning."

"Damn straight."

Rounding the foot of the bed, he braced his hands on the sill of the room's single window and peered out. Merlin's Hill was a dark rise of land beyond an open field. Cybele came up behind him.

"We'll find it," she said. "The cave, and the staff."

"Go ahead and shower first," he said without turning. "I'll wait."

***

Cybele's absence was welcome. Arthur was almost at the end of his rope as far as restraint was concerned. He needed her too much. Her scent lingered in the air, taunting him. He wanted desperately to lay her down on the shabby bedspread and make love to her. But he couldn't risk having another blackout when she was near.

Restless, he left the room and tried the door to the second guestroom. Unlocked. The space was similar to the one they'd been given. The bed was smaller, however, allowing room for a desk and chair. Though the furnishings were old, the room scrupulously clean. Everything was in perfect order—there wasn't so much as a wrinkle on the bed covering or a speck of dust on the desktop. The woodwork shone dully, as if recently polished. And yet Arthur couldn't shake the feeling that something was out of place.

Frowning, he opened all the drawers in the dresser

and desk. He even got down on the ground to peer under the bed. It was a waste of effort. He found nothing.

He went to the window. Across a graveled yard stood a barn and a smaller structure that might've been a chicken coop. He noted a wagon, a pickup truck, and a well pump. A dirt road ran from the near corner of the barn, passing alongside a pasture before disappearing into a tangle of vegetation. Through the branches, he could just make out the collapsed roof and crumbled stone walls of a much older structure.

A sudden spill of light caught Arthur's attention. One half of the barn's double door had opened. A teenaged lad emerged, holding a lantern. He closed the door behind him and turned to trudge toward the house. Just before he passed under the window, Arthur caught a glimpse of his face, strangely illuminated, almost as if from within. Arthur frowned. Light from the lantern? From the window? Or from something else?

"Arthur?"

He turned. Cybele stood in the doorway, wrapped in nothing but two thin towels—one around her body, the other, turban-style, around her head. His gaze took on her bruises—one on her right shoulder, another on her forearm, a third on her thigh. There were bite marks, too. More than a few.

His stomach turned.

"What are you doing?" she asked.

"Nothing." He couldn't lift his eyes from her long, damp legs. He imagined them open, draped over his shoulders.

She stepped past the door and into the room. Immediately, his lust was superseded by a deep feeling of wrongness. He didn't want her in this room. Something wasn't right. He backed her up into the hallway.

He shut the door behind him. "Don't go in there."

"Why not?"

"I'm not sure. Just...don't."

"All right," she said slowly, eyeing the closed door. "If you say so."

Once back in their own room, she unwound the towel from her head. Her hair fell, wet and snarled, to her waist. "Ugh," she said. "I forgot conditioner. It's going to take forever to comb out."

Her bare shoulders, even despite the bruises, mesmerized. He went hard just from contemplating her collarbone. She half turned away. His gaze skimmed over the delicate lines of her shoulder blades. Only to freeze at the sight of three long red scratches, running diagonally across her back. Bloody hell.

His erection shriveled. Snatching up clean clothes, he mumbled a couple words and headed to the shower. When he returned, already dressed, it was to find Cybele sitting on the bed, cross-legged. She wore a flowery blouse and panties, and nothing else.

She'd made slow progress with her hair. Half of it was smooth, the other half remained a tangled mess. She looked up as he entered. "This is ridiculous. I should cut it."

"Please don't," he said.

"It'd be a lot easier."

There was no chair in the room, so he sat down on the bed, careful to keep some space between them. "I like it the way it is."

She huffed. "You do it, then." She held out the comb.

Against his better judgment, he took it. Scooting toward him, she turned and shook her damp hair down her back.

He passed the teeth of the comb through her hair, working up from the bottom. He could feel the damp heat of her skin though the thin cotton blouse. The faint scent of shampoo, the texture of the blond strands between his fingers, the sound of her breath hitching higher. The sensations spread like sparks across his awareness.

His hand began to shake. "I'm not sure this is such a good idea," he muttered.

She glanced over her shoulder. Something in his expression must have given her pause, because she slowly drew back and took the comb from his hand.

"I'll finish it," she said, her eyes sliding away.

He watched her comb through the rest of the tangles, and then braid the lot of it into one thick rope. She hunted through her pack for a hair tie. As she was looping it on the end of the braid, she looked up and met his gaze.

"I wish we could make love," she said.

He stood, abruptly, and put as much distance as he could between them without actually fleeing the room. Which was not, he thought grimly, nearly distance enough.

"Don't you?" she persisted.

"Cybele. Don't push."

She grimaced and pulled the backpack closer, rooting through it for a clean pair of jeans. "Sorry."

"So am I."

She pulled on the pants and stood to zip and button them. "It's just—I can't stop thinking about last night. I'm still reeling. It was..." She blew out a breath. "I can't wait to do it again."

Neither could he, but... He grabbed her wet towel off the bed, shook it out, and draped it over the footboard. "How could you possibly want to do it again? You're one big bruise."

"A few bruises are nothing compared to that orgasm."

"A couple broken bones won't be worth it." He grimaced. "Maybe I should sleep in the other room tonight." Though that was the last thing he wanted to do. The thought of sleeping in that room jangled his nerves.

"So Mrs. Spencer can charge us another fifty pounds?" Cybele exclaimed. "No way. I didn't bring unlimited cash."

"We'll sleep with our clothes on, then."

She looked skeptical. "You really think that'll make a difference?"

"It better," he muttered.

Their gazes met. For a moment, they just stared at each other.

"Will it always be like this?" She hugged her torso. "Will we always want each other so badly?"

"Yes." Arthur had no doubt. "At least, for me it will be. You're the only woman I will ever want."

"You can't know that," she said quietly. "And it's not even likely. Nephilim don't do monogamy."

They didn't, as a rule. But maybe if his parents had been lifebonded, if they hadn't had other lovers, things would've turned out differently. But Tristan's only goal had been to father a child of Merlin's line. As for Alwen, she'd remained at Tŷ'r Cythraul mainly because of Arthur. Still, no matter how unhappy his mother had been, she might have restricted herself to Druid and human lovers. How could she have gone so far as to sleep with a rival Nephil? Had she hated his father that much?

"We will stay together," he said fiercely. "I won't allow anything else."

Her brows rose at that. "It's not for you to allow or not allow. Unless you mean to enthrall me during my Ordeal."

He jerked as if struck. "What? No!" He was appalled she'd even think such a thing. In two strides he stood before her, gripping her shoulders. "I won't control you, Cybele. Ever. If you don't want to be with me, just say so."

"Oh, Arthur. Of course I want to be with you. Only you.

There could never be anyone else."

He inhaled roughly. "In that case..." His eye fell on the faded photograph hanging on the wall. Releasing her shoulders, he grabbed it. The frame cracked in his hands. The thin glass shattered.

"Arthur. What are you—"

"This." He stabbed a shard of glass into the center of his left palm. Blood oozed from the wound.

"Um...I have a knife, you know. Right here." She slid it out of her boot. "There's no need to go breaking things."

He gave a terse shake of his head. "It's done now. We can make our pledge."

She tucked her blade back into its sheath. "You're serious."

"I am." He swallowed. "Don't you want to?"

"Yes." Her chest rose and fell. "It's just...Nephil lifebondings are so rare. And Mab's forbidden them."

"I don't give a shit about Mab. Do you?"

"No, of course not, but..." She eyed the drop of blood welling in the center of his palm. "Who ever heard of an adept bonding with a dormant?"

"So what? I love you. You love me. That's all that matters."

She still didn't look convinced. "Have you ever known a lifebonded pair?"

"My great-aunt, Morgana," he said. "Her bondmate was—still is, I suppose—a human witch."

Cybele eased the shard of glass from his fingers. "Are you sure you can handle the sight of my blood? Yesterday...the deathlust..."

He curled his hand into a fist, uncertainties rushing in on him. "You're right. Maybe we should wait."

"No." She touched his jaw, urging him to meet her gaze. "Forget I said anything. I trust you. If you want to do it now, I want that, too."

"Are you sure?"

She pressed her thumb against the broken glass, testing its edge. Then, with a decisive motion, she pierced her left palm.

"Yes."

The scent of her blood made his nostrils flare. He hissed in a breath through his teeth. A fierce fire kindled in his gut. He wanted to grab her, wanted to... He shut his eyes and touched his mother's moonstone.

"You okay?"

He opened his eyes. She stood before him, wounded, blood dripping down her palm. Her life was his for the taking. And he wanted to take it. Not in death, but in surrender. He wanted to dominate, control, own. The finest of lines separated sex, enthrallment, and death.

But she was Cybele, and he loved her. As long as he remembered that... "Yes," he said. "I'm okay."

She eyed him a little uncertainly. "How do we do this?"

He took her left hand and pressed it to his, palm to palm. "None but Thee, Cybele. Unto Oblivion."

Her fingers curled around his hand. "None but Thee, Arthur. Unto Oblivion."

The archaic vow, delivered in Cybele's soft Southern drawl, caused his heart to clench. The lust to dominate hadn't completely faded—it never would, he suspected—but he wouldn't let it master him. If he did, he'd be no freer than she.

How long they stood there, palms clasped, eyes locked, he couldn't have said. The press of their hands, skin on skin, blood mingling with blood, filled his senses. He held her life pulse in his hand. Each beat entwined their energy, their magic, and their lives.

Cybele was trembling. His own legs felt unsteady. The

longer he looked into her eyes, the more he hated to look away. He'd thought he'd known the depth of his feelings for her. But until this moment, he hadn't really understood how completely she'd become a part of him.

She spoke first, of course. She always did.

"I...your power. Your magic. I can feel it, Arthur, and it's...immense." She swallowed. "I feel like an ant, crawling on a massive oak."

"It's yours," he said fiercely. "Myself, my magic. Everything I am. It all belongs to you."

She wrapped her free hand around the back of his neck. He pulled her flush against his body, trapping their hands and their mingled blood between them. Her chin rose. His head dipped. Their lips met.

She opened her mouth and, moaning, sucked in his tongue. He delved deep, stroking, consuming. His cock hardened. White lights raced inside his skull...

The scent of her blood took on a new quality. No. That wasn't it. It was his own nature, changing. The demon inside him was rising, expanding, demanding life in sacrifice to its power. Magic, dark and fathomless, surged. It tossed his human nature like so much flotsam, to flounder on a stormy sea, past control, past reason.

Deathlust surged, roaring in his ears, flashing in his vision, twisting in his gut. He wanted death. Needed it. But this was *Cybele*. He clung to the thought like a mantra. *Cybele.*

With the last shred of his humanity, he shoved her toward the bed. She slid across the coverlet and smacked her skull against the headboard. He lurched backward; his shoulders hit the door with enough force to crack the wood frame. Opal lights consumed his skin. His vision went red. White sparks erupted in his hands.

Cybele scrambled to her knees on the bed. Their eyes

locked. Arthur's chest heaved, his breath coming harshly. The scent of her blood surrounded him, consumed him. His eyes dropped, drawn to the red smear on her palm. She balled up her hand and shoved it behind her back.

Death tasted so sweet. He craved it. Fuck. He never should have risked this. Would he never learn?

"Bandage," he croaked. "Now."

After the briefest hesitation, she lunged toward him and snatched up the towel he'd draped over the footboard. As she had in Tŷr Cythraul, she used her teeth and her good hand to rip off a strip and wind it around her wound.

He wrapped his fist around the moonstone and forced himself to look away, to shove his demon back into hiding. It was a near thing, but in the end, he succeeded. The lights under his skin faded, his eyes cooled. He slumped against the door. A shuddering sigh of relief left his lungs.

Silence reigned.

"Well," Cybele said eventually. "That was interesting."

He looked up to find her tying off the ends of the bandage. She pulled the knot tight with her teeth.

He laughed weakly. "Only you would call nearly getting your head ripped off 'interesting.'"

"You wouldn't have done it. Not to me."

"Let's hope not."

Her faith in him overwhelmed him. She leaned over and touched him with her bandaged hand. If he'd ever entertained doubts about her courage, they vanished in that instant. Her absolute trust humbled him. Would he ever be worthy of it?

"Arthur?"

He looked up. "Yes?"

"Are we..." The expression in her green eyes was uncharacteristically shy. "We're really bondmates?"

He couldn't repress a smile. "For better or for worse."

TWELVE

"Whatever happened to your hand?"

Mrs. Spencer was not pleased to see Cybele and Arthur appear in the dining room a full fifteen minutes past the appointed time. Mr. Spencer, slightly balding, his expression mild, sat at the head of the table. His grandson, Jack, to his right, had his eyes trained on his empty bowl. The basket of bread and the covered stew pot were apparently untouched. The meal had been awaiting their arrival.

Cybele donned her most conciliatory smile. While the wound on Arthur's hand had already vanished, hers remained bandaged. "I...um...knocked the photograph in our room off the wall," she improvised. "The glass broke. When I tried to pick it up..." She shrugged and looked ruefully at her hand. "I'm afraid I cut myself."

Mrs. Spencer's eyes narrowed. "Is that my towel you've wrapped it with?"

"Uh...yes. Sorry, ma'am. It was the first thing I grabbed to stop the bleeding. We'll pay for it, of course. And for the picture frame."

The promise of more money forthcoming seemed to mollify the woman. "I must say, you made a very poor job of the bandaging. Come to the kitchen and let me do it up proper. Your friend can visit with the mister and Jack."

Cybele darted a look at Arthur. He wasn't exactly in a

social mood. His entire body was tense. Mr. Spencer, who sat at the table's head, waved him into the chair at his left, opposite his grandson. Jack looked up, taking in the visitors with guileless blue eyes. He was probably close to Arthur's age. The thought was laughable. He looked years younger and, somehow, centuries more innocent.

Arthur took the indicated chair. Cybele eyed him uncertainly. Mrs. Spencer was holding open the kitchen door but Cybele couldn't shake the feeling that she shouldn't leave Arthur. Which was ridiculous. He hardly needed a babysitter. He was tense, yes, but nothing in this room was likely to set him off. Except her. He'd probably be better off with her out of sight.

"Please, everyone," she said. "Feel free to start eating without me."

Mrs. Spencer sniffed at that. "I should say not. They'll wait, if they know what's good for 'em."

There was nothing to do but follow her hostess into the kitchen. Once there, Cybele unwound her makeshift bandage and dropped it in the trash bin. "Why, it's not even deep," Mrs. Spencer groused. "I can't imagine why you wrapped it up ten times over."

"Um...I hate the sight of blood."

"Hmph." The woman retrieved a tube of ointment from a cupboard and smeared a bit on Cybele's palm. She followed up with an adhesive bandage. They returned to the dining room to find the men sitting in silence. Mr. Spencer contemplated his empty bowl. His grandson fiddled with his cutlery, a grimace on his face. Arthur's eyes roamed restlessly around the room.

All three looked up as the women entered. Cybele hastily sat in the empty chair at Arthur's right. "The meal smells delicious," she said with what she hoped looked like a sincere smile.

"First, the prayer," Mrs. Spencer declared as she settled in her chair at the foot of table.

Oh, damn. A prayer? Beside her, Arthur muttered a curse under his breath. Cybele hastened to cover it with a comment.

"How...nice." In reality, it was anything but. A religious ritual, even a small one like a prayer before meals, was not a comfortable thing for a Nephil adept. "Do you pray before every meal?"

"Before supper, certainly." Mrs. Spencer gaze narrowed. "Don't you? Or are you non-believers?" Her voice held more than a hint of challenge.

"No," Cybele said. "We're...um...rather fervent believers, actually."

That was absolutely true. In fact, she and Arthur were more than mere believers. They knew beyond a doubt that Heaven and Hell—and all their associated denizens—were real.

For the first time since they'd arrived, the edges of Mrs. Spencer's lips rose. She gave a nod of approval. "Gratified I am to hear it. So many young people go astray these days. Is that not true, George?"

"Aye, my dear. You have the right of it. As usual."

They were the first words the man had uttered. And they seemed to be, Cybele thought with dark amusement, a little sarcastic. If Mrs. Spencer sensed her husband's surreptitious mocking, she gave no indication of it. Her attention had returned to her grandson, who was scratching at the tablecloth.

"Jack," she said sharply. "Stop your fidgeting. We have guests."

Jack's chin jerked up. His gaze slid to Arthur. He froze, except for his hand, Cybele noted, which was suddenly shaking. Realizing it, he made a fist and slumped back in his chair. When his grandmother's frown deepened, he closed his eyes.

"Don't know what's gotten into the lad these last few days," she said. "He's been acting mighty odd." She cast a glance at her husband. "Well, then. Go on."

Mr. Spencer bowed his head over his folded hands. Mrs. Spencer and Jack did the same. Halfheartedly, Cybele mimicked them. Arthur didn't even try. She hoped their hosts wouldn't notice.

"Dear Lord, we thank you for this food..."

Mr. Spencer's prayer was a quickly mumbled affair. Thank the ancestors for that. Cybele didn't want to know what effect a more heartfelt offering would have had on Arthur. As it was, he was gripping the edge of the table so tightly, his knuckles had turned as white as the cloth. A few sparks erupted. Quietly, she laid a hand atop his. When the prayer concluded and Arthur's clenched muscles relaxed, she breathed a sigh of relief.

Mrs. Spencer uncovered the pot, revealing a hearty lamb and barley soup. While the others ate, she bustled back and forth to the kitchen, ferrying sliced beef, potatoes and buttered beans to the table.

Cybele was famished. She ate a bit of everything. Arthur, she noted, ate nothing but meat. No doubt he would've preferred it bloody and raw. He had to settle for rubbery and overcooked. Still, when Mrs. Spencer offered a second helping, he didn't turn it down. Jack, by contrast, ate little. He kept darting glances at Arthur.

Cybele frowned at the boy. A faint but unmistakable glow clung to his head and shoulders. Or maybe it was just a trick of the light. Or a migraine coming on. She rubbed the space between her eyes. Her head was beginning to throb. They should have walked back to the village for dinner.

"Come looking for Merlin, have you?" Mr. Spencer asked.

Cybele's chin jerked up. "What?"

Mr. Spencer laid his knife and fork on his plate. "Merlin. The sorcerer. He's the only reason tourists visit this part of Wales. I suspect that's why you're here."

"Yes," Cybele said, a bit shakily. "That's true." Faced with her host's expectant expression, she added, "I understand he was born nearby?"

"Aye." The farmer pushed his empty plate toward the middle of the table. "The sorcerer's birth is the subject of any number of tales." Leaning back in his chair, he folded his hands over an ample belly. "Merlin's mother, it's said, was the daughter of a local clergyman. The girl was a troublesome lass, shunning the church and her Bible. Some even called her a witch. They claimed she fled into the hills in the night, to practice the dark arts under the stars. Perhaps that was true, because when she fell pregnant, she told her Da she'd been ravished by a demon."

Mrs. Spencer snorted. "Diddling a local boy in a hayloft, rather, and didn't want to confess to the sin."

"That's as may be," her husband allowed. "Her father, however, chose to believe her. Or perhaps he simply wished to err on the side of caution. Merlin was baptized a bare three minutes after his birth, even before the cord was cut. 'Tis said the babe screamed like the devil hisself when the holy water splashed. Didn't quiet down until he was wiped dry. The child was raised a pious Christian, but blood will tell in the end. At any rate, it did with Merlin."

Arthur cleared his throat. He picked up his knife and turned it over in his hand, contemplating the blade. Cybele kicked him under the table. He glanced over at her and put the utensil down.

Would this meal never end? "What happened then?"

"Merlin came of age and studied for the priesthood. One night, as he walked from church to rectory, a sudden storm rose. He was struck by lightning."

"Was he injured?"

"Most assuredly. He lay near death for two days and nights. On the third day, he suddenly sat up in his bed, as alive as could be. His burns, which just the night before had been festering, were healed. Might'a been considered a miracle, if not for what happened a few months later."

"George," his wife interrupted. "I don't think—"

To Cybele's surprise, Mr. Spencer tucked his chin and glared at his wife. "Quiet, Gladys. I'm speaking."

Mrs. Spencer flushed. She rose and began clearing the table with jerky movements, muttering under her breath about sin and damnation as she collected plates and bowls. Jack paled. He slid down even further in his chair and hunched his shoulders.

Mr. Spencer leaned forward, resting his forearms on the table. "Weel, then. This is what happened. Young Merlin, returned as he was from near-death, rose from his bed three months later. Stark naked. Without pausing to don a stitch, he left the rectory, passed in front of the church, and disappeared into the countryside. He came to this very hill."

He swept an arm toward the window, though with night fully descended, all that was visible was the room's reflection in the glass. "For three nights, terrible screams rang out. For three mornings, cattle and sheep were found mutilated in the fields and barns, heads torn from their bodies, flesh chewed clean through. Three persons—two men and a woman disappeared. They were never seen again. And in the sky—"

He paused. Jack began to hum under his breath.

Cybele knew well enough where the tale was going.

She sighed and played along. "What was in the sky?"

Jack clapped his hands over his ears and hummed louder.

His grandfather sent him a frown, and then turned back to his audience. "Many swore to seeing a fearsome creature flying overhead. A winged demon. They said Merlin had sold his soul to his father's kind. In return, he gained dark powers such as mere humanfolk cannot comprehend."

"Merlin used his power for the good of mankind," Cybele felt compelled to point out. "Not for evil."

"Perhaps that was the result," Mr. Spencer allowed. "But Merlin's magic was far from benevolent." He frowned. "Jack. What's wrong with you, lad? Stop that blasted noise."

Jack's humming dimmed.

"Merlin's dark magic allowed Uther Pendragon to seduce another man's wife," their host continued. "A right dodgy affair that was."

"But without that illusion, there wouldn't have been a King Arthur," Cybele said.

"True enough," Mr. Spencer conceded. "Still, Merlin couldn't outrun the devil forever. Ruin caught up with him. He ended up ensorcelled by his own magic, trapped under the Earth by a scheming lover, in the same cave where he'd once sold his soul."

His wife, exiting the kitchen with a pie in her hands, snorted. "That's the way of it, innit? A man never sees a woman's cleverness until it's too late."

"Now, you must admit, dear, I've never doubted your cleverness. Would've been the death of me," he added under his breath.

His wife cut a generous piece of pie and slid it in front of him. Cybele accepted her slice with murmur of thanks.

Arthur declined with a swift shake of his head. When Mrs. Spencer exhaled an offended huff, Cybele gave an apologetic shrug. "Arthur's not one for desserts."

"Arthur, eh?" Mr. Spencer leaned over and elbowed Arthur in the ribs. "Just like the king."

"Not quite," Arthur mumbled.

Jack opened his mouth as if about to speak. At the last moment he seemed to change his mind. He set down his fork, covered his ears, and began humming. Loudly.

"Jack," his grandmother said. "Whatever has gotten into you?" She turned on her husband. "Finish your pudding, husband. 'Tis late. Jack wants his rest."

Cybele very much doubted that he did. The boy looked far too agitated for sleep.

"Gladys. Let the lad be." Mr. Spencer scraped his last bite of pie onto his fork and pointed it at Cybele. "Some say Merlin didna die at all. They say he's sleeping, waiting for his faithless lover to return. They say that if you go up onto Merlin's Hill at midnight, you'll hear him moaning."

"Have you heard him?" Arthur asked.

Cybele looked at him sharply. Was he serious?

"Me?" Mr. Spencer snorted. "Midnight finds me in my bed with my eyes shut and my ears closed. A farmer's up before the sun, you know."

"There's nothing to hear." Mrs. Spencer took Cybele's plate and stacked it atop her own. "'Tis just a heathen tale. There's no moaning in the hills." She rose. She was about to gather another plate when Jack's fist slammed the table. Chinaware jumped. Cutlery clattered. A water glass overturned.

"Jack!" Mrs. Spencer exclaimed. "That was uncalled for. And you—" She glared at her husband. "Let the lad be, indeed. He must be sickening from something."

Jack certainly didn't look well. His spine went ramrod

straight. His mouth fell open. Words emerged at a higher pitch and softer than Cybele might have expected.

"I hear the moans. I see the light." He gestured to the window. "Out there. On the hill."

His grandparents stared at him, mouths agape. Mr. Spencer recovered first. "Those are more words than the lad's uttered in a year," he muttered. "All told."

"Moaning. In the cave."

"Cave?" Arthur said sharply. "Where?"

"Oh, no," Jack said. "Oh, no, oh, no, oh, n—"

"Jack." His grandmother scowled. "Stop that. You didn't hear moaning on the hill. You had a dream."

"No. No dream." He shoved back his chair. "Moaning. Light. Magic. Out there." He jumped up and, before anyone could react, ran out of the room. The outer door opened and banged shut. A moment later, Jack ran past the window, heading across the graveled yard.

Cybele looked from Mrs. Spencer to her husband. Neither had moved. "Shouldn't someone go after him?"

Mr. Spencer sighed and shook his head. "He's likely gone to check on the kittens. There's a litter in the barn loft. Jack likes to look in on them before he turns in."

"He's a good lad," his wife said. "Always has been. Never a lick of trouble."

"Never two words strung together neither," put in Jack's grandfather. "Before now."

Mrs. Spencer looked down at the plates she was stacking. "Lad's been acting mighty odd these past two days. Ever since that German gent stopped here." She looked at her husband. "Maybe he's caught some foreign disease. I'll have the doctor in tomorrow."

Mr. Spencer's expression remained troubled. "Wouldn't hurt, I reckon."

***

Maweth was lonely.

He slumped against the curving quicksilver wall, too depressed to even lift his head. He'd wanted to leave the mirror with Lucky and help him out with the assignment Dusek had given him. The angel had no experience with the kind of underhanded task the master had ordered him to perform.

He was sure to feel guilty about it. But would Lucky do the smart thing and turn tail and fly off? Oh, no. Dusek had vowed to take out his anger on Maweth if the angel left. The cherub had solemnly sworn not to.

Stupid angel.

He sure hoped the little guy was okay.

***

Maybe, Michael reflected, it was a good thing Raphael had called him back from Devon. Things had been getting a bit out of hand. Trouble was, the scene he'd witnessed through the window at Tŷ'r Cythraul was burned permanently into his brain. Getting things back *in* hand wasn't going to be easy.

He was currently in Prague, carrying out Raphael's latest orders. His heart, however, yearned for England. His heart—and another part of his anatomy, which, even though it didn't function properly, insisted on making its needs known.

He couldn't stop thinking of Cybele. Scenarios and dialogues played like video in his brain. In some scenes, he was himself. In others, he was human. In one incredibly disturbing daydream—one that shamed him to remember—he'd cast himself as a Nephil.

Each time, in every scenario, Cybele turned her back on Arthur and took Michael's hand. His hand, and his...

No. He had to stop this. Lustful rumination wasn't healthy. It was, in fact, a sin.

What was she doing this very moment? Bathing? Eating? Copulating? His brain stuttered over that last one. Maybe Gabriel was watching her doing unspeakable things with Arthur right now. The very thought made Michael want to punch something.

His mood was grim as he flew over the old quarter of the city. With effort, he wrenched his mind from Cybele and tried to concentrate on the streetscape below. The medieval city center boasted a veritable forest of church spires. On another day, in another mood, he would have found it beautiful.

He landed on the sidewalk across the street from the Prague Institute for the Study of Man. Michael folded his wings into his back and changed from spirit to flesh form. A bicyclist nearly ran him down.

He leaped out of the way just in time. *Get a grip*, he told himself sternly, turning his attention to the building before him. As schools of higher learning went, the Institute's campus was modest. Its facilities consisted of a single, largish seventeenth century mansion, fronting on four lanes of twenty-first century traffic. He peered up at the baroque façade but could discern nothing that might be happening beyond its windows.

The Institute's main entrance didn't front on the public street. It lay beyond a pair of iron gates, tucked inside a central courtyard. A cobblestone carriageway connected the road to the interior yard via a short, barrel-vaulted tunnel.

He crossed the street, ignoring horns and shouts. The intricate scrollwork on the gates had caught his attention. The pattern on the right formed the figure of an angel. Raphael himself, if Michael wasn't very much mistaken.

The flowing robes and gilded wings were unmistakable. True, the proportions of the Sword of Righteous Vengeance were a bit off. But in general, it was an excellent likeness. The figure on the left was a dark-winged Nephil. The creature rose from a fissure in the earth. It gripped a jagged bolt of hellfire in its left hand, the tip aimed straight at Raphael's heart. Michael snorted and shook his head. As if his brother could ever be bested by a Nephil.

The gates were closed and locked. Michael pondered his options. He could open the lock, or reassume spirit form and simply pass right through the iron bars. He opted for the former. Interacting with the Institute's denizens in the flesh might prove more helpful than just drifting through and observing them unseen. With a touch of his fingertip, he sprang the lock's mechanism and opened the angel side of the gate a couple feet. He walked in and shut the gate behind him.

The courtyard was surprisingly green, planted with trees and flowerbeds within a circular drive. A fountain, topped by a variety of marble statues, occupied the center of the garden. The subject of the artwork was, again, angels and demons, this time locked in hand-to-hand combat. The day was warm for the spring season, with a touch of sun. A handful of students, heads bent over laptops or phones, were scattered about at tables and benches. Nothing seemed out of the ordinary. Michael scanned the ground. If Fortunato had flown this way, he'd left no trace.

He rounded the fountain and approached the main entrance. Twin mahogany doors, ten feet tall and burnished to a dark, glassy sheen, stood at the top of a marble stair. The stone medallion over the door bore the school's coat of arms. He was annoyed, yet unsurprised, to note yet another angel/demon motif on the escutcheon. Really, this theme was getting old.

"Sir. May I help you?" The offer, spoken in accented English to his back, was spiced with disapproval.

He turned to find a darkly handsome young man. Longish black hair, olive complexion, soulful brown eyes. Not a Nephil. A human. He wore shirt and tie, pressed black slacks, and a blazer sporting the Institute's crest. He seemed, to Michael's eye, less than comfortable in the restrictive garb, as if he were used to more casual attire.

Michael stood a little straighter and concentrated on projecting a relentlessly human aura. His black jeans and vintage military jacket presented exactly the look he wanted. For today, he'd added a messenger bag, its strap slung across his chest. A nice, casual touch of human student realism, if he did say so himself.

"This courtyard is private," the man said. "Students and faculty only."

"I didn't realize." Michael offered an apologetic smile. He tried to place the man's accent. Middle Eastern, he thought. Israeli, maybe? "I came through the gate and—"

"Impossible. The gate is kept locked."

"Really?" He added a guileless blink. "I had no trouble entering." It wasn't a lie.

The man looked skeptical. "Nonetheless. You must allow me to escort you out."

"Actually," Michael countered, "I've traveled all the way from England, hoping I might tour the Institute. I'd like to apply for admission."

"Ah." The man's expression eased a fraction. "We have many British students. Some from the United States as well. Most of our classes are taught in English, as the Institute's work is international in scope. What is your area of study?"

"The Ancient Middle East."

"Precisely my interest as well. I suggest you visit the admissions office. The door is around the corner, accessible from the street. They can provide further information and arrange a tour on the weekend."

"Unfortunately," Michael said, "I'll have left Prague by then. Perhaps you could give me a brief tour now? Informally?" He held out his hand. "My name is Michael, by the way. Michael...Santángel. And you are?"

After a brief hesitation, the man shook Michael's hand. "Dr. Shimon Ben-Meir, archeologist. I'm at liberty for the next hour. I suppose it wouldn't hurt to show you around. Come." He nodded toward the mahogany doors.

Michael murmured his thanks as he fell into step beside his host. "When does the next term begin?"

He kept up a steady stream of questions as Ben-Meir guided him through several ground floor passageways, pausing to allow Michael to peer into classrooms, offices, and laboratories. A few passing students eyed him curiously. He nodded in return. The Institute was, as Raphael had said, a bona-fide center of learning, no matter that the director was a Nephil. Its facilities were a curious mix of modern comfort and old-style graciousness. Michael sensed nothing amiss with any of it.

He let his senses roam, seeking any sign that Fortunato's celestial spirit had passed this way. He encountered nothing.

There had to be something. The little cherub could hardly have vanished into thin air. "The Institute's founder is well respected in the international academic community," Michael commented as they climbed a marble staircase.

"That is very true. Professor Vaclav Dusek is a highly respected scholar of antiquities."

"I'm sure he's a busy man, but I'd very much like to meet him. Could you perhaps arrange a brief interview?"

Ben-Meir paused at the top of the stair. "That will not be possible, I'm afraid. The professor is out of the country at the moment. I am acting as director in his absence."

Michael wondered if Ben-Meir knew the man he worked for was a demon. "Do you teach classes as well?"

"Not normally, no. In fact, I've spent the better part of the last year off-site, on an archeological expedition."

"Where?"

"Axum. It is in—"

"Ethiopia," Michael said. "The Ark of the Covenant is said to be preserved there."

Ben-Meir's brows rose. "That is true. Unfortunately, only the high priest of Axum is permitted to view the relic, keeping its true provenance a mystery."

"And the archeological expedition you mentioned? Was it successful?"

"I believe so," he said, but offered no further elucidation. Pausing before a pair of gilded panel doors, he pushed the right leaf open and stood back. "The Institute's library," he said. "A place of study and awe."

The space was impressively lofty. The mansion's former ballroom, Ben-Meir explained, now fitted with long wooden reading tables, glass-topped display cases, and tall oaken bookshelves fronted by rolling ladders. Delicate chandeliers hung from the deep-coffered ceiling.

A few students sat at the table studying various documents. Leather bound tomes, illuminated manuscripts, parchment scrolls, and even stone tablets. All wore white gloves and paper face masks.

"The university's collection of ancient materials is unparalleled," Ben-Meir said. "Our most prized artifacts come from Biblical lands. We take the utmost care with their preservation. Yet we also believe the treasures must be accessible for study."

He guided Michael along a series of cases in which fragments of ancient scrolls were displayed in humidity-controlled compartments. He halted before an especially fragile specimen, displayed alone, in a round case a short distance apart from the others.

"From Israel," he said. "Recovered from a cave near the ancient city of Qumran. It's a fragment from the apocryphal Book of Enoch."

Michael bent his head over the case. The dark bit of parchment was no larger than his palm, its edges ragged, the lettering almost unintelligible. It'd been a couple centuries since he'd deciphered any ancient Aramaic, but, as he scanned the text, one word jumped out as if it'd been written in fire.

Nephilim.

He straightened. No wonder this fragment had been given pride of place.

They left the library, descending the grand stair to a marbled entry hall. The tour was almost at an end and Michael's frustration was growing. Perhaps Fortunato hadn't been here after all. But if that were the case, where in Heaven's name could the cherub be?

The stair didn't end at street level. A narrower flight continued downward, closed off at a lower landing by a plain mahogany door. Michael was about to look away when a glittering bit of something, resting on the second step down, caught his eye. His heartbeat accelerated. When his guide turned to speak with an approaching student, Michael stooped and picked it up. He studied it gravely before closing his fingers around it.

"What occupies the lower floors?" he asked Ben-Meir when the student had left.

"Storage, mainly. A few old laboratories which are no longer in use."

Not likely. Michael sensed a vast amount of open space beneath his feet. There were, at a minimum, four lower levels, each one darker than the one above. But in all that darkness, Michael didn't sense even a single spark of celestial light. Fortunato wasn't there, either.

Ben-Meir escorted him back through the courtyard. The archeologist bid him good day and locked the main gates behind him. Once on the sidewalk, Michael gazed up at the iron angel and demon, locked in eternal enmity.

He opened his fist and looked down at his hand. An iridescent feather, a perfect match to the five already in his possession, sparkled in his palm. This was beyond serious. Fortunato wasn't inside the Institute now, but he had been. How? Why? And where was he now?

The Prague Institute for the Study of Man hid far too many secrets for Michael's comfort. The dark subterranean levels, for example. Nothing good could be going on there.

Michael looked left and right down the sidewalk. No one seemed to be paying him any mind, so he willed his fleshy body to fade into nothingness. Once in spirit form, he drifted through the marble-faced walls of the Institute.

As he suspected, the door to the lower level was locked. He passed through it and found himself in a long corridor. As Ben-Meir had said, the rooms on either side appeared deserted. Michael returned to the stair and drifted down another flight.

This level proved more instructive. He discovered a room that appeared to be an alchemic laboratory. Long worktables were littered with glass beakers and flasks, some with distilling tubes attached, set above gas burners. Cauldrons hung above stoves heated by wood or coal.

Rows of test tubes, filled with powders and liquids of every color imaginable, lined the far wall. Copper pots and urns, and glass and ceramic canisters, stood neatly arranged on a table below. One particularly large glass bottle was filled with a dark crimson liquid. He leaned close and sniffed it. Blood. Human blood.

All this faded to the back of Michael's mind as he focused on a long, golden platform, vaguely coffin-like, which occupied the center of the room. A container, he realized, though the hinges, and the cracks where the lid met the sides were barely visible. Even stranger, the oversized box was constructed of a substance he'd only rarely encountered.

Alchemical gold. Though the material held its shape with perfect corners and precise lines, it wasn't completely solid. The surface shifted and moved. What's more, an aura of...life...surrounded it. Most odd, considering it was the work of a Nephil. He reached out a hand to touch it. It felt like...nothing. Nothing at all.

What was in that golden box? His senses gave no hint. His angelic perception couldn't pass through it. Was Fortunato trapped inside? He thought it unlikely. Even the most powerful Nephil couldn't contain a celestial life force.

Shaking his head, he drifted back to the stairwell. Another level lay below this one, but when he reached the locked door at the bottom of the stair he received a shock. He couldn't pass through. What was worse, the surrounding walls were just as impenetrable. Gravely troubled, Michael returned to the level above and tried sinking through the floor. He couldn't do that, either.

Vaclav Dusek's magic could block the will of an archangel. How in Heaven's name could that be?

THIRTEEN

"Where do you think Jack went?"

Cybele picked up a black and white kitten. She stroked its tiny head and murmured sweet nothings. It tangled its claws in her blouse.

Arthur blew out a breath. The nausea he'd experienced during dinner had faded to a sour taste in his mouth. A vague rage lingered. His body's reaction was all out of proportion to the situation. Yes, religious rituals were difficult for a Nephil to endure, but Mr. Spencer's prayer at dinner hadn't been all that sincere.

Arthur had been reacting to Jack.

He tried to puzzle it out, but it was difficult to think with his nerves angry and jangling. The urge to shift and kill was growing stronger by the minute. He wanted to order Cybele to return to their room while he waged battle with his demon nature. There was a less than zero chance she'd obey, however, so he didn't bother wasting his breath.

They'd excused themselves from the dinner table after Jack's precipitous departure. They waited barely ten minutes before slipping out of the house after him. The litter of barn kittens had been easy enough to find. But Jack himself was nowhere to be found. They'd checked the barn, the chicken coop, and all the surrounding area. The only creatures visible in the bordering fields were sheep.

"He couldn't have gone far," Arthur grumbled.

Cybele paused in the motion of stroking a kitten. "Do you think he really heard moans on the hill?"

"I don't think he's lying. He fairly oozes goodness and innocence." Arthur suspected that's what had made him so nauseous.

"True," said Cybele, frowning. "He's even got a glow about him."

Arthur shot her a look. "You saw that, too?"

"Yes. Faintly." Cybele detached the kitten's claws from her blouse. "So if he's not lying about the moaning, what do you think he heard?"

"Not Merlin," Arthur said flatly. "Maybe a demon." He didn't have much experience with demons—they tended to avoid areas already inhabited by Nephilim.

"A demon, way out here in the middle of nowhere?" Cybele said dubiously. She returned the ball of black fluff to its mother and siblings. "Don't demons prefer populated areas? They can't do much damage without a human host."

"I suppose," Arthur said. But what the hell else could it be?

They left the barn. The night was very dark. An access road started behind the barn and ran between two fenced fields. About a quarter mile down this path stood the stone ruin he'd seen from the window, barely visible through a screen of vegetation.

Cybele's eyes followed his gaze. "Maybe he's in there."

"Maybe."

Their passage down the trail raised the soft bleating of sheep on either side. Though Arthur could see perfectly well in the dark, he knew Cybele couldn't. He called a handful of hellfire, and was heartened to discover he could

contain it in a compact, controlled burn. He released the
sparkling globe into the air. It drifted obediently before
them.

Cybele grinned. "Nice."

As magical accomplishments went, it was a small thing.
Hardly worth the intense pride Cybele's praise sparked.
But the effort marked the first time he'd truly felt in
control of his magic. Maybe there was hope, after all.

The stone ruin turned out to be an abandoned stable.
Half the roof beams had collapsed and the rest looked
ready to go in the next stiff wind. The place was choked
with brambles and saplings. Broken branches and a trail
of fresh footsteps led them past a row of stalls. At the end
of the passage, a fallen beam and a good deal of crushed
roofing blocked their path.

Jack had scraped a path under the debris. Arthur
caught Cybele's quick grimace. She wasn't fond of
enclosed spaces. Evander's preferred form of punishment
for dormants was twenty-four hours locked in the cellar.

"I'll go in and take a look," he said. "You wait here."

"No. I'll go with you."

"You're sure?"

She nodded. After a moment's hesitation, Arthur
ducked under the beam, widening the path as much as he
could as he went through. Cybele sucked in a gulp of air
and made a wild lunge through the barrier. He caught her
on the other side. He could feel her heart pounding.

"I'm fine," she said, pushing him away and standing on
her own. He caused his hellfire to flare brightly,
illuminating the space more evenly. She sent him a
grateful glance.

He looked around. They'd entered the stable's tack
room, and it was a mess. Mold climbed the walls. Rotten
saddles and other bits of disintegrating leather lay matted

together on the floor.

"Ugh." Cybele hugged her torso. "Mouse droppings."

Arthur prowled the space, looking for hidden nooks or exits. He found nothing. "If Jack was here earlier, he's gone now." He straightened, rubbing the back of his neck. "Damn. Where could he have gotten to?"

"Maybe it doesn't even matter," Cybele said with a sigh. "So what if he thought he heard moaning? He probably imagined it."

"Maybe. But his grandparents said he barely spoke before. Something caused him to start babbling."

"The foreign lodger?" Cybele asked. "Do you think the man could have molested Jack?"

"Damn," Arthur said. "I hope not. But something must have happened recently."

"Let's just look for the cave on our own like we planned," Cybele said. She eyed the gap in the debris through which they'd entered. "Though I'm not thrilled about going through there again, that's for sure."

They retraced their path. Once back in the open air, Cybele sank down on an overturned water trough and gulped several deep breaths of clean air.

Arthur laid his hand on her upper back. "You ok?"

"Fine."

That was bullshit if he'd ever heard it, but she wouldn't appreciate him calling her on it. She needed a few minutes to regain her composure, though.

"I want to take a look from above," he said. "Maybe I'll spot something we've missed. Wait for me here?"

She nodded.

He walked a short way down the access road. His neck was stiff. He stretched it, working out the kinks. Then he closed his eyes and spread his arms.

For one long, fluid moment his body was suspended in

time and form. The sensation of shifting, previously a spasm of gut-wrenching agony, now felt as natural as a morning stretch. His demon essence, as terrifying and unpredictable as it still was, no longer felt like a foreign thing. It wasn't, he realized. His Nephil nature was an intrinsic part of his self. His most basic identity.

Heat glowed behind his eyes. Sparks gathered in his hands. Dark opal hues pulsated under his skin. His wings unfolded on a whisper. Energy—fierce, limitless—surged into his muscles.

He took to the sky with his eyes still closed, aware that Cybele was almost certainly tracking his flight. He battled an unholy urge to reverse course and fall on her. To tear off her clothes and plunge into her body.

He wanted her desperately, but for the first time since surprising her at Tŷ'r Cythraul, he felt as though he was the master of his lust. They would make love again, but not just yet. Not while his haphazard skills and the power difference between them threatened her life.

He rounded Merlin's Hill, his expanded Nephil senses absorbing his surroundings in a way his human self could never have imagined. Subtleties previously ignored were suddenly obvious. His ears detected the rustle of the wind, the bleat of sheep, the hoot of an owl. He knew the scurry of rodents and insects, the pulse of life hidden in the heartwood of every tree. Myriad scents reached his nostrils: wood smoke, exhaust fumes, sheep dung. The earliest flowers of spring.

He flew over the summit and banked to the left, then began a slow descending spiral around the site. He and Cybele had tramped over much of the ground below during their afternoon exploration. They hadn't, however, noticed a particular rocky dip of land, overrun with brambles. Nor the hidden face of a boulder, split in two by a deep crevice, just wide enough for a person—a very slender person—to pass through.

Excitement surged. He knew this place. He'd seen it in Merlin's memory. The vegetation was different. A wild wood had given way to cultivated fields. But this was the place. He was sure of it. This was the entrance to Merlin's cave. The resting place of Merlin's staff. The key to Arthur's victory over Mab.

Heart pounding, he dove toward it.

And that's when things got weird.

***

Cybele paced circles in the small clearing, trying to put her finger on why she felt so odd. The moment Arthur had flown off, the atmosphere surrounding the ruined stable had changed. She wasn't quite sure how it'd changed, or why. It simply felt...off. Much like the Spencers' dining room.

She eyed the tumbled-down building. Without Arthur's light to illuminate the darkness, the place took on a sinister aura. The unsettling vibe wasn't in her head. It emanated from the shadows within.

Inhaling deeply, she slipped her hand into her jeans pocket and drew out her touchstone. The braided alder shoots and the peridot within it was hardly any larger than a walnut. But it was big enough to provide a focus for her magic, and a block for her worries.

There is nothing in there, she told herself firmly. *Nothing. We looked everywhere.*

A finger tapped her shoulder.

She cried out and spun about, scrambling backwards at the same time. She caught a glimpse of soft light. Then her foot caught on a stone and she went sprawling. She only just managed not to drop her touchstone.

"Sorry! Oh, sorry!"

She blinked up at the young man looming over her, wringing his hands. "Jack? Is that you?"

The odd aura she'd noticed around Jack's head and shoulders at dinner had brightened. It now cast his entire face in an otherworldly light. He stood, looking down at her with an uncertain expression, hands opening and closing at his sides. His blue eyes revealed fear, apology, and distaste.

Cybele stood slowly, not daring to take her eyes off him. "Jack," she said. "What are you doing here? Where did you come from?"

There was no way he'd been inside the stable. She and Arthur had looked in every corner. Had they missed seeing Jack on the road? Or in one of the fields? That didn't seem likely.

"Come. We must go." He extended his hand to her.

She didn't take it. "Go? Go where?"

He gestured toward the stable's sagging doorway. "Inside." He moved closer.

Cybele resisted the urge to take a step back. "There's nothing in there."

"Come," Jack said again. His hand closed on her wrist.

Hell. She circled her hand, trying to break his hold. His grip held. He was stronger than he looked. She felt a surge of irrational panic.

"Jack," she said sharply. "Let me go."

"Go," he said. "Yes."

He turned and began a slow trudge toward the stable. Cybele set her heels in the dirt and resisted. To no avail. No amount of tugging, pulling, kicking, or cursing slowed Jack's forward motion.

Slowly, inexorably, he dragged her after him.

FOURTEEN

Arthur landed near the cracked boulder. As he touched down, the stone blurred and smeared as if it were nothing more than paint running down a canvas. A different kind of barrier came into view. It looked like golden, sparkling gauze.

He'd never seen anything like it. He tried to move closer. With every step, the stone seemed to move farther away. Strong magic. Merlin's? Arthur discarded that theory almost immediately. This light didn't feel like Nephil magic.

For one thing, there was no hint of death about it. The force was cooler and sweeter than any power a demon could manage. But for all its brightness, it was no less lethal. Its delicacy was like a spider's silk: fragile and deadly.

Heavenly magic? Arthur had no experience with that. As he tried to puzzle out who or what might have conjured such a barrier, a sudden gust buffeted his wings. The gauzy light responded with a ripple. The movement spilled light past the boundary of the stone, past Arthur and down the hillside. The leading edge stopped just short of the ruined stable.

He eyed the glittering blanket uneasily. Whatever it was, he didn't want Cybele facing it alone. He lifted his wings, intending to fly back to her. And then froze as a mournful wail filled the air around him.

The sound seemed to seep from the very stones beneath his feet. It began as a bare whisper, but quickly escalated in volume. The gauzy light pulsed with the eerie melody, as if breathing in tandem with a despairing spirit.

Stranger and stranger. He stepped closer to the pulsating light. This time, it didn't retreat. He extended a hand. The air in front of the disturbance was hot, though not uncomfortably so. He took another step. He was almost touching it now.

He did touch it. His hand met no resistance. It sank into the luminescence. His arm and shoulder quickly followed. His fingertips brushed something solid. Stone. He spread his palm on the rough surface. Whatever this light was, it hadn't dissolved the boulder itself. He probed the stone with his hand. The crack was no wider than two of his fingers.

He took a backward step, peering at the anomaly from a different angle. He could, if he concentrated in just the right way, see the dark slash of the crevice through the rippling gold light. The inhuman moaning pierced his eardrums. Could he get through to its source? He could only try.

He called hellfire into his hands and blasted it into the light. The stone shook at the impact. Encouraged, Arthur sent volley after volley into the fissure. Bits of spalled stone spewed out. On the next blast, a loud crack split the air. Blinding brilliance flashed.

The moaning suddenly ceased. The normal sounds of the night seemed louder in its absence. Arthur approached the stone warily, shading his eyes. The crevice had widened, perhaps even enough for him to pass through. But when he turned sideways and tried to insinuate his body into the space, the light leapt in a scorching flame.

"Bollocks." He jumped back. After a brief hesitation, he tried again with the same result. Frustrated, he took three steps backward and blasted the stone with hellfire. The boulder exploded. Arthur dove to the ground as shards sprayed over his head.

After a moment, he looked up. The boulder was gone, but damn if the light didn't look stronger and brighter than ever. His assault hadn't weakened the magic one bit. He got to his feet and lifted his hands to try again.

"Oh Heavenly angels above. What an idiot!"

Arthur froze. Behind him, very close, someone was laughing. Chuckling and snorting with glee. Cautiously, he turned, sparks sputtering on his fingertips.

He couldn't, at first, pinpoint the location of the laughter. Then he spotted something. A new smudge of light. Not golden, this time. Silver. An unpleasant sensation skittered across his nerves. He took a step toward it. The light promptly vanished. But he knew damn well it wasn't gone.

He felt invisible eyes upon him. He was being watched. Well. Two could play at that game. He called an invisibility glamour, hoping to Hell and back that this time it would work.

Stealthily, cloaked by the glamour, he circled the place where he'd last seen the silver light. At the same time, he projected an image of himself standing in the place where he'd been. It was a tricky bit of illusion, probably the most complicated he'd attempted so far. It seemed to work—at least, he saw no evidence that his unseen watcher was aware of the deception.

As he stalked closer, the silver light shimmered back into his perception. A transparent, pulsing of magic, rising and rippling like heat waves. He narrowed his eyes, and concentrated on seeing its source. Abruptly, a figure melted into view. To Arthur's vast surprise, it was a man. Or rather, a being in the form of a man. With his back to Arthur, his posture was one of utter ease. Idiot. He was staring intently at the illusion Arthur had planted as a diversion. Arthur moved to one side, far enough to catch the amused look on the stranger's face. His very, very pale face.

His hair was like snow, his skin milk-white. His clothing was just as pale. He wore a white linen suit, white shirt, white bow tie, white shoes. Diamond earrings glinted in his lobes. His white-gloved hands rested on the silver handle of a white gentleman's cane. His magic swirled and buzzed about his shoulders in a cloud of tiny, silver sparks.

Arthur walked up to him and tapped him on the shoulder.

The bloke all but jumped out of his pale skin. He whirled about, jaw agape, eyes wide. Those eyes, oddly, were the same shade of silver as the sparks whipping around his head. He looked at Arthur then back at the illusion. With a flick of Arthur's finger, the glamour dissolved.

Silver Eyes spun about, jaw agape. "You...you...you can see me?"

Arthur crossed his arms. "What do you think?"

"But...but...but..." The pale man waved his walking stick. "You shouldn't be able to."

"Why not? Who are you?"

Lowering the tip of his stick to the ground, he placed one hand atop the other on its handle. "Who do you think I am?"

Arthur considered the question. Truth to tell, there weren't a lot of options. "Not a demon."

A huff of disbelief. "I should say not."

"Or a human."

He rolled his eyes skyward. "Only a lackwit would think that."

"And definitely not a Nephil. So you're an angel," Arthur concluded with disgust. "A goddamned fucking angel."

"Certainly not." Graceful silver wings unfurled from the angel's back. "Angels are blessed, not damned. As for the other, impossible. My kind does not engage in carnality."

"No? Why not?"

"What?" The angel appeared taken aback. "Why, because it's not allowed."

"Too bad," Arthur said. "There aren't many things better than fucking."

The angel gave a huff of disapproval, and then adjusted his cuffs and smoothed his hair. "Really. So crass. Pity your race wasn't wiped out in the Flood as it was meant to be."

"If I'm so objectionable," Arthur countered, "why are you talking to me?"

"Well, I'm not supposed to be talking to you, am I?" the angel snapped. "I'm merely supposed to be watching you."

He was under angelic surveillance? This was getting weirder by the second. Arthur crossed his arms. "Under whose authority?"

Silver Eyes let out a long-suffering sigh. "Raphael's."

Arthur blinked. "Raphael? You mean the archangel Raphael?"

"Just how many other Raphaels do you know?" The angel tugged the hem of his coat, adjusted his tie, and winced. "Oh, botheration. He's going to be furious when he finds out I've let myself been seen."

"So don't tell him," Arthur suggested.

"If only that were an option." The angel gave him a pitying look. "Honestly, don't you know anything? You seem remarkably uninformed about celestial matters."

"Maybe I was raised under a rock," Arthur said. "Why don't you provide a little enlightenment? Starting with your name. Who the hell are you?"

Silver Eyes harrumphed. "If you must know, I'm Gabriel, archangel and deliverer of celestial messages." He raised a hand. "You know, as in, 'Hail Arthur, full of sin.'"

"Very funny. You've got a message for me?"

"Um...no," Gabriel said, lowering his hand. "No, I do not."

"Then why the fuck—"

"Tsk, tsk. Language."

"—are you stalking me?"

"That information," Gabriel replied testily, "is available on a strict need-to-know basis. You, I am delighted to inform you, have no need to know."

"Like hell I don't. Listen, Gabe—"

Gabriel's chin jerked. "Do *not*," he said, "call me that. It's Gabriel. *Ga-bri-el.*"

"Fine. Whatever. Why is Raphael so interested in me?"

"As I've said, that information is—"

Arthur had just about had enough of the twit. "Cut the crap, *Ga-bri-el*. Or do I need to blast the answer out of you?"

The archangel laughed at that. "I'd like to see you try."

"Don't tempt me."

"Consider yourself tempted." Gabriel drew a mocking circle with the tip of his walking stick. "Go ahead, miscreant, do your worst." He grinned. "You know, I've always wanted to say that."

Arthur hesitated.

"I'm waaaaaaiting," the angel sang. His arms dropped. "Unless you're too much the coward, of course."

Annoying prat. With a growl, Arthur blasted a stream of spark and flame at his white head. About a foot before the hellfire found its mark, it bent an abrupt ninety degrees downward. The stream splattered harmlessly into the ground.

Frowning, Arthur tried a second, larger blast. Gabriel easily blocked it with his walking stick. Hellfire ricocheted back at Arthur's head. He barely managed to duck before it exploded in his face. The blaze evaporated, leaving behind a trail of sulfur-tinged smoke.

Arthur swore.

Gabriel chuckled. "Don't feel bad. Don't you know a Nephil cannot harm an archangel?"

"What kind of bollocks rule is that?"

"Why, a celestial one, of course. My, my. Your education is truly lacking. But then, I suppose that's the sort of thing a guide teaches a new adept. And you, my dear enemy, have no guide."

"You know about that?" Arthur asked in surprise. How the hell long had Heaven been watching him, anyway?

"Oh, yes, I know all about your sorry situation. Half-mad and all that. More to the point, Raphael knows. And he is not happy, let me tell you. He would've much preferred you to die during your Ordeal."

"Is that why he sent you? To kill me?"

Gabriel's chin went back. "I should say not. I told you, I'm a simple messenger. Not an avenger. Or an assassin." He tugged the sleeves of his suit jacket, first one side, then the other. "And anyway, celestial retribution requires just cause. So far, you haven't given Raphael an excuse to exterminate you."

"But he expects me to."

"Well, yes," Gabriel admitted. "We're all very hopeful."

"Am I so dangerous?"

"Heaven help me, yes! Just look at you." He circled the tip of his cane. "You fairly crackle with power and you can't control a tenth of it. You're a grave threat."

"To what?"

"Why, to nothing less than the equilibrium of the human realm. The balance is delicate." Palm up, he evaluated an imaginary weight. "A little good, a little evil; a lot of good, a lot of evil. Neither enough to tip the scales one way or the other. Everyone muddles on until the final trumpet."

"You believe I'm a danger to that balance?"

"Well, who's to know? Merlin certainly proved to be a threat. Will you be as destructive as your infamous ancestor? I have no idea—even archangels can't see into the future. But I'll give you a bit of advice, free of charge. Abandon this quest you've conceived of finding Merlin's staff."

"I suppose I shouldn't be surprised you know about that too," Arthur said. "If you're so concerned, I must be close." He gestured toward the boulder. "This is the entrance to Merlin's cave, isn't it?"

"One of them," Gabriel agreed. "I can admit it freely, because there's no way you can get in. The cave is blocked by a celestial seal set by Raphael himself. Only Heavenly creatures can pass through."

"Like you?"

"Yes. I suppose so."

"Get me in."

Gabriel uttered an exasperated huff. "Have you heard nothing I've said? You are a threat to humanity. There is no way I'm going to help you enter your ancestor's cave."

"No? We'll see about—" Arthur broke off as, across the

field to the south, the old stable lit up like a beacon. "Holy crap. What's that?"

The angel's pale complexion went whiter than white. "Why...that's impossible, that's what it is. The cave's second entrance is inside that old stable." His silver eyes showed something like panic. "Someone has breached the seal."

An icy chill spread through Arthur's veins. Holy fucking hell. *Cybele.* He was in the air, diving for the stable, before he even drew his next breath.

Gabriel flew close behind, muttering under his breath. "Loopholes. Blasted, wretched, perishing loopholes!"

***

Luc woke to his skull bouncing down a flight of stairs. When his head finally smacked the concrete floor, Rand released his hold on Luc's ankles and kicked his body toward the center of the cellar. Luc rolled once, coming to rest on his stomach. He pressed his forehead to the floor. His thrallstone burned like a hot poker thrust through his throat. Pain filled his head so completely, there was no room left for any thought of resistance. There'd be no point to it, anyway.

Rand bent to manacle Luc's wrists behind his back. He locked a cuff around one ankle and secured it to an iron ring embedded in the floor. "Cybele was a fool, tryin' to escape," he said. "Mab'll find her, faster than fast. And then she'll give her to me." He leaned close, hissing into Luc's ear. "I'll enjoy fucking your sister. I'll turn her into a pathetic thrall, like her twin brother. What do you think of that?"

Luc pressed his lips together.

"Answer me."

He closed his eyes.

"Answer me, thrall." Rand's boot connected with Luc's ribs.

"You're...as much a thrall as...I am," Luc gasped. "At least...I have...some pride."

"That'll be gone, soon enough," Rand snarled. His fist slammed into Luc's ear. Luc nearly fainted from the explosion of pain. He tried to roll away. A hand covered the back of his head, stopping his momentum and grinding his nose and mouth into some unspeakable muck on the floor. Luc choked and flailed.

Just as his consciousness faded, Rand jerked him upright. Luc gulped air, and then gagged on the stale beer breath. He opened his eyes. Rand's snarling smile was barely an inch away.

"You don't fucking disrespect me, you hear?"

Luc spat in his face.

Rand roared. From that moment on, Luc was aware of nothing but pain. Punches, kicks, lashes of fire. He rolled. Rand dragged him back. Luc wasn't entirely helpless. Even shackled, even with his magic muted by the thrall collar, he managed a few solid kicks and a couple of hellfire blasts.

But it was a losing battle, one Luc was insane to fight. Groveling would have been easier. Not to mention smarter. Fuck that. The sight of Rand limping up the cellar stair, spewing curses, was a pleasure worth hurting for.

The door slammed. Luc, his cheek pressed against cool concrete, closed his eyes.

***

Gabriel held an honored position as Holy Messenger of the Earthly and Celestial Realms. He'd been praised in myriad prayers and songs. His most notable communication by far had been one delivered in Nazareth a couple thousand years ago. The event had caused his lofty self to be featured prominently in more works of art than he cared to count.

In short, Gabriel was the subject of endless human adulation. One could logically assume that he enjoyed his profession. This, however, was not the case.

His job, sadly, was not all it was cracked up to be. Sure, he held an exalted title, but he was, in truth, little more than Raphael's errand boy. Certainly, if he had his druthers, he'd never find himself accompanying a disgusting Nephil into a damp and smelly ruin.

Since his druthers were unfortunately nowhere to be found, he let out a long-suffering sigh and followed his charge into the breach. Arthur sprinted through the stable's sagging doorway and dashed past a row of empty stalls. Gabriel picked his way through more slowly, careful to keep the soles of his shoes a few inches above the grubby floor. He didn't care to look too closely, but he suspected a large part of the muck on the stone paving consisted of animal dung.

A fine mess this assignment was turning out to be. *Keep an eye on the Nephil,* Raphael had ordered. *Don't let him do anything rash,* he'd said. Well. Easier said than done, Gabriel thought sourly. Nephilim were the opposite of prudent.

A brilliant light shone from beneath a fallen beam at the end of the passageway. Arthur barely paused before diving under the heavy timber and its associated pile of ruined roofing. Gabriel, grimacing, used his walking stick to lift a section of rot. With a delicate shudder, he faded into spirit form and melted through mold, slime, and a rat's nest. His scalp crawled with revulsion. The things he did for Raphael.

On the other side of the obstruction, he found Arthur standing as if frozen, staring down at what looked like a cluster of braided twigs, lying on the ground amid a small puddle of blood. A few steps beyond, more blood formed a trail of droplets, leading to a pool of celestial light. Gabriel drew up short, not quite able to believe his eyes. Oh, holy...shining clouds above. This was not good. Not good *at all.*

Arthur bent down and picked up the clump of twigs. He stared at it for a moment. Then, with a curse, he shoved it into his pocket and started toward the hole. Gabriel sped past, inserting himself between the Nephil and the portal. "No farther," he said, brandishing his walking stick.

Arthur's jaw set. "Get out of my way."

"No."

A wisp of vapor rose out of the glow. It carried the odor of brimstone. It was accompanied by a faint but unmistakable wail. *Dear Lord.* Worse, worse, and worse again.

A vein in Arthur's forehead throbbed. "That was not a request. That's the entrance to Merlin's Cave and I'm going in. Cybele—"

"Couldn't possibly be in there," Gabriel said. At least, she wasn't supposed to be. "Her entrance is forbidden. As is yours."

"Her blood's on the ground."

"That could be anyone's blood. An animal's, maybe."

"It's hers," Arthur said flatly.

"How can you be sure?"

"I can smell it."

"Oh." Gabriel gave a faint shudder. "Disgusting."

"I found her touchstone. She wouldn't let go of that. Not voluntarily."

"Touchstone? Isn't that some Druid thing?"

"You don't know?"

"If I knew," Gabriel said testily, "would I ask?"

"It's a stone," Arthur said. "Embedded or wrapped in wood. Every Druid has one. It helps us focus magic."

"Ah," said Gabriel, finally understanding. "Stone and wood are elemental to Druid magic. Water is as well, is it not?"

Arthur scowled. "Much as I'd love to give you lessons on Druid magic, I'm afraid it's going to have to wait. Right now, I'm going after Cybele."

Gabriel watched with mild disgust as dark lights burst to life under Arthur's skin. His eyes changed, the gray of his irises dissolving into hellish red. "And. You. Will. Not. Stop. Me."

An epiphany struck. Gabriel's eyes went wide. "Amazing!" he exclaimed. "I didn't think this sort of thing was possible."

Arthur's scowl deepened. "What the hell are you going on about now?"

"Why, you, of course. I'd assumed you were merely in lust with your blond dormant. But it appears..." Gabriel shook his head. "As unlikely as it seems, I believe you're actually in love with her. A Nephil in love. Who would've thought?"

A muscle ticked in Arthur's jaw. "Get out of my way."

Gabriel shook off the oddity of a Nephil in love and returned to the subject at hand. "Listen," he said. "You don't really know if she's in there. She might just have dropped her stone without noticing. And then got tired of waiting. She probably went back to your guesthouse."

"Cut the bullshit."

"It's not—" Well, all right, yes, Arthur had him there. Though he had no idea how it had come about, it was likely that Arthur's lover was inside the cave. But he wasn't about to admit it. Raphael would have Gabriel's wings in a sack if he let Arthur follow after her.

"I don't know what's happened," he continued, "or how your friend was injured. If she went into that cave, I don't know how she did it. No Earthly or Hellish being may pass through a celestial seal. Or at least, not without—"

His mouth snapped shut.

Arthur went still. "Without what?"

"Nothing. Nothing at all."

"You white-faced sot. What were you about to say?"

"Never you mind."

"Fine." White flame erupted in Arthur's palms. Stepping neatly to one side, he took aim and...

"Wait." Gabriel lunged for him. "What are you—"

Hellfire exploded. He whipped his walking stick around—unfortunately, not quickly enough. He deflected only a portion of the attack, and poorly, at that. The lion's share of the fire blasted right past him into the pit.

Gabriel's hair stood on end. He watched in horror as Arthur poured all his fury and fear into the flame. The Nephil's eyes burned red, his skin glowed darkly. The force of his magic was so raw, so pure, and so filled with the power of death, it actually sent Gabriel staggering backwards.

Dear Heavenly Host above! Cherubim and Seraphim aloft! Raphael was right to fear Arthur. The Nephil was a grave menace. What was Gabriel even doing here? He was a messenger, not an avenger. He wasn't used to situations like this. Conflict was Raphael's and Michael's domain.

He raised his walking stick, considering how best to interfere. Before he could act, Arthur's hellfire sputtered and died. Gabriel breathed a sigh. Then he realized his relief had been premature.

Arthur, arms outstretched, flung himself headlong into

the light. As Gabriel watched in horrified shock, a hand rose from the brilliance and closed around the Nephil's wrist.

What? Oh, no. No, no, no, *no.*

His walking stick clattered to the ground. Hurling himself forward, Gabriel grabbed Arthur's nearest ankle with both hands. "Stop. Stop right now!"

Arthur's arm had sunk into the light up to his shoulder. Gabriel tugged as hard as he could, but the Nephil wouldn't budge. "Noooo!" he wailed. "This cannot be happening!"

Arthur smirked at him over one shoulder. "Must be a goddamned miracle."

"Nephilim," Gabriel cried, "do *not* receive miracles."

Arthur's leg slipped from Gabriel's grasp. In a blink of an eye, he was gone. He'd fallen into the cave that he was not, under any circumstances, supposed to enter. For one wild instant, Gabriel considered plunging in after him.

Then he came to his senses and shook his head. Darn it all to holy heck, he was a messenger, not a warrior. What was he supposed to do? Attack the situation with a round of Hails?

"Stupid loophole. Let Raphael deal with it."

FIFTEEN

Cybele sat up and immediately wished she hadn't. Damn. She'd smacked her head so hard she was still seeing stars. Gingerly, she pressed the lump swelling on the back of her skull. She was sitting in a puddle, her jeans rapidly wicking up moisture. Her upper arm stung. She touched the spot, and her fingers came away sticky. Blood. Right. She remembered snagging her arm on a nail or something when Jack dragged her under the fallen beam blocking the old tack room.

And light. She remembered brilliant, golden light.

Whatever that light had been, it was gone now. It was dark, almost totally so. A constant *drip, drip, drip* fell from above. A splash of water hit her nose. An eerie wail rose and fell like a tide through the darkness.

That had to be the sound Jack had described. But as for it being Merlin's voice—Cybele had her doubts. It didn't sound at all life-like.

Still, the place was creepy. She hated suffocating spaces. Reaching out to the right and left, she spread her palms on slick stone. She was in a dark, narrow tunnel. She tried her best to ignore the panic that thought brought.

She levered herself to her feet. As her eyes adjusted to the dimness, she realized she wasn't entirely trapped. A narrow slice of space stretched out before her. What illumination there was seemed to come from above. She tilted her head back. A layer of gauzy light filtered down from overhead. Exactly how far above, it was difficult to judge. And where the hell was Jack, who had gotten her into this mess?

"Jack? Are you here?" She paused for an answer. It came only as an echo of her own voice. She tried again. "Jack! Answer me."

The effort of shouting made her head spin. The cave seemed to waver. Imagination? Or magic? She craned her neck, focusing on the light.

It vanished, plunging her into total darkness.

An explosion of panic nearly choked her. A sudden downdraft drove her back against the cave wall, palms slapping on the slick stone. Just in time. Something fell from above, landing with a thud in the spot where she'd just been standing. A dark opal light illuminated the darkness.

"Fuck," a voice said.

She went limp with relief. "Arthur." She threw herself at him.

"Cybele." A ball of hellfire ignited above her head. His arms closed around her. He was in demon form. His wings swept forward, sheltering her. "What happened?" he whispered frantically, running a hand over her hair. "I saw blood on the ground...I can smell it now..."

She looked up. Arthur's expression, delineated by sharp-edged shadows, was frantic. "I'm fine. A nail or something found my arm."

"Let me see."

"No." She eased from his arms. "I don't need you going into kill mode again."

"Oh, I'm already in kill mode," he said darkly. "But it's not you I want to kill." He glanced at the light far above. "Goddamned coward didn't follow me in."

"Who?"

He told her about his encounter with Gabriel. "So there's the reason none of my ancestors could find this place," he finished. "A celestial seal. Goddamn interfering archangels."

"But...if that's true, how did we get in?"

"I'm not sure. Someone pulled me through," he said.

"It had to be Jack. He dragged me in here, but I don't know where he's—"

"Here," a voice said. "But we need...we need to go..."

"Jack!" Cybele spun around. The boy was huddling in a shadowed nook.

"Get over here," Arthur growled. "And tell us what the hell is—"

"No. Don't say that." Though his voice was rusty with disuse, Jack's speech emerged distinctly. "That's a bad word. Very bad."

Cybele paused, frowning. "And you don't like bad words? All right. Just tell us. Why did you bring us in here? And how?"

"No. No time to tell. You must come. Now." Jack reached out and grabbed Cybele's arm.

Arthur let out a growl. "Get your bloody hands off her." He jerked the boy up by the collar and gave him a sharp shake. "Or I'll snap your neck."

Jack's eyes bugged. A few unintelligible words choked out of his mouth. "Gaaa— Gaaa—"

Cybele easily twisted her wrist free of Jack's grip, and then turned her scowl on Arthur. "Stop it. You're scaring him."

"Good," he said. "Maybe if he's scared, he'll give us some answers."

"Yeah, well, he's not going to tell us anything if he's too terrified to talk."

Arthur gave the boy a final shake and let him go. Jack stumbled and fell, his arms coming up to cover his head.

"You're not helping matters at all," Cybele told Arthur, exasperated.

"Oh, for fuck's sake." He rolled his eyes. "All right. Fine. But he better start talking."

Jack rose to his feet. Keeping a fearful eye on Arthur, he sidled past him. "No time for stories. We have to go. We have to go now." He gestured toward the open end of the cave. "Go this way. We must. We must save him."

"Save who?" Cybele asked.

Jack's words tumbled out. "Save my friend. This way. Hurry. Please." His eyes filled with tears. "He's in trouble. I must bring you. He said so."

"He?" Cybele asked. "Who's *he*? Your friend?"

"No. My friend's...master. If I don't obey...he'll hurt...my friend." The syllables emerged like hiccups. "Come. Hurry. Please."

"We're not going anywhere," Arthur said. "Until you tell us what the goddamned hell this—"

"Nooooo!" Jack clapped his hands over his ears. He dropped into a crouch then fell over and curled into a fetal position. "No!" he wailed. "No more bad talk. No more." He rocked back and forth on the wet ground.

Cybele sent Arthur a repressive look and dropped down on her haunches beside the hysterical boy. She laid a gentle hand on his shoulder. "Jack? Don't worry. It's okay. I won't let him say those things anymore. I know those words hurt you."

Jack sat up. "You do?"

"Yes," she told him. "I do."

His face had taken on a faint glow. Tears dripped off the end of his nose. He sniffed once, and then began to sing in a clear, sweet voice. *"Lo! He comes with clouds descending...Once for favored sinners slain..."*

Cybele rose and took a step back. She didn't know much—or anything, really—about religious music, but... "Um...do you think that's a church hymn?" she asked Arthur.

He pulled her to his side. "I guess so." His voice was strained. "Why's he singing it?"

"Thousand, thousand saints attending..."

"I don't think he's singing it," she said. "Or at least, I don't think *Jack's* singing it."

"What the hell do you mean by that?"

"Swell the triumph of His train..."

"I think Jack—the real Jack—is possessed," Cybele said.

Arthur snorted. "By a hymn-singing demon?"

"Hallelujah! Hallelujah!"

"No," Cybele said. "Not by a demon. Arthur, Jack's possessed by an angel."

***

"The Nephil known as Vaclav Dusek is not currently in residence at the Institute," Michael told Raphael. "His assistant, a human male, gave me a tour of the facility. I found this."

Raphael sat on his cloud throne, twirling Fortunato's lost feather between his thumb and forefinger. "I see."

"I also did some snooping on my own. There are dark forces at work in that place."

"What forces?"

Michael cleared his throat. "I don't know, exactly. When I looked, it was like...like there was a wall. A thick brick wall. I couldn't see past it."

The feather stopped twirling. "Dark magic indeed." Raphael met Michael's gaze, his golden eyes greatly troubled. "Is Fortunato caught up in all this?"

"I think it's likely. I can't be completely sure, but I don't think our lost cherub is in Prague. I suspect Dusek has him."

"Where?"

"I don't know."

Raphael's brows lowered. "How can you not know? It should be easy enough to track the Nephil's movements. He's half human, after all." The feather started moving again, spinning clockwise, then reversing course to spin counter. "Besides which, an angel cannot be trapped against its will by any lesser being. Not by a demon, not by a human, and certainly not by a Nephil."

"Yes. Well," Michael said. "That's official celestial law, of course. But remember, there are loopholes..."

Raphael sighed. "Yes, of course. Loopholes."

"I'll continue my search," Michael said. "But finding out exactly what's going on may take some time. This Nephil is far more powerful than he should be. In fact..." He pulled his phone from his back pocket. "I've been Googling him."

"Goggling?"

"Not goggling. *Googling.* I've been Googling him."

"What in blessed Heaven's name is that?" Raphael asked.

"It's a way to look up information," Michael said. "On the human Internet."

"This Internet thing again. Really, little brother. There are better ways to operate. Magical ways. Heavenly ways."

Michael scowled. "Do you want to know what I've found out or not?"

"Do not," Raphael said, "take an insolent tone with me." But he leaned forward to peer at the phone's screen nonetheless. "What am I looking at?"

"The archives of The Czech Consolidated News Media."

He thumbed through a series of images, starting with the most recent. Each one showed the Nephil known as Vaclav Dusek. "See? This one was taken during Earth's Second World War. Dusek looked then exactly as he does now."

"So? Nephilim are long-lived, and don't tend to show their age past thirty years."

"That's just it. A Nephil's maximum lifespan is one hundred twenty years. Somehow, Dusek's been around a lot longer."

"That's impossible."

"I don't think so. More loopholes at work, I'm afraid." Michael retrieved a second set of photos. "These are from the Czech National Library's historical archives. The record is sparse, but I managed to connect the dots."

"Connect dots? Why would you want to do that?"

"Not literal dots. It's an Earth expression. It means to infer new truth by combining previously known information in a unique way."

"Huh." Raphael waved a hand. "Proceed."

Michael swiped through photos and news articles, one by one. "Dusek's been around for a very long time. The earliest photographic record dates from the 1880s, but I found a few illustrations from earlier periods that also look like him."

"It can't be the same man. The earlier records must refer to Dusek's ancestors."

"I don't think so," Michael said. "I think Dusek's been alive much longer than should be possible. Four centuries, at least. Probably longer." He paused. "He's not native to Prague. Nor is Dusek his original name. He's had several. I've found evidence he may have been alive as far back as the fifteenth century. In the Southern Carpathians. That's a mountain range between Romania and Serbia."

"Five hundred years?" Raphael stood so abruptly, his

golden robes stirred up a whirlwind. Michael's hair whipped around his head. "That's preposterous. A Nephil could amass a disturbing amount of power in five hundred years."

"That's precisely my point," Michael said grimly. "I suggest—*whoa!*"

A sudden explosion of the cloud beneath his feet tossed Michael backward. His phone went flying. He wheeled his arms frantically while the source of the disturbance—his brother, Gabriel—soared skyward. Droplets of fog rained down. Crazy rainbows sprayed in every direction.

Raphael grabbed his throne's armrest, his robes whipping in the sudden tempest. Michael only just managed to unfurl his wings in time to prevent an ignoble sprawl on his own celestial ass.

Gabriel's silver wings flapped furiously as he tried to halt his upward trajectory. A gale-force wind swept downward. It slammed into Michael just as he was getting his feet back under his body. His butt landed in wet, sloppy cloud mist after all.

"Oh, for the love of—"

Gabriel threw himself into a dive.

"Watch out!" Raphael shouted.

Michael rolled. Gabriel landed hard, barely a foot in front of him. Cloud mist sprayed. A solid wave of the stuff slapped Michael square in the face.

"What the f—" At Raphael's ferocious frown, he swallowed the foul word. But holy crap, he was soaked. He got to his feet and glared at Gabe. Who had, Michael noted with some surprise, seemed to have left his beloved walking stick behind somewhere. Not a good sign.

"What in Heaven's holy name is wrong?" he demanded.

Gabriel was bent double, hands on his thighs, panting

as if he'd run a marathon. He looked up and raised a forefinger.

Raphael huffed. "Really, brother. Your penchant for drama is not appreciated."

"No drama," Gabriel gasped. "I came...as quickly...as I...could." Finally, he straightened. "Though I fear...it may already be...too late."

"Too late for what?" Raphael demanded.

"Too late to keep Merlin's staff in place."

"*What!?*" Raphael exclaimed.

"Merlin's cave—" Gabriel panted, still breathless. "Your celestial seal...breached. Arthur Camulus...inside."

Michael's eldest brother, the Holy Steward of Heaven and Earth, looked like someone had struck him with a poleaxe. "But-but-but that's impossible."

"No, it's not," Gabriel said. "Remember? All things are possible. There are loop—"

"Don't say it." Raphael's golden eyes snapped. "I tell you, if I hear that word one more time, I will not be held accountable for the consequences."

***

Arthur shot Cybele an incredulous look. "Are you barmy? Angels don't possess humans. Only demons do that."

"I know, I know. It sounds crazy." Cybele gazed down at Jack, still cowering on the ground. "But you heard what Mrs. Spencer said about Jack's good nature. She even called him an angel."

"Not a literal angel."

"Still. His soul is pure. And he said he heard voices."

"A human doesn't have to be possessed to hear voices." Arthur's own voice was tight. "Just mentally ill."

"You felt nauseous at dinner," Cybele pointed out.

"And you're feeling sick again now. I can tell."

"That was because of the prayers," Arthur said. "And now this damn hymn singing. It's not Jack himself."

"I don't know, Arthur. What else could've pulled two Nephilim through a celestial seal except an angel?"

"What angel would want to?" Arthur countered. "Gabriel nearly shit himself trying to stop me from passing through that seal. No. It's got to be something else."

"Not a demon," Cybele said. "I mean, just look at him." Jack, lying flat on his back on the ground, blinked up at them with wide, sad eyes. "What self-respecting demon would manifest like that?"

"Good point," Arthur murmured. Still, an angel? It seemed so improbable.

"Please. Please come." Jack held up a trembling hand.

Cybele grasped it and pulled him to his feet. "Jack," she said. "Where do you want us to go? Did someone send you to get us?"

He looked at her beseechingly. "Please. Come."

Cybele sighed. "We should just go with him and see what happens."

There really wasn't much choice, Arthur supposed. "All right. I can't say I like this, but...lead the way, Jack. We'll follow."

Jack nodded and darted down the narrow passage. "Here!" he called from the gloom.

The lad was bouncing on his toes, pointing to a narrow crack in the cave wall. The wailing grew louder, clearly emanating from the crevice. Arthur was inclined to dismiss the path as impassible, but Jack seemed determined to get through. He turned his thin body sideways and stuffed himself in. With a sound like the popping cork, he disappeared.

"Bloody hell," Arthur said in exasperation. "How are

we supposed to follow him through there?"

Cybele went down on her haunches and peered through. Arthur let his demon light dip, to better illuminate the crevice. "Can you see him?" he asked.

"No. There's a turn, about ten feet in. I think..." She swallowed, and wiped her hands on her jeans as she stood. "I think...I think it's wide enough to get through. For me, anyway."

Her anxiety was obvious. "Fuck that shit," Arthur told her. He tugged her away from the crack. "Stand back," he said, calling hellfire into his hands.

Cybele regarded him warily. "What're you going to do?"

"Blast our way in."

"Arthur, I don't think—"

He launched a concentrated stream of fire into the crevice. Unfortunately, he'd misjudged the force needed. The explosion was enormous. Cybele cried out. He grabbed her and slammed her into the ground, covering her with his body. Rock and dust rained down all around.

"Can't...breathe." Cybele shoved at him. He rolled to one side. She gasped and then dissolved into a fit of coughing.

"Shit," he said. "Shit. I'm sorry." He helped her to her feet and pounded her back.

She swatted his hand away. "Damn it, Arthur, the entire cave could've come down on our heads."

"But it didn't." He nodded toward the crevice, which was at least a foot wider than it'd been. "And now we can go through."

He plunged in sideways, Cybele close behind. Once around the bend, the passage opened up considerably. Another turn to the right and one to the left. They emerged into cool, clean air.

Arthur let his demonlight sputter and die. He no

longer needed it. They stood on an upper ledge in a light-filled underground chamber. A dark pool filled most of the space. A flat rock rose from the center of the still water, in which a staff of twisted wood, topped by a crystal orb, stood embedded. A stream of sparks shot upward from the orb. The light arced in every direction, spilling to the ground in a many-streamed fountain of brilliance. The eerie moan rose and fell with the light.

Arthur's breath caught. He stood mesmerized, his body frozen, his vision dazzled.

Cybele laid a hand on his arm. "We've found it. We've found Merlin's staff."

Her voice was wavy and indistinct, as if it had journeyed to Arthur's ears from a place far, far away. Merlin's staff, with its massive Druid touchstone, filled his senses. Arthur's most powerful ancestor had fashioned that rod and held it in his hand. He'd used the crystal sphere as a focus to his fathomless magic. And now...

"It's mine," Arthur breathed.

The moaning grew louder, rising and falling with the rushing pulse in his ears. His vision went white, obliterating everything. Everything but the staff itself. Dazzled by its beauty, by its endless possibility, Arthur plunged toward the water's edge. Dimly, he heard a voice call his name. He paid no attention. He was about to dive into the pool when a hand on his belt yanked him back. He spun about, wings lifted, hellfire crackling, left hand raised.

Cybele grabbed his arm with both hands and shoved it up over her head. Hellfire shot from his palm, and hit the cave's ceiling. A shower of sparks and rock shards rained down.

"Arthur! What's the matter with you? Get a grip."

A large stone hit Arthur's skull. "Wha—?" He gave his

head a shake, blinking. Cybele. She stood glaring up at him. His arm was lifted. For some reason, she was holding it above his head.

He blinked down at her. "Cybele? What...what's going on?"

She slowly let her hands fall. "Are you okay?"

"I—" Why was his arm up? He lowered it. His gaze was drawn by the staff, glittering on the other side of the water.

"I need to get over there," he said.

"You need a plan first," Cybele countered. "If you're not careful, that staff could tear you apart. How are you going to approach it? How are you going to judge its power before you touch it?"

"I...I don't know," Arthur admitted. "I guess I'll just—"

"Wait," Cybele said suddenly. "What happened to Jack?"

Arthur looked up sharply. He'd all but forgotten the lad. "He's got to be somewhere about."

"I don't see him." Cybele scanned the cave. "Where the hell could he have gone?"

A maze of rock formations, punctuated by nooks and twisting paths, rose and fell around the pool. "Could be anywhere," Arthur said.

"But why would he hide?"

"Good question."

They moved around the pool, peering into the shadows at the perimeter of the cave. They found a half-dozen or more tunnels like the one they'd come through, but no Jack.

"Damn," Arthur said. "He could be hiding anywhere." He paused. "Or anyone else could be."

"Like whoever told Jack to bring us here."

"Exactly."

They rounded a column encased in ripples of milky

crystal. A dark form lay crumpled behind it.

"Jack." Cybele dropped to her knees and pressed two fingers under his jaw.

Arthur stood over her, every sense alert. No movement, no sound, other than the constant drip of water. "Alive?"

"Yes," she said. "He's just unconscious."

He expelled a breath. "What happened? Did he fall? Hit his head?"

Cybele probed his skull. "No. At least, I don't feel a lump or anything." She leaned close, and gave him a little shake. "Jack? Can you hear me?"

A deep voice, cold and amused, answered. "He has no need to hear you. The boy has served his purpose."

Arthur spun about, hellfire crackling on his fingertips. The speaker remained hidden. "Show yourself," he shouted.

"As you wish."

A figure, clad in black, stepped from the shadows.

SIXTEEN

"Lucky, Lucky, Lucky! You're back!"

Yes, Maweth's foolish friend was back, and he was a mess. He'd burst through the mirror unannounced, tumbled head over heels, and landed in a heap.

"It was so terrrrrible," he sobbed. "So b-b-bad of meeee."

The little guy's halo was askew and, Maweth thought, a duller shade of gold than it had been. He felt awful. "You shouldn't have done it," he said. "Not for me. I'm not worth it."

Lucky's head popped up. "But you are. You're my friend."

"I'm Death itself. I'm no one's friend."

Lucky rubbed his eyes and blew his nose on the edge of his swaddling clothes. "I'd do it again. For you. But oh, I shouldn't have done it."

"That makes no sense," Maweth pointed out.

"It was...so strange...being inside a human," Lucky said, blue eyes blinking rapidly. "Even one as nice as Jack. I didn't want to hurt him, but every time he got near one of those Nephilim..." Lucky shuddered. "He hated it as much as I did."

"So you're out now," Maweth said. "It's over. Try to forget about it."

"I don't think I'll be able to do that," Lucky said

doubtfully. "Jack's still in trouble."

"He'll be all right," Maweth said.

"You think so?"

"I do," Maweth lied. He really, really didn't believe that. Not one little bit. The kid was toast.

"But...what about Raphael?" Lucky said. "I don't even wanna think about how furious he's gonna be when he finds out I pulled three Nephilim—and poor Jack—through his celestial seal."

Maweth shrugged. "Who says he's got to find out? I'm certainly not going to tell him. And I doubt old Dusek's gonna get chummy with him, either."

"That just leaves me," Lucky said miserably. "And I can't keep a secret for anything."

***

A figure stepped from the shadows.

Nephil magic pulsed in waves. The power was so strong, Arthur wondered how he could have been unaware of the adept's presence until that very moment. The newcomer was wiry and tall, clad entirely in black save for the crimson lining of his cloak. The garment billowed gently as he moved.

Arthur experienced a sick jolt of recognition.

"You." The face before him—pale and gauntly beautiful—lived in his nightmares. "You killed my parents."

The Nephil advanced slowly, as if stalking prey. Perhaps he was. A shower of light glinted on an ornament hanging from a chain around his neck. A quicksilver mirror. Arthur had seen a drawing of such a disc in an old history of the Nephilim he'd found in his father's library. The liquid mercury swirled and bubbled, yet somehow retained a solid shape. Strong magic. Alchemy.

He raised his left hand. The middle finger bore a heavy

gold ring, bearing a disturbingly lifelike replica of the Nephil's own face. Its eyes held a glint of amusement. The expression was identical to the one on its wearer's countenance.

"Why, little Arthur. All grown up. Do you know, you resemble Alwen most strongly."

A hot wave of rage broke over Arthur. "Do not utter her name."

The Nephil gave a thin smile. "May I mention your father's, then? I have never, in all my years, met a fool quite like Tristan. Filled with noble ideas about freedom and self-determination. Dedicated to the shelter and protection of his human brethren. Unwilling to bind any Nephil as his thrall." White teeth flashed. "Utterly unable to control his lover. I could never understand how your father rose to alpha status, Arthur. It reveals, I suppose, the essential weakness of the Druid line."

"He was stronger than you."

The Nephil's smile broadened. "Facts say otherwise. Do you know, I very much enjoyed killing your father. Even more, I think, than I enjoyed defiling your mother."

"You fucking bastard."

"Do you know the most pleasurable aspect of that night? The moment Tristan's hellfire struck Alwen. The look on your father's face as she fell is one of my fondest memories."

Grief and rage congealed in Arthur's gut. White light exploded at the edges of his vision. He felt Cybele's hand pressing flat on his back.

"Arthur," she murmured. "Stay calm."

"My father was aiming for you," Arthur told the Nephil.

Dark brows shot up. The patronizing smile vanished. "You were there?"

"At the window."

"I see." The Nephil's lips thinned. "Mab has much to answer for."

"Enough," Arthur said. "Who are you? Why did you send Jack to bring us here?"

"Did I neglect to introduce myself? How remiss of me." He spread his arms and bowed. "I am Professor Vaclav Dusek. Alchemist."

"A descendant of Azazel."

"I have that honor, yes."

"That shame, you mean." Azazel had been the worst of the Watcher angels. Arthur's Watcher ancestor Samyaza had wanted only to be left in peace with his human wives. Azazel, by contrast, had considered humanity an endless source of personal amusement. He'd taught the fledgling race murder, obscenity, and war. Then he'd settled back to watch the show.

Arthur called hellfire into his palms and launched it, full force, at Dusek. The twin blasts hit the Alchemist squarely in the chest. He didn't so much as stumble, or even flinch. In fact, Arthur thought with chill foreboding, his attack hadn't even made contact with the bastard's body. The hellfire had come within an inch of his flesh and simply vanished.

Cybele swallowed a gasp. The sound caused Dusek's eyes to flick past Arthur. Arthur moved to block his line of sight, but not before the Nephil's lips curved.

"Your whore is very beautiful," he said.

"Fuck off," Cybele spat.

Dusek chuckled. "With pleasure, if you will join me."

Incensed, Arthur launched a second blast of hellfire. This one didn't even make it as far as the first. It sputtered and died halfway to its destination. *Fuck.*

Dusek threw back his head and laughed. "Do you truly believe you can touch me? Such innocence. But we are wasting precious time with this banter. Let us proceed to the matter at hand. I went to great lengths to bring you to Wales. I want the task done."

Arthur scowled. "We didn't come to Wales because of you."

"No? Did you imagine your vision of Merlin and Nimue was a true memory? Why, of course you did. I created it most delicately, after all."

If the ground had suddenly shifted beneath Arthur's feet, he couldn't have felt more off balance. "You're lying."

"Am I?"

Was he? The ancestral memory Arthur had been so grateful for...could it have been false after all? Could the vision have been a product of Dusek's alchemy, rather than a glimpse into Merlin's life? He couldn't quite believe it. The images and the emotions had seemed so real.

But Dusek had been in Wales before he and Cybele had arrived. Arthur had no doubt that he was the foreigner who'd tainted the Spencers' second guestroom. But that didn't explain everything. "How did you get into this cave?" he demanded. "It's sealed by celestial decree."

"The same way we did," Cybele said. "Jack brought him here. Or rather, the angel possessing the boy."

"Clever as well as beautiful," Dusek murmured, his eyes flicking down her body. He tapped the strange liquid disc at his chest. "The angel has returned to me now."

"Lies," Arthur said. "No angel would do the bidding of a Nephil."

"It is almost frightening how little you know," Dusek said. "However, I've neither time nor the inclination to enlighten you." He swept a hand toward the island. "Merlin's staff awaits. You, Arthur Camulus, will bring it to me."

Arthur's eyes narrowed. "You can't retrieve it on your

own, can you? That's why you've gone through all this trouble to bring me here."

Dusek's expression darkened. "Merlin has set it into the rock with an unrelenting magic. A most aggravating habit of your ancestor. I suspect the staff will yield to his heir, however."

"Maybe not," Arthur said. "Maybe nothing can remove it."

"If that were true," Dusek said. "Heaven would not have sealed the cave to prevent its retrieval."

That had the ring of truth about it. Gabriel had been desperate to prevent Arthur from entering the cave. Was Merlin's staff Arthur's for the taking?

Dusek's left hand lifted a slight degree, the face in his golden ring blinked its eyes. Arthur frowned. Nothing untoward occurred, however, and Dusek's hand soon relaxed back to his side.

Arthur took a step toward his parents' murderer. "When I retrieve Merlin's staff, I'll keep it. You have to know that."

"That is, of course, a choice you may make. However, know that the celestial seal remains intact around us. Unless you have an angel to help you pass through it, you will die in this cave. As Merlin did." His shoulders lifted and fell in one smooth movement. "I will, of course, regret the loss of the staff. But I will be greatly consoled by my possession of your lover."

"My lov—" Arthur spun about. Cybele no longer stood behind him next to Jack's unconscious body. His heart thumped painfully. "What have you done? Where is she?"

"Calm yourself, Arthur. I assure you, I would not harm as much as a hair on her head." His eyes glinted. "A Druid dormant, especially one ripe for the Ordeal, is exceedingly hard to come by."

Arthur swore viciously. The magnitude of Dusek's magic stunned him. The Nephil had snatched up Cybele and Arthur hadn't even noticed. A crushing sense of inadequacy descended upon him. If Dusek forced Cybele into her Ordeal, she'd become his thrall and his bridge to Druid powers.

Over my dead body.

His skin and eyes burned. His wings rose. Hellfire crackled all in his hands. He was poised for battle, but how could he hope to win? He fought back his demon rage. His mind raced with fury, but he needed calm. He needed focus.

One hand came up to cover the moonstone and press it into his chest. He drew a slow breath. "Where is she? I need to see her alive and well before I touch that staff."

Dusek nodded. "As you wish."

His ring's face moved again, its mouth opening wide. A subtle veil lifted, revealing Cybele. She lay at Dusek's feet, wrists and ankles bound with hellfire.

Arthur stared. Teleportation? That wasn't a power associated with Alchemy. What the fuck was going on?

Dusek smiled at Arthur's shock. "Yes, Arthur, it is true. I have power beyond your understanding. And I might have had more, much more, if Mab hadn't snatched you from my grasp seven years ago. Ah, well. Perhaps it was all for the best. Cybele may not be heir to Merlin, but I sense her power is strong. Enthralling her will be my pleasure."

Cybele's eyes were wide with pain and fear. Arthur didn't move his gaze from her as he said, "Let her go. Then I'll think about getting the staff for you."

"Hand me the staff," Dusek replied smoothly, "and perhaps I will be inspired to release her. Though—" His lashes lowered. "Now that I think on it, perhaps not. Cybele as my thrall may be the greater prize."

Arthur nearly choked on a surge of panic. "I vow, Dusek. You will regret the day you crossed my path."

"Strong talk from a weak man. I grow weary of it. Bring me the staff. Or bid your lover farewell."

And if Arthur couldn't pull the staff from the stone? What then? But no, he wouldn't think of that. He fixed his gaze on the staff's crystal, on the sparks erupting from the orb, only to fall into the black pool. With one slow downstroke of his wings, Arthur lifted into the air and glided over the water. He touched down lightly on the island.

Here, the wailing filled his ears, blotting out all other sound. From across the water, Arthur had thought the island flat and smooth. Now, standing behind the waterfall of light, he saw it sloped to a shallow pit in the center. Merlin's staff, standing upright in the center of the depression, was taller than Arthur expected. The twisted wood, with its orb set in finger-like branches, rose higher than his head. As the vision Dusek had forced on him had shown, the wood was not one species, but three. Oak, rowan, and yew.

At the base of the staff, scattered over the stone, lay bones.

He stared. Ribs and vertebrae. Pelvis. Femur. The bones of two arms. Merlin, unable to breach the celestial seal the archangel Raphael had set over the cave, had died beside his staff. His skull, released from its spine, had rolled a short way to one side. His ancestor's hollow eye sockets seemed to stare straight through him.

A deep chill invaded Arthur's body.

"He got what he deserved."

Arthur jerked around to find Dusek on the island beside him. Damn. The bastard moved as swiftly and silently as death itself. His cloak was gone, as was his shirt.

His chest, hairless and slender, radiated an aura of wiry strength. Black wings rose above his head. Arthur's gaze darted across the water. Cybele still lay in the same place, wrapped and writhing in hellfire.

The Alchemist's voice dripped with contempt. "Merlin was so very powerful and yet so very foolish. The combination of traits seems to be a Druid shortcoming."

"How did you find this place?" Arthur demanded. "It was hidden by Heaven. My ancestors searched for centuries without uncovering a trace of it."

"That," Dusek said, "is a story for another day. For now, you will do as you're told. Retrieve the staff and deliver it directly into my hands."

Arthur darted a glance at Cybele as he weighed his response. She wasn't close by, but did it matter? Distance seemed no impediment to Dusek's magic. What could the Alchemist do with a Druid staff once he had it? In the normal scheme of things, a rival Nephil would require a Druid thrall to perform Druid magic. What power would Merlin's staff bring to Dusek? It was impossible to tell.

Arthur didn't want to find out—he couldn't risk Dusek getting his hands on the staff. No telling what havoc he could wreak with it. Somehow, Arthur needed to get Cybele, the staff, and himself out of the cave alive. He had no idea how all that was to be done. He suspected, however, that his only hope was to grab Merlin's staff and not let go.

He was acutely aware that, as a plan, it wasn't much. What was he going to do with the staff once it was in his hands? Would his instinct and his chaotic magic take over? If it did, he could only hope that he and Cybele would survive whatever the hell happened next.

"Go on." The Alchemist's voice, low in Arthur's ear, vibrated with anticipation. "Take it."

Arthur moved closer. Magic emanated from wood and crystal. The staff was, Arthur realized, the source of the wailing. The sound brushed into his mind. His head lightened; his vision blurred. Something like a long, mournful bell rang in his ears.

He approached the staff. It generated heat as if on fire. Arthur's fingers burned as he reached for it. Touching it, he knew, would be like plunging his hands into a living flame.

He welcomed the prospect. He sensed the fire could—*would*—purify him. Make him whole. Banish his uncertainty and cast light onto his Nephil ancestors' forgotten memories.

The staff was his birthright. It was power and pain, and it would complete him. He reached for it. But just before his fingers grasped the prize, the ground heaved and the cave exploded in golden light.

"Stop." A sonorous voice rang out. "In the name of Heaven, I adjure you!"

What the fuck? Arthur, blinded, grabbed at the place where he thought the staff should be.

His fingers closed on air.

SEVENTEEN

"Luc. *Luc!*"

The call, insistent and tinged with panic, penetrated the haze in Luc's brain. He tried to ignore it and sink back into insensibility. Whatever was going on, he didn't want to face it.

"Luc!"

Small hands gripped his shoulders and shook. Though a spray of bullets healed in seconds, magical wounds, left untended by magical remedies, festered. Luc's wounds responded to the jarring movement. The stripes of Mab's whip and the bites of her vipers burned like fire, sending streaking agony to every cell of his body. His spine arched. His breath hissed through his teeth.

"Oh." His assailant jerked back. "I'm sorry. I'm sorry."

He thought about lifting his hand and waving whoever it was away, but the motion seemed like too much effort.

"Go...'way..." he whispered instead.

"No. I can't. You gotta wake up!" The voice trembled. Its owner was on the verge of tears. How odd. Who cared enough to cry over him?

"Please, Luc. Please. Wake up. It took me forever to get in here, and I don't know how much time we have. I'm so afraid..." A choking sob finally came. "I'm afraid Mab will kill you. She thinks you can lead her to Cybele..."

Cybele.

Beneath the pain and shame, a deep emotion stirred. Cybele. His sister, his twin. Mab's prize. *No.* He would not let Mab have Cybele. He would not see her enthralled to Rand. Not while he still drew breath.

He cracked open an eyelid. Even that small movement hurt. A pale face dotted with freckles hovered inches away.

"Zephyr?"

Her blue eyes went wide. "You're awake!"

"Barely."

He shoved into a sitting position, gritting his teeth against the raw, searing pain. It felt as though Mab's lashes were striking all over again.

"I unlocked the manacles," Zephyr said.

He flexed his shoulders, wincing at the pain. "How?"

Zephyr held up a key. "Can you walk, Luc?"

"I hope so." He eyed the key. "But what about the magical protections?"

"Rand didn't set any," she said. "I guess he figured you weren't strong enough to go anywhere."

"No one's even guarding the cellar door?"

She snorted. "Hunter, Evander, Rand, Starr, and Tempest are all up there. But they started a poker game, complete with snow and hooch. Hunter and Evander passed out."

"Rand and the witches?"

"They went to bed." She made a face. "All three of them together."

"Mab?"

Zephyr shrugged. "She flew off right after Rand threw you down here."

Luc considered the information. "How long ago?"

"About five hours. It's almost midnight now."

Gritting his teeth against the pain, he shoved his body upward. First to his knees, then to his feet. Everything spun. He closed his eyes and grabbed for the closest support, a square brick pier.

Zephyr hovered anxiously beside him. "Are you okay?"

He took a deep breath. "Yes." He had to be, didn't he? He couldn't be here when Mab returned. She'd burn every bit of information about Cybele out of his head. And while he didn't know where she was, he could guess enough about where his twin might have gone to put her in grave danger.

He let go of the brick pier and somehow remained standing. "Let's go."

Zephyr nodded and darted up the stairs. The barest line of light shone between the door and jamb. She peered through the crack, and then motioned for him to follow. "They're still out like the dead."

And smelling almost as bad. Evander, slumped forward over the kitchen table, reeked of whiskey. No wonder. He'd passed out gripping a bottle, and most of its contents had spilled out.

Noise drifted down from the upper levels of the house. The creak of bedsprings from Rand's bedroom, country music and female laughter from the witches' quarters. From the dormants' wing, the tinny melody of video game music.

Zephyr closed the cellar door and turned the lock. Moving with admirable stealth, she slipped the key into the breast pocket of Evander's shirt. Luc, ignoring the pain, just concentrated on moving. His back was on fire. Every movement was agony. It was a good thing Evander was out cold, because if Luc had needed to cast an illusion over his escape, he couldn't have pulled it off.

They passed silently through the kitchen and into the front room. Here Hunter sprawled on his back on the couch, one arm flung over his face, his cowboy boots hanging over the armrest. A fine dusting of cocaine coated his beard. He didn't stir as Luc and Zephyr slipped past.

They crossed the porch and yard, not speaking or stopping until they reached the shelter of a stand of cypress. Once out of sight of the house, Luc steadied himself with one hand on a tree trunk. "Promise me you'll stay out of their sight after I'm gone, Zephyr. Always. As much as you can."

She shrugged. "Mab would kill any male who touched me."

That was true. So few females were born to Nephil and witch mothers. Dormant girls were too important to lose and any male Nephil knew better than to harm one. Still, it didn't make Luc feel any better about leaving Zephyr. His half-sister was canny for her age, but her age was still only thirteen.

"And anyway," she added. "I'm good at hiding. Almost as good as Cybele."

"If Mab finds out about that, there'll be worse hell to pay."

"I know."

"Be careful."

"I will, Luc. I always am."

The night was warm, the air alive with the sound of crickets and bullfrogs. Nevertheless, Zephyr rubbed her arms as if cold. Suddenly, she looked very young. "Where will you go?" she whispered.

"Better you don't know."

"Will you ever come back?"

He wanted to lie, but that would do no good. Zephyr wouldn't believe any made-up bullshit anyway. "I doubt it."

She bit her lip, fighting tears. Like Cybele, though, she was too tough to let them fall. "Good-bye, then."

She slipped into the darkness. One moment she was

there, the next she simply...wasn't. Cybele had taught her well and Luc was damn glad of it.

His legs gave out only seconds after she'd gone. His knees hit the dirt. He didn't stay down long. No telling where Mab had gone or when she'd be back. He half-lurched, half-stumbled down the trail. His mouth felt like dirty wool. The forest was a zig-zagging blur. Flying or even shifting was out of the question. Even if he could summon enough strength to call his magic, he wouldn't do it. If he did, Mab would feel it. She'd be on him like a rat on garbage.

He headed for the old pickup parked by the warehouse. He only just managed to reach it without collapsing face-first in the mud. He wrenched open the door and fell into the driver's seat. The key was under the mat. He just had to get it into the ignition. But what then? There was nowhere to run. Mab owned him, body and mind. He could hide for a while, but in the end, she'd find him.

There was only one place he could go where she wouldn't follow. Oblivion.

He slammed the door and jammed in the key. The engine protested. Death. Except for that one desperate attempt during his Ordeal, Luc had done everything he could to avoid it. He'd turned his back on Cybele, on his self-respect, on his dignity. He'd gone after power and ended up a thrall.

His brain burned with the humiliation of what Mab had done to him. He fought the memories: the whip, the fingernails, the teeth, the vipers... His body and mind manipulated and invaded at his mistress's whim.

Mab. Always Mab. He shifted into gear. His life was shit, and yet on some long-buried level he still couldn't completely accept that death was the only way out. His mind spun, looking for another path out of the mire.

Hunched forward, arms draped over the steering wheel, Luc hit the gas.

***

The ground shook. Golden light filled the cave.

Cybele rolled, hissing with the pain of it. She fought to push her body upright. Dusek's dirty gold hellfire wrapped her wrists and ankles. Halfway up, she fell over again. Light—brilliant, terrible light—blotted out everything. What the hell was happening?

"Stop. In the name of the Heaven, I adjure you!"

Somehow she managed to jackknife into a sitting position. That voice. It vibrated with splendor. She blinked against the glare, trying to see the speaker amid all the glory. The light was shifting, gathering at a single point, thinning everywhere else. Cybele stared as the mass resolved into a shimmering male form.

Golden sandals encased his feet. Long robes, alight from within, whipped about his legs. Glorious wings with gilt-edged feathers rose above his blond head. His face was almost unbearably beautiful, from his amber eyes to the solid jut of his chin. A bejeweled sword, held aloft in his right hand, blazed like the sun.

Holy shit.

Cybele knew a few things about angels, though she'd never actually seen one. Lesser angels—cherubim and seraphim—were nothing to worry about. Cherubim were childlike creatures, eternally at play. Seraphim didn't do much besides play harps and sing.

The being standing before her was no cherub or seraph. Wave after wave of celestial magic poured from his body. Righteous fury flared from his blade. This, she thought dazedly, was the third type of angel. The deadly type.

Archangel.

EIGHTEEN

't trust the archangel. Not one bit. But he
be skewered on the point of Raphael's
At least with the archangels present, Dusek
hands on Merlin's staff, either. That was

away. One tense moment later, Raphael's
d. He lowered his sword.

hipped around. Dusek hauled Cybele up
, his arm across her throat. She fought like
ey were near the edge of the cave. A couple
they'd disappear into the maze of tunnels.
the truth and whatever angel had been
s body was now secure in the Alchemist's
hil could carry Cybele through the celestial
ar before Arthur could stop him.

d for Merlin's staff. This time, both hands
d wood. Bracing his legs wide, he pulled
ngth. With no resistance at all, the twisted
free. Arthur fell backward, clutching the

ael, sword ablaze, leapt across the water.
awled on his arse, swept the head of the
. Hissing steam, shooting from the hole

The word caused her body to go cold. Human children grew up hearing stories about bogeymen and monsters under their beds. Nephil young were weaned on tales of Heaven's avengers. There were three. Arthur's silver messenger, Gabriel. This golden one was Raphael, the warrior who once waged a war of genocide against the Nephilim. His righteous sword had sent countless Nephilim to Oblivion.

It looked as though Raphael sorely wanted to add Arthur to the body count. Arthur, who currently lay sprawled on his ass beside Merlin's staff. Dusek stood nearby. The eyes of both adepts glowed a furious red.

"Arthur Camulus." Golden flame leapt from Raphael's sword, tangling with the sparks of Merlin's crystal orb. "Do not move. Not one muscle."

Arthur jumped to his feet.

The angel went white with fury. "Michael," he barked. Almost instantly, a second figure appeared, heralded by a clap of thunder. Cybele blinked hard. Michael? Could this newcomer truly be the third archangel?

If so, he certainly didn't look the part. For one thing, he wasn't fair, but olive-skinned. Dark stubble covered his firm jaw. His eyes were the color of bittersweet chocolate, his body whipcord lean. Oddly, he wore human clothing rather than celestial robes. Cybele's gaze took in black combat boots...black jeans...black shirt topped by a black vintage military jacket. The jacket's silver frog fasteners, hanging undone, were the only light thing about him.

His wings—dark bronze and beautiful—rose above him. With smooth movement, he slid a switchblade from his right sleeve into his open palm. His fingers closed around the hilt. The blade snapped open. It was no righteous sword, but Cybele had no trouble believing that, in Michael's hand, the blade was every bit as lethal as his golden brother's fiery weapon.

She couldn't take her eyes from him. As if he'd felt her scrutiny, his head whipped around. Their eyes locked. He didn't look away. A wave of heat swept over her, starting at her feet, flowing up her legs, her torso, her breasts and shoulders. Her face flamed. Some vital emotion—she wasn't exactly sure what—flared in his eyes.

The hellfire lashes on her wrists and ankles vanished.

What the—? She scrambled to her feet, rubbing her wrists. She had no time to wonder about her unexpected release, however. Her eyes darted toward Arthur, then back to the archangels. Raw fear sliced through her as Raphael leveled the point of his flaming sword at Arthur's heart.

"Step away from that accursed implement of destruction, demon spawn."

"Bollocks to that." Arthur grabbed for the staff. A golden bolt shot from the sword, striking his wrist. He jerked back, spitting curses. His foot collided with something on the ground. A skull. It skittered across rock, splashed into the water, and sank out of view.

"Leave this place, Nephil. Never to return."

"Merlin's staff is my birthright," Arthur shouted back. "No goddamned archangel is going to stop me from claiming it."

"Make a move toward that staff and your next step will be into Oblivion."

Arthur's wings lifted. "Why wait? Kill me now."

"He cannot." The answer, surprisingly, came from Dusek. "Heaven's punishment comes after sin. Not before." The Alchemist turned mocking eyes on the archangel. "You can't stop Arthur from claiming Merlin's staff. You also know that once it is in his hands, it will be too late to prevent the consequence you fear."

What conseque
reaction, it would
concerned. The a
thundercloud. Was
Cybele's gaze dar
sharply when she f
her. She blinked an

Raphael spoke
embedded his staff
Remove it, Arthur,

"He lies," Duse
will do anything t
yours, Arthur. Tak

Arthur looked
resolve seemed to
water's edge—as if
decide. How could

The moment
pounding beat of h

Arthur stepped
Raphael lower

Dusek spat a
raised,   swept
understood that sh

"Arthur!" She
like a rag doll. H
forearm pressed h
left temple, his bre

Nausea and
couldn't speak. Th
spots blotted the e

She clawed at
across her cheek. '

Arthur didn
had no wish t
flaming sword.
wouldn't get hi
something.

He stepped
shoulders relax

"Arthur!"

His head w
against his body
a wild thing. Th
more steps and
If Dusek told
inhabiting Jack
mirror, the Nep
seal and disapp

Unless...

Arthur lung
closed on gnarl
with all his stre
branch slipped
staff to his ches

"Fool." Rap
Arthur, still sp
staff before hir

where the staff had been, momentarily obscured his view across the water. By the time his line of sight cleared, Cybele and Dusek were gone.

He jumped to his feet, wings aloft, intent on launching himself after them. His flight was blocked by Raphael. The archangel landed before him, brandishing his flaming sword and shrieking with fury.

"Cursed Nephil. What have you done?"

"Out of my way." Arthur feinted left and dove right. The archangel wasn't fooled. Half-obscured by the hissing steam, his sword raised above his head, Raphael blocked Arthur's escape.

Arthur raised the staff, holding it crosswise in both hands like a fighting stick. The crystal orb flashed. The angel's sword came down. Golden blade bit twisted wood. Shock reverberated through Arthur's body. Magic raced up his arms and across his shoulders.

It exploded in his brain.

And with the magic came memory.

***

"You are so beautiful," said Merlin.

Nimue's lashes swept downward, as if to deny her lover's fervent praise. How could she be shy after what they'd just shared? But she was young, Merlin told himself. Young and uncertain. Whereas he was old and filled with regrets.

She made him feel new.

Perhaps that was why he'd brought her to the place where he'd met his Ordeal. Here, on the island in the center of the pool. He'd nearly died here, nearly gone mad. But in the end, he'd triumphed. Magic greater than any he should have been able to possess had come to him.

The underworld was very close to the surface in this

cave. To his attuned senses, it pulsed like a heartbeat. Had his demon powers been worth the price? In the past he had not doubted it. Now, he was less sure. Of a certainty, there had been victories. Important work done on behalf of his human brothers and sisters. In the end, though, betrayal had found the High King—in the guises of his lover, his best friend, and even, most tragically, his son. Fragile alliances had shattered. War and corruption had followed. Merlin had poured his heart and magic into salvaging the wreckage. To no avail. In the end, humanity had ended up no better off than when he had started.

"What are you thinking, my lord?"

He shoved the past into a dark corner of his mind and turned his attention to the light of the woman before him. "Nothing important, my dear. Only of how foolish I have been."

She smiled. "Never foolish. You are a wonder to me. So wise. So strong."

Merlin knew he was neither, but his vanity soaked up her adulation nonetheless. "And you are perfect," he told her.

She sat up, her naked breasts swaying softly. He found it incredible that she was able to give herself so completely. When he'd found her, she'd been close to ending her own life. She'd been ravished, she told him, by a Saxon. She'd left her violator's child at the door of a monastery and entered the forest. She had intended to do herself the ultimate harm.

He'd taken her into his care. After all his failures, it had felt good to bring peace and healing to one woman. A witch, he sensed. He would nurture her magic, he decided, teach her to defend herself from future attack.

He hadn't thought to make her his lover. But somehow, Nimue had burrowed her way into his heart and from there, into his bed. He'd been honored that she had chosen him after all she'd endured.

The sable furs he'd spread upon the stone for her comfort provided sumptuous dark contrast to her fair skin. She crawled across the fur to him on lithe slender limbs. His gaze clung to her rounded bottom. His erection, so recently spent, thickened anew.

She reached him and pressed a kiss to his chest. "Will you show me?" She arched her back and peered up at him through her lashes. "Will you teach me?"

"Magic?" He frowned down at her.

She licked a line up his neck and nibbled at his jaw. "Yes."

Though it was the last thing he wished to do, he set his hands on her shoulders and eased her away. Kneeling before him, her bottom on her heels, she gave him a questioning look. "Well?"

"You are not a Nephil," he said.

She lifted her arms and stretched like a cat, her back arching. Her breasts filled his vision. He reached for her and they filled his hands as well.

She draped her arms over his shoulders, smiling and squirming as his fingers plucked at her nipples. "I have...some small talent."

"Small talent is not enough," he told her gently.

"But...may I at least try?" Her teeth nipped at his earlobe, her tongue teased his ear. Her hands drifted down his chest, his stomach, his...

Ahhhhh. "You make me feel young again," he murmured.

She looked down and smiled. "You are not old."

Not true—he'd lived more than a century. His natural life span was nearing its end. Soon enough, he would enter Oblivion. But just now, as Nimue's clever mouth joined her clever hands, he didn't feel his age. He lay back, enjoying his passivity. Pleasure rushed upon him, blanking past and future from his mind. A welcome relief.

When it was over, she lay curled at his side. She ran her fingers over his chest, tangling into crisp dark hairs that had only recently begun to harbor a sprinkle of white.

"Will you show me how to call magic, my love?" Playfully, she tweaked his nipple. "I promise not to be disappointed when I fail."

He smiled down at her. What could it hurt? "All right."

They rose and pulled on their robes. Merlin was sorry to see Nimue's body covered. But her pale skin and long limbs would be bare again, he promised himself, as soon as this demonstration was over. He retrieved his staff, which he'd laid on the ground nearby. He stood it upright between them and bid her close her hands around it, in the space between his own.

"Can you feel it? Can you feel the magic within?"

Twin lines of concentration appeared between her eyebrows. "Y-yes. Perhaps."

Her fingers tightened. Merlin covered her hands with his. Closing his eyes, he sent his power coursing through her into the wood.

The orb—his crystal touchstone—flared to life. Nimue flinched, as if struck by subtle lightning.

"Too strong?" he asked.

"No," she whispered. "Not too strong. Teach me. Please."

"The magic must flow freely," he said. "Druid magic is fluid. Emotional, yet anchored in solid stone and wood. At its simplest level, it is mere illusion, but when skillfully wrought, it is more, much more. A powerful Druid may cause illusion to become reality. Truth, created at will. Do you understand?"

The word caused her body to go cold. Human children grew up hearing stories about bogeymen and monsters under their beds. Nephil young were weaned on tales of Heaven's avengers. There were three. Arthur's silver messenger, Gabriel. This golden one was Raphael, the warrior who once waged a war of genocide against the Nephilim. His righteous sword had sent countless Nephilim to Oblivion.

It looked as though Raphael sorely wanted to add Arthur to the body count. Arthur, who currently lay sprawled on his ass beside Merlin's staff. Dusek stood nearby. The eyes of both adepts glowed a furious red.

"Arthur Camulus." Golden flame leapt from Raphael's sword, tangling with the sparks of Merlin's crystal orb. "Do not move. Not one muscle."

Arthur jumped to his feet.

The angel went white with fury. "Michael," he barked. Almost instantly, a second figure appeared, heralded by a clap of thunder. Cybele blinked hard. Michael? Could this newcomer truly be the third archangel?

If so, he certainly didn't look the part. For one thing, he wasn't fair, but olive-skinned. Dark stubble covered his firm jaw. His eyes were the color of bittersweet chocolate, his body whipcord lean. Oddly, he wore human clothing rather than celestial robes. Cybele's gaze took in black combat boots...black jeans...black shirt topped by a black vintage military jacket. The jacket's silver frog fasteners, hanging undone, were the only light thing about him.

His wings—dark bronze and beautiful—rose above him. With smooth movement, he slid a switchblade from his right sleeve into his open palm. His fingers closed around the hilt. The blade snapped open. It was no righteous sword, but Cybele had no trouble believing that, in Michael's hand, the blade was every bit as lethal as his golden brother's fiery weapon.

She couldn't take her eyes from him. As if he'd felt her scrutiny, his head whipped around. Their eyes locked. He didn't look away. A wave of heat swept over her, starting at her feet, flowing up her legs, her torso, her breasts and shoulders. Her face flamed. Some vital emotion—she wasn't exactly sure what—flared in his eyes.

The hellfire lashes on her wrists and ankles vanished.

What the—? She scrambled to her feet, rubbing her wrists. She had no time to wonder about her unexpected release, however. Her eyes darted toward Arthur, then back to the archangels. Raw fear sliced through her as Raphael leveled the point of his flaming sword at Arthur's heart.

"Step away from that accursed implement of destruction, demon spawn."

"Bollocks to that." Arthur grabbed for the staff. A golden bolt shot from the sword, striking his wrist. He jerked back, spitting curses. His foot collided with something on the ground. A skull. It skittered across rock, splashed into the water, and sank out of view.

"Leave this place, Nephil. Never to return."

"Merlin's staff is my birthright," Arthur shouted back. "No goddamned archangel is going to stop me from claiming it."

"Make a move toward that staff and your next step will be into Oblivion."

Arthur's wings lifted. "Why wait? Kill me now."

"He cannot." The answer, surprisingly, came from Dusek. "Heaven's punishment comes after sin. Not before." The Alchemist turned mocking eyes on the archangel. "You can't stop Arthur from claiming Merlin's staff. You also know that once it is in his hands, it will be too late to prevent the consequence you fear."

What consequence was that? Judging from Raphael's reaction, it would be bad, at least as far as Heaven was concerned. The archangel's expression went dark as a thundercloud. Was that a hint of panic in his golden eyes? Cybele's gaze darted to Michael. Her head went back sharply when she found him looking not at Arthur, but at her. She blinked and his gaze shifted.

Raphael spoke. "Merlin, for all his nefarious doings, embedded his staff in that stone in protection of humanity. Remove it, Arthur, and you betray him."

"He lies," Dusek hissed. "He fears Merlin's magic. He will do anything to prevent its reawakening. The staff is yours, Arthur. Take it. Claim it. Now."

Arthur looked to the staff, then back at Raphael. His resolve seemed to waver. Cybele inched closer to the water's edge—as if moving closer was going to help Arthur decide. How could it? She had no idea what he should do.

The moment drew out in silence, measured by the pounding beat of her heart.

Arthur stepped back.

Raphael lowered his sword.

Dusek spat a curse. His powerful dark wings, already raised, swept downward. Almost before Cybele understood that she was his destination, he was on her.

"Arthur!" She tried to fight. Dusek spun her around like a rag doll. He jerked her up against his chest. His forearm pressed her windpipe. His mouth opened on her left temple, his breath moist against her skin.

Nausea and panic churned. She couldn't breathe, couldn't speak. The pressure on her throat increased. Dark spots blotted the edge of her vision.

She clawed at his arm. Dusek swiped his tongue wetly across her cheek. "Do not struggle. You are mine now."

EIGHTEEN

Arthur didn't trust the archangel. Not one bit. But he had no wish to be skewered on the point of Raphael's flaming sword. At least with the archangels present, Dusek wouldn't get his hands on Merlin's staff, either. That was something.

He stepped away. One tense moment later, Raphael's shoulders relaxed. He lowered his sword.

"Arthur!"

His head whipped around. Dusek hauled Cybele up against his body, his arm across her throat. She fought like a wild thing. They were near the edge of the cave. A couple more steps and they'd disappear into the maze of tunnels. If Dusek told the truth and whatever angel had been inhabiting Jack's body was now secure in the Alchemist's mirror, the Nephil could carry Cybele through the celestial seal and disappear before Arthur could stop him.

Unless...

Arthur lunged for Merlin's staff. This time, both hands closed on gnarled wood. Bracing his legs wide, he pulled with all his strength. With no resistance at all, the twisted branch slipped free. Arthur fell backward, clutching the staff to his chest.

"Fool." Raphael, sword ablaze, leapt across the water. Arthur, still sprawled on his arse, swept the head of the staff before him. Hissing steam, shooting from the hole where the staff had been, momentarily obscured his view across the water. By the time his line of sight cleared, Cybele and Dusek were gone.

He jumped to his feet, wings aloft, intent on launching himself after them. His flight was blocked by Raphael. The archangel landed before him, brandishing his flaming sword and shrieking with fury.

"Cursed Nephil. What have you done?"

"Out of my way." Arthur feinted left and dove right. The archangel wasn't fooled. Half-obscured by the hissing steam, his sword raised above his head, Raphael blocked Arthur's escape.

Arthur raised the staff, holding it crosswise in both hands like a fighting stick. The crystal orb flashed. The angel's sword came down. Golden blade bit twisted wood. Shock reverberated through Arthur's body. Magic raced up his arms and across his shoulders.

It exploded in his brain.

And with the magic came memory.

***

"You are so beautiful," said Merlin.

Nimue's lashes swept downward, as if to deny her lover's fervent praise. How could she be shy after what they'd just shared? But she was young, Merlin told himself. Young and uncertain. Whereas he was old and filled with regrets.

She made him feel new.

Perhaps that was why he'd brought her to the place where he'd met his Ordeal. Here, on the island in the center of the pool. He'd nearly died here, nearly gone mad. But in the end, he'd triumphed. Magic greater than any he should have been able to possess had come to him.

The underworld was very close to the surface in this

cave. To his attuned senses, it pulsed like a heartbeat. Had his demon powers been worth the price? In the past he had not doubted it. Now, he was less sure. Of a certainty, there had been victories. Important work done on behalf of his human brothers and sisters. In the end, though, betrayal had found the High King—in the guises of his lover, his best friend, and even, most tragically, his son. Fragile alliances had shattered. War and corruption had followed. Merlin had poured his heart and magic into salvaging the wreckage. To no avail. In the end, humanity had ended up no better off than when he had started.

"What are you thinking, my lord?"

He shoved the past into a dark corner of his mind and turned his attention to the light of the woman before him. "Nothing important, my dear. Only of how foolish I have been."

She smiled. "Never foolish. You are a wonder to me. So wise. So strong."

Merlin knew he was neither, but his vanity soaked up her adulation nonetheless. "And you are perfect," he told her.

She sat up, her naked breasts swaying softly. He found it incredible that she was able to give herself so completely. When he'd found her, she'd been close to ending her own life. She'd been ravished, she told him, by a Saxon. She'd left her violator's child at the door of a monastery and entered the forest. She had intended to do herself the ultimate harm.

He'd taken her into his care. After all his failures, it had felt good to bring peace and healing to one woman. A witch, he sensed. He would nurture her magic, he decided, teach her to defend herself from future attack.

He hadn't thought to make her his lover. But somehow, Nimue had burrowed her way into his heart and from there, into his bed. He'd been honored that she had chosen him after all she'd endured.

The sable furs he'd spread upon the stone for her comfort provided sumptuous dark contrast to her fair skin. She crawled across the fur to him on lithe slender limbs. His gaze clung to her rounded bottom. His erection, so recently spent, thickened anew.

She reached him and pressed a kiss to his chest. "Will you show me?" She arched her back and peered up at him through her lashes. "Will you teach me?"

"Magic?" He frowned down at her.

She licked a line up his neck and nibbled at his jaw. "Yes."

Though it was the last thing he wished to do, he set his hands on her shoulders and eased her away. Kneeling before him, her bottom on her heels, she gave him a questioning look. "Well?"

"You are not a Nephil," he said.

She lifted her arms and stretched like a cat, her back arching. Her breasts filled his vision. He reached for her and they filled his hands as well.

She draped her arms over his shoulders, smiling and squirming as his fingers plucked at her nipples. "I have...some small talent."

"Small talent is not enough," he told her gently.

"But...may I at least try?" Her teeth nipped at his earlobe, her tongue teased his ear. Her hands drifted down his chest, his stomach, his...

Ahhhhh. "You make me feel young again," he murmured.

She looked down and smiled. "You are not old."

Not true—he'd lived more than a century. His natural life span was nearing its end. Soon enough, he would enter Oblivion. But just now, as Nimue's clever mouth joined her clever hands, he didn't feel his age. He lay back, enjoying his passivity. Pleasure rushed upon him, blanking past and future from his mind. A welcome relief. When it was over, she lay curled at his side. She ran her fingers over his chest, tangling into crisp dark hairs that had only recently begun to harbor a sprinkle of white.

"Will you show me how to call magic, my love?" Playfully, she tweaked his nipple. "I promise not to be disappointed when I fail."

He smiled down at her. What could it hurt? "All right."

They rose and pulled on their robes. Merlin was sorry to see Nimue's body covered. But her pale skin and long limbs would be bare again, he promised himself, as soon as this demonstration was over. He retrieved his staff, which he'd laid on the ground nearby. He stood it upright between them and bid her close her hands around it, in the space between his own.

"Can you feel it? Can you feel the magic within?"

Twin lines of concentration appeared between her eyebrows. "Y-yes. Perhaps."

Her fingers tightened. Merlin covered her hands with his. Closing his eyes, he sent his power coursing through her into the wood.

The orb—his crystal touchstone—flared to life. Nimue flinched, as if struck by subtle lightning.

"Too strong?" he asked.

"No," she whispered. "Not too strong. Teach me. Please."

"The magic must flow freely," he said. "Druid magic is fluid. Emotional, yet anchored in solid stone and wood. At its simplest level, it is mere illusion, but when skillfully wrought, it is more, much more. A powerful Druid may cause illusion to become reality. Truth, created at will. Do you understand?"

"I...I think so. But how may such a great magic be wrought?"

"Imagine. Then put your will behind the imagining."

Her eyes found his. "That sounds so easy. Is it truly so?"

"It is simple," he said. "Not easy."

"Show me."

He ignored a flutter of unease. "Perhaps something small," he said. "Let us think of...a flower. A red rose in half bloom. Let us send the image into the orb."

"All right."

A picture of a half-blown rose sprang into his mind. He imagined the rose flowing down his arms into his hands, his fingers, into the wood of the staff. From there the image lifted, traveling through the twisted branch. The touchstone flared white as it received the intention. A shower of sparks rained down. Moments passed, intervals of time blending one to the other. Merlin poured his magic into his mental image of the rose. It came to life, first in illusion then in form, shape, and substance. Roots, stem, leaves, petals. When it was done, he let out a breath and released his creation into the world.

A thorny bush, bearing a single, red, half-blown rose, stood before them, rooted in the rock of the cave.

Nimue gasped in wonder. "It is not an illusion?"

"No," he said. "It is real."

She approached the rose reverently and bent to touch its petals. "It is true." She turned to him, her eyes shining. "You are...like a god."

He felt unequal to her praise. "It's a useless god," he murmured, "who cannot order the world to his purpose."

But the girl was not listening. She eased the staff from his hands. "Let me try," she pleaded. "Alone."

"Alone," he said, "you cannot succeed. You are not Nephil."

"Then I will fail," she said, "ever grateful for whatever pale taste of your vast power I may touch." Her eyes pleaded. "I beg you, Merlin, let me try."

He gave the staff into her keeping and backed away. The attempt could do no harm. Nimue gave him a brilliant smile before turning to face the rose. With both hands gripping the staff, she let her head fall back. Merlin watched the cascade of her glorious dark hair. The ends brushed the curves of her bottom, visible through the drape of her robe.

It was, perhaps, because Merlin's attention was on Nimue's buttocks and not her magic, that he did not realize what was happening until it was too late.

His touchstone turned dark. It released a burst of silver-black sparks. Merlin was aghast—his magic was white, pure white. He had no time to ponder the anomaly. The ground beneath his feet rolled and split, opening a fissure between himself and Nimue. The portion of the island upon which he stood heaved sharply upward. He lost his balance. He stumbled backward and landed on his arse in the water.

Hissing steam shot from the fissure. Through the veil of white, he could see that Nimue had not moved. She stood like a statue, her head thrown back, both hands gripping the staff. A dark nimbus enveloped her body. Silver sparks traveled down her arms and whirled like a tornado around the staff.

The steam began to wail. The air exploded with the rotten scent of sulfur. Merlin lurched to his feet only to be knocked down again by the ground's next shuddering tremor. The water was heating rapidly. He crawled on hands and knees onto the stone.

A small figure emerged from the deep. Merlin regarded it in horror. Its body, lumpy and potato-like, was so darkly red as to be almost black. Its head was mostly round, with a pointed chin and ears, blunt horns, and blazing red eyes. Thin, awkward limbs unfolded, aided in balance by a curved rat tail. When the thing at last gained its feet, a pair of bat wings snapped up from its back.

It rose into the air. As it did so, another like it popped out of the fissure. Then another and another until there were too many to count.

"Hellfiends," Merlin whispered. Fiends were minor demons created by the sinful passions of the souls of the damned. Their brains were tiny; their malice was great. The creatures, spawned in Hell, were rare on the Earth's surface. In all his long life, Merlin had not encountered more than a handful of them. Never had he imagined so many in one place.

They skittered over the ground and launched their misshapen bodies into the air. Soon a mass of them had gathered under the ceiling of the cave, wings beating against the rock. Their shrieks pierced Merlin's ears. The stench, brimstone and filth, closed his throat.

In the middle of it all, Nimue stood laughing. She turned to face him, swinging his staff around with her, scattering sprays of dark sparks like so much mud.

He stared. Her face, flushed with triumph, glowed. Her aura and power were blinding. He'd thought her a human witch of meager talent. He now realized she was more. Much, much more.

"What...what are you?" he whispered.

Her lips curled. "You remain blind, even now? Old fool. I am a Nephil. A daughter of Azazel." Her head dropped back, her arms flung wide. She laughed. "And now I am queen of all the Earth, a demon horde at my command."

She spun about, arms outstretched, his staff gripped in her left hand. A hellfiend alighted on her forearm, a second on her shoulder. By all the ancestors in Oblivion, what had he done? What horror had his blind lust wrought? The woman he'd thought was an innocent was, in truth, a Nephil adept. And worse, a spawn of Azazel, heiress to the alchemical magic of the most depraved of the fallen Watcher angels.

The hellfiends flew to Nimue like flies to rotten meat. They buzzed about her head, clung to her robe. Amid the hissing steam and beating wings, Merlin soon lost sight of her entirely. More and more fiends emerged from the depth to swarm with their terrible brethren. And from within the undulating mass, Nimue's triumphant laughter rang out.

With a shout, she launched the fiends toward the cave's ceiling, driven by a stream of hellfire. The horde obeyed her command, splattering their misshapen bodies against the rock, battering the barrier with their wings. As Merlin stumbled to his feet, fine fissures appeared in the stone overhead. Shards rained down on his head. This cave would not hold, he thought. Each fiend was small, but together, their power was formidable. Driven by Nimue's magic, it was only a matter of time before they broke through to flood the human world.

There seemed no end to the invasion. With every beat of Merlin's heart, scores of fiends emerged from the depth, joining the others in their grotesque dance about Nimue and the staff.

She had bested him. He, Merlin, the most powerful Nephil ever to walk the Earth. Proud Merlin, dedicated to the godly ideals of his human grandfather, who had been a priest of the Almighty. Merlin had thought himself capable of teaching and protecting his human brethren, of shepherding them safely past threats of war and destruction. He'd given his life to this cause. Was this to be his legacy? That humanity's self-appointed shepherd would become the instrument of its doom?

Not while he had breath in his body. Merlin leaped into the fray. Slapping at demons right and left, he made slow progress through the horde. Nimue, in her frenzy, did not notice his approach until he was almost upon her. She spun about, trying to move the staff out of his reach. Too late. His hands were already upon the wood.

"No." She yanked at the staff. Pewter hellfire shot from the orb down the length of the wood. Merlin's hands burned, but he did not let go.

Their eyes locked. Their magic tangled and choked, Nimue's hot fury battling Merlin's cold anger. If he had not been able to take back the staff, he was not sure what might have happened. Perhaps Nimue would have prevailed.

But the staff, with its touchstone orb, had been fashioned by Merlin's own hand. To Merlin, it owed its first allegiance. He sent his magic streaming through it, bright white against Nimue's dirty gray. The surge struck like lightning, racing up the twisted wood and into the crystal where it spun with dizzying speed.

"Desist. You cannot prevail."

"You fool," she said. "My power is ten times yours. A hundred times."

One look in her eyes told him she believed it. He, however, did not. A wave of sorrow passed over him as he gazed at her. "Good-bye, my love," he said.

He closed his eyes and gave his fury full rein. A sound like a thunderclap echoed in his ears. The world behind his eyelids went white. When he opened his eyes it was to see Nimue's body ablaze. She opened her mouth to scream. No sound emerged. He caught one final glimpse of her beautiful face, her eyes filled with shock, before the fire consumed her.

As her grip on the staff dissolved, he staggered backward. His beautiful lover was nothing more than ash. His own hand had sent her to Oblivion. The magic she'd wrought however, had not died with her. Hell's fissure still gaped. The fiends still rose. How many now? Thousands, Merlin thought, with more arriving every second.

He lifted the staff, the crystal rising high over his head. This catastrophe was his fault. He must fix it. He blotted all but his magic and purpose from his mind. Hellfire crackled. Sparks flew through the air. Lashes of light, spun from his staff, wound and tangled in the hellfiends' limbs. Slowly, slowly, like a spider binding her prey, Merlin wrapped the shrieking demons in his magic. Inch by slow inch, he pulled the mass of them down, down, down, forcing them back into the fissure from whence they'd emerged.

It was not until the last fiend had disappeared into the bowels of Hell and Merlin had driven the base of his staff into the stone after them, that he realized the portal opened by Nimue's vision would never completely close. If he abandoned this place, the demon horde might very well emerge anew. If the human world was to be spared the horror of Merlin's final mistake, he must pay for the error with his life.

NINETEEN

Merlin's memories smashed into Arthur's brain. The images and emotions took a bare second to absorb and a scant instant more to understand.

Raphael's stunning blow had driven his blade into the heart of Merlin's staff. Arthur, arms rigid, fought against the archangel's advance. Behind Raphael's head, a stream of blistering vapor shot toward the roof of the cave. Clouds of billowing steam spread right and left. Sparks streamed from Merlin's touchstone to entwine with the mist in a glittering fog. Brimstone escaped from the deep burned his nostrils.

What have I done?

With a roar, he twisted the staff, shoving Raphael's fiery blade to one side. Lurching past the angel, he tried to slam the staff back into the hole. It didn't stick. High-pressure steam, spitting into the cave with the force of a fire hose, flung it back into his face.

A golden blur had him spinning to the left. Raphael hovered above him. His blade sliced downward, aimed for Arthur's head. He barely threw himself out of the way in time. He hit the ground and rolled, sweeping the crystal head of the staff before him. The angel's sword struck rock, spraying golden sparks.

Cybele. Dusek might have her out of the cave by now. He had to get to her...

A loud crack rent the air. The hole from which he'd pulled the staff broke open, fissures shooting in opposite directions. The island came apart, just as it had in Merlin's memory. The rock under Arthur's feet split. The portion of the island occupied by Raphael heaved upward. The angel pitched backward in a flurry of golden wings.

The fissure shot off into the water. More cracks opened, filling the cave with a sound like rapid rifle shot. The staff's hole collapsed inward, leaving a treacherous network of crumbling rock. Hot sprays of steam spurted up from below, blasting from every new breach.

Arthur came up into a crouch on the shifting ground. He wanted to dash across the water, to go after Cybele. Raphael had different ideas. The archangel, having regained his equilibrium, swung his blade. Arthur deflected the worst of the blow with the staff. He spun off to avoid the next strike. With a downward sweep of his wings, he launched himself across the water.

Heat flashed through the air. The pool boiled and churned. Eddies formed in the dark water. With a massive sucking sound, liquid drained through the fissures, until the lakebed was nothing but dry stone, crumbling into nothingness.

Unholy screeching erupted from the fathomless deep. *Hellfiends.*

"Noooo!" Raphael's cry echoed off the rock.

The archangel fell on Arthur, his fury as hot as the sulfurous steam filling the cave. Arthur whipped his wings around, rising into the air, dodging the blows. The vapor blasting from the ruined lakebed turned hotter. Sweat poured down his torso. His throat closed on the stink. At least the thick haze hindered Raphael's aim. Unfortunately, it made it just as difficult for Arthur to anticipate the angel's next attack.

He hovered above disintegrating rock, parrying each strike as best he could. White hellfire crackled inside the crystal touchstone. It raced along the wood, shot out in all directions. Arthur tried to direct the magic at his adversary, but in truth he had little control over it. Merlin's staff seemed to have a mind of its own.

Demon shrieks filled his ears. Misshapen creatures, a match to those he'd seen in Merlin's memory, climbed from the deep. Spindly limbs and horned heads attached to round, lumpy torsos were propelled by bat wings and whipping rattails. The fiends streamed past, flinging themselves against the cave's ceiling.

Raphael looked about wildly. "Michael. Kill them!"

But the dark archangel Arthur had glimpsed only briefly was now nowhere to be seen. With a roar of frustration, Raphael spun and whipped his blade downward. Arthur absorbed the impact with the staff, holding the twisted rod above his head. Fragments of rock rained down. *Worse and worse.* The cave ceiling was crumbling before the onslaught of demon wings.

Raphael's blade, embedded in the wood of the staff, resisted the angel's efforts to yank it free. With a scowl, he reversed course, driving his strength forward. The fiery edge of his blade twisted into the meat of the oak, rowan, and yew. With a resounding crack, all three woods gave way.

Arthur fell back, wings flailing, a half-staff in each hand. Raphael dove after him. As his blade rose for the killing blow, another shower of stone rained down. A large rock struck the angel's forearm. The sword's downward arc shifted. The flat of the blade glanced off Arthur's skull.

His head exploded in pain. More rock rained down. The entire cave, above and below, was disintegrating. The onslaught forced Raphael and Arthur apart. A large rock, striking Arthur's chest, drove him downward. He struggled to beat his wings, to fight his way up through the plummeting debris. He raised an arm, the top half of Merlin's staff clutched in his fist. The touchstone was dark. Stones tumbled, taking Arthur down in a furious avalanche. Rocks pummeled his body. One struck his forehead.

The world went black.

***

"Let. Me. Go."

Cybele's pockets were empty. Her touchstone was missing. She didn't know where she'd lost it. She only knew that without it, she had no hope of casting an illusion or making herself fade from Dusek's awareness. Abandoning the possibility of a magical defense, she grabbed her knife out of her boot.

Dusek merely snatched it away. "You won't need this, my dear." Her knife disappeared into a fold in his cape.

"Fuck you." She fought with everything she had left, biting, scratching, kicking. She jabbed her elbow into his gut, slammed the heel of her boot into his knee. Dusek's hellfire re-appeared. She cried out in pain as they lashed her arms to her torso.

His arm, clamped across her chest, kept her body melded to his. When she glanced down, at his hand, the face on the odd ring snapped its eyes open. Twin streams of dirty gold fire shot out, striking painfully on the underside of her chin. Cybele hissed in a breath. The ring grinned and winked at her then closed its eyes. A shudder of revulsion passed through her.

Dusek's tongue licked around the shell of her ear. Cybele struggled, angling her head away from the disgusting sensation. His lips pursued her, whispering wetly. "Useless to struggle. I have you safe now. I don't know how you managed to cast off my hellfire the first time, but rest assured, my sweet. It will not happen again."

Her captor hauled her into a maze of rocky passages. Sulfurous mist followed in their wake. Cybele gagged. The ground shook. An ominous crack sounded. A network of fissures opened in the tunnel walls. Rock spalled and fell. Dear ancestors in Oblivion. Maybe Dusek wasn't her first concern. She might die under an avalanche of stone long before the Alchemist dragged her into the light of day.

Arthur. He'd been battling the golden archangel when Dusek hauled her into the tunnel. She had to get back to the main cave, back to Arthur, before the hill above it collapsed. But Dusek's grip was like iron.

And the rock below their feet was crumbling. Clouds of steam, tainted by the scent of brimstone, billowed up from below. Licks of flame snapped at their feet.

"It begins." The Alchemist's voice was triumphant. He backed to the edge of the passage, under an overhanging rock. Stone fell like rain outside the sheltered nook. His arm tightened, pressing Cybele's spine snugly against his bare chest. A hard, round object pressed into her back between her shoulder blades. Dark, suffocating wings brushed her shoulders.

"Watch, my darling. Watch what I have wrought."

Fire snapped and crackled. Misshapen, rat-tailed creatures, their membranous batwings whirring, rode the flames up from the deep. Reaching the level of the tunnel, some jumped off to roam about the passageway. Others continued upward. They gathered under the cave ceiling, battering the rock with their wings. The gauzy light of the celestial seal became visible amid the crumbling stone.

"Are they not glorious?"

Cybele swallowed. "What...what are they?"

"Hellfiend demons," he said. "Creatures of pure malice, created by the vengeful souls of the eternally damned. The fiends have been prevented from passing into the upper world for centuries, blocked by the power of Merlin's staff and Raphael's seal. Now, at long last, they are free."

Cybele's mind raced. "You wanted this. You planned it. That's why you lured Arthur to the cave."

"You are no fool," Dusek said. "I approve, my dear."

"But...how could you have known what was behind the seal? And the staff?"

His tongue snaked into her ear. She felt his penis harden against her butt. She shivered with revulsion.

"I know because I have seen it," he whispered. "In the memory of my ancestor."

"Impossible. You aren't of Merlin's line."

"That old fool? I would be ashamed to carry his blood in my veins. Have you not puzzled it out yet? Merlin died in this cave. And so did Nimue, at the Druid bastard's hand. She is the one of whom I speak."

Of course. Cybele had been blind not to see it. "Nimue wasn't a witch. She was a Nephil."

"A Nephil and Alchemist. A daughter of Azazel. She opened a path to Hell in this very cave. Her mistake was in not killing Merlin before the demons rose."

He turned her to face him. A flash of reflected light caught Cybele's gaze. An odd, swirling silver disc, swinging on a chain about the Alchemist's neck. It looked soft and liquid, but it couldn't be. Earlier, she'd felt the pendant digging into her back.

Dusek's voice rising above the din of the shrieking hellfiends. "Merlin received his punishment. Trapped by his own guilt and by Raphael's seal, he died a slow, despairing death. And all for naught. Today, Nimue's vision is finally realized." His arm swept the cave. "Are they not glorious creatures?"

They were hideous. Ugly and stinking, their shrieks were like hot needles poking through Cybele's eardrums. Clouds of sulfur followed them, burning her throat with every breath. Dusek's arm, pressing on her ribcage, didn't help.

She felt him searching with his free hand in the red lining of his cape. He pulled an object from a hidden pocket. "Now," he said, "I will see Nimue's fiends launched into the world."

With a flick of his wrist, he released the object from his hand. A golden ball, held aloft by two glittering incandescent feathers. It hovered for a moment, swaying gently on its whirring wings. A wave of Dusek's hand sent it darting off toward the cave ceiling.

The ball moved deftly, dodging fiends and falling stone. Cybele's eyes followed the gleaming gold as it flitted through the yellow murk, climbing ever higher. Spinning through a gap in the stone, it plunged into the golden gauze of the celestial seal.

For a moment, Cybele thought Raphael's barrier would hold. Then a fine network of spidering cracks appeared, spreading darkly from the point of the winged ball's impact. Chunks of golden light began to fall, revealing the night sky behind.

"Yes." Dusek's cry was triumphant. "Yes." He started out of the niche, shoving Cybele before him. As his wings lifted, an angry rumble shook the ground.

The cave floor heaved. Dusek lost his balance. Cybele didn't miss her chance. She let her body go limp, causing her captor to pitch forward at the unexpected shift of her weight. She twisted to one side and, arms still pinned by the hellfire lashes, slammed her head up into his jaw.

His head whipped to one side. His body half-turned

with it. The silver disc about his neck swung sideways on its chain, striking the cave wall. A jagged line appeared down the center. The silvery liquid trembled and separated. The broken halves coalesced into two smaller, perfect circles.

One disc remained attached to the chain. The other fell to the cave floor. A sphere of brilliant light bounced out of it, spinning sharply upward. With a loud *pop!* the light became a baby—a chubby baby with wings and a slightly tarnished gold ring wobbling wildly above its head. Cybele stared at it in amazement.

"Wheeeeee!" the infant cried. Iridescent feathers whirred. Feathers, Cybele realized, that matched those on the golden ball that had broken the celestial seal. White swaddling clothes, quickly unraveling from the baby's chubby form, streamed free.

Dusek uttered a foul cry. He grabbed at the baby. The little creature was too swift. He evaded the Nephil's fingers. Zigzagging wildly, he ricocheted off the cave walls like a demented ping pong ball. At one point he buzzed past Dusek's nose. The Nephil swatted at him with one hand, but couldn't quite catch him.

The Alchemist's other hand, unfortunately, remained gripped around Cybele's upper arm. Again she twisted and kicked, with little to show for it. Until the cherub—that *had* to be what the winged baby was—flung himself at Dusek's chest.

Grabbing hold of the silver chain with one hand, the angel pounded on the part of the mirror still attached to it. "Maweth? Maweth? You in there? Are you all right?"

Dusek swiped at the angel. This time, his grip on Cybele slackened. She wrenched free. Without so much as a single backward glance, she took off down the tunnel.

Running was treacherous. Dusek's hellfire kept her

arms lashed to her sides, making it difficult to keep her balance. She navigated crumbling ground, dodging fire and fiends. It took all her concentration to remain upright as she stumbled back toward the cave's main chamber.

Something caught her from behind. Her head snapped back. "Not so fast, my love."

Dusek. He yanked her head around, his fingers digging painfully into her scalp. *Damn it all to Oblivion.* She should've hacked off her hair when she'd had the chance.

Incredibly, the little angel was still clinging to Dusek's silver chain. "Maweth? Maweth?" His voice hitched up an octave. "Answer me!"

Dusek, ignoring the angel, gave Cybele's head a vicious shake. "You will learn obedience. Starting now."

"Fuck you." She spat in his face.

A fist connected with her jaw. Pain exploded. Her head whipped to one side. Using her hair as a tether, Dusek gave her another shake. He slapped her across the cheek. Her head snapped back the other way.

"You may look forward to more of that," he said harshly. "I know I will."

"You think you can make me obey you?" Cybele snarled. "Forget it. I'll kill you. I'll gut you while you sleep. I'll poison your food. I'll cut off your—"

"Maaaaawethhhhhh!" The angel, apparently oblivious to his surroundings, pounded on the mirror.

Dusek looked down. "As for you—enough." The Nephil tore the angel off his chest and threw him to one side. The angel ricocheted off a falling rock, swayed dizzily for a second, and then seemed to regain his bearings. He looked at Dusek. His expression darkened.

"You!" A missile of incandescent light slammed into Dusek's face. The Nephil staggered backward. His grip went slack. Cybele fell, her knees hitting the ground with a painful jolt. A falling rock hit her on the shoulder. Looking up, she saw a boulder tumbling toward her. She rolled swiftly toward the cave wall. The massive stone crashed down, barely missing her.

Dusek, cursing, clawed at the angel. Pudgy infant legs locked tightly around his throat. One chubby little hand grabbed a fistful of his hair. The other rained choppy blows on the Nephil's nose.

"Take that!" the angel cried. *Punch!* "And that!" *Smack!* "You!" *Slap!* "Bad!" *Thump!* "NEPHIL!"

Dusek fought his tiny assailant absurdly. Hellfire was no use. The little angel seemed immune to it. And each time the Nephil managed to pry a chubby arm or leg off his face or neck, it slipped through his fingers and splatted back into place.

"You hurt!" *Smack!* "My friend!" *Punch!* "Bad. Bad! BAD!"

The sulfurous fog was thickening. Cybele could barely see through it. Her lungs burned. The world was falling rock, leaping flame, beating wings, and unholy shrieking. The ground was cracking beneath her. The entire hill was collapsing into the abyss. If she couldn't find Arthur and get out of here, they'd both fall into whatever corner of Hell the fiends had escaped.

Maybe Arthur's already gone. Her heart pounded furiously. *No. Don't even think it.* She tried again to free her arms from Dusek's hellfire. Finally, giving up, she scrambled to her feet and threw herself down the tunnel.

With all the dust and billowing brimstone, she might as well have been blind. She slammed into an obstacle she hadn't even seen coming. She would have fallen, if a firm grip, just above her right elbow, hadn't kept her on her feet.

"Cybele."

Her head jerked up. He was tall, she thought inanely. Even taller than Arthur. His wing feathers were like glowing bronze velvet. His expression was hard, but somehow his grimness did nothing to detract from his beauty. Slashing cheekbones, angular jaw, aristocratic nose. His hair was dark and soaked with sweat, plastered across his forehead. And his eyes? Even through the murk, she could tell they were the softest brown she'd ever seen. Or had ever even imagined.

He was the dark archangel. Michael. A chill raced down her spin. Had he come to kill her?

"No." She tried to break his grip. He only held her tighter. "No." She struck out. She couldn't reach him. She kicked. Hit his knee. He didn't flinch.

"Calm down." His voice was deep and smooth. "Stop struggling. I'm not here to hurt you."

With a start, she realized Dusek's hellfire lashes were gone. They'd dissolved the instant Michael had touched her. Surely, if he'd meant to kill her, she'd be dead by now. The cave shuddered. A large chunk of rock fell, struck his head, and bounced away. His only reaction was a frown, and she was pretty sure the falling rock had nothing to do with that. He was frowning at her.

"I'm taking you out of here," he said.

"No. No way." Her chest heaved with the effort of breathing. "I'm going back to the big cave. I've got to get to Arthur."

"Arthur's going to have to take care of himself, I'm afraid." Michael turned her around and hustled her in the opposite direction. His wings came up to shelter her from the falling rock as easily as an umbrella dispelled a drizzle.

"Or not," he added under his breath as another violent tremor struck. "As the case may be."

"What do you mean by that? Is he d—" Cybele couldn't

bring herself to say the word.

Michael supplied it. "Dead? No, he's not. At least, he wasn't the last time I saw him. Can't say how long that'll last, though."

"No! I've got to—"

"Get yourself killed?" He slipped an arm around her waist and hauled her along the passage. "Forget it. Arthur's a big boy. Let him sink or swim on his own. This is all his fault."

"It is not!"

"No? Who pulled that staff from the stone? Who opened a portal to Hell and released a horde of hellfiends from the deep?"

"He didn't know—"

"Not an excuse." Michael's tone was grim. "There's no telling what will happen now that those things are free."

"Merlin's staff—it was keeping those things underground?"

"The staff, yes, and Raphael's seal. Arthur's unleashed what's been contained for over a millennium."

"Not Arthur. Dusek. He's the one who broke that seal. I saw him."

Michael stopped and peered at her with an arrested expression. "You did? How did he do it?"

"He used this little golden ball. It had wings made from two glowing feathers. Angel feathers, I think they were. The ball slammed into the ceiling and the light just...shattered."

Michael uttered a word Cybele was pretty sure angels weren't in the habit of saying. She tried to tug free of his grasp. "Listen. Just let me go. I have to get back to Ar—"

"Maaaaaawethhhhhhh! Are you in there? Are you all right? Answer meeeee."

Michael swung around. He'd stopped before a bend in

the tunnel. The voice high and melodious, like a bell, and came from just ahead.

"Blessed Heaven," he muttered. "That sounds like—"

A golden blur of light wobbled around the corner, caught sight of Michael and Cybele, and drew up short. The little angel who'd attacked Dusek earlier hovered in the air, wings whirring. In his chubby hands was the Alchemist's mirror. Its broken chain dangled in the air.

The angel blinked, the sparkling blue of his eyes looking terribly out of place in the yellow murk. "Michael?"

The archangel appeared stunned. "Fortunato?"

"You know him?" Cybele asked.

Michael blinked down at her. "Know him? Of course I know him. He's a cherub, isn't he? I've been looking everywhere for him." He looked back to the angel. "Fortunato, what in Heaven's holy name are you doing here?"

The angel sniffled. "Michael! It's really you." He threw himself at the archangel, wrapping one pudgy arm around his neck. "Michael. Michael. Michael." He thrust the mirror under the larger angel's nose. "Help."

"Help with wh—" Michael cut off as the rock under their feet disintegrated.

Cybele scrambled for footing. There wasn't any. A chasm had opened up beneath her. She shrieked. Michael's grip tightened. She found herself suspended, her legs dangling in thin air. Michael held her easily, with one arm, her back pressed against his chest, much as Dusek had done.

The sensation was as different as night to day. Michael's touch was firm, but not at all threatening. His bronze wings fluttered gently. "Don't worry." His lips brushed her temple. "I won't let you fall."

Fortunato swung back and forth like a pendulum, his

gossamer wings moving so fast Cybele could hardly see them. "Michael. Michael." He held out the disc. "You've got to help my friend."

Cybele could hear the confusion in the archangel's voice. "Who's your friend?"

"He's—" The cherub's reply was lost in an unholy shriek. A pair of hellfiends, careening up from the deep, smashed into Cybele. One tore at her pant leg, the other tangled in her hair.

"Ugh." The things smelled like vomit. If Dusek hadn't taken her knife, she'd slice up the potato bodies and send each piece back where it came from. She swatted at the one in her hair. Her hands came away slimy.

"Disgusting," she spat.

"Stay still." Michael's left arm tightened around her. The switchblade she'd seen earlier appeared again in his right hand. He skewered the creature, lifting it on his knife and flinging it away with one smooth movement. It let out a yelp and exploded into ash.

He dispatched the second one with lethal efficiency. Another explosion struck. Rock and stone crashed down from above. Michael spread his wings over Cybele, shielding her from the worst of the deluge. "Fortunato!" he barked. "To me."

The cherub didn't hesitate. Clutching the mirror to his chest, he leaped onto Michael's shoulder and hooked a chubby arm around his neck. Michael's blade folded and disappeared up his sleeve. He shifted his grip on Cybele.

"Hang on," he told her.

They shot skyward, exploding into the night amid rock, fire, and ash. Michael set a spiraling path through the hellfiend horde. The ground spun in circles beneath them. A low rumble vibrated the air. The peak of Merlin's Hill cracked wide open, releasing a writhing mass of what looked like ash and fire. Cybele knew better. The hellfiend horde had broken free.

Clods of dirt, splintered tree branches, chunks of rock—even a few sheep—rained down. As Michael flew over the Spencers' farm, Cybele caught a glimpse of the couple, rushing into the yard in their nightclothes. For one frozen moment, they clung to each other. Then Mrs. Spencer staggered forward, arms outstretched. "Jack!"

A wave of grief broke over Cybele. Innocent, trusting Jack. There wasn't a chance in Hell that he'd escape alive. At least the boy would have a place in Heaven. Cybele hoped the knowledge would be a comfort to his grandparents.

If they survived, that was. A boulder hurtled into the side of the barn. With a shudder, the entire structure collapsed. As Michael changed course, Cybele caught a last glimpse of Mr. Spencer hauling his wife toward their truck.

Michael flew over the road and the field beyond. He landed perhaps a mile from Merlin's Hill, in the lee of a crumbling stone barn. He set Cybele's feet on the ground. Her legs folded like spaghetti. She found herself sprawled in the dirt, staring up at her unlikely defender.

He frowned down at her. How, she thought dazedly, could this dark, forbidding man be an angel? The notion was impossible to wrap her head around. His face, with its Middle Eastern complexion, and his body, all lean muscle encased in black human garb, was as far from Cybele's understanding of angels as it was possible to get. Michael wasn't pale, noble, or holy. His angelic aura was simply one of power. Raw, elemental power.

His bronze wings appeared almost black against the dawn sky. They might have belonged to one of her own kind—a Nephil. Until they folded down to nothing and disappeared into his back. Through his clothes. That, more than anything else, convinced her of Michael's angel status. No Nephil could melt wings through fabric.

She shoved herself into a sitting position, watching him warily. The little cherub was still perched on his shoulder, one chubby arm clutching the mirror, the other looped around Michael's neck. The archangel didn't seem to remember the cherub's presence until Fortunato leaped from his perch to the ground and kissed Michael's boots.

"Oh thank you thank you thank you thank you thank you."

Amusement flitted across Michael's face as he looked down at the cherub. "You're very welcome."

Fortunato hopped away. Gently, he laid the mirror on the ground. The surface slithered and swirled. Looking up briefly at Michael, the cherub said, "I'll be back in a minute." He jumped and, with a pop, disappeared into the mirror.

"That's odd." Michael frowned at the piece.

Taking advantage of his preoccupation, Cybele climbed to her feet and backed slowly away.

The archangel's head whipped around. "No. Don't go."

Cybele froze, her heart pounding. "Why? What are you going to do with me?"

"Do with you?"

"Are you going to—" Her voice was little more than a whisper. "—to kill me?"

His brows shot up. "What? No! Is that what you think?"

"The thought occurred to me."

"It shouldn't have," he said. "If I'd meant for you to die, I'd have left you under that hill."

"Why didn't you?"

"That," he said, "is a fucking good question."

She blinked. "I didn't think angels cursed."

His expression turned sheepish. "We don't, normally."

She glanced toward Merlin's Hill. The smoke and flame showed no signs of abating. Even this far away, she could feel the ground trembling. "I guess there's nothing normal about this." She drew a breath. "Can I ask you a question?"

"I suppose so."

"Arthur," she said. "Do you think he's alive?"

He shrugged. "I haven't the foggiest."

How could her chest feel tight and like it was cracking open all at once? "But—I need to know."

"Well. As I've said, he was alive when I saw him last. Raphael was trying his best to remedy that, but your lover is a wily fighter. He was giving almost as good as he got."

"So he could still be alive."

"Might be, yes. Though it's not likely."

Cybele didn't give a shit what was likely. She clutched at the shred of hope he'd offered. "You have to go back."

"What?"

"You heard me. You have to go back."

He regarded her with patent disbelief. "Into that mess? To rescue the Nephil who caused it? You've got to be kidding."

"I'm dead serious. Go back and get Arthur. You can do it. I know you can." She closed the distance between them and grasped his arm.

He flinched. For a long moment he stared down at her hand, as if it were a viper, preparing to strike.

"If Arthur's alive," he said slowly, "he'll find his own way out."

"Not if he's unconscious." Cybele's grip tightened. "Please. You have to look for him."

"I have to do no such thing." Michael shook his head slightly as if trying to dislodge something from his brain. "Honestly, I shouldn't even have done this much. I stepped way outside my boundaries when I rescued you."

"Why did you?"

He took a step back. Her hand fell to her side. Their eyes locked. Several long moments spun out.

"I couldn't let Dusek take you," he said at last.

"But—why would you care?"

"I—I don't know, exactly."

She cocked her head to one side, trying—and failing—to understand. But some unreadable emotion in his brown eyes prompted her to go on. "Please," she said softly. "Please go look for Arthur. If not for his sake, for mine."

His lips pressed together, and he looked away. "He's probably dead by now."

Her heart clenched. "Then bring me his body. So I can be sure."

His expression didn't change, but she sensed a subtle shift in his resolve. She held her breath through a long moment of silence.

"Please," she said at last when he didn't speak. "I'm begging you."

He looked at her. "You love him."

"Yes," she said. "Yes, I do."

"Why?"

The question surprised her. "Because...because he's Arthur. He's—oh, it's hard to describe. I loved him—I *knew* him—from the very first moment I saw him. He was twelve. I was thirteen. He was...so much more than anyone I'd ever met. His ideals, his beliefs—before I met Arthur, I didn't know...I didn't realize...that there could be a life outside Mab's dirty little world. Arthur made me dream of a different future. Of a life built on free will."

She paused for breath. Michael remained silent, his expression inscrutable.

She eyed him. "Have you ever been in love?"

"No." He looked away. "I have not."

"I suppose love isn't...isn't something angels need. You can't really understand. But it's true. I love Arthur and he loves me. He...if it were me in that mess, he wouldn't even think about whether or not to look for me. He'd just do it. He went rogue and faced his Ordeal alone for me. He was in that cave, looking for Merlin's staff for *me*."

Her vision blurred. Tears? Damn. She never cried. "Please. Just find him. Bring him back to me. Alive or dead."

Michael touched her cheek. When he drew his hand back, she saw his fingertip was wet. He stared at the drop of moisture—her tears—for what seemed like a very long time. Finally, his hand formed a fist. He lifted his head.

"All right. I'll look for him. Wait here."

His lofty wings, velvet bronze, unfurled. His dark gaze touched on her. *He's so beautiful,* she thought dazedly.

Too beautiful. She looked away.

When she looked back, he was gone.

TWENTY

The wait was interminable. Cybele paced in the rut between the ruined barn and a muddy field where some wheat-looking kind of plant was just beginning to sprout. Every couple of passes, she paused to stare across the valley toward Merlin's Hill. The hellfiend invasion showed no signs of letting up. A seemingly endless horde poured into the sky, spreading out in every direction. The air was thick with ash and sulfur. A deep breath burned. It looked like night for all that she'd caught a brief glimmer of dawn before the unholy murk took over completely. She felt sick, ready to throw up. Would the sun ever shine again?

A popping sound had her head turning sharply. The little cherub—Fortunato?—had emerged from the quicksilver. He looked to the left and right and then, fearfully, at Cybele. "Where is he? Where did he go?"

"Michael?" Cybele felt odd, saying the archangel's name out loud.

"Yes. Michael." The cherub backed slowly away, as if Cybele were a rabid dog or something. His bare foot slipped on a puddle. He fell on his baby bottom, splattering mud all over his swaddling clothes. "Where did Michael go?"

"Back to the cave. What's left of it. To look for..." Her throat closed. She had to believe Michael would succeed. She had to. "For Arthur," she finished.

The cherub's brilliant eyes widened. "And he left me here with you?" His voice rose in a screech. "Help! Help!" His gossamer wings whirred, but he couldn't quite lift himself out of the mud. "Save me!"

"Oh, for the love of—"

Fortunato flung his arms up over his head. "Mercy! Mercy!" His little body trembled.

His terror was real, but Cybele couldn't help herself. She started to laugh.

Fortunato's whimpers stopped. One eye peeped from beneath his chubby arm. "Um...what's so funny?"

"You are," Cybele said. "Geez. Get a hold of yourself. I'm not going to hurt you."

"You're not?"

She sighed. "No."

The cherub lowered his arms. "You could be lying," he said doubtfully. "You're a Nephil. I've recently discovered that Nephilim lie. A lot. And they're not very nice."

"If I'm so horrible, then why are you still here? It looks like your wings still work." She made a shooing motion with her fingers. "Go. Fly away."

"Into *that?*" Fortunato exclaimed, pointing skyward. "Are you *crazy?*"

Cybele rubbed her forehead. "I must be," she said. "I'm standing in a field, in the dark, talking to a mud-covered cherub. Insanity is the only explanation."

"And anyway," Fortunato continued, as if she hadn't spoken, "I can't leave. I need Michael." He pointed to the mirror. "My friend is hurt."

"Your friend? Who's that?"

"Maweth. He's in the mirror, and he's hurt."

"Is Maweth another angel?"

Fortunato shouted with laughter. "Maweth? An angel?" He flopped onto his back in the mud, chortling. "That's a good one. Maweth. An angel." He dissolved in a fit of giggles.

Cybele wondered if all cherubs were as annoying as this one. It hardly seemed possible. Heaven was supposed to be a pleasant place.

Fortunato sat up, suddenly sober again. "I can't get Maweth out of the quicksilver. The Alchemist trapped him in there."

"How did you get out?" Cybele asked.

"Oh, I was never really trapped," the cherub said. "I just didn't feel right leaving my friend."

"That's very loyal of you."

"You think so? I don't know, I—hey, look!" Fortunato leaped up and jabbed a pudgy finger at the sky. "There he is. Michael. He's coming back!"

Cybele's stomach dropped to the ground. She couldn't bring herself to look. "Does...does he have Arthur?"

The angel squinted. "Uh...maybe? He's carrying somebody, anyway."

Michael touched down. He was indeed carrying Arthur, who lay limp in his arms. Cybele rushed at him as he landed, her heart lurching. "Is he—?"

"No." The archangel lowered Arthur to the ground. "Not yet, anyway."

Cybele dropped to her knees. When she'd last seen Arthur, he'd been in demon form, blazing with power. Now his wings were gone, his body reverted to its human state. He was bruised and battered almost beyond recognition. If not for his mother's touchstone, in its apple wood setting, hanging limply on its chain around his neck, she might not have even recognized him.

"Arthur..." She touched his forehead, her hand trembling. There was a nasty gash on the side of his head, and more cuts on his face. His shoulder bent at a strange angle—his collarbone had to be broken. A motley mosaic of red, purple, and black decorated his torso and arms. His jeans were covered in soot. A dark crimson trickle seeped from a cut on his left thigh, visible through a tear in the denim.

He lay as still as death. His skin was cold, his complexion gray under the bruises and dirt. Was he even breathing? Yes. His chest rose and fell, barely. Cybele pressed two fingers to his neck. His pulse was thready, but it was there.

He was alive. For how long, though? A furious rage blossomed in Cybele's chest. "Raphael did this."

Michael didn't deny it.

"You goddamned angels." She wanted, so badly, to look away, to forget she'd ever seen Arthur like this. Somehow, she couldn't. Her eyes and her brain continued to scan his body, cataloguing every wound. Her fingers flexed and unflexed. She wanted to hit something. Or someone.

"What fucking self-righteous hypocrites you are," she said.

"I'm not my brother," Michael said quietly.

She glared up at him. "You might as well be. You're all the same."

"We're guardians of humanity," Michael replied. "What did you expect? That Arthur could pull Merlin's staff from the stone and flood the world with hellfiends, and there would be no consequences?"

"He didn't know it would happen."

"He didn't need to know," Michael said. "He only needed to obey Raphael's orders."

"*What?*" Cybele's vision went red. At that moment, she wasn't sure which was greater, her grief or her rage. Every breath she took stabbed like a knife.

She jumped to her feet, hands fisted at her sides. "All he had to do was obey? Are you serious? Raphael tried to wipe out our entire race. Fuck obedience! Fuck you and your fucking celestial privilege! You righteous prick. Everything on Earth and Heaven—every damn thing—is rigged for your benefit. You have no idea—" Her voice broke. "No idea—" She drew a shuddering breath. "No idea what it's like to be a Nephil. To be cursed before you're even born."

She dropped back to her knees, laid her cheek on Arthur's chest, and sobbed. *So much for never crying.* If Arthur died, she wasn't sure she'd ever stop.

After a long moment, she felt Michael crouch down beside her. He laid a tentative hand on her head. "Does he really mean that much to you?"

She lifted her head. "He means everything," she said dully.

"Cybele," Michael said. "Look at me."

Reluctantly, she turned her head and looked into the angel's eyes. Her first thought was...how could anyone's eyes look so soft? And so forbidding at the same time? It didn't make sense.

He held her gaze for a long moment, until she had the impression that he was no longer looking at her, but gazing inward.

"All right," he said at last.

"All right, what?"

"Just remember, I'm doing this for you. Not him. For you."

Her heart pounded. "Doing what?"

In lieu of an answer, he laid his right hand on Arthur's head. Closing his eyes, he inhaled deeply. On the exhale, he breathed a word she'd never before heard. The sound of it burned her ears.

She sucked air into her lungs and held it there. She was afraid to move, afraid to speak, afraid to so much as breathe. Her eyes were riveted on Michael's hand, on the glow seeping from his fingers.

The light whispered over Arthur's body. His skin lost its grayness. His collarbone shifted under his skin, resuming its normal line. His bleeding stopped. His wounds closed. The bruising faded. Even the blood on his jeans disappeared. Arthur drew a single deep breath. His spine arched and his chest expanded. His body relaxed into a long, deflating exhale. With his next breath, his respiration resumed a normal rhythm.

Cybele felt as if she were in a dream. She opened her mouth. "I—"

"Um...Michael?" Fortunato popped up, out of nowhere, cutting her off. He buzzed over to Michael and tugged on his pant leg.

Cybele closed her mouth. She reached out and cupped Arthur's cheek. It was warm. "Arthur?" she whispered. His chest expanded, and then fell with an audible sigh. Cybele willed his eyes to open. They didn't.

"Michael?" *Tug.* "Michael!"

At some point—she wasn't sure exactly when—Michael had removed his hand from Arthur's head and stood. "Not now, Fortunato," he said.

"But Miiiiichael—"

"I said, not now."

Cybele tipped her head back and met his gaze. "Why...why isn't he waking up?"

Michael closed his eyes and sighed. "Raphael's Sword of Righteous Vengeance struck him on the head. It must have been only a glancing blow, else he wouldn't have survived. But a wound like that isn't easily healed."

"But it will heal, right? He'll wake up?"

"When he's ready."

Cybele looked back at Arthur. His bruises were gone and the color had returned to his face. By all appearances, he was sleeping peacefully. "When will that be?"

"Hard to say. Hours? Days? Maybe as much as a week."

Fortunato popped up again. "Michael?"

Cybele rose slowly to her feet. "And when he does awaken? Will he be the same?"

Michael looked skyward. The stream of hellfiends spewing from Merlin's Hill hadn't abated. If anything, it'd grown thicker. A fine ash fell, drifting earthward like black snow.

"I imagine no one in the world is going to be the same after today," he said.

"That's not what I was asking."

"I know." He shoved his hands into the pockets of his jeans. "But it's the only answer I've got. Here—" He took his hands out of his pockets. "Give him these when he wakes up."

He held what looked like two gnarled sticks. The objects expanded rapidly in his hands.

Cybele's jaw dropped. "Merlin's staff?"

He shrugged. "Such as it is."

She couldn't believe it. "And you're giving it to me? To *Arthur?*"

"It's his, isn't it?" he said irritably.

"Of course it is. But you— I mean, but Raphael— He nearly killed Arthur because of it."

Michael's jaw tensed. "I told you before. I am not my brother."

She stared. "I think...I'm beginning to understand that."

It was the only thing she was beginning to understand about him. The rest of it—his motives, his thoughts, his inconceivable actions—she was at a loss to explain.

"Why?" she asked. "Why did you do all this? Why did you save me? Save Arthur? Bring us the staff? We should be beneath your notice."

"No. You're not. From the first time I saw you, in that house by the moor—" His mouth closed abruptly.

"House by the moor?" She narrowed her eyes. "You were at Tŷ'r Cythraul?"

He avoided her gaze. "Briefly."

"Briefly," she repeated. "What the hell does that mean? Why were you there at all?"

"I was keeping an eye on him." He jerked his chin at Arthur.

"But why?"

"Raphael thought it prudent." He grimaced. "Turns out he was right. As my brother annoyingly tends to be."

"Raphael sent you to spy on us?" Cybele's mind raced. Her voice took on a dangerous tone. "Tell me. What, exactly, did you see?"

He blinked once. A flush appeared high on his cheeks. His lips pressed firmly together.

Cybele gasped as the truth hit her. "Holy shit! Those were your wings I saw through the window. You creeper! You watched Arthur and me doing it."

He didn't deny it. What's more, the accuracy of her accusation was written all over his face. His cheeks went from pink to crimson, and he wouldn't meet her eyes.

The image of what he must've seen through the window—she and Arthur, tangled together on the bed, fucking each other's brains out—sprang into her mind. Her cheeks began to burn as hot as his.

She crossed her arms. "I have to say, that's pretty low. Even for a human. For an angel—"

"I know," he broke in. "I'm sorry."

"You're a miserable liar," she said, eyeing him. "I don't

think you're sorry at all."

He brought his gaze to hers. "I am sorry—" He held up his hand when she opened her mouth to retort. "You're right. I'm not sorry I watched. I'm sorry I've upset you."

Was she upset? Suddenly she wasn't sure. It was all too absurd. Who ever heard of an angel Peeping Tom? She swallowed a bubble of laughter. "So tell me, what did you like best? Was it when I went d—"

"By all that's holy!" His entire face flushed so hotly, she thought it might combust. "What I saw or didn't see is irrelevant."

"Like hell it is. Holy crap! Don't angels understand the concept of privacy?" She huffed out a breath. "Oh, why am I even asking? Of course they don't. Heaven's always watching."

"And you're lucky I was watching. Otherwise, you and this half-insane, over-powered idiot—" He waved the top half of Merlin's staff at Arthur. "—would be dead right now."

"Oh, sure. Take all the credit. Seems to me you could've saved us all some trouble and stopped us from coming to Merlin's Hill in the first place."

"I had nothing to do with that. I wasn't even there when you left. Gabriel was supposed to be watching Arthur. Raphael sent me to look for Fortunato."

At the sound of his name, Fortunato looked up.

"Crap job Gabriel did, then," Cybele muttered.

"We're in complete agreement there," Michael replied.

The cherub buzzed into the air. "*Now* can you listen to me, Michael? Please? Please?"

"In a minute, Fortunato." Michael held out the two pieces of Merlin's staff to Cybele. "Here. Take these."

She did. The wood was cold. Lifeless. "Thank you," she said. "Though...I'm not sure it matters. I'm not an adept, of course, but to me, this feels...dead."

"Maybe Arthur can make it whole again."

Cybele's brows rose. "What would Raphael say about that?"

Michael grimaced. "I don't want to know. Which is why I'm not going to tell him."

"Then...why give Merlin's staff to me at all?"

"Because," he said seriously, "it occurs to me that if Merlin was once able to hold back a demon horde with this staff, his heir may be able to use it to banish the current invasion."

"That's a pretty big stretch, if you ask me." She tipped back her head and looked at the black sky. "How many of those things do you think there are?"

"Hundreds of thousands? Millions? Who knows?"

Her fingers tightened on the twisted wood. "When Arthur wakes up—" She had to believe that would happen. "I'll give him the staff and tell him what you've said. And what you've done. He'll be grateful."

Michael snorted. "You think? I guarantee you, he won't be."

"Why not?"

"If you have to ask," he said, "it's not worth me trying to explain it."

"That," Cybele replied, "makes absolutely no sense."

An explosion rocked the ground. Cybele pitched forward, clutching the pieces of the staff against her chest. Michael's arms came around her, steadying her and holding her close for the briefest of moments.

It was a very odd feeling, being in the arms of an angel.

He released her and stepped away. Cybele felt his gaze on her, but she didn't—couldn't—return it. She looked toward Merlin's Hill instead. Staccato bursts of hellfire arced between billowing clouds of ash.

Fortunato sprang up between them, wings beating furiously. He held out the mirror to Michael. "Now can you do it, Michael? Please?"

Michael's gaze shifted from Cybele to the cherub. "Do what?"

"Get my friend out of here."

"Your friend?"

"Yes. My friend. That nasty Alchemist trapped him in here. Now he's hurt and I can't get him out. Pleeeeease?"

Michael took the mirror. He turned it over in his hands, frowning. "This is very odd."

"I'll say." Cybele ducked around the cherub to get a closer look. "I've never seen a mirror like that. What's it made of?"

"Quicksilver." He frowned. "Salt...fire...and blood. Fused with Alchemical magic. It's solid and liquid at the same time. It's not possible. Or at least, it shouldn't be possible." His gaze found Fortunato. "You say your friend is trapped in here?"

"Yes. That nasty Nephil trapped him. Can you get him out?"

"Let's see," Michael said. He laid the mirror in his left palm and passed his right hand over it.

A wispy creature tumbled out, quickly expanding until it matched the cherub in size. Its body and its wings were dark and insubstantial, a mere shadow. Its pale, skull-like face sent a chill down Cybele's spine. Fortunato caught the odd being in his chubby arms and eased it to the ground.

Michael examined the quicksilver, frowning. "This thing needs more study," he said, slipping it into his jeans pocket.

Fortunato hovered anxiously over his fallen friend. "Maweth!" he called. "Maweth! Can you hear me?"

Michael looked up sharply. "Did you say Maweth?"

The cherub nodded vigorously. "Yes. Maweth."

"Who—or what—is he?" Cybele peered down at the unconscious figure and experienced an overwhelming surge of panic. She wanted to run, to put as much distance between herself and the creature as she could, as quickly as possible. And she wanted, desperately, to kick it away from Arthur.

"Maweth is the Demon of Death," Michael said. "He came into being after Adam and Eve ate the apple. He's the personification of sin and hopelessness." He glanced at Fortunato. "And you say he's your friend?"

"Yes. He's so much fun. We play games together."

"That," Michael said, "is the most ridiculous thing I've ever heard. Angels and demons can't be friends."

Fortunato's bottom lip pushed out in a pout. "That's not true. I'm friends with Maweth." The cherub jabbed a finger at Cybele. "And *you're* friends with *her.*"

Michael's cheeks resumed their crimson flush. Fortunato, however, had turned back to the unconscious demon. "Wake him up. Please, Michael, wake him up. Or at least heal him like you did with that Nephil over there."

Michael muttered something distinctly un-angelic under his breath. He shook his head and sighed. Bending down, he touched his forefinger to Maweth's pale forehead.

The demon's eyes snapped open.

"Maweth!" Fortunato threw himself on his friend, and covered his face with kisses.

"What the—" The demon sat up and swatted him away. "Lucky, cut it out! You know I hate—" He caught sight of Michael and Cybele. "Hell. Who're they?"

"This is Michael," Fortunato cried joyously. "The archangel. He saved you!"

"And that one?" Maweth asked, eyeing Cybele warily.

Fortunato sobered. "Oh. She's Cybele. She's a Nephil."

Maweth scrambled to his feet. "A Nephil!"

"But not a full-grown one. She can't hurt—"

A blast of sulfurous wind snatched the words from the cherub's mouth. A stream of soot hit Cybele square in the face. She gagged and dissolved into a fit of coughing.

Fortunato beat his wings, trying to shake the soot out of the gossamer feathers. "Yuk. I want a bath."

Michael held out his hand. "I'll take you back to Heaven, and you can get one."

"Can Maweth come too?"

"To Heaven? Of course not."

The cherub crossed his arms. "Then forget it." He grimaced. "I don't think it's smart for me to go back there anyway. Raphael's going to be reeeally mad at me. I helped a bunch of Nephilim get through his celestial seal."

"And then your feathers destroyed the seal entirely," Cybele informed him, ignoring Michael's glare. "That's what let the demon horde escape."

"What!?" Fortunato blanched.

Maweth groaned. "So that's what Dusek did with those feathers. I told you, Lucky, that you weren't going to like it."

"That settles it then. No way am I going back to Heaven. Not for a long, long time." The cherub blinked beseechingly up at Michael. "Take me and Maweth somewhere else? Pleeeeease?"

Michael sighed. "Oh, all right. Come on."

Fortunato flew up to perch on the archangel's right shoulder. Maweth, after a brief hesitation, stretched his wings and joined him. Michael bent and, without any apparent effort at all, hoisted Arthur's limp body over his left shoulder. He anchored the back of Arthur's legs with one arm and held his free hand out to Cybele.

Their eyes met. After a brief hesitation, she placed her

hand in his. "Where are we going?"

He tugged her close and wrapped his arm around her waist. His lips brushed her temple.

"Someplace safe," he said.

***

Cybele, I'm sorry.

Luc couldn't have said how many hours he drove. Miles and miles of back road rolled past the pickup. He was aware of turmoil, both his own and his sister's. She was in trouble, he sensed, and there was nothing he could do about it. Another shortcoming to add to his long list of failures.

His gas tank was just about empty. The night was oppressive. A storm was brewing, angry clouds rolling in from the bay. He abandoned the truck on a stretch of industrial highway near a lagoon fed from the gulf. A chain-link fence topped with razor wire separated the road from a field of massive oil tanks.

Lightning flashed. A rumble of thunder followed. The electric-charged atmosphere lifted the fine hairs of Luc's nape. Sultry wind gusted, heavy with particulates discharged from the refinery. Each breath intensified the acrid taste at the back of his throat.

No humans in sight at this time of night. Even so, Luc kept a watchful eye out as he approached the fence. He couldn't afford mistakes. He was done being Mab's slave. If he had to die for his freedom, well then, what the fuck? He'd die.

Suicide didn't come easily to a Nephil adept. With no afterlife awaiting, his race had developed an incredibly strong instinct for survival. Luc had to do this right the first time. He wouldn't have the strength for a second attempt.

The wounds inflicted by Mab's whip still burned though not as intensely as they had in the cellar. He was aware, as always, of the wooden collar constricting his neck. His thrallstone throbbed painfully. The discomfort was manageable. He was sure he could shift through it. And call at least some magic. Would it be enough? *It had to be.*

Up until this point in his escape, he hadn't used any magic. As soon as he did, Mab would feel the power surging through his thrallstone. It would take a while, however, for her to locate him. By the time she did, it would be too late. He'd be gone.

He closed his eyes and willed his demon form to the fore. His vision took on a red cast. His wings erupted from his back. He unfurled them slowly and flew to the top of the nearest oil tank. Its roof bulged, sloping upward from the perimeter to the center where a pipe protruded. Luc landed next it and studied its ventilator valve.

As a child, he'd been taught to fear Oblivion above all else. Facing it now should have terrified him. Strangely, he could only view the prospect of eternal annihilation with mild curiosity. Death existed on the other side of his pain. It represented peace. Peace and...nothingness.

The storm was passing to the south. Luc placed his hand on the valve and imagined it open. Imagination became reality. Some miles away, lightning flashed. Luc looked inward, his mind sifting through the talents of his Druid magic. *Water.* Of the three elements of Druid magic—stone, wood, and water—water was the most difficult element to control. But it was the one he needed.

Come to me.

The clouds obeyed his command, shifting course, streaming north toward Luc's call. Fat raindrops, propelled by driving wind, stung his face and torso.

Lightning cracked like a whip, brilliant in Luc's vision. With an angry hiss, the open valve sucked in oxygen and electricity. A brief, silent moment followed.

The stillness gave way to a roar like a freight train hurtling off its track. The noise whipped into a fury under Luc's feet. The oil tank's steel roof heated. Black smoke burst from the vent pipe, blasting into Luc's face.

Bare seconds of his life remained. A wild urge to spread his wings and fly came upon him. It took all his strength to resist.

A faint emotion stirred in the deepest part of his instinct. Whatever trouble his sister had been in, she'd come through it. She was safe, at least for now. Relief flooded his body. The profound release of tension made it easier, somehow, to face his own end.

He spread his arms. *Cybele, I'm sorry.*

TWENTY-ONE

"Someplace safe" turned out to be a dingy apartment.

She wasn't sure how they'd gotten here. She'd expected Michael to fly. She'd wondered how he was going to cut a path through a sky thick with hellfiends while carrying two Nephilim, a cherub, and a demon.

He didn't even bother to try. The field in which they stood simply vanished. An instant later an off-white wall fronted by a threadbare green couch materialized. It was accompanied by a stained carpet, a table surrounded by mismatched chairs, and a pair of dirty windows with crooked shades. An old television sat at an angle in one corner. Glancing out one of the windows, Cybele saw they were five or six stories above the street in a densely urban setting.

Michael's arm slid from her waist. She stumbled a bit before she found her balance. The cherub and his unlikely friend leaped from the archangel's shoulder, hands joined, to land on the couch. Michael turned and, with Arthur's limp form still slung over his shoulder, strode down a short hallway.

Cybele hurried in his wake. "Where are we, exactly?"

He shouldered open a door. "Southwark."

"Where's that?"

"London."

London was his idea of a safe location? "I'm not sure

that's such a good idea."

"Why not?"

"It's not exactly off the beaten path. Mab's looking for us. She's the Druid alpha and—"

"I know who Mab is." He shot her a look. "And I know what she is."

"Then you know why we can't let her find us. We need to hide."

He lowered Arthur onto a sagging double bed. "The best place to hide is in plain sight."

"What kind of stupid logic is that?"

He turned, eyeing her frankly. "A simple thank you would be sufficient."

"I thanked you already." She went to the side of the bed. Arthur lay sprawled on his back, arms flung wide, face gray. He looked like death itself. Her chest squeezed so tightly she could hardly breathe.

"You're welcome," Michael said. Out of the corner of her eye, she saw him move toward the door.

She turned. "Where are you going?"

"To find Raphael. I've been gone too long. He's got to have noticed by now." He disappeared into the hallway.

She smoothed a lock of hair off Arthur's forehead. She kissed the spot where it'd been. Then she turned away and followed Michael into the flat's living room, where the archangel stood conversing with Fortunato and Maweth.

"You really should let me take you to Heaven," he was telling the cherub. "I swear Raphael won't punish you. There would be no point to it. The damage is done."

"Maybe I'd go home," Fortunato said slowly. "But only if Maweth can come too."

Maweth snorted. "Forget that. They'd never let me in."

"Sure they would." The cherub's blue eyes blinked. "Michael, tell him it's okay."

Michael ran a hand over his head. "Um...I'm going to have to agree with Maweth on this one, Fortunato. Heaven is not going to welcome the Demon of Death with open arms."

"See? I told you." Maweth shook his head. "Honestly, Lucky, do you have even half a brain? Look. Just go to Heaven without me. I'll be fine here on Earth."

"No." The cherub crossed his arms over his chubby chest. "If Heaven won't have you, it won't get me either. I'm staying here. With you."

"Not a good idea," Michael said. "In case you haven't noticed, there's a hellfiend invasion. Earth's not the best place for you to be right now."

"I don't care." The little angel pouted. "I'm staying. Unless—" He eyed his unlikely friend uncertainly. "Unless...Maweth doesn't want me here?"

Maweth looked discomfited. "Of course I want you here," he mumbled.

Michael looked from cherub to demon, clearly nonplussed. "This...friendship," he said, "is highly irregular."

"No more irregular than archangels consorting with Nephilim," Maweth pointed out.

Michael's expression shuttered. "All right, all right. Fine. But please. Stay in this flat until the sky clears."

"When's that going to be?" Fortunato asked.

Michael shrugged. "No clue."

"And when whoever lives here shows up?" Cybele asked. "What then?"

"No one lives here. The flat's yours for as long as you want it. You'll find the keys and a copy of the lease on the desk in the second bedroom. There's food in the kitchen. There's no need to go out, so don't. Mab can't find you as long as you stay inside."

"What? How did you manage all that?"

He shrugged. "I have a few talents. Now I've really got to get—" His brows snapped together. "Cybele? Are you okay?"

No. She felt as though a boulder had slammed into her head. Her ears were ringing. Her chest was tight. She couldn't breathe, and her hands had gone clammy. Cold sweat dripped down her brow. Her legs shook.

"I'm going to throw up..."

She was only dimly aware of Michael guiding her to the couch. His hand, warm and large, came down on the back of her neck, urging her to drop her head between her knees.

She tasted bile. *Luc*, she thought. *Luc*.

Michael knelt in front of her. After a moment, when she thought she wouldn't vomit in his face, she looked up.

"Cybele, what's wrong?"

"Luc," she choked out. "He's..." *Cybele, I'm sorry.* Her twin's plea made itself known, not in words but in a raw feeling deep in her bones.

"Luc?" Michael's brows drew in. "Who's Luc?"

"My twin brother. He's...Mab's thrall. Luc and I, we're...oh, I don't know how to describe it. Linked, I guess you'd say. Emotionally."

"And you feel something about him? Something bad?"

She looked up at the archangel, into his beautiful, concerned eyes. "He's going to kill himself."

***

Luc lay face down on a slick surface amid an overwhelming stink of urine. There was a disgusting taste on his tongue and a painful ringing inside his skull. And behind the ringing... He strained his ears at the noise, which seemed to echo down a long, oppressive tunnel.

Behind the ringing...the sound of...

Traffic?

There was no traffic in Oblivion. In Oblivion, there was no sound at all. No sickening odors. No horrible tastes. No slimy surfaces.

A car horn blared.

This makes no sense. No sense at all. He was dead. Wasn't he?

Maybe not.

He cracked open one eyelid. He was sprawled on his stomach in a dank alley beside an overflowing garbage bin. A door set in a brick wall lay less than ten feet in front of him. A vent above it spewed a greasy odor. It blended nauseatingly with the urine smell. A window, its glass painted black, was cracked open an inch. Luc heard the clank of pots and voices speaking a language he didn't understand.

He set his palms on the ground. A rank substance oozed between his fingers. His head was pounding. He squinted upward. The buildings on either side of the alley were several stories high. The slice of sky above them was gray, spitting a half-hearted drizzle down on his head.

One end of the alley died into a brick wall. In the opposite direction, about thirty feet away, he could see a street. Traffic passed in a steady stream. A pair of pedestrians—two young women—hurried along the sidewalk. They quickly passed out of view.

Where the hell was he? Houston? Dallas? The last thing he remembered was the oil tank exploding beneath him. He'd made sure escape was impossible. Or so he'd thought.

He was in human form. And his back no longer burned. He peered down at his shoulder, where Mab's whip had left a particularly nasty gash. All that was left of the wound was a faint red line. The other marks she'd made on him, what he could see of them at least, were completely gone. His thrall collar remained fastened around his neck. But the ruby had ceased to throb, and the wood felt looser.

Strange and stranger. His mind balked at the effort it required to make sense of it. His wounds might be healed, but his human body remained a long way from full strength. It took supreme effort to push himself into a sitting position. Once he managed it, he sagged against the brick wall, panting. The movement startled a rat that had been busily picking at a rotten rind. The creature froze. It scurried away without its prize.

Well. A least Luc was still able to scare something.

It took another few minutes before he felt ready to stand. He rose unsteadily, grasping at the wall, his breath uneven. Long moments passed before his head stopped spinning. Experimentally, he stood straight. His legs, surprisingly, supported his weight.

He glanced down the alley, toward the dead end. The passage was deserted. Luc had no wish to bang on the door of the greasy spoon or on the only other door he could see, about twenty feet down on the other side of the alley. He turned and took a step toward the street.

"Luc."

A man's voice, low and smooth. Behind him. Where just two seconds before no one had been. He spun around.

A man of Middle Eastern descent—the kind of guy who wouldn't last two seconds in a Texas biker bar—stood not five feet away. He was young and lean, dressed all in black, except for the unfastened silver frogs on his vintage military jacket. The costume should have made him look ridiculous. Somehow, it didn't. The harsh angles of his face, his unshaven jaw, his lean build, and—most of all—the expression in his dark eyes, shouted danger.

Luc tensed. Green sparks crackled on his fingertips. Shifting onto the balls of his feet, he prepared for a fight. One threatening move and he'd blast the guy. But the dark man didn't react. After about a minute, Luc's fighting stance began to feel foolish. He dropped his hands and let the hellfire fade.

"It was a very near thing," the stranger said. "I barely got you out in time."

Luc blinked. "I don't understand."

"That oil tank. It's still burning. It's going to take them days to put it out."

"You—" Luc swallowed, his throat suddenly dry. "Are you saying you...rescued me?"

"Yes."

Son of a bitch. "Why?" Luc asked. "How? Who the hell are you?"

Amusement glinted in the stranger's eyes. "You're welcome."

"I'm supposed to be grateful?"

"It's better than being dead."

"I'll be the judge of that," Luc snapped. Whoever this creature was, Luc didn't trust him. He wasn't eager to test the stranger's fighting skills though. "Who do you think you are, anyway? My fucking guardian angel?"

The stranger laughed at that, his white teeth glinting. "There's a thought." His gaze rested on Luc's neck for a moment, and his expression sobered. "I couldn't remove the collar. It's a pact between Nephilim. I have no power over it."

Luc stiffened. "What do you know about the Nephilim?"

"More than I wish I did. And yet, somehow, it's not enough." He gestured toward the street. "See that building? Go there. Top floor, number 622."

Luc glanced over his shoulder. "Why should I—" The

question died when he looked back at the stranger.

He was gone. Just like that, as if he'd never been there at all. Maybe he hadn't been, Luc thought, rubbing his temple. Maybe he was hallucinating. Or insane. Or maybe he was dead after all, existing in some inexplicable space between life and Oblivion.

With nothing better to do, he walked to the end of the alley and stepped out onto the sidewalk. As he eyed the building the stranger had pointed him towards, a red double-decker bus rolled by. *King's Cross*, the destination sign read.

What the—? Luc's gaze followed the bus until it turned at the corner.

"Jesus, mate! Get out of the bloody middle of the walk."

Luc stepped back to let the irritated pedestrian pass. Not Houston or Dallas. But...London? What was he doing in London?

He crossed the road. The apartment building wasn't locked. He pushed the street door open and walked past a gauntlet of bicycles. No elevator. He took the stairs.

Number 622 was at the very end of the corridor. It was occupied. He could hear someone pacing behind the door. He paused, his apprehension growing. He tried looking through a peephole only to find it blocked on the other side. Finally, with a shake of his head, he knocked and braced himself.

The pacing halted. He heard a faint metallic scrape— someone had uncovered the peephole, he guessed. He stared a challenge at it.

The door flew open.

"Luc!" With a cry and a flurry of long limbs and blond hair, a woman threw herself into his arms. "You're alive! He found you in time!"

He stumbled backward, his arms closing, his heart

pounding so hard he thought his ribs might crack. It was only after a long moment that he grasped his sister by the shoulders and eased her back. Their eyes met. A beat of silence ensued.

"Cybele," he said finally. "What the goddamn holy fuck is going on?"

***

Michael's moral compass spun like a top.

A profound sense of shame pursued him as he glided over London, keeping to a higher elevation than the demon horde. What in Heaven's name was he doing, aiding and abetting a cursed race? Lusting after one of their females? Ignoring Raphael's orders just so he could save her? And he'd hadn't stopped there. He'd let her talk him into snatching her Nephil lover from certain death. And then he'd saved her brother, a bare instant before he ended his own miserable life. Stars above. If Raphael ever discovered even half of Michael's sins, Michael's ass would be toast.

So why was it that he had only to picture Cybele's green eyes, snapping with passion, to know he didn't regret any of it?

For the first time in his millennia-long existence, Michael understood the temptations the original Watcher angels had faced when they lived on Earth. To make matters worse, Cybele was only half-human. Her other half had its origins in Heaven. It was hardly her fault that her Watcher ancestors had fallen.

Dear God Almighty, what was he saying? He couldn't rationalize his behavior on such specious grounds, no matter how many loopholes the situation was riddled with. Cybele was a cursed being. A Nephil. A demon. Michael had been wrong to save her. The deed was done, however.

He just wanted to put the whole sorry episode behind him. He fished his cell phone from his back pocket. Raphael was right. The human device was an abomination. If Michael's attention hadn't been snared by all those videos of human copulation, each one more depraved and more compelling than the last... He jerked his mind back to the present.

Never. Again.

Before he could lose his nerve, he tossed the phone over his shoulder. The hellfiends and ash quickly consumed it. He felt a pang at its loss, but he hardened his heart against it. It was time to get back to the purpose for which he was created: righteous vengeance.

Where was Raphael? After a brief search, Michael found his brother occupying a spot over the English Channel, midway between Dover and Calais. Wings aloft, scything right and left with his golden sword, Raphael cut a wide swath through a field of fiends.

Unfortunately, the field was much, much wider than Raphael's reach.

With a flick of his wrist, Michael's switchblade snapped into his palm. He dove down and took up a position at his brother's right side.

Raphael shot him a glance. "Where in Heaven's name have you been?"

"I was unexpectedly detained," Michael said. "But I'm here now."

Hellfiends were dirty little creatures, formed by the eternal malice of damned souls. Grimly, Michael set to killing as many of the mindless demons as he could. It didn't take long for him to realize the effort was futile. There were just too many of the things, with more arriving every second.

They smelled god-awful.

"This is crazy," he told Raphael. "We're never going to get rid of them this way."

Raphael skewered three at once. He lowered his blade and the carcasses slid off. "You have a better idea?"

"Yes. Wake the Almighty."

"No." Raphael's sword came up with a vicious slash. Five hellfiends died shrieking. "Not an option."

"That's your pride speaking." Michael decided not to point out that pride was a deadly sin, just as much as lust was. Who was he to throw stones? Executing a half-lunge, half-dive, he skewered a red-potato body. Its lumpy head exploded. Fetid remains splattered his coat. *Ugh.*

"We'll never kill all of them in hand-to-hand combat," he said. "Even if we keep at it from now until the End of Days."

"I know that," Raphael conceded. He spun a circle, golden blade flashing. Demon heads went flying.

Michael slashed right and left. Six fiends tumbled earthward. They splashed into the channel far below.

"We need another plan," Raphael said.

"Which is?" Michael inquired.

"I'm working on it."

TWENTY-TWO

The rasp of Arthur's breathing combined with the sound of Luc's pacing made Cybele want to scream. She didn't want to admit it, but she was terrified.

It's the waiting, she thought. *I hate waiting.* She fingered her touchstone, once again safe in her possession. She'd found it in Arthur's pocket. Where and when he'd come across it, she didn't know.

"Could you please stand still? Just for two seconds?"

Luc halted. "Sorry."

The last two days were a blur. They'd showered and dressed in the clean clothes they'd found stashed in the bedroom dressers. While the guys' clothing provided was basic enough—jeans, t-shirts, boxers—the feminine items had been more personal. The jeans were her favorite brand, in exactly her size. The blouses were the flowery, flowing kind she loved. And there'd been cute panties and bras. Not racy, but still. Had Michael picked them out for her? If so, just when, exactly, had the archangel done it?

She and Luc had taken turns sleeping and watching over Arthur. At the moment, they were both awake, standing on opposite sides of Arthur's bed. If not for the scant rise and fall of his chest, punctuated by the occasional rasping inhale, they might easily have been looking at a corpse.

Maybe he won't wake up. No. Michael said he'd wake.

Surely the archangel knew what he was talking about. But if Arthur wasn't dying, he wasn't improving either. His face was ashen, his body lifeless. The room's single lamp, positioned on an old dresser, cast a half-hearted glow in the direction of the bed. Cybele took up the pacing her twin had abandoned. Luc moved to the window, his expression grim.

The new day had dawned cold and gray and had only grown darker as the morning wore on. It was now past noon. The sky was turbulent. A steady drizzle fell. Pedestrians scurried by with open umbrellas. They looked harried but not unduly panicked. They must think, Cybele realized, that what was in the sky was just weather. Stupid humans had no idea that a horde of hellfiends was streaming over their heads.

"I should leave." Luc looked like hell. He had dark circles under his eyes and several days' growth of beard on his jaw. His hair, straighter and a darker shade of blond than Cybele's, was in dire need of a brush.

"No." She left Arthur's side and went to her twin. She wanted to touch him, put a hand on his arm, but something in his expression stopped her. "No," she repeated. "Don't you dare even think about leaving."

His lips compressed into a harsh line. "Every minute I stay here makes it more likely that Mab will find us."

"Let her look. As long as you don't use magic, she can't track you. And this apartment is safe. Michael promised—"

"That's another thing I'm having trouble with," he said. "You and that fucking archangel."

"What about him?" Cybele asked warily.

"You can't possibly trust him."

"Why not?" she said. "He saved me. He saved Arthur. And you."

Luc turned to lean against the wall, his arms crossed.

"It's got to be a trick. Some game he's playing."

"It's not." She shoved a lock of hair out of her eyes. "Michael isn't like that."

"You some kind of expert on archangels now?" He expelled a rough breath. "What he's done makes no goddamned sense."

No. It made some kind of sense. *The archangel's got a hard-on for me.* She imagined saying those words to Luc. Forget it. It would sound preposterous, not to mention unbelievably conceited. Anyway, it probably wasn't strictly true. Angels couldn't get hard-ons. Could they?

Maybe Luc was right. Maybe Michael's assistance was part of a larger heavenly plot against the Nephilim. That certainly wouldn't be surprising, given her race's prior experience with Heaven's finest.

But the fact remained that he'd helped her, and not in a small way. "Arthur'd be in Oblivion right now if not for Michael," she said. "I'd be on my way to being Dusek's thrall, and you'd be dead."

"Okay. Fine. I can't argue with any of that. But I still think you're a fool to trust him."

She shrugged. "I probably won't ever see him again, anyway."

"Let's hope not." His eyes strayed to Merlin's staff. The two pieces lay on the dresser. Leaving the window, Luc picked up the top half and peered into the crystal. "So. Arthur pulled Merlin's lost staff from a rock and opened a portal to Hell."

"He didn't mean to. If he'd known what would happen, he never would've done it."

"Maybe," Luc said.

"What do you mean by that?"

"You said Dusek was dragging you off. If Arthur thought the staff was his best chance to save you, he'd have grabbed it no matter what the consequences."

Cybele looked at Arthur's face, his sunken eyes and dry lips, and knew Luc spoke the truth.

"I really doubt," he continued, "that an archangel would just hand over Merlin's staff to the only Nephil who could destroy the Earth with it. We're missing something here."

"Michael said Arthur might be able to use it to send the fiends back to Hell."

"I can't believe the archangel is so naïve as to trust Arthur to do it. With Merlin's staff, Arthur could become the most powerful being on Earth. Hell, he could probably use it to enslave all humanity."

"Yeah, well, Arthur has no interest in enslaving humanity."

"No man knows what he'll do," Luc said quietly. "Not until he does it."

His voice was flat, his eyes bleak. Cybele bit back her retort. Not for the first time, she wondered what crimes Mab had forced Luc to commit since he'd become her thrall.

Luc glanced at her. "Not even an archangel can predict what Arthur will do with the powers of Merlin."

"Well, at this point," Cybele said, "it's all conjecture anyway. The staff's broken."

Luc fitted the pieces together, and then separated them again. "Maybe your archangel left it here to taunt us. Now that I could believe."

"Well, I can't. And I told you, he's not my archangel." She sat down on the edge of the bed and picked up Arthur's hand. Cold. Her heart constricted. "I just wish he would wake up. I love him, Luc."

"Hardly a newsflash," he said dryly.

"I know. But that's not all. Arthur and I—we've

pledged a life bond."

His eyes widened. "Mab will never recognize it."

"Arthur and I are rogue. Mab can rot in Oblivion."

"I wish I could send her there for you," he muttered.

"Arthur will get rid of her. With or without the staff. When he wakes up. If he wakes up." She rubbed Arthur's hand between both of hers. "His skin is so dry, Luc. And cold." Her voice trembled. "It's like he's dead already."

"He's not," Luc said sharply. He eyed her. "But you know, you hardly look any better. When was the last time you ate?"

She tried to remember. Since she'd arrived in London, she'd been too upset to eat. "I—a couple nights ago, I guess." With the Spencers. It seemed like a year ago. She thought of Jack, and a deep sadness passed through her.

Luc was talking, asking something. Cybele looked at him blankly. "What did you say?"

"I said, is there food in this place?"

"I think so. At least, Michael said there was. I haven't looked."

"Let's go see."

"But— I don't want to leave Arthur."

"He'll wake up. Or he won't. You sitting here staring at him is not going to make a difference."

Reluctantly, she released Arthur's hand. "I guess."

The flat's kitchen was tiny. The refrigerator was crammed full of food. So were the cupboards. Luc had carried the broken pieces of the staff with him from the bedroom. He propped them against the wall by the door. He started coffee in an old electric coffeemaker and proceeded to assemble a couple large sandwiches.

"I couldn't possibly eat that much," Cybele protested as they entered the flat's main room, where a round dining table stood in one corner.

He set the plate down. "Try."

After the first reluctant bite, she realized just how hungry she was. "Thank you."

"Anytime." He consumed his own sandwich in large, efficient bites and washed it down with a swig of black coffee.

She concentrated on his face, on his hazel eyes. Not on the wooden thrall collar and its ruby. "I'm glad you're here."

"You shouldn't be. My presence is a danger to you."

"I don't care." Cybele peered into her coffee cup. The liquid trembled. Her hand, she realized, was shaking. "I'm just so glad you're away from Mab. And Luc—I'm sorry."

His head went back. "Sorry? For what?"

She put down her cup, sloshing coffee over the edge. "For avoiding you, ever since..."

"Since my Ordeal." His shoulders hunched. "I don't blame you for that. You could hardly do anything else considering. Arthur warned me what it would be like. I refused to believe him. I was too much of a coward to go rogue."

"You're not a coward. If you were, you would've gone to Mab the instant I left Demon's Hollow."

"Didn't you think I would?" he asked.

"No. Of course not. That's the only reason I dared to run. But I knew she'd take it out on you. She did, didn't she?" The sudden remoteness in his eyes was her answer. "I'm sorry, Luc."

"Forget it." He rose abruptly and crossed the room to the old television in the corner. The remote lay beside it on the stand. He picked it up. "I wonder if your angel got you a cable subscription, too."

He's not my angel. "Try it," Cybele said.

He hit a button. The screen sputtered to life.

Every single channel had abandoned its regular programming to report on the situation in Wales. Cybele left the table and joined Luc in front of the set. A female reporter stood in a farm field, her sooty trench coat buffeted by a stiff wind. Billowing clouds, interspersed with jagged lightning, filled the sky.

"This is Brooke Markham, reporting from Swansea, Wales, approximately twenty-five miles from the site of the disaster. The previously unknown volcano came to life in the hour before dawn on Tuesday, rocking the countryside and sending a blast of ash into the sky. Two days later, the eruption continues unabated."

"They're saying it's a volcano?" Cybele said incredulously. "In *Wales*? Who the hell's going to believe that?"

"Most people, probably," Luc said. "It's a lot easier to believe in a volcanic eruption than a demon invasion."

"Someone's going to figure out the truth."

"Yeah, a few nutjobs. The same guys who go for chemtrails and aliens. Who's going to believe them?"

The reporter droned on. "... authorities have blockaded surrounding roadways. More than seventy persons are confirmed dead with many more missing. Injuries are overwhelming local hospitals. The public is advised to avoid the area. The ash plume represents a danger to air travel as well. All airports in the UK and Ireland have suspended operations indefinitely. Passengers are advised to contact their carriers for updates."

"How long do you think this'll last?" Cybele asked.

"Hell if I know," Luc said.

"I wish Arthur would wake up." Cybele's eyes strayed toward the hallway leading to the bedrooms. "What if he doesn't? What'll we do? We can't hide in this apartment forever. But we can't leave, not without Arthur. He's the only one who can stand up to Mab."

"Every adept in Demon's Hollow is Mab's thrall," Luc conceded. "Except Evander, of course, but we both know our father is a coward. But...do you remember the challenge after Arthur's father was killed?"

"Of course I remember. The British Druids arrived in Texas barely a day after Mab arrived with Arthur." Cybele had caught only a glimpse of the frightened boy before Mab had thrown him into the cellar.

"You remember any of them?" Luc pressed.

"I remember the one who dueled with Mab," Cybele said. "The Scot. Magnus. The rest of them surrendered their touchstones and flew the hell back to England as quick as lightning after she killed him."

Mab had never called the British Druids back to Texas again. She'd told them Arthur was dead. She hadn't wanted them to discover the truth.

"There were at least ten," Luc said, "including dormants."

"None of the kids were older than us," she said. "They wouldn't be adepts yet. What does it matter?"

"I just wonder where they all are now."

"Who cares? Mab took their touchstones and forced them to accept her rubies. They all pledged fealty to her."

"Fealty isn't like being enthralled," Luc said. "It's not a lifetime vow. The promise can be broken."

"If any of them were strong enough to beat Mab, they would've done it seven years ago. I doubt any of them are going to step up to the plate now. If they tried to kill her and lost, they'd end up in Oblivion. Or wearing a thrall collar."

"No one's going to be dueling Mab," a voice behind her said. "Except me."

Cybele spun around. "Arthur!"

TWENTY-THREE

Arthur braced one arm against the wall. He felt like death warmed over and knew he looked worse. He'd hardly recognized himself in the bedroom mirror. A tap on the shoulder would likely send him crashing to the floor. If a crushing sense of relief didn't send him there first. Cybele was alive. Alive and...his eyes narrowed. Alive and here with *Luc?* What the fuck?

She gave a cry and rushed him. He held up a hand before she could knock into him. She halted, uncertainly, a few steps away.

His chin jerked. "What's he doing here? Where's his mistress?"

"Arthur." Cybele put a hand on his arm. "It's okay. Mab doesn't know where we are."

He eyed Luc's thrall collar. "Unless the bitch is dead, she's searching. When he casts magic, she'll know which direction to look."

Luc's expression went hard, but he made no reply.

"He hasn't cast any magic. And besides, she can't see into—" Cybele tugged Arthur toward a sagging blue sofa. "Sit down and I'll explain."

He let her guide him, because, bugger it all, his legs were shaky. He made it to the couch and sat down heavily. Bracing his elbows on his thighs, he bowed his head and willed the room to stop spinning.

Cybele sank down beside him. An old telly, on a stand in the corner, was on.

"—speaking with Helena Grant-Barclay, professor of geology at the University of Cambridge. Dr. Grant-Barclay, what do you make of this catastrophic situation?"

"Brooke, the eruption in Wales has shocked the scientific community. The notion that an active volcanic system exists in the UK is not something research has heretofore uncovered."

Arthur looked up. "Volcano?"

"But there have been several earthquakes in the UK in recent years," the reporter protested. "Including, I'm told, a tremor in Wales. Weren't those events red flags?"

"Not necessarily," the geologist replied. "Most tremors aren't caused by volcanic activity. Movement is common at major tectonic boundaries, such as those between continents. Minor fault lines exist throughout Scotland, Kent, and the Home Counties. UK monitoring stations record hundreds of tremors each year. Out of these, only ten or so are strong enough to be felt by the public."

"I see. But tremors can be also caused by volcanic activity, can they not?"

"That is very true," Dr. Grant-Barclay allowed. "There are more than sixty active volcanoes in Europe. The Icelandic volcanoes—most notably Eyjafjallajökull and Bárðarbunga—are extremely active on the boundary of the Eurasian and North American plates. A large volcanic system also exists beneath the Cheb Basin on the German-Czech border, which has, in recent years, seen clusters of quakes and evidence of magma moving toward the surface."

"No hint of such activity was detected in Wales?"

Dr. Grant-Barclay gave a terse shake of her head. "No. It was not. The Carmarthen eruption has, in a word, astounded the scientific world."

"The eruption has been going on for more than two days," the reporter continued. "Can you—"

"What?" Arthur jerked his head toward Cybele. "Two days? Is that true?"

"—an idea as to how long it will last?"

"Unfortunately, no," the geologist said. "These events are difficult to predict. It may be days, weeks, or perhaps even months before the eruption subsides."

The reporter received this prognosis with a grave expression. "Thank you, Dr. Grant-Barclay, for your insight. We go now to Glangwili General Hospital in Carmarthen, for a report on casualties. We've received word that the hospital, which lies just two miles from the eruption, is in the process of evacuating all its patients to Swansea—"

"Enough babble." Luc pointed the remote at the TV. The sound cut off, though the picture played on.

"Two days." Arthur eyed the silent screen where a new reporter was attempting an interview with a harried doctor amid a panicked stream of gurneys and wheelchairs. "Two fucking days." He scrubbed a hand down his face. "I've really been out that long?"

"More like a two and a half days," Cybele said.

From the dark circles under Cybele's eyes, he guessed she'd been awake much of that time. "No wonder I'm so goddamned thirsty," he muttered.

Luc disappeared into the kitchen, returning a moment later with water. Arthur drained the glass and set it down on the coffee table. He hoped his stomach wouldn't heave it out again.

"Thanks," he said.

"Do you want more?" Cybele asked.

"Not right now." He rose, swaying dangerously. Cybele

jumped up to help him. He waved her off and made his way to the window. He peered skyward through the glass.

"Jesus fucking Christ." He turned and sagged against the wall. "There must be millions of those things up there. Because of me." He closed his eyes briefly. "Where the hell are we, anyway?"

"London," Cybele said.

"How?"

Cybele and Luc exchanged glances. Neither looked particularly anxious to answer. Arthur's attention sharpened. "What's going on?"

"Go ahead," Luc told his sister, "tell him. See if he can make any more sense of it than I can."

Cybele sighed and did as her brother asked. When she'd finished, Arthur regarded her with frank incredulity. "Let me get this straight," he said. "While I was fighting Raphael, the Archangel Michael saved you from Dusek? And then threw me and Luc into the bargain just because you asked him to?"

"That's what I said," Cybele said irritably. "Because that's what happened."

"I don't doubt that. You could hardly make up something so ridiculous."

"Ridiculous?" Cybele's tone took on a sharp edge. "What's so ridiculous about you not being dead?" She crossed her arms. "You know, he said you wouldn't be grateful."

"He was right," Arthur said. "This whole business is dodgy. No archangel doles out free favors to Nephilim. Michael must have some kind of agenda."

"That's just what I told her," Luc said.

"I have no idea why he did it," Cybele said, her eyes sliding momentarily away. She fiddled with the end of her braid, and then flipped the long rope over her shoulder. "I was too busy worrying about both your asses to ask him."

"The archangel didn't stop with saving our lives," Luc said. "He left us Merlin's staff."

Arthur went still. "The staff? It's here?"

"Yes. Luc left it in the kitchen." Cybele unfolded her legs and rose from the couch. A moment later she returned, carrying the two halves of Merlin's staff.

Arthur stood as she approached. "It's broken?"

"Michael said Raphael cracked it in half with his sword." Cybele handed him the pieces. "Don't you remember?"

"No. Not really."

"Michael also said you might be able to mend it."

"Fucking Michael again," Arthur muttered, ignoring Cybele's scowl as he examined the broken staff. He ran his hand along the twisted wood but felt nothing. The crystal, which he'd last seen brilliant with Merlin's magic, was dark.

"Luc's right. Why would Michael give this to me? His brother nearly killed me over it."

"He thinks that if you can make it whole, you may be able to drive the hellfiends back into Hell. Like Merlin did."

"And die like Merlin did? I'm sure he'd be happy about that." He passed his palm over the upper arc of the crystal, in its setting of oak, rowan, and yew. A spark, like static electricity on a cold day, jolted his thumb. He couldn't be sure, though, if it was magic.

"Do you feel anything?" Cybele asked.

"I don't know." Balancing the lower half of the staff on the floor, he fitted the upper piece to it. The break was jagged, but no wood seemed to have been lost—the pieces matched perfectly. He wrapped both hands around the joining. Drawing focus from his mother's touchstone, he called his magic.

"It's got to be dead," Luc muttered under his breath. "Michael never would have left it here otherwise."

Arthur closed his eyes, concentrating. A current of electricity, faint but unmistakable, ran through his body. His arms went rigid. The moonstone, in contact with his chest, warmed.

"Wait," Cybele whispered. "Luc, look."

Arthur opened his eyes. Tendrils of flame, unfurling from his hands, licked up and down the staff. Magic caressed the ancient woods, weaving a pattern of light.

He tightened his grip. His breath became shallow, barely deep enough to keep him from passing out. Was this magic his own doing? He wasn't quite sure. It almost seemed the staff was the initiator, calling Arthur's magic into itself. But that was absurd.

A glow, emanating from deep within the wood, turned the staff translucent. First, in the vicinity of Arthur's hands. Then spreading up and down along the staff's length. The wood took on the appearance of clear glass. The light touched the crystal touchstone.

Sparks formed in the heart of the orb. Tiny pinpoints of white brilliance wafted to the crystal's surface. Breaking through, they manifested in the air.

The sparks spun wildly, engulfing the touchstone in a sphere of evanescence. Arthur kept his gaze trained on it. His awareness of anything else—of Cybele, of Luc, of the dingy flat—faded to nothingness.

The vibration was slight at first—so slight he didn't understand what it portended. He felt it in his hands, in his arms, in his chest. The moonstone heated and burned. The oscillations mounted. Still, he didn't comprehend what was happening. Not until the disturbance invaded his skull and shook the very substance of his brain.

Memories—dark and light, violent and peaceful,

vengeful and tender—exploded into Arthur's awareness. All that his ancestors had been, all that was left of their brief existence, flashed to life inside their heir. From Alwen to Merlin and farther back still to the first step of his ancestors on Britannia's shore. Years—centuries—flew past. Arthur remembered his ancestors' first northern migration. Before that flight, their home had been in the ancient deserts. They had been cursed—tossed on the churning waters of the Flood—by Raphael's vengeful sword.

It was too much. He couldn't hold it all. Not within his finite flesh. Life, death, joy, and grief. Guilt and shame. Hopelessness. Experience, emotion, magic. The power of Arthur's line and its eternal curse. No one person—even a Nephil—could hope to contain such a legacy.

"Luc! Watch out!"

Arthur was only dimly aware of Cybele's shout. It was lost amid the ringing in his ears and the brilliance filling his vision. Power—power he hadn't called and couldn't hope to control—kindled in his core. It raced down his arms. It streamed into the staff.

Light exploded. A brilliant bolt of magic shot from the crystal. Luc cried out. Something crashed. Another surge of power wracked Arthur's body. It entered the staff, raced upward to the crystal, and sprayed in every direction. A loud cracking sound. Bits of gritty debris, raining down on his head.

More curses. More shouting.

"What the hell is he doing?"

"I don't know, but we gotta—"

"Cybele! Get down!"

A flash of green hellfire erupted. It wasn't Arthur's magic. Whose? Where the hell had it come from?

"Arthur!" Cybele's desperate scream came to him as if

from the other side of the globe. *"Arthur, stop! Stop it now! You'll kill us all!"*

Stop. The word spun in his brain. Could he stop? Or would his magic destroy all? Would he come out of this to find Cybele dead on the floor?

The thought triggered a shock of panic. His magic deserted him. The suddenness of the loss sent Arthur staggering backward.

His hip impacted the floor. Pain shot through his body. He rolled, carrying the staff with him. He ended up with his face in the carpet, his mouth filled with plaster dust, his body curled protectively around Merlin's crystal orb.

For several long moments, silence—complete and utter silence—reigned.

Then Luc's low mutter intruded. "Son of a bitch. What the fuck just happened?"

Arthur turned his head toward the sound and opened his eyes. Luc and Cybele crouched under the dining table, their bodies shielded behind two overturned chairs. One had a round, burnt hole in the center of the seat.

Cybele started to push the chairs away. Luc caught her wrist. "Wait," he said, his voice rough. "Might not be safe yet."

"I don't care. I—"

Arthur pushed up on all fours, head bowed. The staff lay on the carpet under him, amid a crumbling mosaic of plaster and dust. The transparency was gone. The twisted woods no longer looked like glass. But the shaft was whole again, the top melded to the bottom. He looked for a seam where he'd joined the broken pieces. There was none. It was as if it had never been damaged.

He raised his head and dropped back onto his haunches. The air was cloudy. Chunks of ceiling covered the carpet. Cybele shoved a chair aside and crawled out from under the table. Luc followed her more slowly. They looked ghostly, their faces and clothes covered with plaster dust.

"Are you all right?" Arthur asked quietly. He might have killed them.

"Yes," Cybele said quickly.

"No thanks to you." Luc glared at him. "What the hell was that?"

Arthur lurched to his feet. Too quickly—the room went spinning. He pitched forward, avoiding Cybele's outstretched arms and grabbing the edge of the table instead. Cybele shoved a chair under him. He lowered himself into it.

She eyed him uncertainly. "Are *you* okay?"

"Fine," he muttered.

"What happened?" Luc asked.

"Memories." Arthur rubbed the spot between his eyes. "Too many memories."

Cybele eyed him. "Merlin's?"

"Yes. Merlin's. And so many others. They were like...like tornados inside my skull." He slumped against the chair back. "Is that...do I smell coffee?"

"I'll get you some." Luc glanced from Arthur to Cybele, then disappeared into the kitchen.

Cybele, kneeling, retrieved Merlin's staff from the floor. "You did it," she said, looking at him wonderingly. "You fixed it."

"And almost killed you and Luc in the process."

"Luc's hellfire blocked the worse of it." She bent her head over the staff and ran her fingers over the wood. "You fixed it, Arthur. You can't even see where it was broken."

A dull thump sounded overhead. They both looked up at the ceiling.

A second thump. And another.

"What the hell?" Luc, coming from the kitchen, set a steaming coffee mug on the plaster-covered table.

Cybele shrugged. "I guess our upstairs neighbor isn't happy with all the noise we're making down here."

Luc frowned. "There is no upstairs neighbor. This is the top floor."

A rapid volley shook the ceiling, the impacts coming too quickly to count.

"Something's hitting the roof." Cybele ran to the window. "Shit! It's the hellfiends. They're falling out of the sky."

Luc made a beeline toward the door, Arthur close behind. Cybele, after a moment's hesitation, grabbed the staff and followed them. The stairwell at the end of the corridor led up to the roof as well as down to the lower floors. They raced to the upper landing. Luc kicked open the door.

A hailstorm of hellfiends rained down on the roof. Each creature exploded in a burst of ash and flame as it hit. The unholy shower was already abating, perhaps because the demons were learning to avoid the airspace directly above the building. The fiends flew right and left around it, as though aware of some invisible threat.

Fewer and fewer demons fell, until at last the barrage stopped. Arthur strode onto the roof from shelter of the stairwell. Cybele and Luc followed him. He tipped his head back. Dark, roiling clouds of hellfiends covered the rest of the city, but directly overhead, the sky was brilliant blue.

Luc looked at Arthur. "Damn. You killed a shit ton of those things."

"The staff killed them," Arthur replied.

"Michael was right." Cybele's eyes glowed with excitement. She thrust the staff into his hands. "Can you do it again? Can you take out more of them?"

"Wait just a freaking minute," Luc reached out and grabbed the staff, just above Arthur's grip. "I wouldn't be so quick to try whatever the hell that was again. You nearly killed Cybele and me."

Arthur looked up at the sky. Hellfiends, in every direction, as far as the eye could see. Except directly overhead.

"Go back inside," he told the others. "I'll see if I can do it again."

"All right," Cybele said, tugging on Luc's arm. Luc sighed and released the staff. They backed into the shelter of the landing, Luc pulling the door shut behind them.

After a few moments and several deep breaths, Arthur set the staff upright on the roof before him. Legs braced wide, he gripped the shaft, left hand above right, and closed his eyes.

A full minute later, he opened his eyes. Nothing. Worse, he felt no spark, no flame, no life at all. The staff, though no longer broken in two, was nothing but a few pieces of tangled, twisted wood. Merlin's touchstone might as well have been a powerless chunk of coal.

Arthur wasn't sure whether he should be relieved or terrified at this new development.

He strode to the door. Cybele and Luc loitered in the stairwell behind it. "Well?" Cybele demanded. "What are you waiting for?"

"Nothing," Arthur said. "The staff's dormant again. Or maybe it's dead for good this time. In any case, I can't feel a thing."

"What about Merlin's memories?"

Arthur closed his eyes. "I think—" He blew out a breath. "Damn, I think they're gone, too. At least, I can't see any of them. I remember other lives. But Merlin's? No."

"But...you've already seen Merlin's memories. They have to be inside you. They can't just disappear."

At one time Arthur might have agreed, but now? He couldn't be sure of anything. "I don't know what's happened," he said. "Maybe they're still in there. Maybe I just need to find them. But...don't get your hopes—"

A flash of red caught his eye. He broke off, swinging his head around to stare at Luc. "Oh, shit."

"What?" Luc said, frowning.

"Your thrallstone," Arthur said. "It's glowing."

Cybele sucked in a breath. "No. Oh, no. You used your magic, Luc, when Arthur..."

Luc slapped his palm over the stone. The ruby's red light shone through his fingers. Arthur caught his friend's gaze. Luc looked quickly away, but not before Arthur had seen the raw panic in his eyes.

"She's found me," he rasped.

TWENTY-FOUR

"I'm leaving." Luc's eyes were haunted. Cybele wanted to touch him, put her arms around her brother's shoulders and hug him tight, but the rigid tension in his body told her he'd never allow it.

There's nothing you can do," he said. "She's calling me. I have to answer."

They were back in the apartment. Arthur stood by the window, the staff propped against the wall beside him. Luc eyed the door to the hallway, as if ready to bolt through it any second. Cybele leaned against the door. Leave? Her brother would have to go through her first.

"No." Nausea churned her stomach. "You can't leave, Luc. I just got you back. I can't lose you again."

"You never got me back," Luc said tightly. "I belong to Mab. I always will."

"Don't say that."

Her brother's eyes were bleak. "It's true, Cybele. Face it."

She felt as if she were being torn apart. "No, I won't—"

"Cybele." Arthur spoke from his position by the window. "If he doesn't go to Mab, she'll be coming this way soon enough. She has to suspect we're with him."

"I'm sure she does," Luc said. "But Mab isn't one to go into a situation blind. It'd take her twelve hours to fly here from Texas—she'll want to be sure of what's going on before she arrives. She'll want to lay out a plan."

"She might send one of her thralls to investigate," Arthur said. "Rand, probably."

"Luc." Cybele could hardly stand to think of her brother once again in Mab's hands. "Don't go back to Texas."

"I can't stay here. I won't draw danger to you."

"Go into hiding. There has to be somewhere Mab can't find you."

"Oblivion," Luc said. "I tried that one. Didn't work out."

Cybele choked back a bitter taste in her throat. "There's got to be another way."

"There is," Arthur said. "I'll go with Luc to Texas and issue my challenge to Mab in person. You can stay here."

"What? No. No way. I'm going with—"

"Neither of you are going to Texas," Luc said flatly. "It would be suicide. Arthur's not ready to take on Mab."

"I might not be ready," Arthur said, "but issuing my challenge now, before Mab expects it, will catch her off guard." Arthur regarded Merlin's staff with troubled eyes. "I'll show her the staff. It's damaged, but she won't know that. She'll wonder what I can do with it. She'll be wary."

"You can't be stupid enough to think you can bluff your way through a duel," Luc said hotly. "And do what— fool Mab into thinking you've found the key to Merlin's power? When you can't even call a spark into that stone? That's bullshit. She'll see through you in a fucking heartbeat." He paused, and then continued in a quieter voice. "You think you know what she's capable of? Believe me, you have no idea."

But Luc knew. Cybele saw the truth of that in her brother's eyes. Her heart, already bleeding for what he'd endured, broke in two.

"I'm not totally helpless against her," Arthur replied

calmly. "I have my ancestors' memories—hundreds, perhaps thousands of experiences to guide me. I just need a bit of time to sort them out. And I have another advantage—the challenger chooses the battleground. I'll choose Tŷ'r Cythraul, where the magic of my line has been nurtured for centuries. Mab will need to travel. She'll need to call the entire clan as witness. That should give me a day or so to prepare."

"If she follows the rules," Luc said. "What if she doesn't? What if she kills you on sight? No." He shifted his stance. "I'm going to Demon's Hollow alone. I'll deliver your challenge."

"But—Mab will be furious." Cybele said. "She'll take it out on you."

"Most likely," Luc replied grimly. "And while she's doing it, I'll try to stall her. I'll keep her away from Arthur as long as I can."

The stone on his thrall collar chose that moment to flash. Cybele's stomach turned. Images of perversion—dark, degrading acts her brother would be forced to endure—boiled into her brain. The expression on her face must've betrayed her horror, because Arthur abruptly crossed the room to stand at her side. He took her hand and laced her fingers tightly with his.

"I can't stop you, can I?" Arthur said to Luc.

"Not without killing me."

Arthur nodded and tugged Cybele out of the path to the door. Luc strode past them out of the flat. The door closed behind him with the finality of a lid coming down on a coffin. Arthur's hand, warm and strong, came to rest on the back of Cybele's neck. She made no protest as he propelled her toward the couch and tugged her down to sit beside her.

He didn't speak. She was grateful for that. Anything he

could say to make her feel better would be a lie, and they both knew it.

"We need to leave too," he said after a few minutes. "Sooner rather than later."

"Tŷ'r Cythraul?" she asked.

"Yes."

"How?" She was glad to turn her thoughts to logistics. "The trains might not be running, at least not reliably. We could probably steal a car, but who knows what the roads are like?"

"I'll shift," Arthur said. "And we'll fly."

She regarded him gravely. "Are you sure? You didn't want to do that before."

"I...understand my magic a bit more now," he said. "The debacle with the staff notwithstanding. My ancestral memories—even with Merlin's missing—will help me focus. And we need to get to Tŷ'r Cythraul as quickly as possible. I don't know how long I'll have to prepare before Mab shows up."

"What about the hellfiends?" Cybele asked. "The sky is black with them."

"A few blasts of hellfire will get us through them," he said, standing. "Come on. Let's get out of here."

The TV was still on, muted, a silent aerial of the so-called volcanic eruption scrolling across the screen. "Wait," Cybele said as Arthur headed toward the door. "Let me turn this off first." She grabbed the remote off the table.

At that moment, the broadcast shifted from the aerial to a split screen. The left screen showed a reporter. On the right...

Cybele's fingers froze on the remote. "Arthur," she said in a strangled voice. "Look."

"I see the bloody bastard." Angry footsteps crossed the room. He halted by her side. "Dusek."

The sound of the Alchemist's name made Cybele feel dirty. She repressed a shudder. "What's he doing on TV? I thought...I hoped...he'd been killed." Her fumbling finger found the volume control.

The reporter was speaking. "—and now, for a very different perspective on the volcanic eruption in Wales, BBC takes you to Prague. We're speaking now with Professor Vaclav Dusek, Founder and Director of the Prague Institute for the Study of Man. Professor, thank you for speaking with the BBC."

The pallor of the Nephil's complexion was stark against the high neck of his black sweater. He inclined his head slightly. "Thank you, Reginald. I am honored."

"Professor, you've put forth a shocking alternate theory concerning the eruption in Wales. Will you elaborate for our viewers?"

"Yes, of course. I—"

"Just to clarify, Professor. You are not, yourself, a geologist or volcanologist."

"Far from it," Dusek replied. "I am a scholar. A student of Man and his origins. I have devoted my life to the discovery and interpretation of Earth's oldest artifacts."

"How can ancient history possibly speak to today's volcanic eruption?" Reginald asked.

"History speaks, as always, with absolute authority," Dusek replied. "This unexpected event in Wales has stunned geologists and volcanologists for a very good reason."

"Which is?"

The Alchemist looked straight into the camera. "This so-called Welsh volcano is no volcano at all."

"What the fuck?" Arthur muttered.

Twin lines appeared between the reporter's eyebrows. "With all due respect, Professor. I've watched extensive aerial footage of the disaster. I have only to look into the sky to see the ash plume. How could this be anything but a volcanic eruption?"

"Ah, but that is because a volcano is what the denizens of the underworld wish you to see. The truth, however, cannot hide from those with clear sight. That is not volcanic ash spewing into the sky. It is an army of demonic fiends sprung from the bowels of Hell."

Arthur swore again. Cybele could only manage a gasp.

The reporter appeared no less stunned. "Just to clarify, Professor. Are you saying Earth is under attack? By an army of demons?"

Dusek nodded. "Precisely."

"But...but...that's absurd."

"Is it, Reginald?" Dusek leaned toward the camera. "How can you be sure?"

A half-laugh burst from the reporter's lips. "Because...demons aren't real. They're a myth. Creatures created by human fear and imagination."

"Oh, no," the Alchemist replied. "I assure you, demons are very real. They have roamed the Earth since the dawn of human existence. They have ravaged men, raped women, drunk the blood of infants. Their numbers, however, have been limited. Until now. Mark my words, Reginald. The barrier between Heaven and Hell has been breached. A horde of hellfiends is streaming unimpeded into the Earthly realm. These demons will invade human minds on every continent. They will influence and possess billions. Horrible depravities will occur."

"Um..." Reginald looked uncertain as to what reply he should make. Suddenly, his fingers snapped to the audio feed in his ear. He cleared his throat. "Well. Thank you, Professor Dusek, for that...um...unique, if...um...fanciful perspective on the volcanic eruption." Abruptly, Dusek's face vanished from the screen. "We go now to Carmarthen where we'll speak with a number of eyewitnesses..."

Cybele didn't realize how tightly she was holding the remote until Arthur pried it from her fingers. He hit a button. The screen went black. Cybele continued to stare at it. "Not all humans are going to be as incredulous as that reporter," she said. "Now that the idea has been planted, a lot of people are going to realize what's going on."

"What I don't understand," Arthur said slowly, "is how Dusek knew of the cave and the hellfiends in the first place. The false memory he sent me seemed so real. I would have bet my life it belonged to Merlin."

"That memory was real," Cybele told him. "But it wasn't Merlin's. It was Nimue's. She wasn't a witch, Arthur."

His eyes narrowed. "She was a Nephil. An Alchemist." She saw understanding dawn in his eyes. "She was Dusek's ancestor."

"Yes. At least, that's what he told me. He knew about the portal to Hell that Nimue opened with Merlin's staff. And he knew the fiends were still trapped below the cave, waiting to burst out. When he couldn't pull the staff from the stone himself, he tricked you into doing it for him."

"I fell right into his trap."

"You couldn't have known," Cybele said.

"That's no excuse."

Cybele met his gaze. "What I don't understand is why this TV interview? Why would Dusek want the whole world to know the truth?"

Arthur looked as much at a loss as she felt. "To create a global panic?"

"Panic's inevitable, that's for sure. There must be hundreds of millions of those things, spreading all over the globe. Who's going to fight them?"

Arthur shifted Merlin's staff from one hand to the other, his gaze trained on the lifeless crystal.

"I will," he said.

***

The door to the second bedroom squeaked open a crack.

"Are they gone?"

"Yes," Lucky said, opening the door wide.

"Thank the everlasting fires of Hell," Maweth muttered. A shudder ran through him. "It was bad enough when the archangel was here. Then Michael left and things got even worse. Geez." Ignoring all the plaster dust, he plopped down on his back on the carpet. "When that staff exploded, I thought for sure we were goners."

"Um...we can't die," Lucky pointed out, hovering in the air above him. "Either of us."

Maweth looked at him and sighed. "Lucky, Lucky, Lucky. It's just an expression. But even so. We might not be able to die, but we can get extremely uncomfortable."

"I guess," Lucky said, fluttering down to the floor.

"You know what?" Maweth sat up suddenly. "I'm hungry."

"Hungry?" Lucky's blue eyes blinked. "I didn't know you had to eat."

"Oh, I don't have to," Maweth replied. He flew into the kitchen, Lucky buzzing in his wake. "I just like to sometimes. My favorite is the food that kills people," he added. "Especially the newer stuff—you know, trans fats, high fructose corn syrup, artificial coloring. But good old-fashioned sugar, salt, and lard are fine, too."

He bumped about, opening and closing cabinets. "Here, gimme a hand with this refrigerator."

It took both of them pulling on the handle, but the door finally popped open. Maweth peeked into a white paper bag. "Whoa! Doughnuts. Jam ones." He crammed one into his mouth and held the bag out to Lucky. "Wnahnt some?"

Lucky landed on the counter. "No. But thank you."

"Suit yourself. No use letting these babies go to waste." He ate another jam, and then three custards. "Yum."

Lucky frowned.

"What?" Maweth paused mid-chew. "Grossed out by my table manners?"

"What? No, that's not it." Lucky flew to the windowsill and peered out. "I was just wondering where all those hellfiends are going."

"Oh, that's easy. They're going anywhere humans are." He grabbed a bottle of milk and chugged some down. "Especially evil humans. And the angry ones, the hating ones, the grief-stricken ones—"

"But why? What are they going to do with them?"

"Influence them. Or outright possess them. Depending on how suggestible they are."

"And then what?"

Then what? Maweth put the milk bottle down on the counter. He suddenly felt a little sick.

"Then what?" he repeated. "Don't ask. Because you really, really don't want to know."

TWENTY-FIVE

Michael had never seen Raphael so angry.

Or so frightened. His brother's habitual pacing had morphed into a frantic scurry. With each pivot, cloud droplets frothed into Michael's face. He didn't dare wipe them away.

"The pair of you are idiots," Raphael ranted. "*Idiots*, I tell you. I give you one simple task: watch Arthur Camulus. Keep him out of trouble. And what happens? What happens? Trouble doesn't even begin to describe it."

Michael stopped himself from pointing out that watching Arthur and keeping him out of trouble were, in fact, two tasks. As it had turned out, two *impossible* tasks. Wisely, he kept his mouth shut and exchanged glances with Gabriel instead. Gabe, he noted, was once again in possession of his walking stick. Leaning on it, he rolled his eyes. A daring bit of insolence, but luckily Raphael was too agitated to take note.

"And now," he continued, "because of you two, Earth is going literally to Hell."

Gabriel cleared his throat and bravely ventured into the fray. "With all due respect, Raphael. It was bound to happen at some point anyway. The human race is a collection of sinful sots."

"That," Raphael snapped, "is neither here nor there. Certain events have been preordained by the Almighty. A hellfiend invasion is *not* one of those events. Demons streaming in the sky, blotting out the sun. Nephilim running amok." He gave up pacing, in favor of glaring daggers at Michael. "What in Heaven's name were you thinking, pulling Arthur from the wreckage of his own villainous folly?"

Michael's chin jerked up. "Um...you saw that?"

"I did." His brother's voice was cold enough to freeze the fires of the Eternal Inferno. "Explain, please. *If* you can. Which I doubt."

"I...um..." He stiffened his spine. "The Druid Merlin gave his life in that cave, in defense of humanity. He—"

"Merlin caused the portal to be opened in the first place," Raphael pointed out. "And he only died there because I sealed him in."

"Yes. Well. That's all true enough, I suppose. But that doesn't negate the fact that Merlin killed Nimue and used his staff to send the hellfiends back through the portal. Arthur is Merlin's heir, and he—"

"Has unleashed calamity a second time. Even worse than before."

Blessed Heaven. Michael had had it up to here with Raphael's one-note, bigoted bias against the Nephilim.

"Would you please stop interrupting?" he snapped. "If you want a conversation with yourself, go find a mirror."

Raphael's hand flew to the hilt of his sword. "Why you insolent—"

"You want to fight?" Michael flicked his wrist, dropping his knife into his palm and springing the blade, all at once. "All right, I'll give you a—"

"Boys!" Gabriel sprang up between them, hands upraised. "Please. Fighting amongst ourselves is no solution."

"Maybe not," Michael muttered, "but I'm not averse to

giving it a try."

Gabriel glared at him. "We're all on the same side here. I suggest we act like it."

He was right, of course. Michael sighed and slipped his switchblade up his sleeve.

Gabriel's head swung toward Raphael. "And you?" Raphael made a show of sheathing his Sword of Righteous Vengeance. He straightened his robes, turned his back, and let out an irritated huff.

"Maybe," Gabriel said cautiously, "it's time to wake the Almighty."

"I already suggested that," Michael said.

"Wake the Almighty?" Raphael's head whipped around. "*Wake the Almighty?* Are you out of your blessed mind?"

"Raphael," Gabriel pleaded. "Be reasonable. Hell is open. Earth is a mess. Our options are limited. The Almighty is, by definition, all mighty. He can fix this with a snap of his fingers."

Raphael's voice vibrated with terrible force. "The Almighty entrusted me with humanity's welfare. Me. There is no way—*no blessed way*—I'm going to wake Him up and tell him I've mishandled the assignment."

"They say confession is good for the soul," Michael said in a low voice.

Raphael spun about. "*What?*"

"Nothing."

"None of this would have happened," Raphael said dangerously, "if not for the Nephilim."

Cybele's face appeared, uninvited, in Michael's brain. "It's not really the Nephilim's fault," he told his brother. "They're just living their lives."

Raphael's golden eyebrows lowered. "Living their *cursed* lives. What do you mean, not their fault? Everything is their fault."

"But is it really fair that their lives are cursed?" Michael asked. "The current Nephilim, I mean. The sin was committed by their ancestors. They had nothing to do with it."

"Have you gone insane?" his brother exclaimed. "The Nephilim are unnatural, hybrid creatures. They shouldn't exist. That is why they're cursed. Their lives of sin only prove the curse was valid."

"Um...that seems awful self-prophetic, don't you think? If they weren't born cursed, they might not grow up to embrace vice and evil. Maybe Heaven has made them into what they are."

"*What?*" Raphael was regarding him with such a horrified expression that Michael wondered if his head had suddenly sprouted a mass of serpents. "What kind of logic is that?"

"I believe," Gabriel offered, "that on Earth it's called 'political correctness.'"

"Well here in Heaven, we call it blasphemy! Nephilim are cursed, end of story." Raphael's gaze narrowed on Michael. "You would do well to remember it."

"Fine," Michael said, shooting Gabriel an annoyed glance. "But philosophy aside, the current mess on Earth needs a solution. If we're not going to disturb the Almighty, just how are we going to save humanity? Or at the least, keep the human race alive and reasonably unpossessed until He wakes on His own?"

Gabriel buffed his fingernails on his lapel, and then inspected them one by one. "I suspect our elder brother has a plan," he said. "As usual."

"Quite so." Raphael climbed the three steps to his throne and seated himself with a flourish of golden robes. He opened his mouth to speak.

When he finished—some three human hours later,

Michael estimated—it was with a firm nod of self-approval. The plan was a good one, he said. Practically foolproof, he said. The Earth was sure to be saved.

Michael wasn't so optimistic. Sure, Raphael had a plan. That didn't mean it was going to work. There were bound to be loopholes.

***

Mab was in Houston.

Luc flew toward his alpha, his thrall collar straining toward the hand that had created it. Every fiber of his being screamed for him to fly in the opposite direction. But even if he could somehow break the collar's compulsion and flee, the victory would be fleeting. And if Mab had to come after him, her fury would know no bounds.

He landed on the sidewalk in front of Club Tartarus. It was mid-afternoon. Too late for the lunch crowd, too early for clients seeking evening delights. A knock at the door was quickly answered, however. The bouncer—a human male named Carter—seemed to expect Luc's arrival. He nodded with a touch of respect, as well as a hint of pity in his eyes.

"The Mistress is in Circle 9," he said.

In other words, in the lowest circle of Hell. Club Tartarus was filled with fantasy rooms, available to the clientele for varying fees. The rates rose as the elevator descended. Only the richest and most...adventurous...of Mab's clients entered Circle 9. There, attended by the most skilled of Mab's male and female sex workers, their darkest and most daring fantasies sprang to life. The fee was enormous. Satisfaction and inviolable anonymity were guaranteed.

Luc was intimately acquainted with the tortures of

Circle 9. Just thinking about the place made his brow break out in sweat and his hands go cold. His stomach heaved. He very nearly vomited on the spot, all over Carter's expensive cowboy boots. As if to mock his fear, at that precise moment, the ruby in his thrall collar flashed so hotly, he could smell his own burning flesh. How he made it to the elevator, he had no idea. When he came back to himself he was inside it, alone, heading down.

He stepped out into a nightmare. The room was dimly lit, the only illumination coming from a line of snapping, gas-fired sconces. Hissing steam spurted from nozzles hidden in the floor, ceiling, and walls. The audio system speakers were hidden as well. Clanking chains and the snap of a whip mingled with cries of pain and moans of sexual bliss.

He moved slowly, his eyes scanning the room. At first it appeared deserted. Then a ball of crimson hellfire blazed to life high up near the ceiling. A shaft of light cast a tight circle on a figure below.

Mab, seated on a rope sling, swung gently. A shining vinyl unitard encased her lush body. Spike-heeled leather boots covered her legs to mid-thigh. Her hellfire whip handle twirled lazily in her fingers. Its stolen gems sparkled.

Mab's touchstone shone blood red in the valley of her cleavage. "Luc." Her voice was soft and silky, like languid sex. "You have come back to me."

"Yes, Mistress."

She tapped the butt of the whip handle against the opposite palm. "Why?"

"Because..." He licked dry lips. "Because I am yours, Mistress."

"A fine answer that would be," she said, swinging her long legs to the ground. "If it were true." She walked toward him, heels clicking on the floor. Steam caressed her body as she prowled through the dark. "You ran from me, Luc. With the help of that little brat. She sprang you from the cellar."

Zephyr. Luc's blood went cold. "What have you done to her?"

The thin line of Mab's plucked brows rose high above her cold blue eyes. "Why, nothing, Luc. Yet." She stalked closer. "Put her out of your mind."

"Please, ma'am, don't punish Zephyr. She made a mistake, opening the cellar door. I should've sent her away. I'm the one who's to blame."

Mab's sudden smile was, perhaps, even more threatening than her darkest expression. "Ah, the truth. At last. Yes, Luc. You are to blame. Are you very sorry for your sin?" He opened his mouth to respond. She halted his words with an upraised hand. "Do not lie to me, Luc. I'll know if you do."

He met her gaze squarely. "No, ma'am," he said. "I'm not sorry."

"See? The truth isn't difficult. You're not sorry. Of course you aren't." She spun the whip handle between her fingers. "But you will be, sugar. You will be."

She circled a finger and said a word. A dozen or more sconces set high on the walls sprung to life. Waving, licking light flooded the far end of the room, falling upon a sort of low stage. Luc swallowed thickly. A long table against the wall held all manner of instruments. Manacles. Floggers, ropes, candles. A ball gag. Butt plugs. A massive strap-on dildo.

And suddenly...wasps. Thousands of wasps, swarming amid the paraphernalia. A low, sinister buzz filled his ears. Illusion? Or illusion-turned-to-reality? There was no way to know.

His stomach rolled. His gaze darted right and left, as if looking for a means of escape. There was none. He knew that.

"I searched for y'all," Mab drawled. "I couldn't find your sister or her lover. I couldn't even find you, though you wear my thrall collar." She moved closer. "Your sins didn't begin there, sugar. It was bad of you, very bad, not to tell me Cybele and Arthur were fucking behind my back. And what about Cybele's magic? No dormant should be powerful enough to give me the slip. But Cybele did. And you knew it." She pursed her red lips. "You have no idea, Luc. No idea how angry all this makes me."

A single wasp detached itself from the swarm. Lazily, it bobbed across the room, drifting ever closer. Cold sweat trickled down Luc's forehead, stinging his eyes. The insect alighted on his head and began a slow crawl through his hair.

Mab had advanced, too. She was within reach of him now. Every muscle in Luc's body clenched. "But you will know it," she whispered. "Oh, you will. Remove your shirt."

It took a long moment before his muscles unlocked enough to comply. He shucked off the shirt and let it drop to the floor. The wasp, dislodged from Luc's hair, buzzed angrily in his ear.

A long red fingernail touched the center of his naked chest. It scored a light line downward, stopping an inch above his belt buckle. "You knew about Cybele. About Arthur," Mab murmured. "And you did not tell me."

Luc stared straight ahead, eyes focusing on the flickering gaslight. Mab's nail circled once, around his navel. The wasp alighted on the back of his neck. His stomach clenched.

"I suspect they're together," she said. "I suspect y'all have been together these past two days."

"Yes."

"They are hidden by strong magic."

"Yes."

She drew back, her red lips twisting. "So many disturbing events." She tapped the butt of her whip handle against her palm. "Arthur gone rogue. Surviving his Ordeal without a guide. A horde of hellfiends streaming out of one of the places Merlin was supposed to have died." A dozen or more wasps separated from the swarm and flew in his direction.

"Tell me, Luc. Did Arthur find Merlin's cave? Did he free those hellfiends?"

"Yes."

"How?"

He ignored the sensation of the insects alighting on his arms, his shoulders, his chest. "With Merlin's staff. He's found it. Its power belongs to Arthur now."

Mab went still at this pronouncement. Shock, however brief, showed in her dark eyes. Luc couldn't suppress a rush of satisfaction.

"Arthur gave me a message for you," he said.

"Message? What message?"

"The heir of Merlin issues a challenge. A duel to the death for the position of alpha and the right to lead the Druid clan. He awaits you at Tŷ'r Cythraul."

For a long moment, Mab remained silent. Then she smiled and spread her hand on Luc's chest. One of the wasps was trapped beneath it. Its stinger sunk into Luc's flesh.

Mab's voice was dangerously soft. "And does Arthur believe he can defeat me?"

"Yes. Yes, he does believe it." It was not, precisely, a lie. Arthur believed there was a chance he could defeat Mab. A slim one, yes, but a chance, nonetheless.

She smiled. "If he doesn't win, and I succeed in keeping him alive, I will collar him. He'll be my thrall."

"Yes." Luc swallowed. "He knows that."

He couldn't let Mab realize how likely that scenario was. If she knew how unstable Arthur's magic was, she'd be off to England like a shot. Arthur needed every hour, every minute, Luc could give him.

"He's willing to take that risk," Luc said. "That should give you an idea of how powerful he is."

"Should it? Perhaps." Mab tapped a finger against her full lower lip. "But somehow, I'm not convinced. The truth is never so simple. There are always secrets."

She moved closer and pressed her body against him. Her lips whispered hotly against his ear. "Tell me, Luc. Tell me Arthur's secrets."

He didn't move, didn't speak.

She stepped back, her voice no longer teasing. "I can take the knowledge from you. You are my thrall. When the pain I inflict on your body is broad enough, and deep enough, your brain will turn soft. But then you know that, don't you? You remember your Ordeal."

With a snapping sound, a lash of hellfire snaked from her whip handle. As if called by the magic, the entire swarm of wasps rose into the air. A writhing, buzzing mass of dread curdled in Luc's stomach.

"Did you enjoy your Ordeal, sugar?"

Luc forced his reply past dry lips and tongue. "No, ma'am. I did not."

"No? I did. I enjoyed it so very much." Mab gazed at the swarming cloud of wasps, and past it, to her tools of pain and humiliation. "Now I'm fixing to enjoy myself again."

Luc knew his mistress spoke the truth.

TWENTY-SIX

Lightning flashed.

Arthur directed the jagged energy toward a boulder on the moor, a target he'd chosen in advance. The bolt hit precisely in the center. Shards of rock and grit exploded with satisfying fury. Feeling marginally more hopeful than he had in days, he flew back to the garden at Tŷ'r Cythraul where Cybele sat waiting under the heavy clouds. Real clouds this time. The hellfiend cloud had finally dissipated, leaving Arthur a clear sky in which to practice the weather-calling skills he'd gleaned from his ancestors' memories.

Cybele's shirt was wet from his rain, plastered to her chest. Her nipples were hard. He tried not to stare.

"It's getting easier," he told her. He sat beside her on the bench. Closing his eyes, he envisioned the clouds above them moving away. The rain stopped.

"Nice," Cybele said. "I think you have weather down. Your illusions are complex, too. Much more convincing than anything I can conjure."

"Maybe," he allowed. "But Mab's not going to be fooled by a glamour. At least not for long." He leaned forward, bracing his forearms on his spread legs. "How can I fight her? I can't go past illusion. I can't manipulate reality. She can."

He'd tried, over and over, until he thought his brain

would explode. He hadn't succeeded in bringing so much as a speck of dust out of illusion and into the material world.

Cybele shoved a hank of wet hair out of her eyes. "It'll come. It's only been a day and a half since we left London."

"That's more time than we thought I'd have." How the hell had Luc managed to keep Mab away this long? Abruptly, he buried the thought. It didn't bear contemplation. He could tell Cybele's thoughts were traveling the same disturbing path. She shivered, her shoulders hunching as she wrapped her arms around her torso.

"You're cold," he said, though he knew that wasn't the problem at all. It was a warm April night. "I've done enough for now. Let's go in."

He folded his wings into nothingness. In the kitchen, he pulled on a shirt. They set out food they didn't feel like eating.

"At least the hellfiends are finally out of the sky," Cybele said, shoving her sandwich to the center of the table.

"Out of the sky," Arthur said, "but not gone."

His father's old battery-powered radio provided news from the human point of view. The volcanic eruption had ceased. The Welsh authorities were clearing debris and counting the dead. Air traffic and train service had resumed on a limited schedule. Most people were back at their jobs.

Concurrently, there'd been a disturbing spike in street violence. In the last twenty-four hours, eighteen people had been murdered in London—a count fifty-four times the normal rate. Assault and rape were rampant. London wasn't unique—other cities in the UK and around the world reported similar crime surges. Global trouble spots were boiling over.

"The fiends did less harm in the sky," Arthur said. "Now that they're interacting with humans..."

He pushed away from the table and crossed the room to retrieve the staff, propped on the wall by the door. For about the thousandth time, he rotated the shaft in his hands, feeling for a spark, a vibration, for anything that might indicate the wood wasn't dead or the touchstone permanently dark.

Nothing. And yet...he couldn't believe the fault was in the staff. It was in him. He wasn't good enough. Not yet. But was there enough time to learn what he needed to know?

Guilt and frustration crowded in on him. "The fiends are my fault. If I hadn't been so goddamned arrogant and—"

"And what?" She pushed her chair back from the table and rose, her posture angry. "Let Dusek kidnap me? Let him rape me and use my magic?"

"No," he said. "Never that."

"So stop beating yourself up about what you did. Regrets aren't going to destroy those fiends."

"Merlin's magic can destroy them. Or at least send them back to Hell."

"Arthur." Cybele crossed the room and plucked the staff from his hands. Opening a tall cupboard, she shoved the staff inside and slammed the door. "Forget the hellfiends. We need to think about Mab. She'll be here soon with Rand and Evander and all the others." She paused, her throat working. "With Luc." Recovering, she pressed on. "Will she play by the rules and call your British relatives?"

"I don't know," Arthur said.

"Tell me about them. Did you know them well?"

He sensed she was asking out of a desperate need to think about something other than Luc.

"My mother was the last of Merlin's line," Arthur said. "All the relatives I remember were my father's family." Their faces flashed through his brain, filtered through a boy's memory. "The English kin visited Tŷr Cythraul rather often. Great Uncle Percival was my grandfather's younger brother. Brax and Avalyn, my father's full brother and sister. There were two older cousins. Ronan and Harry. Harry lived with a witch whose name I can't remember."

"And...the one who challenged Mab?"

He felt a stab of pain. Locked in the cellar, he hadn't witnessed Magnus's death. "I didn't know him well. That branch of the family rarely left Scotland. There was Collum, a jovial sort. And his cousins, Magnus and Morgana. They were twins—"

At Cybele's stricken expression, he cursed himself and changed course. "If any of my father's kin were able, they would've sent Mab to Oblivion. None of them are powerful enough."

Then again, none of them had possessed Merlin's staff. He looked toward the closed cupboard. "The staff is my only chance for victory."

"What about your mother's touchstone? And your ancestral memories? That all helps, doesn't it?"

"Yes." It did, just not as much as Arthur would've liked.

"The staff isn't your only chance, Arthur. You have power. Your *own* power. Have faith in it."

He gave a short laugh. "Faith isn't exactly a Nephilim virtue."

"Maybe it should be," she countered. "I have faith in you, Arthur. Your magic's stronger than Mab's. It'll be there when you need it. You'll defeat her. I know you will."

The profound sense of gratitude kindled by her words left him feeling curiously fragile. "Thank you."

She leaned up and kissed him on the cheek. "You're welcome."

He caught her hand and pressed it to his chest. He wanted her touch there, close to his heart, close to everything he couldn't find the words to say.

"Let's make love," he said quietly.

She looked up in surprise. "What? Now?"

"Yes. Now." He searched her gaze. "Don't you want to?"

A laugh bubbled up from her throat. "I always want to. You're the one who said it wasn't safe."

"Nothing's safe," he said, his grip tightening. "Nothing's certain. Life is short, and it's all we have. If I'm going to die soon—"

"You're not," she said sharply.

"I need you, Cybele. I know it's selfish. I know I shouldn't ask you, but—"

She stopped his words with two fingers against his lips. "Don't ask. Let me ask you, instead." She wrapped her arms around his neck. "Make love to me, Arthur. Please?"

He knew he should resist, but in that moment, resistance just wasn't in him. Especially not when she was kissing him, her body all but melting in his arms. Her clothes were still damp and clinging to every curve. His cock was hard, his brain was scrambled, and his heart—it was utterly lost.

He glanced toward the stair. They wouldn't make it past the first landing. Her hands swept down his torso and found the edge of his shirt. She moved her palms back up his bare chest, nails lightly scoring his skin. He groaned and gripped her arse. She wrapped her legs around his hips.

He turned and half-stumbled, half-lurched through

the front hall and into the library. How Cybele managed to get his shirt up over his head, he didn't know. Her hands explored his bare chest. Her mouth covered his nipple. She sucked hard.

Had he thought they could make it all the way to the rug in front of the fireplace? Bollocks to that. He turned and pushed her up against the wall. His fingers tangled with the button and zipper on her jeans. He shoved the jeans down to her knees, taking her scrap of underwear with it. She kicked the lot of it the rest of the way off. His fingers explored between her legs and came away wet.

She turned to liquid fire in his arms, kissing, licking. She nipped at his skin, the tiny bites inflaming him almost past reason. Hands trembling, he yanked down his pants, hissing in relief as his cock sprang free. He circled his hips, nudging the head of his cock into the wet slit between her legs. She not only opened for him, she wrapped her fingers around him and guided him home.

He slid into tight heat and slick moisture. She gasped and sank down on him, impaling her body on his rigid flesh. Her scent, musky with her arousal, enveloped him. He grabbed her thighs, thrust once, and pinned her to the wall.

Pleasure exploded, in every part of his body. His magic responded, surging brightly in his brain. Everything flashed white. He felt himself slip. His head dipped until his forehead pressed against hers. His breathing turned harsh.

She stilled. "Arthur? Is everything ok?"

Was it? He felt as though he were suspended in mid-air, legs pumping frantically, like a cartoon character waiting for gravity to kick in. His body and mind were poised on a precipice. In the abyss was unfathomable, uncontrollable magic. Magic that didn't care who it hurt.

Or who it killed.

He couldn't—wouldn't—look over the edge. Instead, he concentrated on Cybele. His love. His touchstone.

The warmth of her in his arms, her smooth skin against his calloused palms. The sound of her breath, moving in and out of her lungs a little too quickly. The smell of her arousal. The faint taste of her sweat as he kissed her temple. He drew back, just far enough to look into her green eyes. And the abyss faded away.

Control. It was his, he realized, as long as Cybele was with him. She didn't destroy the focus of his magic, she enhanced it. With her at his side, he could do anything. Even, he thought, defeat Mab.

A smile spread on his lips. "It's fine," he told her. "Better than fine."

She kissed him. He moved inside her, slowly at first, then with increasing urgency. The world faded away. Nothing mattered, nothing could harm them. Not as long as they were together.

His orgasm hit almost without warning, spinning him into a place of pure bliss. Cybele ground her hips and bore down on him. Her inner muscles spasmed. He found her mouth and covered it with his own, swallowing her gasp as she came.

In what seemed like a very long time after the last jolts of pleasure waned, he loosened his hold on her hips. Her feet slid to the floor. "Don't let go," she said. "Or I'll melt into a puddle on the floor."

"Can't have that." He turned, leaning his back against the wall and pulled her in close, her back to his front.

"See?" she turned her head where it rested on his shoulder and looked up at him. "You didn't lose control. Your magic didn't kill me. You were worried for nothing."

"Not for nothing," he said, his embrace tightening. "It'd

been a near thing, but he'd come away stronger for it. He hadn't let Cybele fall. He was confident now that he never would. She wasn't his weakness. She was his strength. His true guide.

She sighed and turned in his arms. "That was incredible, Arthur."

He smiled. "Give me a couple minutes and I'll do it one better."

She grinned back at him. They did it three more times—on the rug before the hearth, on the wide desk, and after a trip to the kitchen to eat the sandwiches they'd abandoned earlier, in a wide, comfortable armchair.

After that last time, Cybele fell asleep in his arms. It was only as her breathing slowed and deepened that he realized they hadn't used a single condom all night. Shit. He dropped his head against the chair's high back. He just...he just couldn't think about that now. He'd think of it later. If there was a later.

He stared at nothing, brooding over the upcoming duel, crafting and discarding strategies. There was really, he thought, no way to plan. Not against Mab.

He should've slept. He hadn't. Sleep was too much like Oblivion.

Outside, the wind whipped up. It howled over the moors, wailing like the brokenhearted. The shrubs outside the library windows, years overdue for a trim, scratched against the glass. Cybele shivered. He rubbed her arms. The howl outside the window changed in pitch and tenor, deepening to a low, rushing roar.

Abruptly, Arthur realized the sound wasn't wind. Or at least not a natural one. His arms tightened. "Wake up," he whispered urgently. "Get dressed. Quickly. I think they're here."

"Who's here?" She lifted her head off his shoulder,

blinking groggily. As sleep receded, her eyes widened and her body tensed. "Oh." She swallowed visibly. "So soon."

He slid her off his lap. Her arms clung for a heartbeat then fell away. They pulled on their clothes in haste. Leaving the sanctuary of the library, he traversed the hallway and approached the front door. He paused for the space of a deep breath, gathering courage.

"Wait."

Cybele stood at the end of the passage near the door to the kitchen.

"What?" he asked.

"You need to throw her off balance," she said, ducking out of view. She reappeared a moment later, carrying Merlin's staff. "This should give her something to think about."

"For all of three seconds," Arthur muttered, taking it from her. "Until she realizes it's useless."

"Maybe we can trick her into thinking it's alive," she said. "Come on."

She moved past him and opened the front door. The wind was so strong it nearly snatched the oak slab from her hand. She held firm to the brass knob as he came up behind her, his eyes searching the sky. Storm clouds roiled overhead. Dark shapes, only just visible against the turbulent gray, drew ever closer.

Rand landed on the moor beyond the garden's low stone wall. His left arm encircled Zephyr, whose eyes were wide with fear. Cybele stiffened. Arthur grabbed her hand to keep her from bolting.

"Not now. You can't do anything for her."

Evander and Hunter touched down next, followed by Draven, Clayton, and Blade. The three male dormants—Auster, Finley, and Grayson—traveled with them.

"Luc." Cybele's voice was strained. "Where's Luc?"

"There."

Luc stumbled as he landed, going down hard on one knee before lurching to his feet. Arthur sucked in a breath as he took in his friend's appearance. His face was black with bruising. A mass of blistering welts and bleeding whip marks crisscrossed his torso and limbs. He stared straight ahead with blank eyes.

"Damn that bitch," Cybele said. "Damn her to Oblivion. Kill her, Arthur. Kill her for me. For my brother."

"For all of us," he said. If utter hatred were magic, Merlin's staff would be ablaze. Mab would fall dead from the sky.

The dormants moved to one side. The adepts fanned out in a line. Mab touched down last. She took up a position in front of the seven Nephil males. A red nimbus of power crackled about her. She wore full dominatrix garb, black leather and vinyl, her enormous ruby nestled in the valley between her upthrust breasts. Her bejeweled whip handle dangled at her waist. Arthur's lower lip curled at the glint of the stolen gems.

He let anger seep through him. His demon nature rose to meet it. His wings rose and his vision went red. He planted Merlin's staff before him. If the sight of the long-lost relic dismayed his adversary, Arthur couldn't detect it. Her wings swept downward. Her shoulders went back.

"Arthur Camulus." Her cold voice rang out over the moor. "You will not stand against me. Surrender now and I will grant you your life."

"As a thrall," Arthur shouted. "That will never happen, Mab. I'll see myself in Oblivion first." He adjusted his grip on the staff, wishing desperately that he could feel a spark of life in it.

"You will regret that choice."

With an upward sweep of her hands, she launched two

balls of crimson flame. Darting forward, Arthur swung the staff to meet the attack. The crystal caught one hellfire missile and sent it sizzling into the wet ground. The other shot overhead.

"Cybele, watch out!"

The blast struck the door jamb scant inches above her head. Sparks showered. She ducked behind the door. At the same time, a white cloud appeared, whirling about the crystal atop Merlin's staff.

Arthur blinked against the sudden dazzle. His grip on the staff tightened. What was going on? The touchstone was dead...

Cybele. The magic was Cybele's. Illusion only, but a very good one. How long the ruse would fool Mab—if it fooled her at all—was anyone's guess.

Angling the staff high over his head, he strode forward across the stone-flagged terrace. White sparks poured from his palm. He sent the magic racing in spirals up the staff's twisted shaft. The instant they reached the crystal, he redirected the stream at Mab. And hoped like hell she wouldn't see through his ruse.

His hellfire struck the center of her chest. She faltered. If he hadn't been watching so closely, he might have missed the flash of panic in her eyes. The trick had worked. Mab had seen only what Arthur and Cybele wanted her to see—the ancient power of Merlin.

The alpha recovered quickly. She deflected his next blast before it struck. His hellfire disappeared into the grass at her feet.

"Is that the best you can do with your new toy?" she taunted.

Arthur forced a large dose of arrogance into his reply. "It's only the beginning of what I can do. Merlin's magic is mine."

"But, sugar, can a boy like you handle it?"

She fingered her whip handle, and then detached it from her belt. Three sizzling crimson strands of hellfire spurted out.

With a flick of her wrist, she launched the lashes at Arthur. He jerked the staff to one side. Not quickly enough. One lash snapped around the twisted wood. A second stung his forearm, burning like the fires of Hell. The third wrapped his left knee. He hissed in a breath through his teeth.

He twisted the staff, slashing it to one side, trying to free it. Mab yanked her whip back. Pain exploded in his knee. His leg flew out from under him. His arse hit the ground.

Behind him, Cybele let out a strangled cry. Mab threw her head back and laughed. Somehow Arthur managed to free himself and lurch to his feet. His knee felt like it had been pierced by a thousand burning needles. His leg barely held his weight. He leaned heavily on the staff.

The alpha yanked the final lash. The staff jerked. Arthur hung on with all his remaining strength. Cybele's sparks regrouped. Forming a tight ball, the illusion shot toward Mab. Arthur shoved the agony in his knee to the back of his brain and sank his mind into the sky. The instant Cybele's fake hellfire arrived at its destination a bolt of lightning hit the ground inches in front of Mab's boots.

Fuck. He'd meant to actually hit her.

The alpha jumped back, spitting curses. Her attention dropped briefly from her magic. Arthur took the opportunity to wrench the staff free of the crimson lash.

Abandoning her whip, Mab launched a stream of hellfire directly from her palms. Arthur caught it with Merlin's crystal. He sent it ricocheting back so quickly, and with so much furious anger, that Mab barely leaped out of the way in time.

"Mab."

Her head jerked up. Her blue eyes narrowed.

His knee was on fire, his focus close to shattering. If Mab guessed how powerless he really was—how close she was to victory—he was finished.

He summoned every bit of confidence he could muster. Standing with legs spread wide, he held the staff aloft.

"I challenge you," he shouted. "For the right to lead the Druid clan."

She set her hands on her hips and laughed. "Do you really think you have a chance, sugar? Has the Ordeal damaged your brain that much?"

"Do you accept?"

"I won't let you die, you know." She gave him a cat's smile. "Oh, no. You'll submit to me. You'll take my collar. You'll live out your life as my thrall."

He repressed a sick wave of dread. "Do you accept my challenge?"

Her smile grew wider. "If that's what you've got your heart set on, sugar." She lifted her arms.

"No. You know the law. The clan must stand as witness."

She laughed. "I am the law, Arthur. And look around you. The clan is here."

"Not all of it." His gaze swept over her adepts. "My father's family is absent."

"They aren't necessary. Tristan's kin are bound to me."

"Bound, yes. But not enthralled. Their oaths may be broken."

"They won't stand with you, if that's what you're hoping. Sniveling cowards, all of them."

"Then let them watch the contest," Arthur urged. "Let

them witness my fall. They think I'm dead. Let them see I'm alive. Show them how thoroughly you fooled them seven years ago."

Slowly, Mab lowered her arms. "Why, now, that's a thought. One or two may even be angry enough to fight at your side. More fodder for my collars." She smirked. "One can never have too many thralls."

Arthur pressed on, hardly daring to hope. "Summon them." When Mab seemed to dismiss the idea, he added, "Unless, of course, you're afraid of what might happen if you do."

Would Mab take the bait? He braced himself for her next blow. Waited for her to laugh and resume the fight.

"Afraid?" Her brows went up. "Oh, I think not, Arthur."

"Then do it," he shouted. "Summon my father's relations to witness my challenge."

Another long moment passed in which Arthur once more thought he'd lost. Then the ruby nestled in Mab's cleavage flared. The stones worn by her seven adepts responded, gleaming blood red in answer. They took up a pulsing rhythm, glowing like hot coals alight on the dark moor.

The breath flooded out of Arthur's lungs. The summons was not limited by distance. It would reach every Druid who possessed a fragment of Mab's touchstone. Every Druid bound in fealty to the alpha.

"It is done," Mab said. "The clan is summoned. Your worthless kin will soon bear witness your defeat."

Arthur forced himself not to react. His gambit had worked. He'd gained a bit of time. How long before his father's people arrived? A few hours? More? Would they join his challenge, face death and enthrallment in an effort to defeat Mab? None of them had taken the risk seven years ago. Maybe none would now.

He turned toward the house. Cybele stood in the doorway. Their gazes touched; grim understanding passed between them. Then her eyes suddenly shifted to a point behind him.

"Arthur! Behind you!"

He spun around. Mab stood with arms raised high. Not a spark of hellfire emanated from her hands, but he felt her magic nonetheless. It rippled from her body in undulating waves. The ground around her turned dark and began to move.

No. It wasn't the ground that was moving. It was the mass of tiny, writhing creatures upon it. He watched in horror as they surged toward him. The wave reached and crested the garden wall. Spiders. Thousands, maybe millions, each no bigger than a fingernail. Were they real? Or simply an illusion? From this distance, it was impossible to tell.

The leading edge of the horde formed an undulating line. It seeped in his direction like a spill of black oil. Arthur braced himself. White flame leapt into his hands.

"Arthur." Mab's clear voice rang out above the swarm. "Give yourself up. You can't win. Not against me."

"You've broken the terms of the duel. The clan—"

"I told you, sugar. I decide what's going down. If you're hankering so bad for a fight we'll do it here and now. As for your precious kin, the only question is whether they'll find you dead or enthralled when they arrive."

The arachnids swarmed closer, flooding the rose beds. They enveloped the apple tree in a dirty, shuddering blanket. Arthur sent his hellfire up the staff, swirling the magic around the crystal before sweeping it across the garden.

The swarm scattered to avoid the flames. But was it the true reaction of living creatures? Or had Mab simply adapted her illusion to counter his attack?

The door to Tŷ'r Cythraul slammed behind him. Good. Cybele must have taken shelter inside the house. He glanced behind him. No, goddamn it. She'd closed the door, all right, but she was running toward him.

She reached his side. "Holy crap," she said in a horrified whisper. "Do you think they're real?"

"Don't know," he said. "Get in the house."

She shot him a repressive glance. "Fuck that."

The swarm was regrouping. Arthur eyed its renewed advance uneasily. "Sod it all, Cybele. Be reasonable. You don't have hellfire. If those things are real, you can't fight them. "

"I can cover you. Make you less of a target for Rand and Hunter and the others."

The others—? With all his attention on Mab, Arthur had forgotten about her thralls.

"Rand and Hunter to our left," she said calmly. "Evander on our right. Draven and Blade on the roof behind us. Don't know where Clay's got to."

Arthur's gaze darted to the cluster of Druids on the moor. Luc, who was in no condition to fight, was the only adept left among the dormants.

An orange fireball scudded into the ground fifty feet to his left.

Hunter. Arthur swore viciously. "No way is his aim that bad," he muttered. "What the fuck's he playing at?"

"He's not playing." Cybele's voice held a distinct note of satisfaction. "He's confused. I've blurred our position and set illusions of our bodies in seven different spots. They'll be blasting everything but us."

Arthur was damn glad to have Cybele by his side. She might not be an adept, but her magic was uncanny in its inventiveness. He gave up any notion of herding her to safety. Safety didn't exist, anyway. He blasted another round of hellfire at the spiders. This time, they barely paused in their forward motion.

Cybele sucked in a breath. In seconds, the swarm would be on them.

"Come on." He grabbed her arm.

With Mab's laughter following, they bolted for the house. Arthur threw himself at the door and wrenched at the heavy brass knob. It came off in his hands.

"Fuck."

"Hurry," Cybele panted, her hand on his back. "Do something else. They're almost on us."

Arthur poured a blast of hellfire into the door's lock. The metal didn't even heat. He redirected his magic into the door itself. The oak remained uncharred. A line of fire along the edge of the door failed to melt its hinges.

"Arthur!" Mab called. "Give it up."

The spiders swarmed up their legs.

Cybele screamed and slapped her pants. Arthur fought the urge to do the same. The tiny creatures raced up their bodies, slipped under their clothes, scrambled into their hair. They burrowed into ears and nostrils. It was hard to see or even breathe. Cybele made a choking sound and ducked her head inside the neck of her shirt. The creatures were real. Horribly, terrifyingly real.

Hellfire blasts landed on their right and left. Too close. Cybele's illusions were faltering. She dropped into a crouch, shoulders hunched toward the door, arms shielding her head. An inch-deep mass of spiders swept over her. It was the last thing Arthur saw before the things swarmed into his own face.

"Ready to surrender?" Mab called.

Not quite. Arthur turned his magic to the sky. Angry weather rushed to his aid. Dashing spiders out of his eyes, he tilted his head back and steered the clouds into a single dark formation directly overhead. Lightning cracked. Thunder boomed.

Rain poured down, pounding with all the intensity of Arthur's rage and fear. The drenching downpour succeeded where hellfire had not. Spiders dropped out of his hair and fell off his arms. They slid down his legs and disappeared into cracks and crevices in the ground.

He wiped the last of the creatures from his eyes and lifted his head in time to see Mab land in the garden. She faced him with wings high and eyes blazing. A word summoned her favorites to her side. Rand and Hunter touched down on her right, Evander on her left. Their alpha's crackling red nimbus expanded to envelop the three men. Within it, their eyes burned red and their bodies blazed with opalescence. The rubies at their necks glowed.

Upon contact with the heat of Mab's power, Arthur's rain hissed into steam. Rand handed something to his mistress. She accepted it, and then turned with arms outstretched, lifting the object into Arthur's view. With a jolt of horror, he beheld his enemy's offering: a ring of twisted wood set with a glowing ruby sphere.

"Arthur Camulus, this collar is your destiny. Accept it freely and I will allow you to stand at my side. Reject it and you will grovel at my feet."

"Get this through your thick head," Arthur shouted. "I will never be your thrall."

"You'd rather go to Oblivion?" Mab tilted her head as if considering. "I'm so sorry, sugar, but that's just not an option. I want you alive."

Beads of sweat broke out on Arthur's brow. He angled Merlin's crystal toward his enemy and fought to keep his voice steady. "Forget your threats. I hold the power here."

"Do you?" Her white teeth flashed. "For someone who's holding all the power, you're talking a mighty lot of bull. That ol' staff might as well be a stick of dead wood, with a lump of coal set on top, for all the damage it's done. You know what I think? That thing in your hands is nothing but a prop. And a piss-poor one at that. Give it up, Arthur. Admit you've lost and salvage at least a little of your pride." She held out the collar. "Here. Come and take it. If you know what's good for you, you won't make me bring it to you."

Arthur brushed her words away, as if they were stray cobwebs. He let them seep through the crevices in his awareness, barely noticed. He turned his focus inward, where myriad ancestral memories drifted in his murky subconscious. A preternatural calm descended upon him as he sorted through the remnants of his forebears' lost lives.

A single thought—a vivid snatch of a memory spoken in the voice of a long-dead ancestor—caught his attention.

Power is weak.

It made no sense. Not at first. Then, in a flash of insight, Arthur understood.

Mab possessed powerful magic. She ruled the clan with brutal purpose. Viewed through the eyes of the boy he'd once been, she'd seemed invincible. Now, as a man, Arthur pushed aside that frightened boy's nightmares and considered Mab in a new light. Weakness propped up her power. What fear had driven her to amass such terrible strength? What lack within herself drove her to rule with such vicious might? What horror lived in *her* nightmares?

The answer came to him. He saw it clearly, because he recognized it so intimately. Mab shared Arthur's own worst fear.

Betrayal.

Arthur didn't know what lay in Mab's past, but whatever it was, it had driven her to rise above her peers, and then use her position to curtail every freedom of the Druid clan. She craved control. She made slaves rather than releasing new adepts to freedom. She wrapped collars around their necks and tethered their magic to her own. She had no friends, only subjects. She stood alone and trusted no one.

He darted a glance at Cybele. Her expression was solemn. But not panicked, or even despairing. She trusted him, Arthur realized. She still believed he would win.

"I need you to make Rand and Hunter think they're blind," he said tersely. "For ten seconds. Maybe fifteen. Can you do it?"

"Yes. Just say when."

Arthur nodded, then lifted his eyes to meet Mab's contemptuous gaze. "If you want me to wear that thing you'll have to place it around my neck with your own hands."

As he spoke, he concentrated on Evander. Cybele's father was the only free adept in Mab's circle—the only Druid Arthur could use for the ruse he had in mind.

"Now," he muttered.

Cybele released her magic.

"What the fuck—?" Rand and Hunter staggered backward, looking wildly about. Mab's head swung toward them.

Arthur launched his own illusion. Evander seemed to lift his hands. Dirty brown-green hellfire crackled on his fingertips. "Forget those idiots!" Evander bellowed. "Look at me, you bitch." He flicked his wrists, flinging two burning lashes at Mab's head.

"Wha—" Mab spun around. "Why, you fucking bastard!" She loosed a stream of hellfire at her lackey.

Arthur launched himself at Mab, dropping the staff as he leaped into the air. Magic couldn't defeat her? Bugger it, then. He'd break her bloody neck—if he could get his hands on her before she realized what was happening.

He'd nearly reached her when her Mab's magic broke through his illusion. The false Evander abruptly evaporated. The real Evander was on his knees, screaming, his body alight with Mab's burning magic.

"What? Why—?" He stretched out his arms to his mistress.

Mab spat a curse. She swung around just as Arthur's fingers closed on her neck. He twisted with a savage motion. His fingers slipped as Mab's hellfire blasted him into the air. Flailing his arms and legs, wings flapping wildly, he sailed up and backwards. The ground race beneath him.

He slammed into the house, his spine flattening painfully against unforgiving stone. His skull smacked the sill of a third floor window. He heard something crack; pain lanced through his wings. Mortar and bone, snapping together.

The agony left him gasping. For what seemed like an endless moment he hung suspended, arms and legs flung wide, his body pinned against the stone facade of Tŷr Cythraul. A strangled cry came from below. He looked down. Cybele was staring up at him with wide, frightened eyes, both hands covering her mouth.

The stone wall at his back shuddered. An ominous vibration ran up his spine. He started to fall. He tried to resist the pull of gravity—tried to fly, tried to rise through the tumbling stone. His broken body would not obey.

He plummeted heavily. Tŷr Cythraul fell with him, its stone facade splitting apart like a giant jigsaw puzzle. He hit the ground amid a crushing wave of jagged rock and broken mortar.

He rolled with a furious roar, flinging the wreckage of his childhood home off his back like a dog shaking water. Dragging his broken wings, gasping with pain, tasting mortar and mold, he clawed his way to the top of the rubble. Cybele. Where was Cybele? He looked about like a madman. His heart seized when he spied a pale arm protruding from the debris.

Spitting curses, he scrambled over the rocks. A firelash yanked him back. He tumbled down a slope of stone and landed on his back. More wing bones snapped. A fresh round of stabbing agony left him gasping.

Mab loomed over him, a nightmarish smile on her face. The collar destined for Arthur's neck rested in her hands. The light of the ruby thrallstone stabbed his eyes. Firelashes coiled agony around his body, binding his limbs and pinning his torso to the ground. He peered up at Mab through a daze of pain and despair.

"You belong to me, Arthur. Your body, your mind, your magic. All that you are is mine."

The twisted wood turned crimson. The collar gleamed wetly, as if slick with blood. Sparks spun around the ring. Gathered. Separated. A gap appeared in the circle.

Mab pulled the arc of wood apart, widening the space Arthur's neck would pass through. He cursed and tried to strike out. His body refused his command. He was caught in the web of Mab's power more securely than any hapless insect was ever trapped in a spider's web.

A groan passed his lips. Satisfaction flared in the alpha's eyes. "Seven years of waiting," she murmured. "Now, at last, you're mine." She glanced to her right and left. "Come and look, boys."

Hunter's grinning face moved into Arthur's line of vision. "Can't wait to play with you," he chortled. "Once that collar's in place."

"Fuck off," Arthur growled.

Hunter's grin widened. "Oh, ho. Big man."

Rand shouldered in beside Hunter. Arthur's heart stalled. Rand held Cybele in his arms. Her body hung limply, one dangling arm swinging slowly back and forth. A nasty gash on her forehead dripped blood.

Mab frowned. "Dead?"

"No, ma'am," Rand answered. "But as near to it as I reckon a person can get."

The alpha shrugged. "I'll leave her survival in your hands. If she lives, she's yours to guide and collar."

"No worries. I'll take fine care of her." Rand's teeth flashed. "Maybe I'll let even Arthur watch me do it. If he's a good boy."

"Oh, he'll be a good boy." Mab smiled down at Arthur. "Seein' as he's got no choice in the matter."

Arthur lay helpless and panting, awash in pain. His heart raced as Mab bent over him. The collar came closer. The alpha's magic flared. His vision turned red. He twisted his head, desperate to avoid the heat of the ruby and the touch of the slick, crimson wood.

A white spark caught his eye.

Merlin's staff. He'd dropped it before going for Mab's throat. It lay now half-buried in the rubble of Tŷr Cythraul. The crystal, caught between two stones, was just visible. White sparks swirled inside it.

Not illusion this time. True magic. Magic that Arthur hadn't called.

Magic that called to him.

Mab's eyes blazed a triumphant red. The collar was just inches from his throat. Rand loomed behind his mistress. He'd flung Cybele's battered body face down over his shoulder. She swayed slightly. He steadied her weight with his palm on her arse.

That hand tipped the scales. That big hand with its fingers spread wide over Cybele's buttocks, squeezing, kneading. The sight flipped a mental trigger in the darkest part of Arthur's consciousness. Hatred—raw, scorching, elemental fury—boiled forth. It spilled through his chest. Invaded his limbs. Flooded his brain.

A high, piercing tone filled his ears. Mab's hellfire restraints snapped like twigs. Arthur leapt to his feet, roaring like a beast. He flung his left hand up, swatting the collar out of Mab's hands. The force of his blow knocked her to the ground.

A word Arthur had never heard before—guttural, unimaginable sounds—erupted from his throat. The syllables reverberated like a gong struck by a god's hand. Merlin's staff vibrated. The rubble weighing it down shook, then simply disintegrated. Its crystal touchstone exploded in brilliant waves of hellfire.

The relic rose from the ruins of Tŷr Cythraul. It hovered in the air, spinning and spitting white fire. A second word—as unknown and unbidden as the first—left Arthur's lips. The staff shot like an arrow toward its master. It slapped into Arthur's open palm. As his fingers closed on the twisted wood, a nimbus of brilliant power enveloped his body.

He caught one clear glimpse of Mab's terrified face through the chaos of his magic.

Then his vision went white and he knew no more.

TWENTY-SEVEN

Cybele woke to a pounding temple and a stabbing agony in her lower left leg. Her ribs hurt like a bitch, too. Must be a few cracked bones in there.

She was fiercely glad.

Glad, because pain meant she was alive. Not dead and gone, lost forever in the gaping black abyss of Oblivion.

A chill invaded her body. She'd looked into the heart of that endless void. The velvet nothingness had wanted her. And she had wanted it. Only the thought of Arthur—still alive, still fighting—had given her the strength to resist. Every ounce of her life force, every spark of her magic, had gone into the battle for survival. And since she was now lying on hard ground, her body hurting like a sonofabitch, she must've won.

She was awake, but she hadn't quite gotten up the courage to open her eyes. What was she going to see when she did? She'd survived the collapse of Tŷr Cythraul. She'd resisted the uncanny lure of Oblivion. But had Arthur won his battle with Mab?

How much time had passed? Her mouth felt like cotton. She tried to swallow and almost gagged. She moved her hands over the surface under her. Damp grass. She couldn't bend her left knee. Her leg was in a splint. Broken? That would explain why it hurt so damn much.

She wasn't alone. Someone nearby was breathing

roughly but steadily. Asleep, maybe. Who?

Steeling herself for the worst, she opened her eyes.

The ruins of Tŷ'r Cythraul rose before her. The top half of the front facade had fallen, leaving the interior of the upper floors exposed. The floors, having lost support on the front end, sloped sharply downward. A jumble of furnishings lay broken atop a pile of stone rubble.

Arthur was sprawled beside her, lost in fitful slumber, his back half-supported by the garden wall. Cybele's gaze flew to his neck.

Bare.

Her breath vacated her lungs in one long swoosh. The rush of relief was so intense, so exuberant, she couldn't immediately catch her next inhale. When she finally did, she sucked in a lungful of musty air and dissolved into a fit of coughing. And shit, how that hurt her head and ribs. She stifled a moan.

Arthur jerked upright, his head turning sharply in her direction. Their eyes met. For several long moments, they just stared at each other.

"You're awake," he said finally. The relief in his voice was palpable.

"Yes."

"How do you feel?"

How did *he* feel? She looked him over. He sported an assortment of scrapes and bruises, but it didn't look like anything was seriously wrong with him. Except his eyes...they were red-rimmed, as if he'd been crying. For her? She struggled to sit upright, only to freeze when fresh pain stabbed her ribs.

"How do I feel?" she said through gritted teeth. "Like shit."

He moved to help her sit up. "Here. Lean against me."

She did, gratefully. "Dang it. I think I might I'd hurt

less if a truck ran me over."

"Can't be that bad if you're bitching about it." The lightness of his words belied the seriousness of his tone. He ran a hand down her arm, as if trying to convince himself she was whole.

"I guess I'll live."

A beat of silence ensued. Then he said, "I didn't think you would."

She twisted to look at him, ignoring the pain the movement brought. "What happened after the house fell on me?"

Arthur grimaced. "I'm not exactly sure. Luc said—"

"He's okay?"

"Yeah."

"Zephyr? Auster? The other dormants?"

"They're fine," he said. "Clay, Draven, and Blade are okay, and helping out. They're on the moor building a temporary shelter."

"What about Rand and Hunter?"

"Gone. They took off when Mab fell."

Every muscle in Cybele's body unknotted. "She's really dead, then. You defeated her."

"Yes. Merlin's staff—it woke up. I called and it came flying at me. I caught it and then..." He shrugged. "Apparently, I blasted Mab into a pile of ash. The thrall collars disintegrated. I don't remember any of it. Luc filled me in when I came to."

"Evander?" Cybele asked.

He avoided her gaze. "Your father didn't survive Mab's hellfire. That's my fault. I used him—"

Cybele caught his hand and pressed her palm against his. "Don't regret it, Arthur. You did what you had to do." Evander might have fathered her, but he'd not spent a subsequent minute of his life caring about her. He'd stood by Mab, enforcing every one of her vicious rules, even though he hadn't been bound by a thrall collar. It was only fitting that he'd died at her side.

She laced their fingers together. "So. My leg—I guess it's broken?"

"Just fractured. You've got a couple cracked ribs, too."

"I figured," she said wryly.

"You came so close to dying. Did you..." He turned their joined hands over and ran his free hand up her arm to her shoulder. "Did you see Oblivion?"

"Yes. I did. It was—" She shivered, remembering.

"I know," he said quietly.

"I feel—different now, somehow. It's hard to describe. I'm in transition, aren't I?"

He nodded.

"Two months, maybe three, before my Ordeal comes." A knot of apprehension tied itself into her stomach. "Oh, Arthur," she said. "I don't know if I'm ready for it."

His fingers tightened on her shoulder. "No one is ever ready for it. But you won't be alone. I'll be there, every minute. Trust me to guide you through it. To keep you safe."

"I do trust you. With my life. And my heart."

His touch glided along her jaw. His finger lifted her chin. When she tilted her head up, his mouth came down on hers. Hard and urgent, and yet tender, too. The combination opened an ache in her heart.

She wrapped her arms around his neck and deepened the kiss. The discomfort of her injuries dropped from her awareness, pushed aside in favor of a more pleasurable agony. Their tongues tangled; she gently bit his lower lip. When they finally broke apart, both of them were gasping.

Cybele closed her eyes against a searing wave of lust. Their eyes met and joy bubbled up inside her. They were alive, free, and together. She slid her arms up around his neck.

"I might be battered, and I might have more cracked bones than I care to count, but dang it, Arthur." She pressed her lips close to his ear. "Just say the word and I'll go down on you so hard you won't know what hit you."

He chuckled, and then laughed outright. Cybele pulled back and drank in the sight. The world might be an uncertain place, but as long as Arthur was in it with her, she was content to take the bad with the good.

His gray eyes danced. "I love how you're always full of such brilliant ideas."

She smiled back at him. "I know."

"And I love you," he said. "Only you, Cybele. Always."

"I know that, too," she said, and kissed him again.